PRAISE FOR

BLIGHT

"A compulsive read: angry, articulate, and lyrical. Somehow, even its horrific fantasy elements only add to the sense that Blight presages tomorrow's headlines (or it would, if those headlines were written by poets and the newspapers themselves weren't all owned by billionaires). Rosen is rapidly proving herself to be the twenty-first century's answer to John Brunner. In fact, this whole trilogy is shaping up to be a minor masterpiece.

"In the unlikely event that we shake off our collective stupidity and cowardice enough to fight against the current trajectory of our society—not to mention that of the whole damn biosphere—I want Rachel Rosen leading the revolution." — Peter Watts, author of *Blindsight*

"Rachel A. Rosen is a superb prose stylist and an incisive social commentator. Her post-apocalyptic Canada will haunt you forever. Predicting the future is supposed to be science fiction's job, but Rosen shows that urban (and rural!) fantasy can do it, too, with sharp-edged commentary and real-world relevance. Look for this one on the award ballots." — Robert J. Sawyer, Hugo Award-winning author of *The Downloaded*

"Suffused with masterful horror and black humour and compassion for its beleaguered and all-too-human characters, this spellbinding chronicle of leviathanic magic, political intrigue, and righteous insurrection hurls a molotov cocktail at the evil lurking in humanity's banal appetites for control." — Dale Stromberg, author of *Maej*

"Rosen's ability to create such a beautifully vivid picture of a vicious world as it slowly chokes to death is simply breathtaking." — Rohan O'Duill, author of *Cold Blooded*

MORE PRAISE FOR

BLIGHT

"The second book in the series is even better than the first ... Deftly showing that collective action, not individual heroism, is the only way to fight fascism, *Blight* is a book I know I'll be coming back to. Rosen is a daring voice in Canadian SFF, and she'll break your heart while making you laugh." — Michelle Browne, author of *Meaning Wars*

"'Any ship can be a submersible if you don't care about coming back up.' Dotted with laugh-out-loud gallows humour, *Blight* is supernatural horror with a distressingly prescient narrative. Its disparate (and desperate) cast of resistors, revolutionaries, and reluctant heroes are pitted against a particularly Canadian fascism which is all too believable, even as it comes to power through a response to the resurgence of magic in the world. Fast-paced and populated with characters to fall in love and hate with, Blight is a compelling, entertaining, timely, and thoughtful read." — M. Darusha Wehm, author of *Hamlet, Prince of Robots*

"These are hard times and a lot of us are swamped in burn-out and frustration. BLIGHT isn't the piece of escapism to distract from what is going on right now. It is raw, stained with grief, full of broken bones and buildings, but it is a book to remind us that we have to keep pushing, because what else is there? Maya says: "This isn't the kind of fight we win—it's the fight we fight." Did we ever think the self-proclaimed Princes would give it all up without a fight? No matter how dark it gets, BLIGHT is full of tenacious, acerbic hope." — Ryszard Merey, author of *Read and Then Burn This*

"This is the book about monsters rising from the deeps (of Ottawa) you need in these times. A weird, bleak, startlingly hilarious story about how to keep on fighting after the end of the world. — Ursula Whitcher, author of *North Continent Ribbon*

BLIGHT

The Sleep of Reason
Book II

The BumblePuppy Press

OTTAWA, CANADA
2025

The BumblePuppy Press

The quotation from Dennis Lee's poem, "Civil Elegies," is gratefully used with the permission of his publisher, House of Anansi Press.

Cover design by Rachel A. Rosen.
Cover illustration and map by Marten Norr.
Sigil design by Kit Fisher.

Blight is published by:

The BumblePuppy Press
Station E, P.O. Box 4814
Ottawa ON K1S 5H9
Canada

National Library of Canada cataloging in Publication Data:

Rosen, Rachel, 1979 -
Blight/ Rachel Rosen

ISBN: 978-1-7387598-8-0

Electronic editions of this book are also available.

First edition

For anyone who has ever punched a Nazi.

Contents

BOOK I — THE SONGBIRD

BOOK II — THE RETRIBUTION

Book III — The Maple Spring

Dramatis Personae

The Mackenzie-Papineaus (Mac-Paps)
Ontario-based resistance movement, named after the Canadian battalion that fought in the Spanish Civil War

Gabrielle "Gaby" Abel: Disgraced former Member of Parliament and widow of Prime Minister **Patrice Abel**, now leader of the Mac-Paps
Monique Abel: Her older daughter, commander of the Scarborough cell
Martine Abel: Her younger daughter, an MAI
Junior Abel: Her son
Maya: An MAI, formerly known as **Sujaya Krishnamurthy**
Shadi Al-Abdallah: Maya's husband, a former engineering student
Jonah Augustine: Formerly a consultant for the Party, now an arms dealer, ex-husband of **Blythe** and father of **Laura**
Felipe Pereira: Gaby's advisor, a former Canadian Army captain
Anton Yannick: Gaby's advisor, a former steelworker
Various gang leaders, anarchists, and miscreants

The Last Call
Loosely affiliated with the University of Victoria, though officially independent

Blythe Augustine: A climate scientist, ex-wife of **Jonah** and mother of **Laura**
Bailey: A refugee from Alberta
Kenny Ocampo: Bartender at the Last Call, **Blythe's** partner
Edgar Yip: Team leader of **Blythe's** department
Omid and **Kitty**: Edgar's grad students
Various fishermen

The Dominion

Government of the Dominion of Canada, formerly the Opposition

Quinn Atherton: Director of the Dominion
Miriam Atherton: His daughter, presumed dead in the Blight
Alycia Curtis: Atherton's advisor and MAI, formerly a philanthropist
Reid Curtis: Atherton's advisor, formerly a media baron
Amelia Fatimatou: A nurse
Colette Greene: An MAI researcher
Lucy Fletcher: An opera singer, known as the Songbird of the Dominion, widow of **Tobias Fletcher**
Eric Greenglass: A research analyst at the Walsingham Institute
Cal Harrison: A senator and former venture capitalist
Simon Yamashita: An MAI composer
Various apparatchiks and collaborators

Others

Nothing to see here, move along

Ian Mallory: MAI, former consultant for the Party, presumed dead in the Blight
Mitch Pruitt: SVAR liaison to the University of Victoria
Luther Sears: President of the American Free States, Defender of the Faith
Natan Surkov: MAI, President of the Russian Federation
Various civilians of no particular political inclination

The story so far

Twenty years ago, a rapidly warming climate melted ice caps, raised sea levels, and returned magic to the world in a mass event known as the Cascade. Since then, the world has struggled to cope. The United States has fractured into several countries and, in the power vacuum left, Canada's profile and influence on the world has considerably risen. The left-leaning Party currently clings to power with a minority government, led by the scandal-plagued Patrice Abel, and propped up by his precognitive wizard advisor, Ian Mallory, while the right-wing Opposition decries the influence of magic.

Ian is increasingly cornered by fate and politics. Having foreseen the Blight, a disaster that will come within months, he attempts to use magic to delay and control it. Along with Eric Greenglass, his liaison, and Sujay Krishnamurthy, his apprentice and intern, he tries to maintain the government's minority rule. He pulls in Jonah Augustine, an old friend from his activist days, to map out the areas most likely to be affected by the Blight and to work with his Indigenous contacts to avert the worst of the damage.

Jonah's ex-wife, Blythe, a climate scientist in Victoria, is tapped for an experimental deep-ocean expedition, using an MAI child to navigate magically-disturbed waters. She encounters an ancient, gigantic skeleton that reaches into her mind and renders her co-pilot comatose.

Tobias Fletcher, a photojournalist with the right-leaning *Post*, goes on assignment to photograph Ian for a newspaper profile. Urged by Lucy, his opera star wife, and Reid Curtis, the media magnate behind his paper, Tobias uncovers a series of scandals. But it's the discovery of Ian's spellcasting, apparently aimed at Parliament itself and caught on Tobias' camera, that proves to be the government's undoing.

An election is called, which the Party loses. Ian informs a brokenhearted Sujay that they are running out of time, and tells her to go home to her family. He's arrested on an obscure anti-witchcraft statute. All this is quickly overshadowed by a terrorist attack by a disgruntled MAI on the Canadian Parliament, killing most of his cabinet, sparing only Quinn Atherton, a long-time political operative whose daughter is killed in the blast. The magic spreads, following ley lines that Ian and Jonah had mapped, and consuming the country in fire and earthquakes.

Atherton, backed by the Curtises, uses the chaos following the Blight to institute martial law, expelling foreigners and cracking down on political opponents. Patrice is executed after a show trial. The government's far-right shift is too much for Tobias, particularly given his recent discovery that Alycia Curtis, Reid's wife, is an MAI herself. Tobias is arrested and ends up in a black site in the cell next to Ian, who reveals their shared fate. Knowing what awaits him, Tobias tries to escape and is murdered by the prison guards.

Blythe flees in a refugee boat with her and Jonah's daughter Laura, but they are set upon by mercenaries from the SVAR who sink their ship, drowning the girl. Blythe is rescued by a giant tentacle emerging from the water as the creature destroys the SVAR ship.

Sujay escapes to her home in Toronto, but finds her family murdered by the Cleaners, a paramilitary organization loyal to the government. She's rescued by Shadi, who reveals that he was sent to recruit her to the resistance. She performs a spell to bury her name, hiding her from the enemy's magic, and takes a new one: Maya.

*T*he corpse's skin is grey, a contrast to Lilith's living-dead flesh, and Jane lets it hurt a little. More than she thought it would.

"What's the point?" Jane murmurs. "Of all this magic? All this power, everything we are, if we can't protect them?"

"Oh, puppy," Lilith replies, the affection in her voice unguarded. "Not everything needs to have a point. Some things just are. And so much the worse for them...and for us."

— Sujay Krishnamurthy, ***https://not-your-chosen-one.tumblr.com/***

Book I

The Songbird

The Glass Child

Even sitting in her favourite chair, the glass child was never still. Her muscles, grotesquely extended, rippled and pulsed beneath the hard, translucent shell of her carapace. The bristling hairs on her arm shivered, her yellowed eyes searched out patterns in the fingerprints and smudges on the window. She waited.

The black car in the distance looked no larger than the flies that smashed against her window. It beetled, determined, along the road that cut through snowbanks to the parking lot of the hospital. Maybe it was Him, was today His day to visit? She tensed at the uncertainty. It had been hours since she'd seen Him, but sometimes she asked the nurse, and Amelia would gently explain that those hours were really days, months.

He and Amelia did their best. In her moments of lucidity, she could appreciate the mural on the wall, the mermaids and unicorns that had been her obsession as a little girl. The soft toys, carefully chosen to ensure nothing with sharp edges, nothing that could be used as a weapon, nothing that could cause an infection, replicas of identical toys that her talons and teeth had shredded. These were beloved playthings, murdered and resurrected, in hopes she would forget she had destroyed them in the first place.

A wire cage wove between the panes of window glass. She could bite through it. The glass wouldn't penetrate her palms, what remained of her lips. She could wait until Amelia came, four times a day, any one of those times, she could sink her claws into that soft, trusting flesh, and run, and run. She could kill Him, her world, her God, and she would be free, and all the snow and the gravel and the tall bare trees would be hers. But she would be alone.

The sun shone through her, casting shadows on the floor that echoed the shapes of her bones. She moved slowly though she could feel, in her distended muscles, the potential strength and speed. She had learned about potential energy in school, how an elastic band contains its own painful snap against the skin. She wondered if she would feel nothing. If what her skin had become would shatter. Her arms were longer now, knuckled to the ground like an ape. Amelia said she was beautiful, that beauty was subjective. Amelia told her what subjective meant.

But the glass child was a monster, a demon, not an idiot. She saw how He looked at her. There was nothing subjective in His face, in the way He would quickly turn if she caught his eye.

Her heart, a melted, deformed wreckage that nestled inside a partially reabsorbed ribcage, pulsed harder at the sound of footsteps. But it was only Amelia at the door, soft-voiced Amelia, who kept her head low and her fingers splayed before her, as if the seconds her caution would buy her could spare her from her charge's rage. Amelia, in her nurse's scrubs, all cotton and velcro, the laces removed from her shoes.

Amelia didn't call her by name, or ask her how her day was. She was a prisoner just as surely as the child herself, a ghost of a girl who lived or died on His sufferance, the same as anyone else. Amelia was scared of the glass child whose shell she sponged clean daily, who could snap her neck in a whiplash tantrum. But that was nothing beside the fear she held for Him.

"I think He's coming to visit today," Amelia murmured, and the glass child's heart, that misshapen coil held together by magic and will, might have exploded out of her chest. She didn't recognize it as a seizure, not at first, until the fit came over her and she toppled from her chair, twitching and convulsing on the floor, her consciousness flickering in and out like a broken lightbulb.

She pissed herself. She vomited. She heard Amelia swear as if from a great distance.

Dragging herself upwards, she saw that she had vomited on a shoe. Patent leather, shiny black. *Him. Sorry sorrysorry.*

"Is she dying?"

"She—she does this sometimes. It's part of her condition. Here, let me..."

"*Don't touch me.*" He was kneeling, wiping the vomit from His shoe. Then turning, He dabbed her cheek clean with a handkerchief. Carefully, He slid a hand under her elbow, and He and Amelia helped her back into her chair. "You tell no one, you understand? No one."

Amelia, quaking, swallowed hard, and nodded.

His smile, when He unleashed it on the child, was charming. Pitying. He placed His large hands over hers.

It was His cruelties that defined Him, but His acts of mercy would undo Him every time.

1

Deep in the Rockies, under the claw of a months-long superwinter, Blythe Augustine led a band of six refugees out of the Dominion of Canada towards freedom in the west.

Spines of translucent shriekgrass moaned, their wails amplified through the mountain pass. Filmy streaks of daylight through the clouds painted their protruding tendrils, which swayed, flinched from Blythe as she stomped through the patch, scraping sticky residue from her boots on the rocks as she went. The shriekgrass was invasive, poisonous, and in spore season, drove people mad en masse, but it wasn't the worst of her concerns.

No, the worst was that the goddamn baby wouldn't stop crying.

They had travelled by night from the Prairies, picking their way across the broken highway. One couple, both of them Cree, headed for the Iron Alliance, knew a little of the land, how it had been, how it was now. The others were useless—the girl with her baby, an older man who complained endlessly about it, and a skinny nonbinary kid with a grown-in undercut who hadn't brought the right shoes for a three-week long hike across the snow.

The night vision gear turned her flashlight beam acid green as it darted in thin seams over the snow. When dawn threatened, they veered off the road and hid amid the pines, in the sharp angles of the mountain's shadow, praying that the snow would fill their tracks and the shriekgrass would cover the sounds of their movement. Blythe had made the pass in winter nine times now, a psychopomp leading the dead from their fallen cities and towns in the east, over the Rockies, to whatever freedom the beleaguered West Coast would afford them before it sank into the sea.

Her mask kept the shriekgrass blooms from getting their claws in her. To supplement the caches stowed along the route, Blythe had her mother's pemmican, wrapped in wax paper and more durable than heartache.

She still skidded on the ice every goddamned time, her heart racing and insistent on the danger long after she'd steadied herself against a trunk. The pack, with its camping stove and clunking cans, pushed her into a hunch and made every fall harder. She still underestimated the bone-deep chill high above the world, how her head and her legs and her fucking ward tattoo thrummed a song of pain and cried out for the salt weight of the ocean. Her body was a stubborn animal, determined to keep breathing and shitting and moving long after her spirit had withered.

But the baby. The baby was the worst of it.

Her daughter Laura had been a colicky baby. Blythe and her ex, Jonah, had intended at first to smash the heteronormative, patriarchal nuclear family, had crowdfunded for pumps and quality earplugs and worked out a spreadsheet, and all of Blythe's careful planning went to hell the moment they had come in contact with an actual living, squalling infant. Laura, with her impeccable newborn taste, had preferred Blythe to Jonah, and particularly preferred Blythe when there was a morning lecture, or a report due, or a conference call with a colleague in a different time zone. Sleep-deprived, ears ringing, Blythe would scroll through mommy blogs, where, in the dead of night, anonymous parents admitted that maybe they didn't love their children as much as they should. Just when the 3 am self-loathing would roll in, Blythe would hold her tiny, wrinkled-bean daughter to her chest, and weep from love for her.

She'd thought—back then, with a naivety sickening in hindsight—that a baby who wouldn't stop crying was an Abu Ghraib-level atrocity. She'd thought if she could survive it, she could survive motherhood.

"Can someone shut that thing up?"

Blythe sat up, wrapping the blanket she'd been pretending to sleep on around her shoulders. It was the old guy doing the whining, a man who, despite being a refugee had been charmed enough not to know how much worse silence was than a baby's howls. She didn't ask for anyone's backstories. None of them had lived a life, before the Blight had remade the world, that had prepared them for a death march over the mountains in the grave of the superwinter.

She didn't punch him. A glare, a hand brushing her parka where her pistol was holstered, was enough to silence him. The blanket caught under her boots as she shuffled over to the mother and baby.

The girl couldn't have been older than 17, a child herself, rocking the baby in its sling against her scrawny chest. Under a hood, black hair spilled from her ratty toque, frozen into hard spikes at the tips. The baby was sallow, almost yellow, its tiny lips pursing and releasing between sobs.

"I'm sorry," the girl was muttering, "I'm so sorry." Her eyes, when her head jerked up at Blythe's approach, were wide and vacant.

Blythe slid the blanket off her shoulders and wrapped it around the girl, as if the moth-gnawed shroud could make up for the oppressive cold of the superwinter or the sharpened teeth of the mountain pass.

"I shouldn't have come." The girl's voice was a dry twig threatening to snap in half. "We were safer, back—"

Blythe crouched across from her, evaluating the sliver of the girl's face visible above her mask. She wouldn't have been scooped up in the first purges, not if she kept her head down and did what she was told, not if she lived somewhere big enough to disappear or remote enough to hide, but the Dominion noose was tightening. Soon they'd be rounding up anyone with too deep a tan, too questionable an internet history. The Vancouver Archipelago, under the benevolent thumb of the Silicon Valley Autonomous Region, drowning in free speech, investment opportunities, and homeless encampments, didn't have a high bar to clear when it came to safety.

"I knew someone who thought like that once," Blythe said. She kept her voice low, gentle. She had spent the bulk of her career as an environmental scientist doing everything she could to not sound reassuring. It was a hard habit to kick. "It went pretty badly for her. Trust me, you're doing the right thing."

Even if the baby didn't make it, the girl would be better off than Blythe was. At least if it died here, she'd have certainty.

"Do you want to hold her?" the girl asked. "Her name's—"

"No names," Blythe snapped. "Names have power." Not hers, of course, hers had been buried for two decades. Frozen, like blue whale DNA in a biobank. It was some protection, not just from Dominion checkpoints but also from the demons, rumoured to call out to their victims before claiming them. "And I don't do babies. Just try to keep it quiet, okay?" She searched her pockets for something the baby could chew and came up short. Her legs, stiffened by the cold, protested her attempt to stand up.

"If the Dominion are chasing us, they'll find us," the girl said.

Blythe gestured up at the snow-draped peaks, splashed in bloody dawn. "The highway's still a mess. The tracks, too. They can get planes over, but it's gonna be costly, and worse if they try it over the Free States. There are advantages to having three warring powers with a claim to land none of them own." Technically, the SVAR counted as dozens of warring powers rather than three, and the ones that had set up shop on the Pacific Coast didn't always agree amongst themselves. Not that the kid would care.

"I heard Japan's opening up again."

That particular prayer swirled around the Dominion's work camps, in the demon-haunted bush, in the parts of the cities where the hunted would risk a shriekgrass infestation over being rounded up and shot by the Cleaners. It was manifestly untrue. The paragons of freedom that had occupied what was left of the Island had no interest in letting anyone leave, and Japan had no interest in boatloads of desperate foreigners.

Twenty years ago, the Cascade had changed everything. It had returned magic to the world, rendering everything she knew as a scientist, as a human, obsolete. She had only just begun to understand this new world, to learn its rules, when the Blight had upended life once again, killing millions in a cataclysm of earthquake, fire, and flood. The last spasms of a tortured, dying earth, shaking as much of humanity off its back as it could manage.

"You and the kid survive to make it to the other side, you'll be as safe as it gets. There's nowhere to run to after that. Unless you want to run headfirst into the sea."

· · ·

The Milky Way stretched across the sky like a wound.

They had rolled up their camping gear in the failing light of dusk, hiked the trails adjacent to the road. It was the more difficult route, but it rendered them nearly invisible to surveillance drones. At moonrise, the outcrops of rock became crooked old men, a giant fist raised, in rage, to the heavens.

What conversation there had been, was only a breathy, "this way" or "watch for the branch," quiet enough to hear six sets of breaths, ranging from the infant's snuffles to the man's irritated rasps, to hear the swishes and sighs where the forest gave way to them.

Quiet enough to hear when something else was moving through the trees.

These are the things that, according to common wisdom, kept away a demon: salt, fire, wards, bullets, prayer. A large enough flamethrower, if you could find the gas to power it. Concrete walls.

These are the things that, according to Blythe's experience, kept away a demon: absolutely fucking nothing, if it really wanted to get at you. It would unhinge its jaws and swallow you before you could reach for your gun. It would have claimed your mind long before that. You would walk, smiling, into its rotting arms as it sang your name.

She felt their presence before the temperature dropped, a needle-bright jab that danced over the labyrinth tattoo on her shoulder. Leave it to Ian fucking Mallory to bestow her with an advanced warning system that told her only of a fate she couldn't avoid.

Blythe flashed her light—once, twice—counting on her charges to remember the arranged signal. The girl with the baby huddled close, as did the Cree couple and the kid. The older man hung back, and Blythe hissed under her breath for him to get closer.

There were at least three demons. She couldn't see them, but the snow shivered and the trees recoiled at their passage. They moved quietly, but not silently, the snow crunching under their malformed feet. They didn't sing, as the sea did, but the wind rattled them as it glanced off the sharp facets of their diamond skin, whistled like breath on glass. They reeked of decaying meat.

Flashlight off, she pushed forward, stepping heel to toe, the snow still too loud under her boots. The only way past was to fall beneath their notice, to blend in with the trees and rocks before the darkest part of the night. To exist mindlessly afloat in space, without a consciousness for them to close their jaws around.

One of the demons cried out, a high-pitched keen that rattled the branches of the pines. The girl jerked, inches from Blythe, whether from fear or desire to run towards it Blythe couldn't tell. Blythe grabbed for her sleeve but found the edge of the baby's blanket instead, brushed the fragile, squirming bundle within.

Blythe froze. The demon's voice was joined by a second, then a third, and then a chorus of shrieks and wails, a cacophony that echoed off the mountains. It curdled in her marrow, in the spaces between blood cells. The thickened air stuck to the cilia in her lungs. Her tattoo came to life, bristled under the layers of clothing that had suddenly become a prison.

Be useful, she told it. *Hide us.* As if Ian had been powerful enough to tame the wild magic and corral it into service on her skin. It wouldn't protect her, not this far from the ocean. With all his future sight, it would never have occurred to him that she'd be foolish enough to blunder into the Mordor-hellscape of the Rockies.

The reek of putrefaction was a fetid cloak seeping over them. The girl was close enough that when she stopped moving, the top of her hair tickled Blythe's nose. Over her rapid breathing, something clicked and chittered, the sound of dry exoskeleton brushing against itself. Millimetre by torturous millimetre, Blythe pulled her arm away from the baby.

The baby gurgled, sucked at the air like it was working itself up to a scream. *No no no, not now.* Of all the stupid ways to die, among strangers, far from home and catastrophically outside her area of expertise. Even the ocean, her impossible protector, bound to her by Ian's spell and Laura's blood, wouldn't save her.

They were close enough for ropy shadows to dance between the black pines, scattered and amorphous in the flat, dead light. Close enough that if the demons could still draw breath through their long mouths and sagging throats, she would have heard them.

Guns were no good against demons, but she reached for hers, tucked into an old holster. It would work on humans, if it came down to it.

Blythe didn't pray, not these days, not when she wasn't sure what would answer.

The pulse of blood through her skull drowned out the demons' approach. If the baby started crying again, she wouldn't hear it. Her senses closed in on her, wrapping her in cobwebs. Some stray neuron flicked, fired in search of a receptor, and, in the dark, found something else.

A gentle vegetable heat twitched by her ear. Lichen crept over the bark of the tree closest to her, coating the trunk in delicate ruffles. It pulsed, the soft seaweed green deepening to blue, an inhale and exhale at a floral pace almost too slow to perceive.

Blythe tilted her head, followed the faint bioluminescence that crept over the trees and rock face towards a narrow pass that led away from the road. She couldn't make out what lay beyond it.

Why not? Lichen was a symbiosis, an algae carried by fungi and yeast to every corner of the world, and the mountain, too, had once been the bottom of the ocean. She wasn't alone, even this far inland. The sea kept its promises. Even here.

Blythe motioned towards the glowing trail, though God knew if it was glowing for anyone else. Undercut nodded first, prodded the young man next to them. Slowly, Blythe led them forward, one finger tracing the lichens as they passed from the safety of first one tree, then the next, a grateful propagule dispersal to scatter her saviours across the rocks. The howling wasn't any closer. They were going to make it.

The older man broke from the group before Blythe could stop him, stumbled for the tamarack sentinels laden with the last snow. They whisked him in behind him.

The nonbinary kid reached out an arm and Blythe slapped it down, hissed, "Stay!" Then, "Move!" and hurried the little group forward.

The sound of overlong teeth tearing through flesh, of muscle sucked and slurped free from bone, followed their flight down the ridge or the black line of the road below. She stumbled in the descent, nearly sliding sideways and losing sight of the girl. She pressed into the rock face, snow sliding from the movement of the refugees climbing down after her, now minus one.

"Keep moving," she hissed. "Put as much distance between them and us as we can."

The baby heaved great hitching gulps that the girl did her best to muffle against her collarbone. It almost covered the sound of meat slapping wetly on snow. Blythe tucked her gun back into her belt and stumbled down the long expanse of ruined highway.

2

In the darkest part of the night, when demons came out to play and the curfew began, a woman in a ballgown woven with stars fled across the suspended city.

Lucy Fletcher, shivering in an overcoat and headscarf, picked her way over a bone-crusted street that hovered over the wreckage of downtown Ottawa. The sheer back of her gown was embroidered with glittering thread, meant to catch stage lights and scatter tiny rainbows of light at her feet. Now it threatened to catch beneath her heels. She picked up the train in one hand and bunched together the fabric in her elbow-length velvet glove. Less than an hour ago, performing a spell-entangled opera, she had been the centre of attention. The audience's applause had been an assault. Now, she was just another thin shadow, slipping in and out of the austere marble columns that stood stark in the swing of the searchlights.

In the old world, the walk from the National Arts Centre to ByWard Market had taken a dozen minutes, not even worth an Uber. The half-floating city interrupted much of the downtown now, filling in the chasms opened by the attack on Parliament three years ago. Festering veins of magic, unfurled by the Blight, bled under the pavement of the old city, threatening to devour it as they had so many other parts of the world. They glowed where they ran closer to the surface, the cement molten and unstable. The upper city, a fever dream of Classical columns and arcades, was connected to the salvageable parts of the lower city by marble staircases and delicate filigreed bridges.

If Lucy turned her head at just the right angle, away from the wreckage that hugged the river, away from the hanged men at the end of the arcade, away from the great concrete sarcophagus that shielded the city from the many-mouthed Abomination that had burst forth from Parliament Hill, it was almost beautiful.

"There's something you need to see, dear heart." It had only been a week ago. Simon Yamashita, world-famous Magic Affected Individual and composer, hadn't been sleeping. He had placed both his hands over hers, bowed his head. "I think everything is about to change, and not for the better."

Lucy stopped between pillars to catch her breath. The stone, magic-forged, blasted into being from broken concrete and crumbled brick, from flash-burned corpses, was warm against her back, like a living thing. She lifted her ankle out of one shoe and rubbed at it. At her heel was a line of pain, sliced where the back of her shoe had bitten into it. Her ridiculous stilettos would have to take her a little further.

The searchlight swung across the columns, flashing sharp geometries over the frosted ground. Lucy hugged herself, fighting the urge to run back, down the long spiral staircase to the old city. Instead, she waited for the shadows to gather themselves back together to move on, through the unforgiving de Chirico landscape that she'd had a hand, however unwillingly, in building.

She did not go to ugly places. Her life, now, was that of a glamorous swan, gliding from concert to party, the life that she had dreamed of as a girl. It was diamonds and velvet and carefully hoarded champagne. It was everything that the Cascade, the great magical flood that had turned the country inside out, had denied her. It was what the Dominion of Canada, in its quest to rebuild the nation, had given her back. As she toured the country, she did not see the sordid underbelly of the new world, its prisons and its mass graves. Neither did Simon, who laboured long hours to turn the regime's desires into music. But he had seen something, and returned to her haunted.

At the corner, a billboard, bordered in marquee lights, showed her in profile, resplendent in crimson. It was the size of a building storey, Photoshop-smooth, the shining daughter of the revolution. The Songbird of the Dominion. She turned away, unable to meet her own eyes.

She had to keep going. She owed that much to Tobias. Lucy would never have a decent night's sleep as long as she lived, but if she kept running, at least she might be able to look at herself in the mirror one day.

Inside the black site, it was too dark to see. Why had they let Simon in the first time? He'd mentioned something about testing. A doctor there was researching MAI, and so they needed his blood, needed every last drop of magic they could squeeze from him, but Lucy, an ordinary woman, had no such excuse. They knew her, though, recognized her loyalty and the blue of her pass card, and let her in. Taken past rows of closed doors, where prisoners shouted and catcalled, to the cell at the end of the hall with the long scratch across the door.

Not much was open this close to curfew. The yellow beacon of a café that catered to the government's functionaries and cronies stood apart from rows of shuttered windows and gated storefronts. She was on the very doorstep of the enemy, and the hidden eyes that dotted the city were watching her.

She was being followed. She was going mad, and jumping at shadows.

"The people love you," Simon had told her. "They love both of us," she'd replied, but she knew as well as he did that the love of the people was fickle, one misstep and it would devour them.

Lucy let the headscarf fall to her shoulders and wrapped it over the spore mask. She willed her hands not to shake, straightened her posture, and entered the café.

Little bells above the door announced her arrival. She noted the clusters of mobile office workers hidden behind laptops pretending to work. Eric Greenglass was already waiting for her in a booth by the back. He had come from the Walsingham Institute. Without the spotlight of her celebrity, he might have been a model citizen, just another blandly attractive cog in Director Quinn Atherton's PR apparatus, meeting a pretty girl for a nightcap after a day that had gone on far too long.

Lucy wore a floor-length gown and a coat that cost $5000 in the Before Times. Anonymity wasn't an option.

She bought and poured a mushroom tea with regular cash, paying a surcharge for use of one of the café's mugs. She had Dominion Exchange Credits, and hadn't been gone long enough for the bank to cut off her access to her funds, but those would be tracked. Free States coffee, advertised on the menu but buyable only with DEC, remained torturously out of reach.

Judging by his suit, Eric had set a high price on his soul. He'd tamed his floppy hair with some kind of product, and his lanky frame had filled out with a gym routine. He looked good. Confident. At least until he greeted her with that familiar dopey expression that he thought she didn't notice.

"Pornhub," he said as she slid into the booth across from him.

"Sushi," Lucy replied. "You said Pornhub last time."

"What can I say? I miss it a lot." Eric reached across the table, squeezed her fingers, and let go, too briefly to claim they'd been holding hands. "Toronto Raptors." She must have made a face, and he laughed. "What? I can contain multitudes."

"*Do* you, though? Medicare."

"*Night Beats.* You're not supposed to make this depressing."

"It's good to see you, Eric." That wasn't part of their game. She was breaking the rules, and she didn't care. She hadn't seen him in months, since the last time the Train had stopped in the ruins of the city they'd once both called home. The walls were pressing in on her. She wasn't the Songbird who dazzled a packed house at the National Arts Centre with another Yamashita original designed to frame her voice, to elevate

Atherton's regime. She was the Lucy Fletcher who twisted a napkin between her nervous fingers, who still woke up with a start to find the other side of the bed empty, who still waited for her husband Tobias, camera in hand, to walk through the front door.

And she was running out of time.

"It's good to see you too." Eric said it like a question.

Everyone knew that Ian Mallory had been dead for three years, killed in the paroxysms of the Blight, the Cascade's violent aftershock that had splintered the earth into burning shards and propelled the Dominion to power. Simon had barely recognized him, nor had he understood, years after his Party had fallen into obscurity, what purpose there was in keeping him prisoner.

She made another darting scan of the room, but no one was watching them, at least in any obvious way. She took a sip of her watered-down tea. She'd have to add *untraceable coffee* to her list, if they ever met up again after this.

If she survived the week.

"If you weren't completely useless with VPNs and stuff," she babbled, "you could probably still get Pornhub."

"*Lucy,*" he said, and how had the world changed so much that he could be the serious one?

Inside the cell, a dead man had called her name. Had he known to expect her? Never one to waste his time with small talk, Ian said, "I know how that husband of yours died."

"I want to come in," Lucy said.

• • •

Lucy Fletcher had sung the new world into being.

She hadn't stood on a firing squad. She hadn't raised Ottawa's Ionic columns from the rubble of its staid, uninspiring brick. She hadn't dug a mass grave or herded anyone into the back of a truck. She was allowed a place on the Train that carried Atherton's cabinet from coast to almost-the-coast, but she did not dictate its course.

All she had done was sing. Even after she'd known the purpose woven into the notes, the value she held to Atherton and his masters, Reid and Alycia Curtis, she had sung for them. Simon had given their ideas a shape, and she had given them a voice, and together they had drawn the nation back together. There was only one way to protect humanity from the monsters, from the demons and the rogue MAI and the entirely mundane, entirely human terrorists who would not stop until they'd burned the country to the ground. She had believed her song would save Tobias, and when it hadn't, that it would save her.

The graveyard streets and the black sites gave the lie to her innocence, her good intentions.

• • •

"You *what?*"

Lucy flinched. "Not so loud," she hissed. "You heard me."

"This isn't a LeCarré novel, Lucy." Eric rubbed at his face, frowning. "What makes you think I can help?"

"Oh, don't be *coy*, Eric. It doesn't suit you." The napkin was shreds in her hands. She rolled it into tight little strings, knotted them together and braided them, one strand over the next. "I can pay."

"They don't want money," he said. Then, "I don't think."

"Of course they want money. Everyone wants money. You can't have a people's uprising without cash. But I didn't mean—" There was a Post-It note, carefully transferred from purse to clutch. She shoved it at him, and his laugh was awful, a high-pitched giggle.

"Oh," Eric said. "Just how stupid do you think I am? No, don't even answer that. Just how stupid do you think *they* are?" Her mouth opened, and he shook his head. "I don't have anything to do with them anyway."

"Could you," Lucy said, and she heard her own voice the way an audience must, steel-sharp and gleaming. She'd never given much credence to the acting part of opera, but she knew her role to play. "For once in your life, attempt to be something like a decent human being and pass that along to those people you have nothing to do with anymore so that maybe, just maybe, they can make up their own minds what they want to do about this? Because you're literally the only chance I have."

"It's suicide," he said, ramming the note somewhere in his too-expensive jacket.

"We're both on borrowed time."

Despite what he'd said, she knew he wasn't stupid. But he'd get sloppy if he were backed into a corner, and that was the last thing either of them needed. He had a plum appointment at the Walsingham Institute, spinning Quinn Atherton's increasingly bizarre policies into PR gold. A valued tool in the government's arsenal, and a loyal son of the regime.

He was also a mole, and he'd been playing a dangerous game for the last three years. He'd navigated the morass of secrets that lay between Atherton's government and the pockets of terrorists still fighting against it without getting drowned by either. If Lucy was compromised, so was he.

"Lucy," he muttered. "You just couldn't stay out of it, could you?"

"I was *there*." She flushed, heat prickling over her skin. "If you care at all. I've seen what they're hiding." She couldn't continue. For years, Tobias Fletcher had been a martyr for the Dominion, a lone voice of journalistic integrity silenced by the terrorists. The moment she spoke the truth aloud, it would crush her.

She could hear Eric trying, and mostly succeeding, to control his breathing. He was doing better than she was. Maybe he had grown up a little after all. "Why?"

"I've been honest. I always was. I can't take it anymore. Your friends can make their own decisions." She tried again. "It was terrible. No one...no one deserves that. Not even Ian Mallory."

Whatever Eric Greenglass had once been was buried beneath years of calcified lying, but for the first time, his smile turned into something less fixed, something that might have passed for genuine empathy. It was enough to crack open the floodgates. Sympathy, these days, was a rarer commodity than Pornhub or sushi. She curled in on herself, buried her face in her arms, and sobbed.

"Lucy, shit, Lucy, not here, okay?" Her eyes squeezed shut, she could hear the frantic shuffling as he scrambled to see if she'd exposed them both. "Come on, Lucy." Then louder, in case anyone *was* paying attention, "He can't have been worth that. He wasn't worth your time."

She sniffled, reached for the tattered ends of the napkin to wipe her eyes and nose. Mascara streaked across it, brushed with the galaxy of her metallic eyeshadow. *Makeup that holds up to emotional emergencies,* she silently added to the list.

"Can I come home with you?" she asked. "I don't want to be alone tonight."

His arm around her, he led her out into the street. A searchlight spun across them, just as he lifted her chin so that her tearstained face was just below his, a mockery of a normal young couple, in a normal time. Lucy squinted against the burst of white, their shadows dark as they passed her billboard. Black had always suited her. Far more than red ever had.

"Maybe you won't need to." When the sweep had passed, he started walking, still keeping her close to him. The night seemed somehow warmer than it had when she'd arrived.

"Can't believe you're crying over—you know. He'd laugh at you. Or worse."

"It's not about *him*. It's about what he told me. About Tobias. I can't just shut up and be a good little girl, not anymore."

"It's a bad time to grow a conscience."

They kept walking, his own apartment in the opposite direction. Lucy told herself that her grip on his arm had everything to do with appearances and was nothing at all like a drowning woman clinging to a life raft.

The city, cleaner and crueler than it had ever been, took no further notice of them.

• • •

Accustomed to the white noise of the Train, exhausted from her performance and desperate flight, Lucy drifted off in the quiet of Eric's Prius, stirring only as they hit a bump on the off-ramp. No one repaired the exits into Exclusion Zones, nor was there any point in maintaining the barbed wire that sealed off the city blocks abandoned for lost. Those would just end up being torn down by scavengers, and Alycia saved her architectural flourishes for raising the salvageable places from the dead, not for walling off Scarborough.

"How long was I out?" More of Lucy's mascara came off on the back of her wrist as she rubbed at her eyes.

"It's the last good sleep you'll get for a while," Eric said.

Lucy's neck cracked as she straightened in her seat. "I don't know about *good.*"

"Yeah, well. You haven't seen where we're going."

He slowed, the flashing lights up ahead signalling a checkpoint. She stiffened, fingernails digging into the leather of the door handle.

"I'm visiting my family. You haven't been reported missing yet." He repeated it like a mantra, like she was supposed to find it reassuring. She dug through her purse for her ID, the royal blue card that meant safe passage, even beyond curfew. But blue cardholders had been shot too. All it took was a jumpy kid at a checkpoint. All it took was Alycia to be awake, to look for her, and find her gone.

The guard at the command post was a Cleaner, not a cop or soldier, one of the young patriots who'd leapt at the opportunity for steady employment, a low-grade ward tattoo, and a noble mission to keep the city streets free of criminals, rogue wizards, and terrorists. He might have been seventeen. Eric handed over his own card—red, restricted class—and motioned for Lucy to do the same. His hand was visibly shaking, but that was good, wasn't it? You were supposed to be a little afraid of the Cleaners, or else what was the point of them?

"Lucy Fletcher, eh?" His face, pale in the flashing red and blue, went vacant, searching for recognition. One of his hands hovered over the gun holstered at his hip. How long would it take him to draw? Faster than Eric could start the car, anyway.

"She's a famous singer," Eric said. How did he keep his voice so even? If she spoke, it would have been a squeak of fear.

"Never heard of you," the Cleaner said.

"Ask your mom about the Songbird of the Dominion," Eric said with a terrifying lack of deference.

"I can give you an autograph." Her voice quavered. Vibrato, torn from the throat of a dying hummingbird. She forced her lips into a demure smile. Her entire life had been a performance; why change course for its finale? "Might be worth something someday."

"Hold on." He was looking for a superior. He was dialling in, through the old-fashioned land line phone in the booth, a report of a defector, a traitor to the Dominion, to the friendship of Alycia Curtis and to the memory of her martyred husband. He had found a little matchbook, flipped it open, and handed her a pen. "My mother didn't make it through the Blight," the Cleaner said. "My dad's name is Ronny."

She scrawled her name across the inside of the matchbook, and the young man handed them back their passes, and the gun stayed snugly beneath his uniform.

Eric drove down identical side streets, washed in the blue of early dawn. The suburban tract housing there had been built for speed, not permanence. It had already fallen to ruin, damaged in the earthquakes and the aftershocks, in the street fights and purges that had followed, then, at last, dealt the mortal blow by shriekgrass that had risen to reclaim those beige fortresses for the earth. They were driving into a blackout. Those streetlights that hadn't been smashed had been left dark.

He parked behind a strip mall. "This is as close as they'll let us get," he said. "Hope you brought a change of shoes."

Lucy glared at him. Eric shrugged, innocent. They each dutifully donned a mask, even though it wasn't spore season. The air was breathable in the deep freeze of an October superwinter, low risk according to the monthly bulletins. Still, she hadn't seen this much shriekgrass in years. The big cities she toured were kept mercilessly free of the invasive plant and the madness it wrought. Here, removed from the Dominion's watchful eye, it grew everywhere, its mauve, spiked spines pushing through cracks in the pavement, chain-linked fences, the failing highway.

Outside of the car's peaceful ecosystem, the screams were louder, a wall of suffering that swelled and sighed as the wind steamrollered over the grass. Eric took her arm again, and she followed him across the broken sidewalk, her heels twisting under her with each step. The sun had already begun to splash the windows of the high-rises in rose and gold.

Someone must be watching them, even here. The grim towers gave nothing away.

"Is it safe?"

Eric shrugged. "On a scale of Dominion Cleanup squads to demons," he said, "how much do you want to nope out right now?"

More than anything else in the world.

The authorities hadn't wanted to release Tobias's body for the funeral. Hadn't wanted to let him come home. She'd had to hire a lawyer to claim ashes that might not have even been his.

"You wouldn't have wanted to see, Lucy," Reid had assured her. *"There wasn't much left."*

She'd let herself believe that Reid and Alycia, especially Alycia, had her best interests at heart. Wanted to honour the memory of her husband, their friend, and to keep his widow safe. They'd *said* so. They hadn't wanted her to see the ruin that remained after the terrorist attack, beyond the skill of any embalmer, to see his face caved in, reduced to shards of bone and blood. It wasn't him, he wasn't there.

Silly girl. You always knew that wasn't why.

Everyone had lied to her, to protect her, to shield her delicate feelings, to bend her to their will. This might have been yet another lie, but—

—someone who lied always had something to gain. Ian Mallory, professional liar that he'd been, had nowhere farther to fall.

Shriekgrass be damned. She'd take the risk of madness, of transforming into one of the demons that stalked the strip malls and crumbling high-rises, over betraying Tobias yet again.

"No," she said. "I'm definitely in. Why aren't you freaking out?"

"I'm warded as fuck. They say it helps. Don't tell my mom. She'd sit shiva for me."

He really didn't seem like the tattooed type. "Where?"

Eric grinned. "That's a second-date kind of question, don't you think?"

They stood at the rim of a crater, the ground jagged with twisted rebar and piles of rubble. No one guarded Exclusion Zones. There were warning signs posted, and barbed wire, but they were old, and there were enough gaps in the fence that slipping through was easy. Even the stupidest of Scarborough's most downtrodden had long since jumped ship. Between the parking lot and the shambling ruins of another strip mall, well past the safe no-man's land with its battered shriekgrass alert symbols, they didn't encounter a single human being. It occurred to Lucy that the Dominion already knew where the terrorists' bases were, and was just waiting patiently for them to turn into demons and hobble off to pick each other's bones dry.

Eric knocked on the smoked glass door of a pho restaurant, long shuttered. The door opened a sliver, first to the barrel of a gun, then to a boy's face, Black, a hoodie pulled down to his eyebrows and a bandana tied just below the bridge of his nose. To Lucy's eyes, he might have been about twelve, but she didn't spend much time with kids. He must have been older if they let him have a gun. He admitted Eric but held up a hand to stop her, then slammed the door.

The sun, stubbornly, continued its upward progress, exposing her treachery.

After some time, Eric reemerged, the kid at his side.

The boy eyed her expensive dress, her stiletto heels. He was still holding the gun, but as they stared each other down, his grip slipped so that it was only his finger through the trigger-guard holding it up, the orange cap clearly visible under the paint. A simulacrum of a gun for a simulacrum of a resistance.

"You've gotta be shitting me," the boy said. This time, though, he left the door open. There were two girls behind him, a teenager with pink spun in her 'locs, and an older one with wire rimmed glasses.

"Coat and purse," the older girl said, and Lucy supplied them. The younger girl rifled through her purse, and pocketed a tube of carmine lipstick.

"If you walk in here," Eric said in a low voice, "you don't walk out. So be sure."

"What about you?"

"I'm in town for a weekend to see my family," he said. "I'll drive back Sunday afternoon. And Monday morning, I'll be back in the office, same as always."

He was waiting for her to change her mind. She could spend a weekend with him, claim a wild affair, and return to her old life. She could tell herself that Tobias had died a hero. That the Dominion's will would be done regardless, even if Lucy refused to give her voice to Alycia's spells.

"Eric says you have a story for us," the older girl said.

Lucy had never been good at speaking; she'd had other people to do the introductions for her. "You believe there's an order to the world. Like music. A predictable pattern, a proper resolution. Your life has a certain form. I was the Songbird. I did what was expected of me, and I was rewarded. And when everything broke it was easy to believe that the disharmony came from outside. They murdered Tobias. We needed to bring them to justice. They caused the Blight; we had to fix it."

"They," the younger one said.

"You." It seemed absurd now. The terrorists were illusory, just children playing make believe with toy guns. "Your...movement."

The younger girl made a show of applying Lucy's lipstick, and the older one said, "Which you now wish to join."

"They lied," Lucy said. "About Tobias, and everything else. My friend Simon Yamashita—the MAI composer—he went to one of their facilities. He took me there too. They have a prison, and they're doing experiments, and there's torture, and..." She had performed often enough that she could tell when she was losing her audience. "Ian Mallory is alive," she finished. "And I know where he's being held. If that's not enough to buy your trust, I don't know what is."

3

The rhythm of the factory was a living entity, a machine-gun pattern that battered against Maya's spell. Floating above its steady and sharp thump like milkweed floss caught in a cold autumn breeze was music, minimal, haunting in its simplicity, a woman's voice in a minor key over a stately piano. Maya had found it beautiful the first half a dozen times she'd heard it, incongruous as it was amid the clanging of the conveyer belt. On repeat it was a violation of the Geneva Conventions—not that the Dominion paid attention to those.

Twenty seconds to slide the circuit board along the belt and ready the next one before the transformer was stamped onto its surface. A robot would have done the job a few years ago, but the Dominion had ramped up its radio production just as the levels of ambient magic made high-tech manufacturing nearly impossible. Twenty seconds to have her hands in the right places or they'd be caught under the stamp, like poor Savannah last week. Twenty seconds to herself between the heavy *thwump* of the heating element descending, to tease apart the spell that wove over the factory floor.

Savannah had been kind to her. She'd offered half a cigarette on break, a ration bar when Maya had nearly fainted on the shop floor. The new girl, Taz, barely spoke a word, despite Maya's best efforts to act like a normal person, one who didn't plan on shitting up the plant's ability to manufacture everything from radios to drone systems. Taz was determined to keep her head down, get her paycheque, and not wind up swinging from the ruins of the Gardiner Expressway for illicit labour organizing. June, on her other side, was more promising, a longtime *Night Beats* fan who missed the show as much as Maya did. Organization and recruitment, according to Gaby Abel, were secondary goals, but it never hurt to make friends.

Jonah, her old colleague, would have made better use of the cigarette. He'd once bragged to her that he could radicalize anyone over a smoke break, but he'd known how to talk to people. These days he was out west, running guns or running from trauma or whatever you did when your wife left you and your kid drowned.

Everything hurt. Her fingers were swollen into painful cones that threatened to slip or fumble the boards. Her eyes, behind glasses that weren't quite her prescription anymore, burned from the dust. She had four real pads and a rag-stuffed monstrosity left to last the rest of the week. At least she hadn't been carried out screaming with the skin of her mashed fingers bubbling like old film the way Savannah had.

"God, I have to piss," June groaned.

"Always." If she'd been a better organizer, or a decent friend, she'd have given up one of the pads. Not that June would have time to cram it down her pants during her twenty seconds of freedom. Their five-minute break, during which they'd have to queue with every other girl for the single washroom, wasn't for another three hours.

She didn't know what had happened to Savannah. The girl was a green pass, like Taz and June, like Maya was pretending to be, and unless she was hiding some massive stack of generational wealth under a mattress, she was stuck with mangled hands, no healthcare, and no work.

Shadi had tried to find out, but no one at the factory used their real names and they all got paid in old dollars, not traceable DEC.

Shadi stood by one of the machines on the line closest to the office. He kept glancing at the door, which wouldn't stop the manager or an assortment of guards from moving in and out every few minutes. He shouldn't have taken his eyes off the line. She could imagine him slipping up, the machine dragging his arm under the belt, and it would be worse than Savannah, not just because she loved him but because his green pass wasn't any realer than Maya's. Both of them were one slip-up away from giving away the location of a safe house and dooming the nascent revolution before it started.

Patience, she urged him, urged herself; the manager's shift would end soon and then Shadi could make his move. She would have to content herself with studying the spell in the meantime. It was a taut, thorny knot that resisted her attempts to tug at its loose ends, the work of a genius or a sadist or both.

Thwump. The machine fell and she slid the circuit board forward and the next one into place. She reached, explored the periphery of the spell. More resilient than any of the wards she'd made, which crumbled in weeks, or illusions, which lasted only hours. It had to be carried in the music—why else would they have allowed this small, strange pleasure? *Thwump.* She moved the next circuit board along. The mask clung to her face, sucked in and out of her nostrils and mouth with each breath. It reeked of off-gassing plastic. *Thwump.* The magic couldn't just be about passivity—the twelve hour shifts, the guards' electric batons, and the ever-present threat of starvation were enough to ensure a compliant workforce. There was something else at work here.

The spell, too, was a secondary target. Gaby Abel, the leader of the Mackenzie-Papineaus and the Dominion's Public Enemy Number One—even if they didn't yet know her name—had personally recruited Maya. She'd gone so far as to send Shadi to whisk her from certain death at the hands of the Cleaners who'd butchered her family and everyone in the apartment building and along with them. Still, Gaby understood magic, and Magic Affected Individuals, only slightly more than the average person. Maya was there to provide cover for Shadi, and Shadi was there to make sure that once he was done with the computers in the office, the company would have to reconstruct their schematics from bits of files stored on archaic floppy disks in a vault somewhere. New technology functioned poorly around magic, and the post-Blight levels of ambient magic forced the Dominion to rely on decade-old CAD files to keep their production lines moving.

Maya couldn't breathe. The smock was a noose tightening around her throat. Beside her, Taz wiped at her face with her shoulder, moving her component into place at the last possible second.

She closed her eyes for a split second and bright flames burst behind the lids.

"Fuck," Maya hissed. "Not now."

The flames spelled out: COME BACK.

"I'm busy," she added, though Martine Abel, the half-feral teenage daughter of their Fearless Leader and, grudgingly, Maya's apprentice, was unable to hear responses. Her eyes snapped open in time to move the piece.

On the opposite wall, past the last line of weary workers, the flames spread out into death metal spikes. ITS RLY IMPORTANT.

Maya glared at the writing. No one else could see Martine's messages. Probably. I already have anxiety. You don't need to make it worse. Normal people send a text. She forced herself to keep breathing, in sync with the rhythm of the machines and the rise and fall of the music. Glanced again at Shadi, but if the message was for him as well, he gave no indication.

"You okay?" June asked. "Stay awake." That was how Savannah had gone, one moment of inattention. The Dominion had no time for the tired, the hesitant. A line of green passes outside ensured that the machines wouldn't take a breath.

"Talk to me," Maya said. Thwump. Move. Thwump. Move. "What did you do before this?"

"Line cook," June said. "You?"

"Intern for a mad wizard bureaucrat in a Party that's now illegal under Dominion rule" was the kind of response that got you pulled into a quiet office until the cops showed up, so she said, "Barista," which was technically true as well. "Did you like it?"

"I liked the people." *Thwump.* They all rationed their peeks at the clock on the wall, measuring time in twenty-second increments, not the hours that stretched ahead of them. She caught June looking now. "What'd you want to do?"

"Write for *Night Beats.*" In hindsight, she could probably have done it. They didn't have MAI writing for the show; she had nothing to offer, no experience, but she'd had no idea how easy it was to dazzle people with magic and turn off their critical faculties. The world as she knew it would still have ended and millions of people, her family included, would still have died, but right up until then, she might have had an easier life.

The minute hand inched upwards in painstaking ticks. The flames curled up the wall, oblivious to her nerves, to the ache in her calves. *Maya maya maya.* A guard strolled past, stopping behind each work station in turn. His baton whisked softly against the stiff fabric of his uniform. When he stood behind Maya, his sour breath puffed hot into the back of her skull, evaporating into mist in the cold. At a downbeat in the music, she felt his body shift, straighter. Pride, belonging. It was a bitch of a spell and she almost respected its caster.

"Listen," June, halting, pitiable, between beats of the heating element, "if you want to grab a tea with me after work—"

Which was when, at long last, Shadi gave her the signal. Two finger guns like the dork he was.

Maya had charged the emoji spell before she'd started her shift. She moved the circuit board—*thwump*—unlocked the burner phone—*thwump*—and cast. The air shimmered around him, warped a little around the speaker where the music was coming from. It would have to do.

Her spell, barbed and alien, peeled itself free from her. It couldn't wait to be let loose. Magic had been unbridled joy to her once, easy as breathing. That was before Ian had made her look into the future, before the earth had split open before her, before she'd found her father's blood splashed against the glass coffee table in their apartment. Before she'd flensed her true name out of her chest and buried it in a Scarborough parking lot to become Maya, outlaw and a foot soldier in Gaby Abel's ragtag army of shitbird terrorists.

Now it fought her at every turn, and breathing wasn't much easier.

Shadi hadn't told her how long the job would take. She envisioned him sitting in front of the console, rolling up his sleeves, sliding in a USB to run through permutations of passwords. If he was lucky, they'd left the system unlocked. Very little was networked these days, which meant that the files probably lived on the local machines and wiping their drives would set production back days, weeks even. Or they could have just wasted the last month, faking job qualifications, burning fake IDs, for nothing.

A guard passed the open door without turning his head. Maya exhaled.

"Why's your phone out?" Taz asked. The girl spoke so seldom that Maya took her words for a trick of echoes. Machine slamming on circuit board bisected her sentence. "You shouldn't have that—what the...?"

Martine's signals were invisible, and the glamour Maya was casting, while it didn't hide Shadi, rendered whatever he was doing beneath notice or interest. But she had never gotten so skilled as to prevent a stray spark of magic or two from fluttering out of her fingertips when she cast.

"Keep your eyes on the line," Maya warned, but Taz had seen, Taz was opening her mouth to state the obvious, that Maya was an MAI, a wizard, she was doing a spell *right now* in the middle of a factory with Level 1 security clearance, and no amount of clever forgery or subterfuge was going to get her back in the building tomorrow. If she even made it out today.

Maya come home, the flames said.

Shadi wasn't going to get any more time. She jammed the burner phone onto the belt and the heating element came down, smashing it in a grinding screech of misplaced metal and molten plastic. Shadi bolted from the office, past the long row of machines towards her.

"Under the Bloor St. Viaduct, any time after 10 on Friday night," she said to June. "It looks like the valley is too steep but just keep walking and you'll find the pathway down. If you want that tea, I mean, or if you're just sick of living like this. Tell them Maya sent you."

An alarm screamed over the music. Guards came pouring out from each of the doors, batons at the ready, and *shit shit shit* she was going to have to fight her way out of here, which was *definitely* something that a person could do if they were John Wick, and not a short, fat wizard-ex-bureaucrat specializing in emoji spells and Somebody Else's Problem fields.

Shadi's hand closed around her wrist. "Run."

She pulled away from the conveyer belt and followed him down the aisle, around a corner and towards the wall. There were guards on either side of them, the tips of their batons glowing white.

Fuck it. She'd already blown her cover. She took a deep breath, pulled Shadi close to her, and dragged them both through the painted cinderblock and into the wall.

She gagged, the uncertainty of her molecules and the molecules of drywall and wood and asbestos in a precarious dance around each other, her magic a thin skein between existence and absence. If the guards were smart, they'd have surrounded the parking lot so no one would be able to get in or out. She couldn't think about that, not with the effort it took to keep them from phasing out wrong.

"Did you get them?" Maya asked.

"I got some of it," Shadi said.

She could tell he was pretending that whatever it had cost them was worth it. She pressed a kiss to his lying lips. Then, still holding him, she pushed them both forward, navigating the spaces between molecules. The burst of magic had drained her like an old battery. A handful of steps forward, and she was greeted by cold, crisp air, the acrid stench of the dumpster behind the factory.

They ran for the car, her lungs seizing, and, as Shadi threw the car into gear and the tires squealed, she dug through the glove compartment, and, finding nothing, said, "I need a phone. Martine."

Shadi handed her a burner.

The girl answered on the second ring. "What the *fuck*," Maya said.

"You need to see what we got," Martine burbled.

"Shadi nuked the schematics for the Dominion's radio systems," Maya said. "No thanks to your little messages."

"A defector," Martine continued. "You're not gonna believe who. Wait, really?"

Shadi's expression said that no, he hadn't really. "Uh huh."

"How many of them did you get?"

"Files? Just the—"

"Cleaners."

Her heart was still thumping out of control, every instinct in her telling her to turn around, to fight, to take from them in blood and flesh what they'd stolen from her, from Shadi, from the world. "None," she said. "They were company security, not Cleaners, and they'd have kicked both of our asses. Why?"

There was a pause on the other end, and were it not for the hum of interference on the burner, she'd have thought that the girl had hung up.

"Oh Maya," Martine whispered. "When you hear what she told me, you're gonna wish you killed them all."

4

Colette Greene woke at five to jog around the block. Nate and the twins were still asleep, but a quick hand gesture that traced beads of light above her head muted her footsteps. She padded down the carpeted staircase, grabbing the door with one hand as she arranged her hair into a loose ponytail with the other.

Frost hung in the air. Summer hadn't really come this year; people joked that time had no meaning, the superseasons playing havoc with the order of months until everything blurred together. Colette liked the crispness, the sudden death that had frozen lawns into beds of crystalline spikes, made permanent the dew on a flower, the cracks in the road. It felt clean, invigorating, even as her lungs struggled for breath.

Five years ago, she might have passed another jogger on her route, the early shift hauling garbage to the curb, people out walking their dogs. These days, people mostly stuck to their homes, did the route from home to school to work to home with as little exposure to the outside world as possible, as if the air itself was poison. An early riser since childhood, Colette rarely saw anyone in the neighbourhood, and it was easy to imagine that she was entering a new world each morning, the layers of the old pulled back to reveal, beneath, a fresh and shining skin. Alone, cold, and utterly free.

She finished her circuit and managed a quick shower. Nate was making coffee downstairs. Colette had been off caffeine for three weeks, and she had yet to create a spell to mute the inviting smell. She ducked into the twins' room. Jasper was already stirring; Noah was barely visible under the pale blue blanket. She pressed her face to their heads, breathed in the soft toddler scent of their fine hair. Readjusted the hand-painted driftwood sign she'd hung on the wall between the children's beds (*in this house, we do second chances, we do grace, we do mistakes, we do prayers, we do I'm sorry, we do loud really well, we do hugs, we do love, we do family*), and left them to their gentle wake up. She donned a flowered blouse and tight, fading jeans. She passed by Nate and held her breath when she kissed him, lest temptation break down her month of willpower.

"Stay for coffee," Nate said, sadist that he was.

"Can't," she said. "My cleanse."

"It's your coffee." There was no resentment in his tone. Minimal resentment. Her job paid partially in DEC, which meant access to luxuries like real coffee. Nate hadn't had work that paid in anything since the early frost in October put a premature end to road repairs. There'd been bad harvests too, not just in Ontario but all over the world, and more and more food was restricted to DEC only. It put more pressure on her, on her job and her cozy relationship with Alycia Curtis, and more pressure on him to not get left behind.

"Give me that." Cleanse be damned. It tasted all the better for being forbidden, bitter, almost smoky. She told herself to taste it mindfully, though the first rush of caffeine tempted her to down the entire thing in a gulp. "There'll be something, Nate. You just need to be patient."

"Always positive." He reached across the table to brush away the stray strands of hair that had come loose from her ponytail. "I'm going down to the job centre this morning. Bruno said there's lots this week. Can you reach a sitter?"

He was a strong man, self-reliant, used to working with his hands. It didn't sit well with him that she was now the sole breadwinner for the family, that she was in the position to constantly reassure him that there were cities to rebuild, that under the Dominion there would be plenty of work soon enough. Already, the radio had reports on the steps taken to address the shortages, on negotiations with the Free States that the old government had neglected.

Things would get better. They always did. Colette retrieved her coat, hung just below Quinn Atherton's portrait, and left for work.

. . .

Back in high school, Colette's biology lab partner was the weird kid in the class, a girl named Wendy who wore all black and drew skulls and snakes on her arms and was a vegan. She had produced, a month into the semester, a note exempting her from the dissection portion of the course. Colette hadn't minded doing the frog herself, but she'd resented that the other girl had gotten the same grade for crocheting her project, a lime green frog with a button-up belly that you could open to reveal a set of tiny pink organs, ruffled yellow layers of fat, red and blue yarn veins and arteries, despite also submitting it to their art class as some kind of postmodern critique on animal cruelty.

Now, in a mildewed cell with her subject splayed before her, stone grey except for where colourful embroidery threads flowed from his heart chakra like blood, Colette wondered if that's where she'd first gotten the idea.

"Hi," she said.

The mass of shadows that formed the rough impressions of what had once been a man didn't stir. He hadn't needed to be restrained in months. The cell was dark enough to render everything but her bright embroidery in washes of grey. She insisted on hygiene—the cell was washed down daily—and the walls gleamed white when she threw the light switch. He flinched at the assault but otherwise gave no reaction to her presence.

"Are you going to cooperate today?" She took up one of the loose strands between two fingers. "I hope you will." She could hear his breathing, a tight rasp that grew faster and shallower as she looped the thread around her index finger. He was a gaunt spectre of a man, whittled into sharp edges by a privation that had begun long before his imprisonment. She, and those above her, had spent the last few years breaking him down further, chipping off the surface stoicism and bravado until the core of him lay exposed.

And still, he held out on her. He'd lasted eight minutes under interrogation before spilling everything he knew—which was in no way useful. Whatever gift of prophecy that had propelled him to power had an endpoint, and he had, at long last, reached it. Atherton might have wanted a public execution, but he wasn't even worth that.

Except to Alycia Curtis. Except to Colette.

He was hers, and hers alone, in the way that Nate wasn't, that even her children would never be.

The Pattern was marked in a colourful labyrinth across his skin, each stitch neatly sewn through grey flesh with a crewel needle. It spread outwards from his heart, its whorls and spirals rendered in oceanic jewel tones, thinning into tributaries over his shoulders, winding under the jutting cliff of his ribs. There were scars where she had removed previous spells, accrued over weeks and months of intricate work, but this latest iteration was her masterpiece. Wendy might have fainted, but she'd have been impressed.

When she was tired enough, she saw meaning in the labyrinth, could almost believe that there were answers hidden in it. But Ian Mallory, and the Pattern, gave nothing away for free.

She tugged at the edge of the thread, enough to get his attention, to send a spark of lightning across their connection. His body spasmed, and he screamed, and she was already tired of this, the weak, failing human, the biological interface between Colette and enlightenment. He rolled to one side, balled up, wheezing. She cut the connection and waited for him to recover his breath before running a finger over the sharp edge of his jaw.

"Let's talk instead."

Ian spat blood onto the metal surface of the table. He must have bitten his lip during the seizure. She always expected a darker shade of grey than it actually was. It looked more innocuous than it should have.

"Fuck you." His voice, too, was a grey thing, frayed and broken. "I don't knows ya. You're nothin', you don't exist."

"Ian." The blood didn't bother her, only the initial dissonance. She wiped it off his cheek with her thumb, the way she did whenever Jasper pitched himself off the porch in a burst of enthusiasm. "We're the same. Useful prisoners of a greater power, in service of our own ends. We might be friends."

There was nowhere he could hide from her in the cell, but he coiled as tightly as he could away from her, a shuddering heap of jagged bone. Colette frowned, the thread a bright line across her palm. For his stubbornness, she incinerated him again.

When he had finished screaming, she said, her voice as even and measured as she could make it, "Let me make this clear. We have won. The only magicians standing are the ones who stand at the feet of Director Atherton, the ones who serve this great nation. We do our duty, just as you did, in your day. But that's no excuse for a deficit of *imagination*."

He had somehow managed to twist away from her. She touched the back of his head, avoiding the urge to recoil. She leaned close, whispered, "I thought I could ask your advice."

He didn't meet her eyes. He stayed curled on the table, his hands shaking violently, and didn't respond.

"I have a project," Colette continued. "Three projects, actually, except they've barely given me anything to go on, no real support. Eat, Pray, Love—that's what I'm calling them, I made up those names. They don't give me nearly enough information. They want me to do something with magic and they think throwing me in a room with you will do it. As if I can just...pull it out of you, and shove it into someone else of their choosing. As if it's that easy to control."

At first, she thought that the ragged, broken noises that wracked his body were sobbing until Ian, slowly, painfully, pulled himself up to face her, his pale eyes blasted and burning with hatred, but dry. She took a step backward, dropping the thread before she pulled the entire spell loose.

Ian wasn't crying. He was *laughing.*

Colette called for the guards.

5

The Trans Canada had been flooded for kilometres, the glaciers bled and reshaped by one unprecedented weather event after the next. The superwinter had frozen it into sheets of dirty ice that rose and fell with the uprooted concrete, like a still frame of the ocean. Shriekgrass burst through in places, providing a foothold with one step, only to wrench it away the next. Even in the cold and the dark, it swayed and groaned and pushed upward in thick, ugly tangles.

A trailer was half-submerged in ice, the roof of what might have been a roadside motel several metres away protruding above a smooth expanse of snow. Most of the lower mainland was long abandoned. The Train hadn't reached this far, and the cities and towns had been built for weather far less chaotic, for winds less vicious and winters less punishing. There were nomadic groups picking off the ruins—criminals, and the occasional temporary outpost of the Iron Alliance living off the land and watching for incursions into Skwxwú7mesh-ulh Temíxw territory—but nothing grew besides shriekgrass and spindly, dying trees.

The forest watched her. Stars caught in the sagging branches of the pines, slashed by their needles. The trees breathed at a slower rate than humans, slower than the shriekgrass' frenzied, violent eruptions, but they were never still. She flinched at the crack of a branch, the soughing of the wind past the trunks.

Blythe walked carefully, almost bowlegged, tilting her head to catch the gloss of starlight over the ice. The treads on her boots were wearing out. She'd found new boots six months into the Blight, on the second floor of a flooded outlet store near Sidney. Three years in, the Canadian Tires and Wal-Marts and Bays and Chinatown shops had been picked clean, and she'd been making do with duct tape, nails, and chains scavenged from old bikes. She feared the demons the most, but realistically she was most likely to die of exposure.

"Pēh ēkwāna kā-kicikāwit." Blythe's brain, overtired from the hyper vigilance of keeping the remainder of her little group alive, parsed the words as English-but-incomprehensible for a moment before blinking at the young man. He huffed, gestured at the kid whose long legs slid, ungraceful as a baby deer, over the ice.

"Apisis piko ni-nistohtēm nehiyawēwin." That was one of the few phrases she'd managed to burn into her memory. Her pronunciation was off. Laura had had a better ear for the language than either Blythe or Jonah.

The man smirked. "Not bad." They both slowed, watched the kid fall twice and collect themself each time, the pale oval of their face a stunned lamp in the darkness. His partner was a few paces behind with her arm draped over the young mother, curled around her strangely quiet infant. "You did well back there. With the—"

"Not well enough," Blythe said.

His head bowed ever so slightly. It wasn't that life was cheap. Life was life. The first deaths had names, faces, memories attached to them. The first deaths left bulky scar tissue that ached when the barometer shifted and split bloody years later. The ones that followed—acquaintances, co-workers—left cumulative damage, termites in the wood unnoticed until the house collapses. Within days, whole neighbourhoods, small towns, entire ecosystems, tragedy writ too large to enumerate, let alone mourn were gone. After three years, other people were shadows, sliding away too fast to register.

"Something's wrong with the baby," he added, as if she hadn't noticed. The girl couldn't produce enough milk. "Can your magic protect it?"

"I'm not an MAI," she said. "It's just a ward tattoo. A really good one."

"That lets you talk to trees?"

"Lichen," she mumbled. She had meant to save her breath, conserve her words. Conversation attached itself to refugees like clouds of midges until they took shape, coalesced into personalities. *Where are you going* quickly became *where did you come from* became *who's your family* became stories, and ties, and tragedies. When Ian told her that names had power, he'd meant it more literally than that, but he hadn't been wrong. "It doesn't. Care about humans. Besides me."

He took this in, and didn't waste words arguing or asking. Magical intrusions, with their chaos and whimsy, were commonplace enough, especially in remote places. Someone got eaten, someone was spared, someone raised a city into the clouds. Applying reason to it was an exercise in cruelty.

Her foot landed in something pulpy. The mountainside was nearly perpendicular to the highway, jagged outcroppings of mossy rock slick with ice. Her ward hadn't fired, but there was a seam, like the Lichtenberg figures the initial strike of the Blight had left in the landscape. It was a mere trickle compared to the rivers of magic that slashed through oilfields and suburban tracts and clear-cut forests, but it hadn't been there on her last pass.

The seam cut through the highway, a bulbous protrusion where the concrete and a slice of mountainside had turned to flesh. Raw and angry, it breathed in time with her own breaths. Liquid seeped from its surface, steaming in contact with the snow. She gagged, raised her arms to signal to the others to stop.

But there was no path other than across the ridge of mutilated landscape, not up the sheer rock face, or into the thick brush where shriekgrass seethed and tangled. She could only step lightly, as she did around her own scars, cursing the madness that had manifested them into being.

. . .

They were a day out from Abbotsford, camped in an abandoned gas station, when she finally worked up the courage to check on the baby. The girl whimpered and turned towards the counter, blocking Blythe's approach with the point of her shoulder.

"Please," she said.

"She's okay," the girl said.

"I'm sorry," Blythe said. "I really don't think she is."

The other young woman slid closer to the girl. She murmured something, and the girl shrunk harder into her worn coat, her back a taut curve over the small, silent bundle. Blythe and the other woman exchanged glances.

Blythe was the oldest, the guide, the human smuggler. The leader. It was her job to take control, by force if need be, to do what was best for the girl and the group. To dispense whatever words of wisdom she had.

As if the girl's life weren't already over, as if she hadn't lost the one thing in the world she had fought hardest to keep safe. As if Blythe had anything to offer besides the stark physical example of how grief had weathered her, sunk her cheeks in where teeth were missing, bent her forward around the hollow place in her chest and filled her skull with the ocean's singing.

"It only gets harder," she said. "You might as well know that now."

The girl's head turned. "What happens when you become one of—those?"

"No one knows," Blythe said. "Sometimes they. Well. You saw, or heard. And sometimes you become one. And I think the part of you that's you goes away."

"Hmm," the girl said. "Sounds nice." She twisted, enough that Blythe could see the crown of the baby's head.

It must have died more than a day or two ago. The skin was wrinkled, dark grey. The winter's sole mercy had been to preserve it, or the gas station would have already been unbearable.

"We should bury her," Blythe said.

"Fuck, not *here*." That was the nonbinary kid, who was pacing aisles marked with Hiroshima silhouettes where chips and Twinkies had blocked the grime on the display shelves. "At a *Petro-Can*?"

"In the forest," she amended. "We'll find someplace beautiful."

But, of course, the ground was too cold to dig, and they had nothing to dig with, and no time for a funeral or a wake and there was nothing of beauty left in the world. The Cree woman sang and Blythe unrolled one of her carefully rationed cigarettes to lay down tobacco. They piled rocks and fallen branches and parts of shelving over the little body while the girl wept. They took turns watching her through the day, each no doubt asking themselves, as Blythe did, how they planned to stop her if she stood up and walked out, meeting the woods as so many others had.

Blythe waited for her own shift to end before she broke from the others to huddle in the ruins of a McDonald's. Even winter, with its dead hand over the mouth of the world, was never silent. No birds sang, no insects thrummed, but the moans of the shriekgrass rushed through the gaps they'd bored through the forest.

She'd quit smoking for Laura, besides the odd cigarette she'd swiped from Jonah, until the bender she'd gone on after washing up on the shore three years ago. She lit one now, the smoke winding in a thin stream before dissipating where the giant M slouched into what had once been a parking lot.

She touched the dry, wind-blasted skin under her eye. The others had cried—not in front of the girl, who didn't need their tears adding to her burdens—recusing themselves to the washrooms and returning with smudges under their eyes. There were words trying to imprint themselves over her own story, words like *PTSD* and *trigger* and *persistent complex bereavement disorder*, words that didn't belong to her, words that were meant for someone else, someone the sea didn't sing to.

A clumsy burst of movement smashed through the crusted snow behind her, and Blythe said, flatly, "If you try to run, I'll have to knock you unconscious and carry you, and that endangers the whole group."

The girl kept walking. Her face was scrunched and reddened, like she'd bit into a particular type of lemon the sourness of which no one before had ever tasted. She didn't move with the frenzy that had impelled the man to his death, or in the serene trance Blythe had seen in others. She was instead defiant, as if she expected the forest and the demons to answer for the crime committed against her.

Joints grinding, Blythe climbed to her feet and followed her.

The demons were already gathering, drawn by despair like sharks to blood in the water. One paced in convulsing lurches over the brindled snow at the edge of the trees. It moved on two rear-facing limbs, a thick, kite-shaped fan of a tail flapping wetly behind it, splashing viscous liquid up into the trees. It had a woman's face, the mouth pulled down in a sharp frown over a jutting chin, the eyes hollow and bristling with black hairs.

The girl swallowed but kept walking towards it, even as Blythe caught up with her and grabbed her by the arm.

She said: "You don't get it."

"The fuck I don't." The girl might want to play Demon Roulette, but Blythe was ambivalent enough to take in one more meagre sunrise. "Why do you think I'm ferrying you people across the Rockies instead of waiting this out like everyone else?"

This caught her attention, at least. The girl swallowed. "Oh."

The demon stopped. It raised its head, the skin bunched at its long neck stretching, and let out a long, rattling sigh. It looked like something Blythe could outrun, but she knew better.

"Get back inside," she said, not out of any real conviction that it would save the girl's life but out of some vague superstition that dying huddled together with strangers was preferable to dying alone.

"What about—"

"Back. Inside." Blythe shoved her, roughly, in the direction of the McDonald's, and waited until she'd disappeared into the service door before taking another few steps towards the demon.

"You want me, come and get me. Say my name if you can find it." It was barely a faltering whisper. Her tattoo burned. The demon chittered. Louder, she cried, "Come on!"

She ran at it, screaming, arms flailing above her head. You were supposed to stand your ground with a bear and make yourself look like more than it could swallow. Her skin was fervid, incandescent. She stopped, abruptly, metres away.

"Do you think you can take away more than they've already taken?"

The head, curiously tiny on its long neck, tilted, teeth bared slightly. The hairy eyes shivered. It seemed to consider Blythe for a moment before turning and retreating back into the forest.

"Yeah," Blythe said. "That's what I thought, too."

. . .

Abbotsford, or what was left of it, was a crossroads. It was the meeting place for the various Iron Alliance bands, those tenacious Cree, Métis, Saulteaux, and Assiniboine communities who had taken to the forests and mountains, too scattered and too remote to fall easily under the Dominion's thumb. Free States and SVAR traders came through too, the surrounding foothills bristling with demons and heavily armed factions.

The town itself was mostly underwater, the roofs of greenhouses and barns and megachurches trapped in ice between the criss-cross of roads. You could skate across it in a superwinter, or canoe the rest of the year, but this close to a thaw, the ice was hungry, ready to swallow a stranger who did not walk lightly enough on the earth.

At least it was quiet. Shriekgrass gasped, distantly, but sought deeper rootholds than the ice could offer it.

The young Cree couple peeled off from the rest of the group almost immediately, with barely a goodbye, though the woman who'd come to meet them took a long glance at Blythe before Blythe smiled at her, regretfully and dismissively. Her Métis-Cree mother could trace her ancestry back to the Red River Resistance but Blythe herself had left, gone to the West Coast and lost herself to the world of academia. She wasn't Native enough for the Iron Alliance to trust, any more than she was white enough to exist under Dominion rule.

She didn't see what happened to the girl once they got into town.

The nonbinary kid stuck around, shadowing her. There was still another long trek, and the ferry to the island, before she reached the Archipelago. She'd fulfilled her responsibilities to the little band of refugees. Whatever happened to them next, she'd gotten most of them across the mountains. It had to be enough.

"I'm Bailey," the kid said. They were sprawled on a stump in front of a fire, the flames darting lucent over their pale moon face. "Yeah. I know. No names. But you're heading to Victoria, and so am I, so. Names."

Blythe shrugged.

"I want to fight them."

"You should have gone north then. Learn to live in the bush and shoot rifles. Or east to Quebec to fight with Vaillancourt's separatists."

Bailey side-eyed her. "I was three years into a marine engineering degree at Dal when the Dominion took over. And I don't speak French, or Cree. Besides, that's not what you're doing."

"Well," Blythe replied. "I'm working for the enemy. And I'm not exactly trying to get old." She shifted her ass on the stump, the pistol digging into her hip. She'd be home soon enough, and then the sea could howl its unreasonable demands at her along with everyone else.

She heard the commotion too late to flee. There was nowhere to go anyway.

Above the sunken roofline, a flock of starlings shook loose from the bowed tiles. Behind their scatter, the shingles groaned and cracked.

She reached for the gun at her belt, even as the sound of electric vehicles rumbled behind her.

They didn't know her real name, but it didn't matter. The SVAR had no magic, nor did they need it, with patents on generations of surveillance tech and troves of data on anything that moved and breathed.

On the roof was a security robot, a headless dog that moved with all the sleek precision that the demons lacked. It bounded to the edge of the overhang, then crouched, whirred, its targeting eye honing in on her. She froze.

From each corner of the building, two more emerged.

She didn't need to look behind her to know she was surrounded. There were innumerable private security firms on the island, contracted to the SVAR conglomerate that ruled over the Special Economic Zone. Half a dozen men in plate carrier vests flanked her.

She could shoot, she could even run, but not before stun guns and batons came out. Not before the dogs were on her.

"Blythe Augustine," the robot dog said. It wasn't a question. She stepped forward, hands splayed on each side of her head. "Your supervisor reported an unexplained absence three weeks ago. It's a $10,000 fine, plus expenses."

"Thought so," she said. Edgar wouldn't be happy, but at least he hadn't been suicidal enough to try to cover for her. Still, a ride home was a ride home.

She made a show of letting them handcuff her, and squeezed into the truck of the carrier, warm for the first time in weeks.

6

The girls were Monique and Martine. The boy was named Junior. They were the three children of Patrice and Gabrielle Abel, the treasonous former Prime Minister and his equally criminal wife. Lucy remembered Martine from one of the stories Tobias hadn't filed, saw in her cruel, knowing smile, her sprawling posture, the echoes of the teenage hellion she'd been. Monique, the older one, was in charge of this little outpost of the revolution, at least until she got back.

Who *she* was wasn't immediately apparent, but all three of the kids seemed to hold her in enough regard that were Lucy to ask to speak with a manager, apparently she'd be directed to this mystery woman.

She waited for hours and watched the dirty children play poker around the table for little gold empty Werther's wrappers, laughing and shoving at each other. Their half-hummed songs, their snapping fingers, their affection shrouded in insults, filled in the silence.

Her stomach grumbled with the memory of bún chả hà nội. When food was eventually produced, it came in a wrapper stamped MRE, and the kids carefully divided each serving in half. No wonder they were so thin. The boy hesitated before placing it in front of her, clearly debating whether or not she was worth feeding.

Lucy hadn't eaten since the grapes and cheese cubes before the concert, twelve or more hours ago, and then, her nerves had been too tightly strung for her to manage more than a few mouthfuls. Instinct insisted that the lumpy rectangle before her, despite the smell, was not food, was not going to taste anything like beef teriyaki, and it seemed a mockery of the Pho King's laminated menu to acknowledge it as such. Her stomach had other ideas, and hesitantly, she maneuvered a corner into her mouth.

Her instincts had been right, but before she could decide whether a second bite was worth the risk, the lock rattled and a woman entered, followed by a man. She was short and squat and he was tall and lanky, both in their 20s and wearing pale uniforms and baggy parkas, pulling blue dust masks off their faces. They were talking, arguing about a phone and a wall and only fell silent when they caught sight of her.

Lucy quashed her disappointment at her first glimpse of the young woman's brown cheeks pinked from the cold, her hair in loose, damp tangles and thick glasses splattered with melting rain. She had been expecting—or hoping, at least—that the mysterious *she* would turn out to be someone she knew.

The woman dropped her bag on the table and scrutinized Lucy, her lips, bloodless and chapped, moving in mockery of words, then trembling almost imperceptibly. There was no doubt that the woman recognized *her.*

She motioned for Lucy to follow her, through the filthy kitchen and past piles of trash bags outside. Lucy fumbled for her own mask, though the delivery area behind the restaurant was such a desolate stretch of concrete that she doubted even shriekgrass could get a foothold.

The air crackled around them. Layers of wards and glamours blanketed the strip mall. Beneath them, the woman herself was faded, ordinary, despite the shine of magic over her fingers.

"If you were any more obvious," the woman said, "you'd need to be watered."

"What?" Exhaustion had overcome tact.

"You're a plant."

"I'm not," Lucy said.

"I'm Maya," she said, offhandedly. "And you're Lucy Fletcher. I've seen you on a billboard. The life you had is over now. You're a Mac-Pap or you're our prisoner."

"Eric said as much." She swallowed. "My life—the life I cared about—it ended when Toby died. Tobias, my husband, you know..."

"I knew him," Maya said, and though Tobias had been dead for three years, Lucy couldn't entirely suppress the jolt of jealousy. They had both kept secrets in those last few months, but Lucy didn't want to imagine him concealing any woman, even this one. "I didn't like him much. He died a martyr, didn't he? Killed by vicious anti-government terrorists."

"That's what they told me." Screw the fancy dress; Lucy leaned back against the brick wall. "Except it wasn't you."

"Might have wanted to." Maya smoothed her mess of hair, pushing it behind her shoulders. "Don't think it was, though."

"Tobias died in prison. Scared and hurting and alone, and all for telling the truth." Her breath hitched in her throat.

"So a hero all the same. Tell me." Maya leaned forward, one hand splayed by Lucy's face. "I want you to look me in the eye and tell me exactly what you know, in detail, and who you heard it from. If you're lying, I'll know. If you're leaving anything out, I'll know. If I think, even for a second, that you're feeding me bullshit, I will make your heart play John Cage's "4'33." I will *flay your fucking face off and sew it into a new purse.*"

Lucy told her.

"And you're sure?" The illusion slipped, just for a moment. Under the poised, self-confident MAI soldier was a scared orphan barely older than the kids inside the restaurant.

"Trust me," Lucy said, "I'm sure."

Maya's fingers tightened into the brick, fingernails bending with the pressure. Her breath was hot and quick by Lucy's ear. Then she pulled back, suddenly, as if struck. "There have been three people in my entire life that I've ever trusted. One's dead, one is—according to you—languishing in a secret prison, and if he's dead, Lucy Fletcher, if your hellspawn fascist puppet masters have killed him, I swear to *actual fuck* that I will find out whether there is anything to this whole blood ritual magic thing and sacrifice you in his honour. I think he'd like that, don't you?"

Who was *she?* Lucy told herself that it didn't matter. Lucy, too, had been a different woman before the Blight. "He's alive," she said. "Last I saw."

"You'd better hope he stays that way," Maya replied. "We haven't had a lot of chances to test out human sacrifice." She drew back, folded in on herself, and Lucy once again saw the frayed edges of her magic. It must have been six am. She must have been going all night, like Lucy had. "You report to Monique now. Don't listen to anything Martine says—that girl will fuck with you for the fun of it. Step out of line and either one of them will strangle you."

Maya had a yellow rubber duck in her hand. She fiddled with it between her fingers, fast enough that Lucy could pick out the tiny whispers between the squeaks. Her dark eyes clouded leaf green, and Lucy was once again on the outside of some shared communion.

"Maya?" she tried.

"Quiet," Maya said. "Don't fuck up the magic."

Nothing much happened. She didn't know what she had been expecting. Whatever Maya had done, or seen, left her frowning when the fog over her eyes retreated. She sagged against the wall, pale and drained.

"So you'll pass this on?" Lucy shouldn't have cared. She'd done her part, played her role. Sang, as Eric, as Alycia, had expected her to. The rest of it didn't matter. "To the actual leader?"

Maya snorted. "The actual leader has enough problems. I'm headed out tonight; I'll be back in a few weeks. Or not, I guess."

"You can't go alone." Maya had just expressed a strong desire to gleefully murder her, but the idea that Lucy had casually condemned yet another person to death was too much for her to bear. "There are guards. It's stupid—it'll be suicide."

"I'm not going alone," Maya said, "I'm going to find an arms dealer."

7

S hadi, being Shadi, hated everything about the idea.

Also, being Shadi, he did not immediately tell Maya that, even though, as she explained, his expressive features broadcast what he was far too polite to say until she finished. He was draped over one of the massage chairs in the nail salon, scuffed Adidas sneaker propped on a sink, while she paced.

"Okay." His nail-bitten index finger pressed up against the border of one thick eyebrow. "Or, and just hear me out on this, we ask Gaby to borrow ten or twenty guys and a bunch of grenades and we just kill the shit out of everything in our way until we find your friend. One night, in and out."

Three years underground, hiding in the enclaves abandoned to shriekgrass and monsters, with the Cleaners breathing down their necks and the full force of the *Emergencies Act* behind them, and sometimes Shadi still acted like it was all just one of the first-person shooters he'd loved until the day he'd had to pick up a gun for real.

But even as Maya shook her head—in the handful of timelines where Gaby agreed, something went wrong: the guards saw them coming, she couldn't hold a Somebody Else's Problem glamour over that many people, someone always died—he didn't question that no, of course she had to leave the Mac-Pap cell they'd built together, the kids who counted on them, their little strip mall temporary autonomous zone, to walk headfirst into a Dominion trap. How effortlessly he folded himself into her fucked up past. He just assumed he'd be there at her side. "A bunch of grenades are our only grenades, and Felipe won't risk them or his guys on the off-chance that we can get to Ian. This is the only way that works."

She had stayed up all night watching herself die. And Shadi die, and that kid from Rexdale who'd shown up at Fort Utopia with bleeding feet and a yearning for vengeance, and the guy from UofT who'd have made the Olympic shooting team if not for the Blight, the boy with the same jacket as her brother Anoj who made her stomach drop when she saw him out of the corner of her eye. She had seen all of them scattered like dry leaves on the floor of a black site.

But she'd seen Jonah Augustine, who'd analyzed zoning documents when they'd worked for the government at the Broom Closet, walk through the corridor to the door with the scrape on it, unscathed.

She hadn't seen Jonah since he'd gotten wind of Ian's master plan and fucked off to wait out the apocalypse with his family. It hadn't gone well for any of them. The last she'd heard he was in rural Manitoba, running guns to the western resistance groups. He hadn't left a forwarding address.

"What happens next?"

"Looking more than a week ahead is pushing it, Shad." At least alone—she'd seen farther, back when she'd worked with Ian, but she couldn't bring Martine into this without Gaby finding out. "We don't get shot this way."

"We'll have moved by the time you got back. What if you don't find us?"

He was reaching, but she'd win, every time. "When have I ever not found you?"

"Lucy said this place is half an hour away. In the opposite direction."

"You're always saying I need a vacation. Think of it like the world's most depressing road trip."

"I don't trust *her*. Why defect now, after everything?"

Shadi dealt in certainties, in if/then statements. He'd been halfway through a computer engineering degree when the Blight hit, used to thinking in terms of systems and logic. He'd have trusted Maya that the heartbreak and grief on Lucy Fletcher's face was not a sophisticated performance for her benefit. That she had loved and been broken hard by that love as certainly as any of them had. But he'd still want proof, and there wasn't a spell for that.

Maya stopped pacing. She sat on the wide leather arm of the chair next to his, leaned across to place her hand over his arm. "It probably is a trap," she said. "I still need to go."

"We," he said. "You don't get to risk your life like that without me."

They were alone in the nail salon, and she'd thrown on an extra ward for privacy. She had enough time, with only Shadi as witness, to indulge herself in a quick cry.

He shifted gears immediately, jumping up to press her head against his skinny chest, wrapping his long arms around her. His sternum, conspicuous from malnutrition, was a sharp stone against her cheekbone. He waited as one would through a flash rainstorm for the tears to pass.

"I want you there, more than anything," she said. "But you can't be. Someone needs to help Monique keep the kids safe, and find out what else Lucy knows, and if something goes wrong—I could lose you."

He snorted. "What about me? You think I'd survive losing you?"

She had to stand on her tiptoes to kiss him. "Yeah," Maya said. "You'd fucking better." Her hands dropped to clutch his, squeezed tightly. "This will work. A week, maybe two. And I'll be back. Hold down the fort and keep Martine out of trouble."

Shadi swiped at his cheek with his shoulder. Were they just going to have a massive cry-fest and never blow anything up? "That's an impossible task," he said.

"Then," Maya said, "I guess I'll just have to come back alive."

. . .

She borrowed an SUV from Fort Utopia, the most obnoxiously bland suburban soccer mom ride she could find, and warded the shit out of it. By the time she hoisted herself into the driver's seat, Maya's limbs were longer, what little excess weight that food scarcity had left her redistributing itself. Her skin tightened, mask-like, forcing her mouth into a rictus grin. Her long hair, dry and frizzy from the superwinter, snaked into spirals. She watched her signature wingtips sprout in the rearview mirror.

"I hate that you have to do that," Shadi said, hanging on the open door, as though in the middle of her dead-of-night desertion, she'd change her mind and let him come with. "Hey. You know you're beautiful the way you are."

"I can't get through checkpoints the way I am."

"Oh, don't get me wrong," Shadi said. "If I had magic, I'd totally make myself look hot. Actually, wait, make me look hotter too?"

Maya laughed, and Shadi put a hand on her knee.

Softly, he said, "Why'd I have to marry someone so brave?"

"Just stubborn and sentimental." Seated in the hulking mom mobile put her at about the same height as him, enough that she could kiss his lips and draw back just as quickly. She sat the rubber duck—a focus for her magic that he'd found to replace her worn-out Panic Pete stress toy—on the passenger seat beside her.

It was too easy to find reasons to stay. Maya started the engine before she could settle on one.

. . .

Maya, before she'd been Maya, had loved driving. She'd ignored math class to study for her G1, spent her tech class on the computer running the clunky simulation as she negotiated parallel parking. Alone among her friends, she'd passed her exam on the first go, and had subsequently launched into a protracted war with Anoj for custody of their parents' car. Her intern's salary after she'd moved to Ottawa barely covered her bus pass, and she missed the wide open highways of a suburban sprawl where pedestrians were an afterthought, where she was just another little ant crawling on the borders of the world.

That was Before. When there had still been parents, still been Anoj. When she'd been able to plug a phone into the USB port on the dashboard and blast Janelle Monáe with the windows rolled down. Now, Dominion propaganda and staticky broadcasts from the American rump state were her soundtrack, and she shivered in the over-large seat, hunched in anticipation of first the Canadian Pacific crossing before Kennedy, then the checkpoint leaving city limits, and after, the wide and haunted road northbound to Sudbury.

The men at the Scarborough checkpoint were soldiers, not Cleaners, motivated by grudging obligation rather than ravenous, fanatic devotion to the cause. They seemed happy enough to wave her tall, blond, skinny ass through. She was headed out into the deadly wilderness, not in from it, and therefore not their problem.

Maya. Where TF u at? She ignored the foot-high letters burning above the checkpoint. It wasn't as though there was any way to send a message back.

Her glamour held, but she didn't relax until she was on the 400. If she drove until dawn, she'd reach Sudbury, and from there, carve her crooked path north to Thunder Bay, hugging the swollen lakeside and forest fallen to the Blight. There would be almost no patrols; the soldiers and Mounties and Cleaners feared the wilderness as much as she feared them. There, she could drive, geasing herself to stay awake, until the forest swallowed her.

. . .

Thin places dotted the Trans Canada Highway, places where you could easily nod off and awaken months later, places where magic reached its osseous fingers for the isolated traveller, the weak, the reckless. Places where Maya could lose her resolve and emerge hollow and hungry, another one of the doomed haunts standing stark in the snow that fell harder the further north she drove.

They didn't worry Maya. Shadi would think her careless, but Ian had once promised her MAI couldn't become demons no matter how hard they tried. No, it was the Cleaner patrols that scared her, the bored boys, hard-faced and cruel beyond their years, with nothing to occupy their time beyond stripping cars and their occupants to the bone, peeling away skin and muscle and fat in search of the barest breath of sedition. Magic would have to fight a cosmic battle for her soul, but the Cleaners would just shoot her.

At least they might have kept the roads in better condition. It was their stated Worthwhile Canadian Initiative, after all. To sew the fractious nation together, to chain it by force if necessary, lest it collapse into the same anarchy that reigned below the border. And yet the highway showed the wear of three years, two hard winters and a superwinter, ravaged by ice and thaw, its path like a frayed vena cava cutting the country in half. The SUV's shocks were up to it, but only barely.

Stupid, stupid, stupid. Ian might be dead by the time she made it back. Fuck knew she'd been too late to save him once.

Maya was used to stealing sleep when she could, on a dirty mattress or a pile of coats. She jerked awake almost immediately, hearing a Cleaner patrol, a demon in the forest, the cold light creeping around the edges of the windshield cover. Her glamour had failed, her car was marked.

But the noise was just other cars, the desperate and brave, the people who thought there still might be hope further north, further west. They rushed past and didn't stop. Her eyes ached but sleep, when it came, was as cruel as waking. Curled under a space blanket, Maya dreamt in flashes of memory, highways that split apart to reveal the bone beneath them, and a future washed in blood.

Her nose and fingers and toes were frozen when she woke, and she hastily turned the engine to flood the car with heat that didn't reach her core.

On the radio, Director Atherton talked about the project to restore Belleville, reclaim it from the damage the quake had wrought. A beacon of hope, he called it. All Maya could think was that they were closing in, that there were fewer and fewer wild places where the Mac-Paps could hide and build their strength. The next story was a triumphant report—the superwinter, despite its severity, had failed to ice over the openings in the Northwest Passage that climate change and the Blight earthquakes had widened.

Sure. What's a few starving polar bears compared to reduced shipping costs? She switched to a barely audible country station, then gave up on the radio altogether.

Two and a half days in, at Ignace, she stopped and pulled off to the side of the road. A thin line of trees separated the highway from the CP Rail line, and in the void left by the treacherous radio, she could hear a train. *The* Train.

The pines that still clung to the narrow strip of land that separated the highway from the railroad were bleached white by magic, choked by the mauve shriekgrass that waved its spines and howled through the swirl of snow. Past them, the rusty tracks quivered in anticipation. Maya ducked low in her seat, one hand tightening around the steering wheel, the other by the keys, always prepared to run.

Ottawa the city and Ottawa the political force had existed by a gentleman's agreement, an old pact shattered by the Blight, by the terror that had followed, by Atherton and the Dominion's ascension to power. It would never be enough to control a fractured, traumatized country, its supply and communication lines disrupted by the Blight, its populace divided against each other. And so the Dominion governed by travelling court, an omnipresent brute force that ensured compliance along its circuit.

The security convoy came first, black armoured vehicles that stuttered in advance of the Train, checking for sabotage along the rail line by Mac-Paps or land defenders or the trickster land itself. There were about five of them, little railcars and APVs, travelling in a tight wedge that hugged the line.

She should have brought guns. She'd have a clear shot through the trees. She'd made harder shots, but they had the kind of remote weapon systems that would vapourize the SUV before she'd had time to squeeze off a malicious thought.

And then came the Train. Like Atherton himself, it was in no hurry. Through the ruined trees, across the blasted landscape, the Train rolled forward, a scarlet streak, Red Ensigns flapping in the wind.

One shot. One perfect act of destruction, and all their problems could have been over.

The Train of course, unlike the ancient rail it travelled, was as state-of-the-art as it could be while still bearing an MAI or two when necessary. Fireproof, bulletproof, explosion proof—oh, they'd *tried*, they'd tried and lost a hundred times. Its geas was so strong that the very thought of striking against it made her head ache.

She had to give credit to the malevolent intelligence behind the curse. For a regime that rose to power on anti-magic sentiment, riding the wake of an MAI terrorist attack and the Blight that had followed on its heels, they had some badass wizards working for them. The *Emergencies Act* had done that, drafted every willing MAI into service. Which, as it turned out, was more than she could have guessed.

Maya pushed the seat back and stretched out, head rolled to one side to watch the Train huff past in clouds of unsettled snow and steam. She barely took a breath until it had passed. Even then, it took all her willpower to turn back onto the highway.

8

You're a field mouse. A fuckin' field mouse. And at first, you have nothing but choices.

From your low vantage point in the tall, golden grass, the sky is azure and big as God. Your tiny mouse heart flutters, your tiny mouse brain incapable of contemplating the infinity that dwarfs you. You can run in any direction. The grass is a forest, an ocean; you grasp a stalk with your tiny mouse hands to hoist yourself to the surface. Here, a hawk swoops; there, the steel teeth of a combine lie in wait to crush your small body in its jaws. Here a creek sings to pull you under; there, a snake scents your blood.

In each direction, a death, inconsequential to the murderer, apocalyptic for you. In each direction, a closing of possibilities, an extinguishing of your small selfhood. And what was once an open field is now a labyrinth, through which you may scurry, hunted by the world, and from which you will never escape.

Until the day that steel slams shut on all sides of you, and there is only the gleam of cold metal, your own starved and deformed reflection stretched in its sheen, only one path forward. Not a labyrinth of bad choices but a trap of none, *no longer a field mouse but a lab rat. No longer a thing to be hunted but a thing to be vivisected, to lie pinned and flayed at the world's mercy. To live, and suffer, and die, and live again, the air forced into your lungs and your heart squeezed into beating. And you marvel, a skinless, bleeding nub, thrashing beneath the scalpel, at how powerful you once thought the hawk.*

· · ·

Colette took Ian to see her other experiments. There was no pattern to it, or purpose, as far as he could see. Her cruelty was accidental, barely conscious, damp wings unfurling from the cocoon of her work. Sometimes she came with her needles and a pain that blinded him and tore him in half, and sometimes she came to talk. Sometimes she'd have him shackled at the wrists and ankles, as if he had a chance of running away, and he would have to shuffle after her, his gait an old man's. Down the hall. Past the open door that revealed a plastic recorder on the bed, and the door that wasn't open where the screaming came from.

Ian had listened to that warbling melody, that trapped little mouse-song as it grew thinner and thinner by the day until it faded altogether. He was too consumed by his own pain to wonder who had held the plastic instrument in their hands, who had somehow choked out the notes even as the breath evaporated from their lungs. Just another layer of shit in the shit millefeuille.

Colette's interest in the dead was limited. Whatever the player had been, the detritus they had left behind barely warranted a glance. She led him forward, pushed him into a different cell.

Ian almost missed the other prisoner squeezed into the corner. The man had clawed deep grooves into his face and arms and thighs, had scratched the whitewash from the walls and painted his scrawny, naked body with it, streaked with the grime that accumulated in the corners and creases of the cell. Only when he moved did he become a living thing. His spidery arms wove one over the other, twining under a bent knee, and his browning teeth bared in an anguished hiss.

Colette, his jailer, his tormenter, his guide, barely came up to Ian's shoulders. Her skin was unblemished, its deep gold tan receding to winter-pale. She wore jeans under the waxed canvas apron that kept the blood from splattering her cotton blouse. It would have been impossible to take her seriously in another context. She watched the prisoner with pursed lips, a solemn child studying a fat, shiny beetle as it scuttled across the sidewalk, waiting until it had nearly reached the grass before smashing it to shards of shell and white paste.

"That's new," Colette said. "Is it me or is he starting to look like you? A mimic reaction, perhaps?" She circled the prisoner, frowning. Ian slouched into the wall, letting it support the weight of the iron tugging him towards the earth.

"Ya got a face on ya like a hen's arsehole in the northwest winds." When someone had masticated your heart, you got to tug their pigtails now and again. "Your little experiment's not goin' so well?"

Her head swung upwards. Her irises, dark blue, a sky ready to burst into thunder, were her only exceptional feature. There was never warmth in them, no matter how broadly she smiled.

She wasn't smiling now.

"Why didn't it work?" Colette might have been asking Ian, or she might have been talking to herself. "It should have worked. Everything *felt* right."

The prisoner lunged. He jerked forward in his manacles, the chains extending just far enough that he could snap at Colette's dolphin-tattooed ankle. The keening wail started low in his throat, ballooning out his larynx, working its way free from his cracked lips. His bloodshot eyes bulged in hollowed-out sockets. He reeked of piss and infection, gangrene crusting the borders of raw wounds.

Poor bastard.

"What am I missing?"

Now it was Ian's turn to study the wraith, halfway to demon already, picking him apart in search of the human beneath the broken mesa of filthy skin. There was an adolescent gawkiness to him, the remnants of acne, a high-and-tight haircut. *Oh. A volunteer.*

"Ideological compatibility," Ian said, and laughed.

The little muscles in her jaw tightened, and he had enough time to see her reach into her apron, the flash of jewel-toned thread, before she drew the knot tight and sharp.

His heart seized. Bronchial tubes calcified into tree bark, bottling the breath in his chest, blood turning to iron daggers that spiked into his veins. He fell to his knees, palms scraping the cold concrete floor.

You're not dying you stund sowing potatoes fuck get up get up and fight.

Each line of labyrinth, painstakingly stitched into his skin, pulled towards its completion, tugged sinew and nerve and bone in its wake, wrenched him into a universe-spanning web of debased and bleeding flesh. He was drowning, burning, she was inside of each one of his cells.

He retched as the spasms ebbed, each coming farther apart until they subsided altogether, leaving him hollow and boneless. He'd barely eaten; there was nothing left in his stomach to vomit, just a thin line of white froth on the concrete.

Colette cupped his chin and yanked his head upwards. Her other hand still held her embroidery, loose threads tangling where they spilled between her fingers, setting off stray sparks of pain between ribs, in the furrow of a hipbone. "What went wrong?" she asked.

You did. They were the earth's last gasp, the flailing immune response of a dying organism, and she used the immense power visited upon her to pick apart bodies until they gave up their secrets. But his mouth, emptied of screams, produced no more than a rattle.

"Magic obeys rules," Colette insisted, a claim Ian considered a massive assumption. "It chose you. It chose me. And it didn't choose him. It made him—" The prisoner—if he was that, if he hadn't mere weeks ago been a bright young goosestepper, eager to serve the Dominion of Canada—moaned and chewed at his own bony fingers. "—This."

Still on his knees, Ian met the poor bastard's vacant eyes. If there was any connection between them, any white-blue spark that bound them to one another, it eluded him. The prisoner watched him back, now incurious and placid as a cow for whom the pop of the captive-bolt gun is simply a distant noise.

Colette's fingers idled at the thread, taut then loosened into echoes of pain that scraped the surface of his nerves. Barely pain, compared to having your soul fleeced from your bones, but he shuddered nevertheless.

What task had she been given? Alycia Curtis had the country bunched like crumpled paper in her lace-gloved fist, had every non-compliant MAI at her mercy, had even killed poor Tobias Fletcher for daring to squeak out the most milquetoast objections. What was left? Eternal life? Raising the dead? Turning magic from a wild and untamed thing into a predictable meritocracy, to be doled out as a reward to the virtuous, the well-heeled, the deserving.

This little Kekistani hadn't passed muster, in that case. Just like his mother used to say. *One of these days you'll wish your cake, dough.* He'd asked her what she meant by that and she'd smiled between the bruises his da had left on her, like he'd figure it out on his own, eventually. And, eventually, he had.

Colette must have been under pressure. Alycia Curtis, on one of her inspections, had interrogated Colette on her progress. *His* lack of progress. Kneeling by him, where he lay wheezing blood on the floor of his cell, she'd mused, "Such immense power. And such little ambition. To settle for a mere *country.*"

The hand holding his head upright thumbed his cheek. "I don't think he has much longer," Colette said. Already searching out a new mouse. "Maybe the next one will go better." The string pulled tight, and he was on his feet, threaded on a giant fish hook. Back to his cell, the dying boy flopping like a newly severed limb behind him.

9

The highway, glossy with ice, cut sharply into Scylla monotony to sing vehicles to their deaths. A lone tractor trailer whipped past Maya's SUV, nearly driving her into the ditch.

"Where the fuck're you going so fast?" She rubbed at her forehead with the back of her wrist, blinking heavy eyelids.

And then she saw it.

It moved like they did in all the footage. Its gait was jerky but it somehow managed to keep pace with her car though none of the limbs were in sync. It should have slid and broken on the icy road, but its thick undulating body kept it upright and steady in her rearview mirror.

It was also fucking *huge*.

The mirror couldn't capture the whole creature, no matter how hard Maya tried to put distance between them. She saw it only in glimpses. Here, an exposed spine, there a threadbare hide stitched together by the barest of skin cells. Antlers that caught the moon in their rack, and eyes that shimmered, mother-of-pearl, caught in the shine of her tail lights.

No human, not even a wizard, could fight a thing like that. Couldn't outrun it. To surrender would be unthinkable. She could only accept its existence, this slow, alien sentience that watched her, moved alongside her until it was in her blind spot, then parallel, humping arrhythmic beside the SUV.

You're here, you're here and I can't stop you from being here, I can't stop you from being, but I'm also here and we can just be here, in the same existence, me over here and you over there, we can just be—

One great, pale eye caught her in its baleful radius. Her entire body stiffened under its gaze.

You couldn't ascribe motivations to demons, any more than you could assign them to shriekgrass, or magic itself. It wanted, it *longed*, in ways stronger and deeper than humans could want or long, but that desire was something unknowable, incomprehensible.

It reared, and she saw the shapes of it that had been smashed and reassembled into monstrosity. A moose that had wandered too close to a wellspring, probably, some hapless creature bending its muzzle to what had looked like the clearest of moonlight streams, burning from the inside as it was transformed into a lurching horror. Maya met its eye. She let herself feel, briefly, an ache of pity, for what it had been, and then pushed outwards at it with the edges of her glamour.

It shuddered and balked, then broke off from the highway, lumbering into the woods.

Maya drove until the white-knuckled adrenaline dropped out of her system. She pulled off and stopped the car, her breaths short and sharp. Far from any town, the cleft of the Milky Way arced through the spray of stars above the tops of the trees.

Shadi would like it, she thought. He'd lived his whole life in Scarborough, which was sorely lacking in epic views, and most of that locked in his room playing video games. It might have been a whole other universe from this one. She took out her burner phone and tried to get a shot, but the whole frame came out either all black or all white, depending on how she angled it.

Martine's flaming words wouldn't leave her scope of vision. *Maya Maya Maya*

Are u dead??

Resigned, she crawled into the back seat, lit a tea light, and tugged the space blanket over her nose. Her neck protested even this, but she was short enough and the seat long enough that she could lie sideways, the buckles of the seatbelts digging into her hip and shoulder. Tired as she was, she told her body, unrulier than the glamour she wore as armour, to stop complaining.

The sky watched her with the same cold impassivity as the demon had, and as she raised her hand to adjust the blanket, pinpricks of stars pierced her palm.

•   •   •

"What a feckin' waste."

He was standing on the other side of the ditch, up to his ankles in the snow that drifted over the cracked two-lane highway. Facing away from her, to the tree line, he was dressed like he'd been the last time she'd seen him, in the suit he'd worn to purge the Broom Closet before they'd come to arrest him. It wasn't his best one, he wouldn't get a chance to visit a dry cleaner's any time soon and what was the point of dressing well, given that, but he looked put together enough to retain a modicum of dignity. No coat, but the cold didn't seem to bother him. He was already the colour of something dead and long frozen. Flecks of snow caught on his hair, the pale outer shell of an ear, and didn't melt. If it kept falling like this it would bury him.

"Excuse you." Maya shoved the door open with her foot and hopped to the ground. "Speak for yourself."

He turned his head. "I died to buy you time," he said. "And here you are, tossin' it all away."

Maya crossed her arms over her chest, tucking her hands under her armpits. Even dreaming, her fingers were frozen stiff, the tea light long burned out. She was convinced she wasn't going to be warm ever again. "Don't be such a drama queen. You're not dead."

"But you're dying. I can sees right through ya, darlin'."

It wasn't so bad. Even Shadi hadn't noticed yet, and he had catalogued every millimetre of her beneath her glamours.

"Life comes at you fast," Maya replied. She stretched, back and neck cracking. "I have a plan. I'm finding Jonah and then I'm on my way to get you."

There was none of the animation in his grey face that she remembered. Fuck whatever this was, the real Ian Mallory would want to be rescued. Would want to know that for all that she'd forgotten, for everything she'd buried and burned, that she still remembered him.

This Ian just watched her. She'd had nothing but ghosts for company since she'd left Toronto. One more was hardly a burden.

"I didn't ask you for time," Maya told him. "I never asked to be saved." And definitely not to be another sacrifice, like Ian had been, lighting herself on fire to serve as a torch for an ungrateful nation.

"And yet," Ian said. "Here we both are. You're not gonna like what you find."

"When do I ever?"

Another snowflake landed on his cheek. He brushed it away, along with the skin that had been beneath it. His flesh cracked and split apart, exposing night sky beneath, stars, the tall, ragged spines of trees. The hand too, crumbled, blew away in the cold breath of wind. A labyrinth burned across his chest, through his shirt, not the white-blue spark of his own magic, but the searing red of someone else's.

He mouthed words, but no sound emerged. Her true name was long buried, unspeakable, and as he dissolved into sparks of light, she almost thought she heard him call it.

.   .   .

Maya drove through the whiteout, the road slippery and deserted but for the trucks and armoured personnel carriers that flashed bright eyes behind her, lighting up the snowflakes, then red as they swerved past her, skidding snow in their wake. The geas propelled her forward and kept her from passing out, but she hunched into the steering wheel, shoulders tucked up by her ears and hands so rigid that she decided that their transparency had been part of the dream.

The narrow thread that spooled and curved around lakes and rock cuts was a murderous drive, an obstacle course of spilled granite and black ice, but as she broke free of the tangle into the straight line of snow-blanketed prairie, the fear she'd been ignoring since the last checkpoint at last settled over her.

This was the part that killed you—not the hazards of the deadly stretch before the Manitoba border, but the hours of open road, broken only by a farmhouse here, a scattered settlement there. The rumours of road bandits were as exaggerated as they were unnecessary. The Mac-Paps had done reconnaissance, and it was an impractical lifestyle, there were other ways to be desperate in this world. She was never going to end this trip with her throat slit and thrown in a ditch. It was the boredom that got you in the end.

When she'd been young, when every day was ordinary, 25 had seemed impossibly adult. Now, alone, the expanse of the world pressing down on her, she desperately wanted someone more adult to step in.

She'd talked about doing this road trip, years ago, after watching some CBC documentary in her survey geography class. She'd envisioned summer, and a convertible, and golden fields of prairie wheat swaying in gentle soft focus. And Jamila. The two of them going coast to coast, telling competitive dad jokes to keep each other awake at the wheel.

We could liveblog the whole thing.

No one would care.

It'd be awesome, fam. Two third-culture girls versus the Myth of Canada.

Your mom would kill you, S—

Maya blinked herself back into alertness. It must have been days. Years. What happened to people who died on the highway? The road she'd walked after the Blight was a dotted line littered with mementos and broken-down cars and a corpse or two. But the Dominion had made cross-country unity a priority, and while the highway trembled and faltered in places, battered raw by the superwinter, it was clean. Someone must have been dragging the dead away.

She stopped to charge the vehicle outside of Winnipeg, ignored the stare of the trucker across from her. She'd gone shorter and dowdy this time, and turned the SUV a dark blue. A pretty woman with carefully applied makeup turned too many heads out here, though apparently any woman at all was enough to draw attention.

A slate grey car pulled in behind her, and she froze. The man in the passenger seat shambled out while the driver remained at the wheel, eyes focused on a point somewhere past her head.

Cleaner uniforms always fit badly. She'd grown up with dapper Nazis on film, but the Dominion's paramilitaries didn't have even a bargain basement knockoff of Hugo Boss tailoring their suits. They were always a little too long in the sleeves, or too wide at the waist, accentuating the youth and awkwardness of the boys who wore them. The Red Ensign sewn onto the sleeve was too complicated a symbol to really pack a visual punch. This particular exemplar of the master race couldn't have been 20, a thin attempt at a moustache peppering his upper lip.

He could still kill her without hesitation.

The Cleaner lifted his head to stare at her. She ducked her head and swiped the pre-paid debit. He was still watching her, probably warded to shit, probably looking back and forth between the suburban mom and the trucker trying to guess who was pinging his tattoo.

Not today, asshole. Maya cast him one backwards glance and climbed back in the car.

• • •

Maya played with the radio dial. If she tilted her head the right way, she could just get CBC. They were playing that ponderous classical music that the regime seemed to consider the zenith of Western civilization.

She suffered through it, waiting for the news. When that inevitably disappointed, she resorted to singing songs from the *Night Beats* musical episode.

We put the PSI

In that Psi-ence CSI

At the crime scene

Not the scream team,

We're the dream team...

It sounded better in context. And sung by someone who could carry a tune.

She flipped down the sun visor, and, when it proved insufficient, threw her elbow over her forehead to block the glare of the sun dropping towards the horizon, turning the snow to glittering knife edges in orange and rust. Maya silently apologized to her teenage driving instructor for not going hand-over-hand as she fiddled with the screen, shifted herself in the scoop of the seat to find an angle that wasn't blinding. The highway and the sun schemed together against her, drawing her deeper into the prairie's heart.

Night fell like a mercy.

She had been driving forever, lightheaded despite the geas keeping her conscious. She tasted ozone. How the fuck did she know it was ozone, how did she know what ozone tasted like, sharp and crisp—

—the sky had turned from black to acid green.

She didn't have time to spare but her hands moved without the consent of her brain, swerving her into a rest stop, legs spilling her out of the car, into the snow. She stumbled, aware of the cold soaking into her knees and palms, as if it was some abstraction outside of herself. The dampness pressed to the border of pain. The viridescent spiral in the sky stretched a tendril to yank her face upward.

In retrospect, she shouldn't be surprised that the sky, too, could hold a Pattern.

She became less and less, no longer able to delineate where her skin ended and the Northern Lights began. They corkscrewed through the thin membrane that stood between her and the world. Every vein was a tripwire, burning white hot. An electric shock arced across her tongue.

She could let go, now. Become not-Maya, the way she had been not-*someone else*. Just a speck of light, to be wished upon by a child, wrapped forever in a fold of the shining cloak that settled over the snow.

In all of it, she thought to glance at her phone, the time displaying a series of letters and runic symbols, blurred together in pixels that failed to quite register. She had somewhere to be, a ticking clock, but she was three years ago, twenty years from now, at an orthogonal angle to linear time.

She was in Anoj's room, getting her ass kicked at Super Smash Bros. Melee, drunk off the vodka he'd smuggled in the Coke, sock feet digging into the duvet as she swerved with each of Samus' moves. She was on the couch with Jamila, tossing popcorn at each other during the *Night Beats* season 3 finale after Jamila expressed the *tragically wrong* opinion that Jordan looked good in that leather jacket, actually, and was showing some *genuine growth* as a character and maybe season 4 would be less of a garbage fire as a result.

She was forty-two years old, and Shadi had grey at his temples, and his beard was fuller, cropped close along his jawline, and he wore glasses now that he raised and lowered over his laptop because he was too stubborn to get bifocals. There was coffee brewing, thick and just this side of burnt, the way she'd decided she'd liked it these days. *Coffee that tastes like coffee.* Some podcast chattered from the tablet charging on the counter of the galley kitchen. Maya strained to hear the conversation, something about re-seeding wild rice in what had been cottage country, the hosts so hilariously intense about sustainable agriculture that Shadi insisted they subscribe. He cared a lot about gardening these days, unironically. Shadi leaned into middle age in a sweater vest, puttering in the backyard. She checked her phone. Jamila had texted from her break, promising a truly hideous ER story, and something bright and sharp unfurled in her chest.

The light from the window caught the bottoms of the pans hanging above the sink—good pans, Shadi had made fun of how excited she'd been to get decent cookware, and then, the first time it was his night to cook, had to admit that she'd been right—and she flinched away from the flash across her glasses. No matter which way she turned, the glare followed her. She squeezed her eyes shut, but it danced violent and green in patterns over the inside of her eyelids, the afterimage of the lights, the prairies, the labyrinth.

Stop it. Stop it stop it stop it

I want to stay here I don't want to go back

Magic cupped her cheek. Draped itself around her shoulders, butted itself up against her forehead. Whispered the name, her true name, the one that she could still feel, beating weakly, where she'd abandoned it under the concrete.

It promised her that she could stay.

The Pattern branched before her, this possibility, and others, where her mother and father had lived, where Anoj had, where the Blight had been sparked elsewhere and its ripples lapped against her home as gently as the Cascade's had. Where they'd somehow muddled through, where the world changed as it always did, but more slowly. Where the spark of her magic was too weak to conjure a future, where it was strong enough to save them all.

For the first time since she'd sat in her teenage bedroom and blown up her phone with an emoji spell, the Pattern's desires for her took shape and will.

She could inhabit all of those realities at once. All it took was ceasing to exist in this one. As far as magical pacts went, she could do worse.

Or she could find Jonah and the cache of firearms her visions had suggested, and save Ian Mallory's life.

There was a string through the labyrinth. She followed it, backwards, upwards, in directions she hadn't seen it go before. The tug on her hands was a plaintive child, begging her for softness, for rest.

And here she'd thought burying her name had hurt.

She fell out of the lights, kneeling in the snow as its cold fingers grasped for her ribs and needled through the thick denim of her jeans. Maya groaned, frost in her throat, pushing herself up on her elbows until she'd gathered the strength to stand.

The sky had gone dishwater grey, paused, indecisive, before committing to sunrise.

Sure. Why the fuck not?

If you kept driving, kept moving, the sunrise would eventually come. The borealis reached for her like a forsaken orphan, but Maya followed the ice-slick pass north.

10

Nearly two weeks after her defection, no one had bothered to take down the giant portrait of the Songbird. They'd buried her treachery like they had buried so much else, wary of the effect it would have on public morale. The view from Eric's office was a neat encapsulation of the new order—the billboard, its shining promise of a glorious future ahead, and just past it, the gallows and the poured concrete wall that kept the city safe from its own nightmare heart.

The Abomination was part of the landscape now. It was a Brutalist concrete silo, caged by scaffolded ward symbols that flickered, molten with enclosed magic. Eric passed it daily on his way to and from the Walsingham Institute. On a morning like this one, bright and merciless, he might even have been grateful for the shade that it cast in his office, and he angled his chair to take the most advantage of it.

Symbolic, really. They hadn't been able to kill the writhing terror that democracy had become, and so they sealed it off behind an iron-lined cement wall, lest it spill out into the streets and devour everything in its path. He wouldn't have expected them to keep the billboard, though. Reid Curtis had never taken betrayal well.

Eric had his rituals. He took off his respirator, hung it on the hook on the back of the door. Brewed himself a Nespresso and sat at his desk, savouring the wages of a guilty conscience, before his first scan of the news. The Dominion's Great Firewall extended to his apartment, but within its own fortress, he could run the state-sanctioned VPN and access the rest of the world.

For the good of the nation, of course.

They watched him, and even expected a baseline of treachery and deviousness. If he didn't step out of bounds a little—a dip into Walsingham's intraweb, a quick scan of *Al Jazeera* headlines, a Facebook search for distant relatives in Europe who might have been willing to sponsor him—they would have suspected far worse.

"You're late." Alcott, his manager, swung the door to Eric's office wider, and he nearly jumped out of his skin. But the other man was grinning as Eric spun in his chair. "Five minutes. You look like shit by the way."

"Thanks?"

"It's Kelly's birthday. There's cake."

He wasn't getting skinned alive today. He duly followed Alcott into the break room, where six department members he'd studiously avoided getting to know all that well were gathered around a birch veneer table. They'd stuffed Kelly into a children's party hat and she was blushing madly.

"Cake time," Norm said, making a beeline for the fridge to retrieve a tall cake. It glistened with rich, dark chocolate, as much a relic of a lost world as Minoan statuette. Kelly was deeply ordinary, a red pass, same as Eric, on the same restricted trickle of DEC. Where had she gotten such a thing?

In his head was the dire Human Rights Watch report he'd scanned. Photographs, blurred by necessity, of the demon infestation that had taken so much of Quebec City after the riots. He sang halfheartedly with the others while Kelly ducked her head and covered her eyes.

Canada had never drawn much attention before the breakup of the United States, but today's news had Luther Sears, President and Defender of the Faith in the Free States, decrying the Dominion's alleged atheism, and one of the SVAR CEOs delivering a TED talk about how the pass policy stifled innovation. Fascists, all of them, despite their disagreements. They were the carcinization of politics, the tendency of every government, regardless of ideology, to eventually evolve into something that would crush you in its pincers.

Nowhere, in any of it, had the Songbird's flight been mentioned.

Kelly, giggling, sliced the cake, managing somehow to get a dab of chocolate on her nose, which Jason whisked off. Eric didn't hate these people any more than he'd hated the Party brass, for the most part. At least no one was turning into a bear or walking through walls.

There should be something by now, a denunciation or a denial or some whisper. It was inconceivable that Lucy Fletcher, the Dominion's voice and weapon, could simply flee to the enemy's doorstep, vanishing without even a diminuendo. Someone must have noticed. Someone must have seen Eric's hand in it.

Had Lucy died before passing on her message? But no, the Dominion would have seen the opportunity presented by the murder of one of their own. They would have paraded her like a martyr, as they'd done with her husband, celebrated her beauty and talent and patriotism whether they or the Mac-Paps had been the author of her death.

"That looks amazing," he said, because he was expected to say something. He was rewarded with a thick slice, the interior just as rich and decadent.

Alcott leaned over. "Be warned," he whispered conspiratorially. "It's carob."

Eric snorted at his manager's sudden stroke of camaraderie and made a show of taking a few bites anyway, working his mouth around the waxy lumps of culinary surrender, enjoying, despite himself, the few moments of casual banter among the people who greased the wheels of the Dominion's death engine.

. . .

Eric's prison was well-appointed. He had a glass-walled office—*all the better to see you with, my dear*—space on his desk for state-approved personal effects: the cactus, still miraculously alive after three neglectful years, the photo of his family. Their continued survival was far less miraculous. *All the better to blackmail you with, my dear.* Jakie's very existence was evidence of Eric's good behaviour and his ability to be Useful. His allotted monthly visits home consisted of more time spent driving than with his parents and brother, and were interrupted by barrages of phone calls and emails. He was reminded on a regular basis that their DEC allowance, their access to seizure meds for Jakie, were rewards for his compliance.

The Walsingham Institute wasn't the Train, but it was as close as anyone got to the centre of power with only a moderate amount of blood on their hands. He didn't have access to the Ninth Ring of Hell—that was reserved for a private LAN, limited to the Train and cloaked in military grade security—but he had access to nearly everything else. He ran weekly clones of the surface-level files. Even a deeper look was often easier than it should have been—there were more than a few mid-level functionaries whose passwords were written on sticky-notes on their monitors, or who hadn't changed their voicemail from the default.

There was a request for tender for repairs to water treatment facilities, a second for rolling stock. Eric collected the names of the current bidders, which ranged well beyond the Dominion's borders. He tracked the shipments across the borders—grain, bananas, and critically, fresh water, to the parched and starving Free States: robusta and firearms in exchange. The latter were bound for western Alberta and an RCMP outpost in the Northwest Territories. Eric was no military strategist, but the play was obvious, and Cal would want to know.

Trouble with the Natives. Trouble with Surkov's Russians, forever eying the Arctic. Trouble with the separatists in Quebec and some businessman named Henri Vaillancourt who was bankrolling their constant little rebellions. Trouble with the Mackenzie-Papineaus, those jumped-up rebels setting off petrol bombs at Cleaner checkpoints. The Dominion, despite commanding one of the largest continuous landmasses in the world, was beset by threats from all around it.

His phone vibrated with an encrypted text. Unknown number, as usual, with just a name in the message body. Eric groaned, slid his glasses down the bridge of his nose, and pressed down on his eyelids until tiny constellations of light danced across his vision.

Cal wanted him to access Norm's files. If any justice existed in the universe, Norm would be as bad at infosec as the average bureaucrat. He had, however, changed his password from the default, and wasn't quite stupid enough to use a birthday.

12345678

password

letmein

Wait. *Shad0wr3alm*. Jordan's password on *Night Beats*. Eric appreciated a trip down memory lane as much as the next guy, but the show had been abruptly cancelled three years ago and it was time to move on.

Thank fuck for nostalgic dweebs. The revolution would have been lost without them.

Cal could want anything on the guy's drive. Eric clicked through the files, scooping spreadsheets, convinced he was being sent to look for a needle in a sewing equipment factory, when he felt a tug at his wards.

He wasn't the magitech genius Cal was, but he knew a geas when he felt one. He hovered over the folder, and his tattoo responded, a tightening of his skin almost to the point of pain. He opened the folder to find a single Excel file, which, upon clicking, turned his screen to an avalanche of Windows XP trails. The document would resist copying to his encrypted USB, or come out as a corrupted mess of ASCII characters. Ian used to do that to files, sometimes even on purpose. It would resist copying and emailing, and generally required irritating workarounds.

Well. Fuck. He took a deep breath, and hit print, his heart hammering so loudly that barely registered the knock on his office door.

"Can I bother you for a moment, Eric?"

Simon Yamashita took his yes as a given and let himself in before Eric could answer. This was as far as the man's confidence could take him. Eric had enough time to Alt+Tab a decoy spreadsheet tracking a respirator shipment from the SVAR. Simon, lost, gormless, an elderly artist trapped in the steel maw of a fascist regime, showed little interest in whatever task he'd interrupted. His skin was papery, his shoulders stooped, as if the weight of his lanyard was too heavy a burden. They didn't let him out in public much these days; he worked behind the scenes to write the music that Lucy made famous.

"What is it?" Eric did his best not to glance at the screen. The printer for Eric's floor was in the copy room, not his office, and each device had a unique watermark and ID number.

"I'm supposed to get the talking points for Atherton's National Unity Tour." Simon thrust a folder in his general direction. "He wants to rein in the separatists."

"And he thinks a song will do what a constitution and four referendums couldn't manage?" Eric had never been a good man, as such, but he had done nothing so terrible as to deserve a job translating between the world of politics and the world of magic.

The print job was at 40%. Anyone could walk by, see page after page of some document classified enough to warrant a geas spilling from the copier's mouth.

"The right song," Simon said, and that was reason enough to be sweating. Quinn Atherton was fucking terrifying, and the Curtises were worse.

Eric glanced at the progress—82%. He shifted in his chair. His bladder gave a painful, insistent twitch.

"Reid thinks a morale boost will help keep Quebec in line. He says we need a win." The slightest uptick in his voice, and Eric's earlier scorn evaporated. Simon was under as much pressure as he was, maybe more.

"Sure, Simon." He searched for the memo he'd gotten from Alcott. He was supposed to work it into something appropriately populist, something to match the emotive, staccato bursts that characterized Atherton's speeches. But the bare bones would do for Simon's work. Finding it, he slid it into the folder.

The print icon flashed at him. The copier was out of paper, the job stuck at 88%. Would the Dominion even bother trying him for treason? He wouldn't last 30 seconds under torture—he'd give them Lucy, Jakie, Cal, he'd give them his parents, everything. Not that they needed information. Every traitorous thought he'd ever harboured might as well be tattooed on his face, prison-gang style, every drip of sweat leaked his guilt over the papers in front of him.

"Everything okay? You look a little peaky."

And here he thought Simon was the one about to drop. "Fine," Eric gritted out. "Look, can you excuse me for a second?" His tongue sat thick against his teeth, unwilling to supply a decent alibi, and they might have both sat in awkward silence forever had his phone not pinged.

Youth and stamina were all that kept Eric from pissing himself. He waited for Simon to make it halfway down the hall before darting for the copier room. Kelly was on her way out, and she might have seen, any number of people might have seen, but when he at last brushed past her and let himself in, the pages were lying, seemingly untouched, on the output tray. He shoved a new ream of paper in, waited, then scooped it into his briefcase and only barely made it into a washroom stall where he at last allowed himself a slow, steady breath.

· · ·

On his lunch break, Eric walked to the Abomination, a respirator pulled tight over his face. The sky was rust, the sun, near-peak, an incandescent penny. The snow, catching the light, gleamed crimson.

His ward tattoo lit up this close to the silo, the lines of ink turned to something living, wriggling over his ribcage. Cal was already waiting, his next-gen respirator flashing an uncanny-valley smile on its digital interface.

"That's not going to catch on," Eric took a seat beside him on the park bench. "Please tell me it won't." How it functioned with the levels of ambient magic was beyond him, though he supposed there was nothing cutting edge about the tech involved. He snapped open his briefcase and passed the spreadsheet to his contact. "I almost died in the stupidest possible way for this," he said. "I hope it's worth it."

Cal eyed it, flipping through the first few pages. "Good work," he said.

"It's *brilliant* work," Eric said. "They're all watching me, every second, waiting for me to slip up, to do something wrong. Have you heard anything about the visa?"

"It's not a straightforward process," Cal said. "They'll screen him at the border, you know, and there aren't many countries that are taking anyone. Let alone someone—"

"And Abigail?" Eric cut Cal off before he could say something unforgivable. He had kept his promise to the woman who had cared for Jakie for most of his life. He hadn't stopped searching for her after the cops had dragged her away. It was just that his search continued to be fruitless.

"I'm sorry, Eric. I wish I had better news. Talk to me about Walsingham."

"They're all unbearable? None of them can stand each other—it's just petty shit, everyone trying to get one up on the other, collecting blackmail, thinking if they impress Reid Curtis enough, they'll move up high enough in the ranks to be untouchable." But Cal knew that, Cal lived for that kind of junior-high bullshit.

"No one is untouchable," Cal mused. "Not even me. There's only one Reid Curtis. It takes a fleet of Quinn Athertons to run a totalitarian regime."

"They're in luck, then." Eric replied. "Our country has a desperate shortage of food, arable land, and functioning infrastructure, but one thing we're not lacking for is men who put the banal in banality of evil." His eyes lingered on the file. "They'll know it came from me. What is it?"

"I believe," Cal picked around the words like a sapper through a minefield, "it's someone's tax information."

It took all of the restraint that Eric had painstakingly cultivated, in three years of his cursed double life, to not leap across the bench and yank the file out of Cal's hands.

"I didn't almost land myself in front of a firing squad for someone's T4s."

"If it's Reid Curtis' T4s, it's worth it."

"Maybe to you."

"Breathe Eric," Cal said, and Eric seethed. It was enough for Cal to stay calm—he was the right kind of white, ancient money, the kind that lubricated the gears of the political machine no matter who was at the wheel. "We're all on borrowed time. It's at least likely that Messrs Dubois and Yamashita have borrowed less of it than you." He slid the papers into his own briefcase. "Are the Curtises on the Train this week?"

Eric nodded. This was safer ground.

Cal's respirator now displayed a series of question marks, which was somehow worse than the smile had been. He shifted on the bench, as if about to get up, and Eric's heart lurched. He didn't like Cal, or their spy games, which felt both like too little and too dangerous, but in between hours of analyzing strategic plans and polishing quarterly reports, it was all he had left to remind him that he was one of the good guys. He breathed a sigh of relief when Cal merely crossed one long leg over the other. "And the other thing?"

He meant the big question, the one that kept them both up at night. The Dominion had won, in nearly every way that counted. Though the west coast was occupied by the SVAR, and Quebec always threatened to cut them off at the East, with multiple MAI in their ranks and dozens of untapped wellsprings at their command, they were on the verge of becoming a global superpower, and more than capable of going toe-to-toe with the Free States. If they finalized the SVAR deal, they'd be practically untouchable. But if anything, the Curtises' research team was more frantic than ever.

Ian had asked what magic wanted. Cal wanted to know what Reid Curtis wanted.

"Pull a coup like that and you're always watching your back," Eric offered.

"It's more than that," Cal said. "Atherton is easy to figure out. He's smart enough, but he's not creative. He got lucky and tripped and fell into the leadership."

"His daughter *died in front of him.*"

"Maybe lucky's the wrong word. But the Curtises have always been the power behind the throne. If it hadn't been Atherton, it would be anyone else."

Eric had stolen enough classified reports and procurement orders to fill a bookshelf, and he knew enough about magitech to decode at least 75% of what he'd read. Reid was interested in psychology; he had commissioned work into faith, what makes people go to church, or join cults, or believe conspiracy theories. He ran the press group at arm's length these days, and Walsingham had taken over much of its duties. News was much more of an automatic process when there was no pretense of freedom of the press. The Dominion, meanwhile, ran its MAI biologist into the ground, dissecting and nitpicking at the nature of magic, at what made one person a magician and another a lurching monstrosity with an endless hunger and too many eyes.

A wave of nausea gripped him. He always assumed that Cal knew more than he did, had somehow been looking over his shoulder when he brought Lucy to the Mac-Paps, somehow knew Eric's next move before Eric did.

Eric had worked for the invisible, all-seeing, all-knowing eye. He should have known better than to assume omniscience.

"Cal," he said. "You don't know, do you?" It must have come too late, like every other spark of hope that the Dominion had managed to stomp out. Almost two weeks had passed, and if the Mac-Paps had tracked Ian down and freed him, Cal would have said. Given the success rate of the experiments, he probably hadn't made it. "Ian is alive. Or at least he was, as of a few weeks ago. That's why Lucy's gone—she's not battling laryngitis or whatever they're claiming. She's defected."

Cal's eyes were on the winding contour of the Abomination, and his respirator display was blank. "I've heard nothing," he said, his voice tight. If he had any urge to track Lucy through the anarchic network of the resistance, to follow her lead to a secret prison and go out in a blaze of glory, it didn't show on his face. If he had any residual feelings for a man who, if Parliament Hill gossip held a grain of truth, he'd dated on and off for years, he tamped it down along with every other sign of sentimentality. "Keep pushing," Cal said at last. "They want something, and it is our patriotic duty, our duty as *human beings,* to find out what it is and ensure that they never get it."

"Yeah," Eric said. He stood up. "Happy reading."

11

Past the mountains, squeezed between empires and drowning in tides, was a paradise built above the gaping maw of Hell.

The Dominion had held its grip on the Vancouver Archipelago for three blood-soaked weeks as the rising ocean claimed it. The RCMP had erected makeshift camps and checkpoints and murdered hundreds. As Jonah had predicted—before he'd shoved Blythe and Laura onto a leaking boat and thrown them to the sea's capricious mercy—the Cleaners had delighted in lining up the resisters and the undesirables and shooting them.

What the Dominion hadn't counted on was the land's response, the Blight, turning the ocean to glass, shaking mountains like a child's toys, hurling spears of magic through wilderness and town alike. The Big One, always predicted and at last fulfilled, severed highways and gobbled everything below 500 metres. The Dominion's shock troops had strained under the burden of blockades and road failures and the strategic marriage of fertilizer and fire and then, once the various fighting forces had been exhausted, the SVAR crossed the border to scavenge the remains.

The Archipelago was a barely healed scab, flooded and depopulated, its cities splintered, its infrastructure unsalvageable. Rather than fight, the Dominion had—here, and nowhere else—retreated, leaving a conglomerate of SVAR companies to establish a Special Economic Zone. Order was held by phalanxes of private security, all with an eye to opening up the province's economy to the world beyond the Dominion.

Blythe's cell was barely smaller than her own coffin apartment on campus. It was newer, though, sleeker, manufactured in one of their off-shore factories. She admired the compost toilet in particular. It flipped up into the wall when not in use, allowing the cot to extend from the opposite wall. She amused herself by pushing the latch open and closed, catching a guard's eye through the plexiglass barrier.

He was company security. He wasn't going to kill her. She wouldn't even take a severe beating before she'd paid off the several lifetimes' worth of debt on her account. Small mercies. Edgar thought she was tempting fate by running away as often as she did, but really, she was just increasing her value, something the company shareholders should have appreciated. She'd said "*Otipemisiwak*" when he'd asked her for a name and company affiliation. The wine-red ID that Jonah had nearly died for was long gone, lost to the sea like so much else. It didn't matter; both sides of the new Cold War knew who she was.

The toilet's latch would wear eventually. SVAR engineering was impressive but not particularly sturdy. She might be able to snap it off before someone paid for her release, though that could still leave her with hours of inhaling decomposing shit. Smell travelled through the vents in the plexiglass—pissing off the guards was probably worth it.

Truly, she lived in the freest place left in the world.

They'd given her a jumpsuit made of some papery material that crinkled when she moved, and was insufficient against the chill. The summer had been cold, and October had swept in with brutality uncharacteristic of the Archipelago's microclimate. The Dominion had declared it a superwinter while the SVAR quibbled about details, but either way, Blythe was sick of it.

The first year, she'd convinced herself that the panic would subside. The grief wouldn't, the hollowed-out weariness that she wore around her shoulders like a shroud, this would never fade. That was the secret that demons knew, the thing that made them strip away the human pieces of themselves and let themselves be devoured by magic.

But the sense of balancing on a precipice, where Wile E. Coyote looked down but had yet to begin to fall, that should have faded by now. What was there to fear? Her daughter was dead, and the world had already ended.

"Blythe."

The latch had won the bet after all. "Hey Edgar," she said without looking up.

He'd been her group leader in the Before Times, supervising her research into the Cascade's effect on ocean currents and salinity. He'd been the one to ask her to strap into an experimental bathyscaphe with an MAI child to investigate the abnormalities they'd discovered on the ocean floor first-hand. He'd believed in her, backed her results to the department chair, and he seemed to consider her enough of a friend to bail her out of jail. He'd even brought a coat. Had she wanted to live, she would have been grateful.

The sunlight was a spike through her skull, no less cruel than the thrum of the fluorescent lights in her cell. "How pissed are you?" she asked. "Give me a number on the pain scale."

"Your bail fee is coming out of the department meal budget," Edgar said. He ran a hand through thinning black hair. If he kept tugging at it like that, he was going to be bald even faster. "I'm not pissed. You're too valuable to them to rot in jail. They just needed to squeeze the thumbscrews a little tighter."

"You can have my dinners," Blythe said. Edgar didn't look like he was using his, anyway.

"I can't replace you," he replied. "And I wouldn't want to. But I wish you'd stay out there, in the wilderness. Away from all this." Whether he meant the SVAR-occupied islands, the university, or the ocean itself, she didn't ask.

Her mother had said the same. She'd talked to Jonah, apparently, on one of his latest runs into the bush. He, too, was clinging to the remote places where the Dominion's authority wore thin, running guns and supplies up from the border to the various Iron Alliance factions. They both wanted her home, despite Victoria being her home for the last fifteen years. Despite Laura being the only thing that had held their little family together for most of that.

She belonged here, watching the ocean. At night it sang to her, invaded her dreams with glimpses of a black-haired girl with seaweed in her hair.

"The big man wants to talk to you." Edgar never learned the names of the rotating cast of upper management, had made no attempt to memorize the org chart. Making sense of the often contradictory directions of the company brass was a different beast than dealing with various vice-presidents and provosts when UVic had been a proper university. She admired that about him, but that was also why the bean counters ended up inevitably finding her.

Blythe wanted a drink, a fuck, and ten uninterrupted hours of sleep. Instead, she had another meeting.

The walk from the detainment facility was over rough terrain. The Archipelago had been a spiderweb of canals and bridges for a decade, but now the earthquakes and flooding had eroded most of the lowlands. The occupiers viewed this crisis, like any other, as an opportunity, erecting road tolls and high rents in the hilly regions. They had swiftly erected a wall where Ring Road had encircled the campus, protecting one of the few institutions left intact from the rabble who might have taken shelter there.

Abutting the prefab concrete wall was a sprawling tent city. A bright neon patchwork, straining under mud and snowmelt from the last storm, sloped from the barrier down the hill, broken only by a maze of narrow walkways and bursts of spiny, sticky shriekgrass. Fires in oil drums burned too close to the nylon tents for Blythe's liking, and a flight of drones kept careful watch over the slum's denizens. They were the last standing in the game of musical chairs that had followed the Blight—the hungry and desperate, as there had been for Blythe's entire living memory, but also the more recently unlucky. She'd pulled strings to get her own ex-students bedspaces behind the walls, but it wasn't the case in every department. She couldn't walk through the makeshift streets without recognizing someone, so she hid in Edgar's wake, her head down, the fur lining on her hood a blinder to the misery. The stench, a thick, bubbling miasma, swelled from plastic barrels and rivulets of sewage that streamed into the muddy paths. She hated herself for holding her breath.

Her digital ID beeped ominously when the guard at the southern gate scanned it. Blythe waited for their system to process it. She tracked a line of spray paint along the concrete wall, imperfectly cleaned. *Oh no, your fancy wall has writing on it.*

The guard glared at her, but let them both pass.

Inside the barrier was a different world, a shining citadel of glass and metal, a shrine to R&D and a future that no longer existed. The big man—Mitchell Pruitt, *call me Mitch*—was waiting in the lab, terrorizing Edgar's two ex-grad students, who hovered around a series of heat maps. Back in the day, a casting room would have called him "an Elon Musk type." She had other names in mind.

"Had a good adventure, did you?"

Mitch was seated on a stool, rocking back and forth like a hyperactive teenager. He looked like a teenager too, even more than the students, in an oversize grey hoodie and blue jeans. Blythe stayed standing, deluding herself into believing it was some kind of power play.

A murderer. Maybe not personally—she'd never learned who had been on the ship that had sunk the *Empress Willow*, blasted Laura and hundreds of refugees into flotsam and jetsam. It didn't matter. No amount of decentralization erased their complicity.

"Thought you believed in freedom."

Mitch grinned. "Not during your contract hours, Dr. Augustine. You seem hellbent on drawing out your debt as long as possible."

"I'm also drowning in data," she said. She'd never managed that cold, waspish professionalism that the handful of women in the occupying forces cultivated. "We had twice the staff before the Blight. Was there something in particular you needed from me?"

"We need to get the fisheries operating at peak efficiency," Mr. Move-Fast-and-Break-Things said. "The plant manager is saying that one in ten fish is testing positive for contaminants."

"Talk to the fisheries about it, then."

"Glass," Mitch said. "And...other things. The rate of change is accelerating with a hypothesized mobile point source of pollutants. Triangulation suggests it's tracking ocean currents along the Cascadia subduction zone."

Funny, how uncomfortable these SVAR bastards were with magic, even now. She had a Ph.D and a first-author *Nature Communications* paper to her name but to the SVAR she was a Native sea witch, in tune with some primal eldritch force beyond their comprehension.

"Tell you what," she said. "Find some willing volunteers in Agricultural Science, fund them for a postdoc, and get them to publish a few peer-reviewed papers on the interactions between piscean population density and wellspring magic, and maybe then, you can find someone with the right background to boss around." At his carefully blank expression, she added, "It's not my area of expertise. I don't know if it *can* be fixed. You're better off cultivating rice. It'll feed people more efficiently and we don't have a shortage of swamps."

Edger drew in a hissing breath. The two ex-grad students, Omid and Kitty, were watching her with saucer eyes. You didn't talk back to the money. That was an old rule of academia, and all of them were so deeply indentured that it wouldn't have even occurred to them it was an option.

She'd told only Edgar the full story of what had happened during her desperate aborted exodus on the *Empress Willow*, in halting, choked installments. He'd borne the brunt of keeping the fragments of herself collected in one body, grounded in the research. The others had to piece it together, based on what everyone had endured, from the unmarked mass graves and the markers with no bodies beneath them, the walls devoted to the missing and dead, the hand-picked wildflowers and muddy teddy bears. From the sole personal item in her workspace, the unfinished, beaded werewolf from *Night Beats* on a strip of brown hide pinned to her cubicle. From the tightening of her jaw and fists when anyone mentioned the proto-state that had sponsored her daughter's murder.

"I'd like to speak to you alone, Dr. Augustine," Mitch said.

Well, that never boded well.

"It's his lab." She cocked her head at Edgar. "You know I'm going to tell him anyway, and he'll tell the kids, and then it's all over the university. Might as well eliminate the middleman."

Mitch shook his head, but didn't insist. "I don't care about fish," he said. "Or rice. We can import what we need. We've serviced the seasteads for a decade now; if your city sinks, it's not my problem. I want to know how to harness the forces acting on this place. And you're the woman to do it, if the rumours are true."

She couldn't help laughing. At her last meeting with whoever his predecessor had been, she'd told him that such things were impossible. And now he was asking her to do the impossible even harder.

"The Dominion has an MAI scientist," Mitch said.

He'd snapped from jovial to deadly serious in the time it took her to process what he'd told her. There hadn't been many MAI—at least not living openly—before the Blight, and no one was in a position to take a survey of them now. The condition didn't lend itself well to anything in the STEM fields; Blythe could still remember Ian blowing out people's laptops from proximity alone.

"That seems like the Dominion's business," she said.

"Until it's ours." He wheeled his office chair closer. They had the heat on as low as possible, and puffs of his hot breath dissipated millimetres from her face. "You may not appreciate it, Dr. Augustine, but we have a good thing here. You've been free to carry out your work—at the university, in safety, not in some filthy labour camp. Adolescent paramilitary gangs aren't beating down your door or shooting you in the street. Like it or not, this is what liberty looks like."

Liberty looked like hundreds of thousands of dollars in debt, lifetimes of interest, every time she crossed the mountains to ferry people to safety, and a coffin apartment in a company town. Her daughter, drowned and lost, with no body to bury and no gravesite to mourn.

"We're a peaceful people," Mitch said. "We never fought a war, unlike the Free States. We negotiated. Do you believe the Dominion of Canada can be negotiated with?"

"No," she admitted. "But I'm not an MAI. I can't help you."

"Make no mistake," Mitch said. "They haven't ceded BC. They'll blast their way through the mountains a second time if that's what they need to take it back. You've seen what they will do with tanks and guns; what do you think they'll do with magic?"

The Dominion had pushed Laura to the edge of the world, but it was the SVAR who had blown her into the ocean.

"You can both murder each other over the scraps for all I care," Blythe said. She might have been handy with a bolt-cutter back in the day, but she'd never learned how to play politics.

"And what happens to all of those refugees you brought over? Who do you think will be first in line for the firing squad?" He stood up and walked over to her. She could only sit there impotently while her daughter's murderer enlisted her in a game of magical realpolitik.

"They have a new weapon," he said. "They're learning how to harness magic. They want more than a country—they want the world. We can counter with our own, or it can get much bloodier." He patted her shoulder. "Think it over, Dr. Augustine. But don't take too long."

12

The two-lane highway had dwindled under the weight of the superwinter, evaporated into the landscape, which in turn smeared into an anemic sky. The route was, at best, a divot in the sea of white, a mere suggestion of a direction. Only skeletal aspen and black ticks of birch, and the occasional battered highway sign, cut through the noise.

The SUV had been overkill in the city, but out here the wind was more than a match for it, nudging it towards one ditch, then the next. Maya strained to see through the wedge of cleared windshield.

She hadn't got a flaming word from Martine in hours. Maybe there was a signal range on them. The messages only went one way, but she sent out hopeless little prayers anyway. *If I die out here, find me.*

She wasn't going to die. She *didn't* die, didn't spin out and wrap the SUV around a tree, didn't jam into a snow drift that piled higher until her gears spun into dust, until she waded out into the dunes, until the snow consumed her.

She held the lodestar of her prognostication in her head. Shadi's rubber duck sat in the passenger seat, oblivious to the gathering storm. The other vision, the one the borealis had gifted her, crept in along the edges. Somewhere, amidst every wrong turn they'd taken, was a world where they'd both been content, and safe, and happy, the kind of happy Maya didn't even remember, the kind that bubbled citrus and smelled of cardamom and cloves, a radiant jewel amid the ash and ruin of the Blight.

She kept driving, until delusion turned to certainty that the landscape matched that of her visions, until she was positive of it.

The huddled gravestones of civilization hugged each side of the road. A line of flatbed trucks, buried up to the rim in white. A grey fence, with a sign for a housing development that had never materialized. A gas station, stripped to its bones. The twin grain silos that marked the turnoff towards a smattering of squat bungalows, a firehall, and an elementary school that passed for a town.

The town's very existence was an act of spite. It was too small to stand on its own, too spread out and vulnerable. They would have had to call in the army or the Cleaners on a regular basis to keep the shriekgrass incursions from overwhelming the fields. The Dominion loved to talk about hardworking rural Canadians and national self-sufficiency, but this was a dying town, fated to be absorbed into a farming protectorate or ground into ruin.

She slowed, driving past vinyl-sided houses, their low roofs dusted with snow. The town had been small even before the Blight had torn through it, just one main street downtown. In the gaps between boarded-up shops, mauve shriekgrass wailed, but pollen season was at least a supersummer away. The church was the tallest structure in the town, a yellow brick monstrosity sandwiched between a thrift store-cum-food bank and the equally ugly parish hall. An old Canadian flag fluttered just below the Dominion's butcher's apron.

The first human beings she'd seen for miles were spilling out of the church as she approached, and, gripped with paranoia, Maya drove past it and parked behind the Esso. Concealing her out-of-town plates wouldn't do her much good. And even casting a veil of nondescript whiteness over herself, a stranger's face would stand out here.

The church was in better repair than most of the other buildings, the walkway and steps swept of snow and the brick sturdier in the face of the elements than the slapdash construction of the rest of the town. It was crowded, and the emptiness everywhere else suddenly made sense. The parishioners who caught her eye, unmasked, offered smiles nearly wide enough to bridge the uncanny valley, but Maya hung back, too accustomed to shadows. Some Dominion sorcery had touched this town, turning its populace into Stepford wives.

She didn't see Jonah among them. It took long minutes before she could work up the courage to walk through the grand arch of the door. The handle stuck in her grasp and it took all her strength to push it open.

The stained glass windows turned the thin grey morning into strips of jewelled light. The priest was talking to an elderly couple by the altar, the nave otherwise emptied. She blushed under the priest's alert glance—apparently, you didn't need to belong to a faith to feel an instinctive twinge of guilt.

Her boots echoed up the tall columns to the domed ceiling. No buttresses or vaulted ceiling for this church—like everything else she had seen in the town, it was more functional than beautiful. The painted wall panels and ceiling skirted transcendence, depicted the stations of the cross with minimal suffering in insipid pastel.

Her vision had showed her this place. The strange proportions on the painted figures were unmistakable. But Jonah wasn't here.

She waited for the old couple to leave. The priest turned his attention to collecting his things, ready to shuffle off to wherever priests went when they weren't preaching. She cycled through a series of excuses and surreptitious ways of asking if he wasn't, perhaps, concealing a wanted arms dealer somewhere on the premises, but settled for a limp, "Sorry, Father, I was just. Um. Do you have a bathroom?"

This got a soft chuckle out of the old man and she was gripped by panic that he might seize on her inconvenient bladder as an opportunity to evangelize, but he only said, "Downstairs and to the left. The light's out, watch your step."

Children's crayon drawings, grey in the bleak light from the stairs, flapped as she passed, crudely rendered Bible scenes and hand turkeys leftover from Thanksgiving. The door to the bathroom was ajar, but she turned the other way, the fragments of her vision haphazardly superimposed over the narrow hallway.

"Excuse me!" The door opened at the top of the stairs above her—was the priest following her? She froze, bracing to throw herself into the wall, her duck out of convenient reach in her pocket, when a second voice, familiar, said, "It's okay, Father Byrne. I know her. I think—" Jonah stepped out from a door in the hall, squinting at her, as if he could force himself to see through her illusion, her buried name.

"Maya," she supplied. "We worked together at the Broom Closet."

"Right," he said, drawing out the word as he worked through the process of matching the person before him, with a different face and a different name, to the memory of an overqualified intern who believed magic would make the world better.

He'd changed as well. The short black fade at the nape of his neck must have been freshly done. The dress pants might have been the same ones he used to drag out when he had to be near a camera. His jacket didn't quite match. The cuff on one sleeve was frayed, but he was far more formally dressed than she'd expected. The haircut rendered his jaw harder and squarer.

"You look good," she offered. He'd been handsome before, and the grief and weariness added gravitas, not age, to his face. What docility permeated the rest of the town had spared Jonah Augustine. If there was still a god that would listen to his prayers, it didn't appear to have granted him any peace.

"Talk," he said, the word flat, barely a challenge. She glanced at the priest, who shook his head and closed the door. "He knows who I am."

She didn't need prognostication to predict what would get his attention. "Ian's alive," Maya said. "He's being held at a Dominion black site."

Jonah's reply was an outpouring of colourful obscenity, much of it uncomfortably blasphemous with a priest in hearing distance.

As she had asked Lucy, he asked if she was sure, only with more "fucks" thrown in.

"I don't think she was lying," Maya said. "She was scared, but—"

"Have you told your Glorious Leader?"

"If I had," Maya said, "do you think I'd be here?"

"Jesus fucking Christ." That priest must absolutely love him.

"So you're in?"

"There was a time I thought if I ever saw him again, I'd kill him. I don't know what about me makes you think I need convincing. Maya." The name sat heavily on his tongue.

"I buried my name." Its absence tugged at her chest. Under the parking lot, abandoned, did it still wonder if she was coming back for it?

"Of course."

She'd never seen him stand still for so long. She waited for him to manifest some of the fire that had put him in front of bulldozers and excavators, but he only stared ahead, at a child's crayon interpretation of Easter, a bunny nailed to a crucifix. Maya knew as well as anyone what had knocked the fight out of him. If wheat fields and the Virgin Mary gave him some comfort after everything he'd been through, she could hardly begrudge him that. But she wanted divine wrath, and she hoped to hell that this hollow shell had it in him.

"You know," he said. "I actually like it here. Sometimes I catch myself going on, living like a normal person, like none of it happened, like I never had—" Only now did the corners of his lips curl up in mockery of a grin. "Battle stations, eh?"

He led her upstairs, into the sacristy—"I'm Hindu, is this even allowed?"—and tugged aside an old rug to reveal a loose floorboard. Father Byrne, standing by the closed door, merely cast a glance in their direction. When she caught his eye, he winked.

Now it was her turn to swear, copiously, and with a ferocity and variety that would have made Ian proud. Beneath the church floors was a small armoury: assault rifles, ammunition boxes. Her vision at last made sense. "Where did it all come from?"

Jonah shrugged. "The Free States want to destabilize the Dominion, the American rump state wants to destabilize the Free States—more than they already are—the SVAR pirates want everyone to stop harshing their plundering mellow, and the Cree and the Ojibwe want their land back. Lots of guns floating around these days. It's easy pickings if you know where to look."

Her own cell had three guns between three dozen people. That Jonah, with his brown skin and his checkered past and no magic of his own, had accumulated a cache of firearms under the Dominion's nose beggared belief. "Why haven't the Cleaners murdered you yet?"

"Ward tattoo and the blessings of Father Byrne. I'm surprised you even managed to find me." He tugged the first gun loose and threw it in her direction, as though he had no doubt that she'd easily catch it. Neither of them had adapted well to a retreat from political life, and she suspected him of spending as much time as she did drilling with illegally smuggled guns. "Plus, they haven't come for the Catholics. Yet."

"I'm full of questions."

"It's a long drive to Bowmanville," Jonah said. "We can talk in the car."

• • •

The black site looked like it had been abandoned for years. Jonah flinched, and Maya knew his ward tattoo must have caught the same sour note that was rolling around in her stomach.

"Stop here," he said. On one side of the road was a stretch of suburban tract housing choked with frost-stiffened shriekgrass. They stashed the van in the driveway of a beige detached house, and Jonah climbed up onto the garage, then onto the roof, for a better view. Maya was fitter than she had been back when they'd worked together, but it was a struggle to clamber up after him. They lay on their bellies behind the peak of the roof, looking out at the stretches of windswept, muddy ground separating the neighbourhood from the shimmering plane in the distance. Between them was a patch of overgrown forest, a snake curve of a river that had dried to dots of frozen ice patches.

"Why me?" Jonah asked abruptly. The late evening light, diffused by snow, illuminated every windblown crevice in his face. "You could have been here weeks ago."

"You have guns," she said. "The Mac-Paps don't."

"If you can walk through walls and turn yourself invisible you don't need guns. And there aren't that many guards. Look."

She squinted through the ward. Several low brick buildings squatted amid overgrown forest beneath the shadow of the guard tower. A searchlight swung and the snow sparkled like broken glass in the wake of the beam. But Jonah was right; there was little movement between the six decrepit buildings, all but one encircled by a road and separated by unbroken snow.

"I had a vision," she admitted.

"You drove halfway across the country because of a *vision?*"

Jonah was no MAI, but he'd been around Ian—and Maya—long enough to understand the monkey's paw bargain they had with magic. Denial was a reflex, a holdover from the time before the Cascade, when it might have made sense.

"Because everyone died. Unless it was just you and me."

"Why?"

Maya had seen blood and fire in her vision, but there was no light in any of the buildings, no sign of soldiers playing cards with guns across their laps as they watched the highway on surveillance cameras.

"It's that one," she said, instead of answering. She pointed to the long, two-story bunkhouse Lucy had described. It wavered in and out of her vision, the way she did when magic had the upper hand in their relationship.

The forest would give them cover, and she watched Jonah plot out a path. It was so close. Ian had been less than two hours' drive away this whole time. Maya pushed down the sick giddiness in her stomach. She hadn't given up, that was the important thing. She hadn't forgotten.

Was it a trap to ensnare the Mac-Paps? Or to prove, beyond doubt, that the Songbird of the Dominion was leaking more dirt than a punctured colostomy bag? If it was, it was a bizarre gambit. Gaby Abel was never the biggest cheerleader for the man who had manipulated and at times torpedoed her political career, and they couldn't have counted on Lucy's reaction either. Maybe they told themselves that the big, bad resistance wasn't coming for Ian Mallory after all?

She had to count on their confidence in their own wards and commitment to lean staffing and fiscal responsibility. Her existence was as closely guarded a secret as Gaby's identity. They wouldn't be expecting Maya, and nothing could have prepared them for Jonah Augustine.

Jonah lined up the rifle's sight with the guard tower. Too far for a useful shot, especially with the haze of the ward and the shaking of his hands. He had been calm on the drive, distressingly so, but it was as if a switch had been flicked, kindling whatever latent propensity for violence lurked beneath the ill-fitting business casual.

"How do you even know how to use one of those things?" she asked. "*Do* you know how to use one of those things?"

"I wasn't always a pencil-pusher," Jonah said, then, sharply, "Did you know?"

"About what?"

"Laura. Did your visions show you that too?"

She bit back her initial response, that she'd barely known he had a daughter for all he'd ever mentioned her at work. She'd only remembered when he wore short sleeves and the little handprint amid a whorl of flowers showed amid his many tattoos. And, of course, when word from out west had finally trickled back, via the broken telephone of resistance networks, came that she'd been aboard one of the many refugee boats drowned off the coast. "I'd have told you."

"Would Ian?"

"You came all this way. Maybe you can ask him yourself."

He lowered the gun. "They'll be on us before we get to that

bunkhouse. How well does your way work?"

Maya's fingers, unprotected by her fingerless gloves, squeezed the rubber duck until she found the familiar rhythm. The air congealed and hardened. She focused on Jonah, whose presence beside her was less tangible, less solid, than everything around him. Her Somebody Else's Problem field, however precarious, stuck to both of them.

Her hands, too, had gone insubstantial. A heavy weight pressed down on her skin, her chest, resisting forward momentum. Resisting breathing.

"Something's wrong," she whispered. It wasn't just the wards. It felt like a magnet whose pole pushed at hers, an intangible tripwire laced over the prison's grounds. None of it, she knew, would stop Jonah from bursting in like the Kool-Aid Man if he got any more restless.

Whatever the source choking out her magic, warping it into something barbed and cumbersome, they'd come too far to let it stop them.

The climb off the roof was easier than up, though she tripped on the last two feet down and rolled into the snow. They moved quietly, in bursts, taking cover between the patches of spruce and black ash, until they stood at the edge of the ward.

A body, at least several days old, sprawled face-down in the snow. The man was wearing a maroon jacket, faded to nearly brown. Bloated cheeks, dotted with foam, fluffy auburn hair and beard. At first, she thought he was merely dead.

He was neatly bisected at the waist; below the jacket was a scattering of fleshy cubes, trailing from the side of the road to the edge of the woods. Shriekgrass was already pushing through the exposed pelvis. Probably one of the many drifters who scavenged off the highway, making his way towards the town when he'd gotten ensnared in the ward.

A few feet away, a second body, this one a woman's, draped over the edge of the road, the skin loose and sagging, the organs and bone liquified and then frozen into a pool around the empty bag of her flesh.

"Jesus Christ," Jonah said.

She smacked his shoulder, where the stick-and-poke ward tattoo was. "We're fine," she said, though it would have chewed up anyone else she'd brought with her. This was why there were barely any guards. This was why it had to be Jonah, why her other comrades would have been doomed. She was suddenly grateful the vision hadn't given her details.

"You sure?"

"Thought you had faith."

He crossed himself, muttered, "St. Michael the Archangel, defend us in battle, be our protection against the wickedness and snares of the devil..."

Maya beside him, whispered, "The Force is with me, I am one with the Force," and walked through the veil, not waiting to check if Jonah was behind her.

The ward sizzled over her skin, but the prison camp resolved into clarity when she stepped onto the road. Jonah pushed through a second later, and she gathered the illusion mantle around them both. The distant figure in the guard tower appeared oblivious to their presence.

She mouthed, *Quickly.*

Maya walked, footsteps too loud in the snow, but she forced herself to move slowly, deliberately, until temptation won and she broke into a skid a few metres before the bunkhouse door. She overshot the ground, sliding and skipping over the last feet of frozen ground to collide with the brick wall, palms out to absorb the shock. Jonah, substantially more graceful than she was despite the heavy armament strapped across his back, landed at her side.

She would pay for this later, her magic slowly stealing her from the world. But it was better than getting shot. She grabbed Jonah's arm and pulled them both through the brick wall.

They were in a long, narrow corridor, recently repainted, a sloppy enough job that decades of accumulated graffiti broke through the whitewash. Towards the front, offices ran off the main hallway; further down the hallway, the doors were reinforced. In the closest room, a man watched glitching surveillance footage, but her field held, and they passed by unnoticed. She looked for the third door from the end, the one Lucy had described, with the scrape under the lock.

She didn't expect the seismic shock of the rifle. She hadn't even seen Jonah whip it off his back and fire. The soldier behind them, a startled deer in the headlights no older than she was, staggered into the wall and sank, twitching, to the floor. Now they would all hear, and come running. She ran for the door, boot sliding sideways in the spreading puddle of blood.

"This one." She reached it and touched the lock, testing its materiality, ignoring the creep of cold over her skin. Jonah's ink-black eyes, wider without his frame of wild hair, were fixed on her. They stood on either side of the narrow corridor, inches from the locked door.

"Maya." Her ears were still ringing. She had to strain to hear him over the tinnitus and the sounds of movement from the other side of the door. "Stop."

She couldn't stop. Hadn't stopped. For three years, she'd pushed through, because if she didn't, if she paused, and breathed, and *thought*, she'd notice things like the bloodied footsteps he'd left all the way down the hallway, or the gaping hole below her ribcage where her family and her friends and her name had lived.

"He's not in there," Jonah said.

"Yeah, he is, Lucy told me, she—"

Jonah shook his head. "This place is *fucked* with magic but it's not his. Trust me, I'd recognize his signature anywhere."

Maya ignored him, reached past him, through the lock, fingers trembling almost too hard to work its mechanism. The lock popped. Maya stepped through the door.

The cell was a shade of grey that barely registered, stained by splashes of darker grey. There was a guard, armed with a baton and a taser, and Jonah shot him before Maya could even reach for her pistol. He stumbled, but didn't fall, and she was flailing for her gun when Jonah rushed past her. He wrestled the guard into the corner, where a rudimentary sink and toilet jutted out of the wall while Maya spun.

Apparently, it was possible to bash someone's skull against the floor until it exploded like an overripe watermelon. Good to know.

Curled against the wall was something skinny and crooked with a sack over its head. She told herself that she could still hear the whistle of breath under the hood like air sucked through a crushed straw.

Maya holstered her gun and dropped to her knees beside him. The slap of meat against cement continued but it was distant now, pushed into the background by the ringing in her ears.

The prison uniform was a shroud, and she grasped more fabric than arm as she tried to haul him into a sitting position, commanded him to breathe, to be *alive,* and was rewarded for her faith with a shuddering heave so violent she thought it would tear him apart.

She tore the bag off his head and then she *knew.*

It was Ian, under the tangled mangrove roots of matted hair, the grey caveman beard that added two decades to his emaciated face. His skin was ash, the cut at the top of his cheekbone dripping diesel oil. But it wasn't *him.* His pale eyes were empty, staring at some point past her head, and in the thin space that defined him apart from eight billion other humans, she felt only a void, a hole slashed in existence itself.

Maya lifted her gaze. Jonah had moved to the other side of the door, flattened against the wall, gripping his rifle in raw-knuckled fists. "We need to go," she said. "We need to go right now."

Jonah blinked, as if for the first time realizing where he was, why he had come in the first place.

"Shit." He stumbled over to where she knelt at Ian's side. "Ian. Ian, can you walk?"

Ian's cracked lips mouthed something, but she couldn't make it out.

"I don't think so," Maya said.

"Fuck it," Jonah shoved the rifle and the duffel bag at her. "Take this." As she fumbled with them, he hoisted Ian fireman-style, up and over his shoulders. She'd never managed to hit a moving target. But as long as her field held, as long as the guards couldn't pinpoint the exact location of the shots, they had half a chance of making it out.

Three guards spilled out of one of the rooms between the cell and the front door, guns aimed right at them. They'd been seen. The shield that had kept them concealed from the SUV to the prison fell apart like piss-soggy toilet paper.

She gathered the shreds of the glamour around them, but it wouldn't hold. The magic dissipated as soon as she pulled at it.

Well, *fuck.*

She aimed the rifle in their general direction and fired. The kickback almost knocked her off her feet. They could go through the wall, but if it was Ian doing this, if the dark-matter mantle that churned around him was interfering with her own magic, they could just as easily end up skewered in a mess of framing and drywall.

She couldn't see if she'd killed any of them. She moved the way she'd been trained to, erratic, fire and duck, until she pulled the trigger and nothing happened.

There were two more doors off each side of the corridor, concealing clown-car levels of fascists for all Maya knew. She switched to the pistol, and when that hammer fell on an empty chamber, she slid out over the concrete floor, grasping for the gun on one of the corpses. Her fingers encountered something tacky, and she crawled closer, the arm of the dead man impossibly heavy, the pistol tucked at his side. She was going to get shot, flailing for a gun on the floor like someone after a lost contact lens. She grabbed it at last, pulled it to her chest, and waited for Jonah's head bob to move.

Outside, the snow was a blinding sheet, and her footprints, pink-tinged, filled in with each new step. The row of houses across the road, separated from them by a field and the patchy forest and, most unnervingly, the guard tower, was lost under the barrage of white.

They crouched in the lee of the bunker, Jonah shivering in his frayed jacket, Ian unmoving.

"Can we make it?" she asked.

Jonah was watching the tower. "How fucked is your magic?"

"Pretty fucked."

"How fast can you run?"

She shrugged. "They always picked me last in gym class."

"Okay," he said, eyes flickering briefly towards Ian, who was draped over him, the slight rise and fall of his chest the barest indication of life. Jonah reached across him to zip open the duffel bag. "Get ready to win a participation trophy, then."

He had the grenade out and the pin pulled before it occurred to her that she was expected to move.

They were halfway across the field when the side of the bunkhouse exploded behind then. Heat seared across her back and she stumbled once, a stray shard of cement glancing off her shoulder, before forcing herself to keep moving. Her lungs were crunched up balls of tinfoil in her chest. There were shots from the tower echoed over the fields obscuring how close a bead the guard had on their location.

They raced across the road to the line of houses and a shimmering oasis—the warded SUV.

She tossed the gun in the back and climbed into the driver's seat. Jonah, tenderly for someone liberally splattered with another man's blood and brains, lay Ian across the back seat.

"We good?" Jonah asked.

She glanced back at Ian, a violent rupture in her magic, in reality itself. There was a crack in the world. Nothing would ever be good again.

She slid against the seatback, groaning. The magic settled in her body, turning her blood to sludge and her skin to vapour. "Yeah." She forced herself to steady her breath, slow the racing of her heart, and slam her foot on the accelerator. "Yeah, we're good," she said, and drove until the prison was a distant haze at the edge of the horizon.

Interlude

This time, it hadn't been Colette who came for him, and it hadn't been anything that could even euphemistically be called an interrogation.

He hadn't seen Colette for days. It was the soldiers who came. They didn't even try to persuade him, as Colette had, to politely ass kiss his way to a slightly less rancid cell in return for his sage advice to the Shitler Youth's Wizard Corps. They wanted only to watch him thrash against his restraints, and his only consolation was that they were settling for torturing him because something had gone horribly wrong for them on the outside.

It wasn't much a consolation, though, not with the cold water filling his nostrils and mouth, the suffocating, clawing agony in his chest. Who'd have thought that drowning would feel so much like being set ablaze from the inside? The wet cloth over his eyes prevented him from so much as seeing his tormenters, and he choked and gagged and tried to scream but the noise that came out instead was a death rattle, the sound of his already-fucked lungs deciding that was it, they were done with him for good this time. When there was a pause, the breath didn't come. Instead he sobbed, and tried to retch, and of course this was how he'd die, eyes bulging, the air throttled out of him, every thought and word burned from his throat, stripped of authority and dignity and horribly, wretchedly alone.

They came and went over what might have been hours, or days, and their moments of absence were somehow even worse. The bag over his head, damp with sweat and tears and snot and bile, sucked into his mouth with each breath. He clawed at it but faced with his twisted, useless fingers, the drawstring held firm.

His body had seldom been more than an inconvenience for him, a skinny sack of bones and not much meat that he dragged behind him like a millstone, but he nonetheless raged at its betrayal, its weakness. He was dying, and the distant shouting down the hall, the pop of gunfire, barely registered: the last fantasies of an oxygen-deprived brain, still dreaming of rescue when the rest of him had given up. Even the crash of a door being kicked open wasn't happening, or if it was, it was happening somewhere far away from him.

After a lifetime in politics, he didn't believe in miracles.

Someone shouted a stream of invective in which his name bobbed, just out of reach. More gunshots, somewhere above the surface, a minor disturbance compared to the roaring in his ears. The sound of something breaking, a wet slap of flesh against concrete, and the clink of shells hitting stone.

And then he was being released from his restraints, propped up into a sitting position, hands shaking him with desperate, pleading force. "Breathe!" And he was truly dead, or irreparably deranged, because it sounded exactly like—

Like—

There was a name in his head, short-circuiting over pain-damaged neurons, a name that had meant something to him once, a nuclear detonation in the body of a girl, a sister or a daughter or—

You're a fucking field mouse, squeaking against the plow.

But squeak you must.

He somehow found a last flicker of strength to inhale, and it hurt like hell but his respiratory passages opened enough to admit air, and the person who in no possible way could be the girl with the severed name put her arms around him and murmured, "Oh, Ian."

It was the first time in over three years that anyone had held him. He collapsed against her, into blessed darkness.

Book 2

The Retribution

Company Profile: Tartarus Technologies Inc.

Business Sector: Magitech, Deep Ocean Exploration, Defense
Operating Geography: Silicon Valley Autonomous Region, SVAR Special Economic Zone (British Columbia)
About Tartarus Technologies Inc:

Tartarus Technologies Inc. is a publicly traded SVAR company that develops magitech components for submarines and other deep ocean submersibles. It is headquartered in the Nautilus Seastead. Tartarus is a technological and innovation leader in the integration of wellspring shards with state of the art navigation, defence, and security solutions. It has over 10,000 employees operating out of 20 seasteads. It boasts both corporate and state contracts. Tartarus's mission statement is "trusted, innovative solutions to disrupt the future."

SWOT Analysis

Strengths
• Magitech shards 1000x more efficient than nuclear power
• Strong R&D capabilities
• Highly diversified business segments

Weaknesses
• Inexperience with wellspring energy source
• Dependence on external supply chain based in the Dominion of Canada
• Pending lawsuits

Opportunities
• Rising demand for deep ocean mapping in response to Blight activities
• Economic instability in the Dominion of Canada
• Increased geopolitical conflict

Threats
• Competition from Russian Federation's magitech solutions
• Competition from other SVAR companies operating in the sector
• Domestic unrest in the Dominion of Canada

Tartarus should aim to diversify its portfolio as it continues to forge partnerships with the Dominion of Canada, with an eye to expansion and acquisitions.

13

The Last Call stood on what had been a hill and was now an island. The rest of the city block had been drowned by the floods. A ramshackle bridge connected the small knot of dry land to the beached corpse of the city.

Three years after the Blight, its windows were still boarded up instead of being replaced. Through the gaps in the planks, a lookout—Bailey, the enby kid that Blythe had brought over the mountains—kept watch. In the muddy green harbour, the SVAR gunships circled like sleek, black sharks where the Legislature, built on gravel and land theft, had sunk into the ocean.

The occupying forces seldom visited the hill. It was an unviable sector, the roads washed out, and an hour-and-a-half by bike over questionable bridges. Hoar-frost clung to the ragged patches of shriekgrass, the only living thing that had thrived after the floods and quakes. Blythe, bent on a milk crate scraping sticky residue off the worn soles of her boot, both cursed it and was grateful that it kept the little bar free from drunk libertarians and armed mercenaries alike. The Last Call was the fairy tale they told themselves about surviving the apocalypse.

The long lab shifts left her hollowed out, but she had no desire to return to her bedspace in the walled campus city.

The options at the bar had improved lately. The SVAR occupation and its hard-on for trade meant that the Last Call wasn't reliant on Kenny Ocampo's experiments in bathtub moonshine. Blythe wiped down her soles with a splash of ethanol and a prayer. It wasn't spore season, but the precautionary principle held even in the safety of the last bar in the world.

Kenny brought her a bottle of red wine and Bailey joined them. It wasn't going to calm the shaking in her limbs, but it was the only thing that kept the sea to a dull roar in her head. Made her feel, if only temporarily, that Laura had been someone else's daughter, lost to some other grieving mother, in an ancient and distant age.

"I need a boat," Blythe said, as if that were a normal way to open a conversation.

Kenny slid onto the seat across from her, the bottle between them. He thumped the big knitting bag he kept stashed behind the bar for slow times down on an empty chair.

"This is Victoria." He rooted through the bag until he found the needles. He was stitching another sweater, a patchwork of garish colours in chunky yarn that he insisted confused facial recognition technology. "It's not like there's a shortage. What do you need it for?"

Helplessly, she wished she could talk to Jonah about it. He wasn't kind, not like Kenny was kind, but he understood, at a viscera-deep level, what it was to want something powerful enough to crush you before it even noticed you were there.

"If I go off on my own, they'll take it out on Edgar," Blythe said. "Mitch said as much. I'm unreliable, performance evaluations, department cutbacks. Everyone has to do a little belt tightening. They'll work Edgar into a heart attack." There was no real way to tell if Mitch meant anything by it. She still had half a dozen grad students who'd be on the chopping block before she was, and it wasn't research the SVAR wanted from her, not really. When Edgar had first asked her to strap into the bathyscaphe and chase down recalcitrant ocean currents, it hadn't been her Ph.D. research that had qualified her for the job.

In the end, it was never about anything but what they could extract from her. If she lived, she'd have time to savour the poetry of that.

"That's not the question," Kenny said. She told herself she could be grateful that he was a pragmatist, or at least not hate him for it. Someone had to be. "What brings us closer to getting rid of them?"

The air in the bar, a geological epoch of dust, was suddenly oppressive. This was how it felt to surrender. The weight of a well-meaning paternal hand on her shoulder pushing downwards, murmuring to her that secret meetings in the wolf's hours did not a revolution make. The reminder that had she been patient, had she held out for longer, Laura might still be alive.

You could get used to anything after long enough. The SVAR didn't have the will of the people, but it had their acquiescence. The squalid tents outside of campus, surrounded by reams of barbed wire, *were* shelters, weren't they? The Dominion had camps. Mass graves. Public executions. If they rid themselves of the SVAR tomorrow, it wasn't going to be the scattered little revolutionary cells and the mutual aid networks that inherited the Archipelago.

She didn't have the fortitude to ask Kenny if he still believed they could win. If he saw anything beyond their tiny pockets of resistance squeezed between sociopathic powers and the vengeful ocean.

Carefully, she said, "If we don't know what's out there, what it wants from us—" *From me.* "We won't have a home left to liberate."

It was a weak argument and she saw it in Bailey's face, in Kenny's quick glance downward at the dance of his knitting needles.

"No one can have this," Blythe said. "The Dominion, the SVAR, they're all working on harnessing magic. Dominating it. Monetizing it. The first one that does it successfully, we'll never be rid of them."

Kenny said, "Just for the sake of argument, what kind of boat?"

. . .

Blythe took the long way down to the docks, through the tangled nest of footpaths and bridges, tapping the toe of her boot on pools crusted with thin ice to feel the crack of it giving way. The ocean and the shelter of the mountains should have warmed the city, but the superwinter had struck deep. Kenny had distributed his stupid sweaters and masks to her little rebellion of three, but she eyed the drones overhead uneasily as they perambulated the former downtown.

She had slept badly. The coffin wasn't meant for rest—the single bed was too hard, too single, so unlike the bed she'd kept when Jonah had left, larger than one person needed. But too large was still better than too narrow; she'd never gotten used to being caged, and the compound was cramped, and loud. The university ran 24/7 without the staffing to run it 24/7, and through the thin walls of her room she could hear the techs stumbling around on their way to the lab, coughing in the cold hours of the morning.

The ocean had taken over the old harbour in its first convulsions. Bits of wall and glass littered the shallows half a mile out from the new coast; the scavengers who tugged salvage from the icy water sometimes found a femur or a waterlogged child's coat. Blythe navigated the new, violent topography by the sea-green tortoise of the old Legislature submerged up the coast.

The icebreaker's bulk dwarfed the flotilla of sailboats and canoes that speckled the harbour. She was a ruin of a ship, gone to rust and scavenged for parts, pockmarked with barnacles and draped in sludge. The *Love Craft* dangled like a condemned man from her crane towards the ship's stern. Its entrance tunnel was visible behind the ship's davit. The cables, like everything else, had seen better days.

The ship must have, briefly, been part of a rescue mission. Now she lay tipped to her side, beached like a dead whale. At least she was still there, and the bathyscaphe with her. Whether either was usable remained a mystery. The crane apparatus was bigger than it had been in her memory, rusted through like everything else. Bolt-cutters and a prayer weren't going to free it, assuming it was even still operational.

They waded out in the shallows to the icebreaker, frigid water seeping through her boots. There was an emergency ladder about a metre above the surface. She grasped the bottom rung, the metal so cold that it burned through her gloves, and kicked and pushed upwards until she could hoist herself up onto it. A few years ago, she couldn't have managed, but the Blight had whittled her into sharp relief, muscle and sinew and burning resentment. She reached a hand down to Kenny. Bailey, with the agility of youth, scrambled up easily behind him.

They weren't the first to have explored the wreckage. There was little on the deck, anything useful and portable—rope, wood, life preservers—had been scavenged. Blythe picked her steps over discarded, half-frozen blankets and fishbones scraped clean and piled into tiny altars. Salt crusted the deck and taffrail, and she breathed in its sharp, mineral pitch.

"They might give me something more seaworthy if I made a business case," she mused. Even as she said it, she was shaking her head. No brilliant PowerPoint was going to make a libertarian see reason. Mitch wasn't the kind of boss who'd let her go out unsupervised, and while she wouldn't cry tears for the occupiers meeting the same fate as her old colleague Dahlia West, there was always a possibility that he'd insist she take Kit or Owen or one of the other grad students with her as hostages. No one was warded besides her and there was no MAI to do it. Not to mention that if the entity was as deep as it had been the last time she'd gone looking for it, not even the most sophisticated ship the SVAR could spare would get her close to it.

Besides, the entity knew the Love Craft. It knew her. She stretched out her hand, inches from the farthest swing of the submersible. The metal vibrated by her fingertips. The ship knew her as well. It warmed to her touch like a family dog greeting the prodigal daughter when she returned home on summer holiday. The last time she'd been aboard the Love Craft, she'd been dragged out of it unconscious, the ancient god of the deep ocean claiming squatter's rights in her skull, her MAI guide traumatized, and her pilot braindead. But it was just an object, a means to an end, its skin blistered, no matter how loudly it called to her.

Kenny, to his credit, wasn't the kind of person to tell her she shouldn't strap herself into an experimental sub alone and pilot it into the gaping maw of an undead eldritch god, assuming said undead eldritch god could even be located. But he was practical enough to ask irritating questions about her lack of a plan. "*Can* you even pilot it?"

"I did it before," she said. Which was to say that, after Dahlia, unwarded and exposed to the entity's cruel geometries and blithe disregard for the laws of nature, had gone unconscious, Blythe had scrambled over the controls and slammed buttons until the ship rose close enough to the surface for a rescue. She asked Bailey, "Could you show me?"

The kid shrugged. "This is some Jules Verne shit. Maybe. But if you run into any problems down there, you're fucked. No radio, no rescue boat."

"I'll risk it."

"Blythe," Kenny started.

"Any ship can be a submersible if you don't care about coming back up." She said it too lightly, and she saw his answering wince. The loss, for him, had begun well before the Blight. "If it wanted me dead, it had multiple opportunities. I'll take Cthulhu over Shitpost Galt any day."

"What's really out there?" Bailey asked. "What's so important that you'd—"

"Giant tentacle monster," Kenny said before Blythe could.

Bailey's eyes widened.

"Oh come on," Blythe said. "After everything you've seen, that's what's weird for you? It was dead, and then it was very much not-dead, and now Mitch thinks he can reverse-engineer it to nuke the Dominion, but he won't even fund the monitoring station that picked it up in the first place, which is typical. And the only thing worse than seeing a wasp in the room is knowing that there's a wasp in the room and not being able to see it."

Bailey squinted up at the bathyscaphe, dormant in its cradle, a teetering wrecking ball of a ship.

"What are you planning to do," they asked. "When you find the giant fucking tentacle monster?"

Blythe inhaled sharply. What did this odd person expect from her? Did they think she was going to toss a harpoon at it, dragging them both to their watery deaths? Pray to it? Ask it for tea and then demand an explanation? "That's a later problem," she said. "Can we get it into the water?"

"The icebreaker would need a team of engineers working on it for months to stay afloat," Bailey said. "I don't even think that kind of expertise exists anymore."

"I can talk to the fishermen," Kenny said. "Everyone drinks at the Last Call. Maybe one of the better boats can give you a tow out. If they think it'll help get rid of the SVAR."

Bailey's attention had been captured by something else now, the omnipresent polyp of the SVAR seastead at the horizon. Blythe was one of the few islanders who'd encountered one at close range. At once a weapon capable of flattening a neighbourhood and a mobile component of one of the behemoth corporate city-states lurking in the Pacific, it had the heft and sociopolitical outlook of a feudal fortress. She still woke up at night from dreams of its Frankenstein towers, the spider leg bristle of cannons at its flanks, the oily smear of corpses in its wake.

"Will it?" Bailey asked. "Help us get rid of them?"

Iron contorted, crunched. A deck impaled by a spear of bone. The city desperately firing its cannons even as bodies spilled into the churning water. Laura's hand, slipping from hers as the *Empress Willow* heaved and split apart.

Blythe couldn't help it. She laughed, as if Bailey had just asked her which would win in a fight, an 18-wheeler truck or God Almighty.

"I don't think it would even notice them coming before it inhaled and ate them," she said.

•   •   •

Three days later, Kenny met her by the ship. The cold never seemed to affect him as it did her, despite the holes in his barely-patched greatcoat. The wind was harsh, withering, but his attention was only on the fluctuating tension of chafed mooring lines.

Bailey and some of the fishermen were already on the deck, lowering the *Love Craft* from the crane. The cables complained with every inch, screaming as someone ratcheted the winch by hand.

"Thank you," she said, quietly.

"For enabling you?"

"For being a charming bartender. You're basically my scientist-to-human translator."

"Thought I was here for moral support." He slid his arm around her waist. They both went in to lean their heads together and ended up colliding. He laughed at her abrupt, "Sorry," and she almost joined him before she remembered where she was.

The thing they had going on was new, evolved from Kenny always being there, serving moonshine at the Last Call, and somehow that became after-hours dips into his private stash, meanspirited imitations of their SVAR overlords, drunken fucking in the little room above the bar where he lived. He hadn't asked her about what had happened in the time between her drinking sessions with the lab working group and the night she'd washed up alone, ragged and sobbing and daughterless, on the shore. She'd never asked him about his scars or the soft-focus terms in which he alluded to a past before the Blight. How that had become enough of a relationship that he'd be willing to face the wrath of Mitch and his company goons when she didn't turn up for her next shift was another mystery, though one she didn't exactly mind.

"It's stupid, though," he said. "It's shortsighted and reckless."

"We're a SVAR protectorate now," Blythe replied. "That's basically our motto."

She winced under the groan of metal on metal, the bathyscaphe scraping the deck as the fishermen maneuvered it awkwardly over the railing. She squelched down the brief panic at the thought of the thing unmoored, smashing into the men working to free it.

"We're better than the SVAR," Kenny said. He would follow her, if she asked him, would bleed out his own brains on the floor of the observation chamber just for a chance at glimpsing the thing. She would need to excise him from her life just as messily as she had every other attachment she had—Jonah, her mother, her team at the university, Laura's shade that plunged beneath the waves every time she closed her eyes.

Someone shouted up the shore. The bathyscaphe was free, half-submerged in the shallows, a dull, dormant thing, the cables hanging from the doomed icebreaker like an umbilical cord. She squeezed her arm around his waist, mumbled, "It has to be worth it," and let the wind swallow her words.

. . .

The lifejackets had long been plundered for other ships, but there was a pressure suit crammed into a workbench. It looked hideously uncomfortable but might buy her a few minutes if the *Love Craft* ran out of charge at the bottom of the ocean. Blythe found a rag and swiped dust from the instruments, while Bailey ran the world's fastest maintenance check. It was bleak, clumsy work that should have demanded precision, conducted by amateurs in the dead of night.

The bathyscaphe was battery powered—did the battery still work? Had it rusted out and dissolved the casing?—but it had gasoline flotation chambers, which had long since been siphoned out by the scavengers. The charging cable was still there, though, and Blythe and Kenny hoisted its python length out along the shore, where some of the fishermen had a generator. Gas was a harder problem. The SVAR controlled the supply and charged a premium for it. They'd stolen what they could, refilled tanks and made empty promises. But convincing ten or twelve subsistence fishers that they needed to part with even a small amount during a superwinter was asking a huge sacrifice.

Not to mention what she knew, what each of them knew. Which was that the floats were for coming back up.

She crawled back into the ship's aortic chamber to hide from the noise.

At the base of the console was a spot of blood—Dahlia's, or maybe her own—that whoever had cleaned the ship had missed when they'd brought it back to the surface. She slid to the floor, head throbbing, arms draped over her knees. She was giving it what it wanted, another blood sacrifice, but it still didn't seem satisfied.

She went over Bailey's instructions. Power, ballast. Left right, up, just like in a video game. The switches for the various release magnets and the floodlamps. The walkie, which would lose contact with the surface long before she needed it.

After her first ill-fated descent, she'd read up on the history of submarine rescues, of which there had been a grand total of four, ever. And this time there was no little Celene with her recorder, no Dahlia with her brash joy, no Edgar and his cool competency waiting in an icebreaker above her. She could still back out, keep up her strange double life of ferrying refugees and wasting the SVAR's time. At least until her brain exploded or her heart went from overwork.

Electricity thrummed through the observation sphere and the lights revived with a clank. Blythe drew in a sharp breath and scrambled for the pilot's seat. Through the observation bubble, Kenny and Bailey were tiny insects scuttling up and down the beach, caught in the bright circle of the *Love Craft*'s beam. She waved at them, the gesture gobbled up by the distance between them.

Blythe pushed out of the hatch to stand on the beach. The wind had died down, and the flotilla of little boats broke longer pauses between the short slashes of moonlight over the waves. She landed too hard on an ankle as she climbed out to disconnect the cable, foot catching on something that might have been the chunks of glass fish that the ocean still vomited up, might have been bone or driftwood.

"Fuck," she hissed, and limped over to where Kenny was negotiating with one of the fishermen. Bailey, meanwhile, was hitching the submersible's cables to two of the ships in the harbour.

"She's the one going out?" The older man looked her over. He clearly wasn't impressed.

"She's our expert," Kenny said, needlessly gallant. "Unless she's changed her mind."

"She hasn't," Blythe said. "Are we good to go?"

"They'll tow you out near where the seastead is," Kenny said. "But no further. These ships aren't built for open ocean, and they'll all shit-scared of the SVAR."

The old fisherman frowned.

"I'll be above you the whole time," Kenny said.

"I know you understand how three dimensional space works," she said. She reached over and seized his hand, squeezed tightly. "Thank you."

"They're going to ask where you went," Kenny said.

"Why do you think I didn't tell Edgar?" she replied. "But they're welcome to look for me. If they think they can find me."

"Don't drown, okay?"

Implosion was more of a risk than drowning—without Celene and her magic protecting the craft, the pressure was likely to kill her before any leak did.

"I really think it has other plans for me," Blythe said. And then, impulsively, *recklessly*, she didn't know that the sweaters worked, that the drones might capture evidence of his complicity, she threw her arms around his narrow shoulders and buried her face against his neck. "Either way, we keep fighting them. Even if there's nothing left. Especially if there's nothing left."

"Always," Kenny said. "Fucking always."

She watched him, and Bailey, in their element, working out the routes that would take them as far out as possible while avoiding the seastead and the known locations of the boat patrols. The fishermen, with their swollen joints and threadbare windbreakers, counting on her to liberate them from quotas and drones, placing a faith in her that she absolutely did not deserve.

She wanted a snappy line, a "let's do this" or "engage" or some big speech. Instead she nodded to all of them and climbed back inside, descended to the observation sphere. It was long minutes before she felt movement. The bathyscaphe moved in fits and starts, with the creaks and sighs of an ascending rollercoaster. She couldn't hear the shouts of the men anymore, or the sloshing of the water around the ship. Her stomach plummeted in advance of the fall.

The instruments purred and the floor quivered. She slid into the pilot's seat—Dahlia's seat—and lifted her eyes to the rattling window.

She should have brought a book or something to distract herself from the monotony of being towed out to sea, the jerking motion as the waves tormented the small vessel. She'd killed the exterior lights, and whatever sights passed before the observation window were no more than shadows against the near-pitch depths.

Hours passed. Days. It was still dark—she told herself that she was just bored, restless, cramped in a little bubble where her friend had died.

The walkie crackled to life.

"We're about to release the cables, over."

She'd forgotten what words sounded like. Snatching it, she said, "Do it. Over."

The cables detached with an unexpected violence, jerking the vessel from bow to stern. For a moment she hovered, suspended above the abyss, a tight coil of potential energy.

And then she fell.

14

The Train rumbled through the wilderness like an avatar of hope and stability uniting the country from coast to coast, its engine clean-running and nearly as advanced as anything the SVAR had at their disposal, albeit with a speed limited by the ancient rails over which it travelled.

Despite the quiet, she only heard some of the precise, but no less deadly, evisceration happening in the Curtis' carriage.

Colette wasn't eavesdropping. She had her own business with Alycia Curtis, and she was supposed to be here. She hadn't failed. She *hadn't*. She just hadn't succeeded yet. She sat in the alcove outside the sliding doors, stabbing silk stitches into a bolt of linen. Alycia had *summoned* her to board the train at Oshawa the previous week. Nate was stuck minding the twins in a passenger car, well away from Atherton or anyone important.

God knew she loved her children, but the peace and quiet came as a blessed respite, at least until Simon Yamashita shuffled past her, into Alycia's on-train offices.

Colette, for her part, kept her face neutral and her gaze on her embroidery. Alycia's political games were vague and amorphous, always shifting and changing, with no clear rules or metrics. Simon's purview, the work of purifying and elevating the arts, was even more esoteric.

The twins were in a phase where all they wanted to watch was *Caillou* reruns, so that was all that anyone heard around the house, but when she was out jogging, she'd put on the soundtrack to *Phantom* or *Wicked* and find her lips moving to the words, her heart soaring with the orchestration. Simon's music moved her too, but it moved everyone, and when it was over, she went about her day.

Nothing Simon did seemed enough of a big deal to make Alycia's voice go from its usual soft to quiet-scary. Oh, Colette would never *admit* that she found Alycia Curtis utterly terrifying, but no one wanted to hear the woman lower her voice. Still, she *did* take opera very seriously.

Colette took a deep breath and focused on the little things. That was Mindfulness 101. She concentrated first on her breathing, the contraction and motion of her diaphragm, the passing of air between her slightly parted lips. On the automatic motion of her fingers as they dipped and wove through the spell, the thrumming connection of the silk like a pulse. The miracle of the material itself, the mass sacrifice that it entailed, thousands of wriggling larvae boiled alive in their cocoons to produce the soft thread that slid over her wrist, that gave only the faintest resistance to the linen. The slightest tug and answering spasm of a nervous system, kilometres away. The burnished cedar woodwork of the train car, elegant scroll details framing the doors and the portrait of Quinn Atherton mounted between Dominion flags.

Words like: *defected, destabilizing factors*, occasionally broke through, but she resolved to ignore the discussion. It probably didn't concern her, anyway.

Ten minutes later, Simon emerged, deflated, managing no more than a thin smile in Colette's direction before inch worming his way to the door between cars. "Come in," Alycia said.

Alycia's office was as sumptuously furnished as the rest of the car, with the Atherton portrait above her desk and the silver laptop the only concessions to the world outside. In one corner, a gramophone, its horn polished bronze, played Mozart. The walls, furnished with original Lawren Harrises and Cornelius Krieghoffs, were the same winter white as Alycia's suit. She looked up, pushed her reading glasses up the bridge of her nose, and motioned for Colette to sit.

"Everything okay?" Colette asked. It hadn't occurred to her that she might be in trouble, even with a continued lack of results. But Alycia's face, normally so animated, was drawn. Haunted. Colette folded her fabric and tucked it into her purse, wishing she had something, anything, positive to report.

"Such small-minded men," Alycia said. Colette couldn't help thinking that she was picking up the thread to some previous conversation. "Simon, of course. Even the Director himself, on his worst days. Oh, they can be useful enough, when they have to be, but they lack vision." She rubbed one manicured finger against each temple, shutting the laptop. "Forgive me, Colette. It's been a very long day."

"I'm sorry?" She hadn't meant it to sound like a question, and Alycia's huffing laugh in response felt very much like mockery.

"All the Director cares about is transference," Alycia said. "And reversing the demon condition, and shriekgrass growth. All very practical concerns, to be fair, but unambitious. I don't suppose you—"

"I'd have reported positive results," Colette said. "Immediately. I was able to transfer energy from the original subject to a volunteer host but." *But the host is a gibbering maniac chewing off his own skin in a pile of shit.* "It might not be possible. There's so much we still don't understand."

She stopped there, because she might not follow politics closely, but she knew a landmine when she had her foot scant inches above it. If magic was encoded in DNA, some vestigial code activated by the Cascade, it was possible that the volunteers simply weren't genetically compatible. Both Alycia Curtis and her husband cared a great deal about genetics, as did Director Atherton. To admit that it was entirely random was heresy, even if the evidence suggested it.

Reid Curtis traced his lineage to the Family Compact; he was the scion of a dynasty that went back to the Robinsons and was as close to aristocracy as could be found in a country that stubbornly refused to grant titles—and he had no magic. Filthy, half-mad sewer rat Ian Mallory had, conversely, been bestowed a gift his betters were denied. They had demanded a genealogy test despite his murky family history and the shoddy state of DNA ancestry labs, as if somewhere a verifiable loophole existed that could turn an upstart nobody into a lost prince. There could be no congenital justification for such a cosmic oversight.

Ideological compatibility. It made no sense, scientifically, but it was easy enough to test for, if the Cleaners were willing to round her up a few terrorists with a minimum of bullet holes in them. She had a strong suspicion that Mallory had just been messing with her.

"It may be possible," Colette managed, a band-aid on a gaping wound, "to use the same transference process to remove magic from a demon. If we don't care as much what happens to it afterwards. And if we could. You know. Actually capture a demon for testing."

"I'll see what I can do," Alycia said, so dryly that Colette couldn't tell if she was joking or not. She erred on the side of not. Alycia had managed to capture Mallory, after all, dragging him off his throne as the country's most powerful living magician and turning him into a shrivelled wretch huddling in the corner of a prison cell. Alycia's attention already seemed to have moved onto something else, a distant horizon behind Colette's head, another, future problem. "Poor Quinn," she said. "The most he can imagine is a ceasefire with magic. My plans, my husband's aims, are vastly more ambitious."

Colette leaned forward, close enough that she could almost feel the place where the energies swirling around each of them met. "What are they?"

Alycia's red lips, a contrast with her pale skin, pursed in thought. She wasn't herself. Alycia, like Colette, threw herself into her work fully, as devoted to the minutiae of repairing a broken country as she had been to her philanthropy before the Blight had rendered charity a moot point.

Unlike Colette, she didn't have the distractions of family to divert her attention. Something else was on her mind.

She at last, settled on a non-answer. "Keep up the good work," Alycia said, "and you'll find out soon enough." She stood, parted the velvet curtains to reveal the window. They were deep into a Blight-scarred stretch of wild, some undifferentiated wasteland marked by farms gone to ruin, downed power lines and jagged granite pushed into crooked hills by earthquakes. Shriekgrass pushed through the crusted mantle of snow, a mauve blur as the Train rolled past.

Nothing lived out here anymore. Nothing but poison weeds and demons. Maybe Alycia did plan to capture one.

"I should get back." The Train moved too quickly for that, and she caught her error before the words were out of her mouth. They were headed for a war zone. Colette hated the high tilt that nerves gave her voice. "The work won't wait."

Alycia's nails clipped lightly against the glass. "This time," she said. "I believe it will."

·   ·   ·

Alycia had dragged Simon out for a rally on the route east, playing piano while the Dominion's top officials slid daggers into each other's backs. Normally Lucy would have been singing; alone, the music was charged, but the actual sound was too thin for the spell it carried.

The wind kicked gusts of fine snow in front of the platform they'd set up by the Train, jolting the flames of the torches. The space heaters ringing the crowd barely offered any warmth. Colette, seated with a cluster of Dominion wives who chattered through the performance, shivered, her back to the Train's warmth. Despite the cold, Simon had patches of sweat under the armpits of his suit, in the centre of his back. He had been untouchable at the outset of their journey, neat and silver-haired and trim, but the confinement was taking its toll on him as well.

Kingston was an echo of the creature it had been before the Blight. Its leaders had set up the stage at the back of the station, in a wide plaza, to spare everyone the sight of the Dominion's failures. The crowd was thin, the storm keeping all but the truly patriotic in their homes. A few Red Ensigns fluttered half-heartedly, lambs' blood on closed doors. The omnipresent torches had proved more popular—for warmth if not for ideological fervour.

Everyone was tired, and irritable, and restless, most of all Colette, who had the most reason to be. An MAI with no magic to do was as useful as an MAI with no magic at all.

Colette's attention was on the riser, where Atherton stood with Reid Curtis and the rest of the Dominion bigwigs. Nate was among them, in the one suit he owned, a plough-horse among wolves. She couldn't follow their conversation over the chatting of the wives. She didn't belong here with these sleek, well-dressed women, couldn't follow their inside jokes or the intricacies of their lives.

"They've reopened Havergal," Mrs. Maitland was saying.

"I ended up with a tutor for Harper," Mrs. Rowe replied. "The teachers aren't what they used to be."

"But the children have missed out on so much learning and socialization." Mrs. Maitland turned her attention on Colette, the newcomer. "Where do your children go?"

"Oh," Colette said. "They're still young. Nate takes care of them during the day." Should she admit that he was out of work? They were connected, they might put in a word with their husbands—but then, why did Mrs. Rowe look like she'd swallowed her twin? DEC payments or not, if Nate didn't find work soon there'd be no money left over for tuition or anything else.

As it always did, the conversation mercifully drifted to fruit and coffee and perfume and microprocessor chips and Mrs. Maitland's problems with her housekeeper. There was a pause in the conversation, and Colette blurted, "I don't drink coffee anymore," a non sequitur that the other women quickly glossed over. Mrs. Rowe laughed, musical and knowing, like the girls in junior high who'd found her fascination with insects and rocks somewhere between a curiosity and a crime against femininity.

"What did you do before you met Alycia?" Mrs. Silberton, her blond waves declaring her access to contraband, folded her hands over her napkin. By the front, she saw Alycia break away from the head party, Reid's eyes tracking her as she strode for the knot of women at the back.

"I was a student when the Blight hit," Colette said. "Kinesiology." At Alycia's approach, she said. "This has all been an incredible opportunity for me, really."

"Ah, that's why you're in such good shape," Mrs. Maitland said. "You should join us for a yoga class, dear."

"I need to talk to you." Alycia had suddenly appeared at her side, then steered her away from the crowd. Atherton was talking, but from her position behind the amplification, all Colette could hear was vowels. Alycia led her away from the wives' table. When she was out of earshot, Colette whispered, "What am I doing here?"

Instead of answering, Alycia said, "Ian Mallory is gone." Colette's heart might have been pierced by one of her own needles. "Missing," Alycia added, and Colette remembered to breathe again. "There was an assault on the facility last night. We have reason to believe Lucy Fletcher gave his location to the terrorists."

Lucy was an insubstantial creature, fluttery and distinguishable from the wives only by her Margaret Keane eyes and her black shroud of widowhood. To imagine her, of all people, running off with Ian Mallory defied belief.

"Act calm," Alycia said. "It's nothing to concern your companions about. There's nothing left to him; the man's a vegetable. And Lucy won't get far."

"I still had—things to do." The older woman couldn't understand; she was an MAI as much as Colette was, but her magic was cool, remote, refined through Simon's compositions and Lucy's singing. She hadn't thrust her hands into magic's churning innards, felt its guts slide between her fingers and its blood dry under her nails. "Have. I need to be back at the facility, not here."

"You belong here. You must start to act like it. You wanted power, and this is where you find it. Not the crude politicking of men—these are desperate times that we must participate in it at all—but the value of a woman's wise influence."

She couldn't imagine being one of these women, stuck nattering about lingerie and living room furniture when the mysteries of the cosmos had burst forth from the earth, crying out to be explored. She had been freed from that by her powers. Some of the sentiment must have come through on her face, because Alycia put an exquisitely soft hand on her shoulder.

"How do you think the world will look like, sweet girl, when we've finished with it?"

"I just—I have work to do. And politics—"

"Isn't your thing. So you've said. You have children, Colette."

"You don't?"

"I always thought it an impediment, unfortunately." Her chuckle was the closest thing to self-deprecation Colette had heard from her. "Such an irony, do you not think? We promote this doctrine, that the highest purpose of a woman, her most sacred duty to the nation, is to birth the next generation. To repopulate this sad, depleted country of ours, that we might as a people be strong again. And yet this has never been my purpose—nor your natural one."

"This is for them," Colette replied, too quickly. Was it a dig about her boys being adopted? "Noah and Jasper. And Nate. All of it is for them. It's not one or the other."

Now Alycia's laugh was broader, and Colette was not convinced of its target.

"It's sweet that you think that." Alycia made brief eye contact with Reid, winked. Married couples had their own language, their private code. She and Nate, after two years, were still learning theirs.

"Then again," Alycia said, "a new world is a birth of sorts. Perhaps one greater than a child. And unlike a child, it doesn't need to be an attachment that weighs you down."

She gave Colette a small, secretive smile.

"Your research is the highest purpose anyone could be tasked with, my dear. Man or woman. To answer the greatest questions of our age, to unravel the knot of magic, and thereby witness the face of God."

. . .

Reid was now calling it Simon's Grand Apology Tour, wherein the disgraced composer attempted to redeem himself for his inadvertent act of treachery. Colette wasn't sure what good it would do, besides reminding him of his place. It could be Alycia's attempt at a consolation prize for Colette after the disappearance of her primary project. It wasn't a very good one. Colette found the music soporific and the art pointless. Her dress, which Alycia had stage-managed with the precision of a musical-theatre mom, pressed painfully into her sides, stiffer and more structured than anything she would have chosen for herself.

She wasn't on display—the spotlight was saved for Simon, who dutifully performed with all the enthusiasm he could muster. He was the vulnerable, human face of the Dominion, and where he played funding and reconstruction projects rained on the shattered cities.

Alycia's mouth was close enough to Colette's ear that the light blossom of her perfume flooded her nose when she inhaled. "Look at him," Alycia stage-whispered. "We are the nation's last bastion of defense against the forces of barbarism, the very face of civilization, dignity, and honour, and this is my raw material."

He played, the notes caught in the wind's fury, held and then extinguished. The crowd cheered regardless. The towns the Train stopped at were battered and hollowed out, their farms smothered by shriekgrass. Were it not for the Walsingham Institute's opulent feats of charity, people would starve, though of course no one was supposed to know that. The Train promised renewal, justice. A future.

Answers.

And so Colette was here, fighting just as bitterly as Simon Yamashita for her place at Alycia's side, instead of in her lab elbow deep in blood and spellwork in search of those answers.

On the stage, Simon played furiously, the little blonde soprano they'd hired to replace Lucy a pale cipher for Alycia's spell. Reid coughed and gave a minute shake of his head.

"They're loving it," Colette said. She barely knew Simon, but she'd learned early in life that there was immense value to having someone below you in the pecking order.

"Hmm," Alycia said. Her taut mouth was inscrutable. Colette might have said something perceptive, sliding in just the right kind of small talk to secure her place in Alycia's inner circle, or she might have indicated an unwitting eagerness to be her next disappointment.

Though, probably not. MAI, let alone MAI with any sort of STEM background, were difficult to come by. There was immense value to scarcity, too.

"I wanted to talk to you," she said. "About the other projects?"

Project Eat had ended with a guard's head smeared across the floor of Ian Mallory's prison cell. Project Love was highly theoretical at best. Alycia, so generous with her funding, was stingy on the details of Project Pray. Colette was a blind woman at the side of an elephant, fumbling in the dark for a tree trunk, or a snake, or a spear.

"Is this really the place for it?" Alycia's answering whisper was arch, if amused.

Project Love had her reconstructing demons from the only samples available, the rare, highly contained samples of wellspring overflow, severed blades of shriekgrass that, though plucked, still writhed and wept faintly on her table. There were no captive demons to take apart and study, even if her scalpel could cut through glass and sclerites. She possessed only demon-adjacent things, the detritus magic left in its wake.

Project Pray was even more elusive than that. Colette had no more than outlines, like those she had once sketched with a marking pencil before the Pattern took over for her. She was to push through magic's resistant membrane until she broke through to what lay beyond. Oh, certainly, both Reid and Alycia had attempted more prosaic phrasing, inventing jargon and specifications seemingly on the fly, but she grasped some of the truth that underpinned their words.

"Until the subject is returned," Colette said, "or a suitable replacement is found. It makes sense for me to move on."

Simon's fingers lingered over each note, an anemic through-line picked out over the keys. Colette's own magic bristled at it, like two angry cats circling each other. He was messing with her. Had to be.

At the first pop of gunshots, she thought it was part of the rally, even looked up to spot the fireworks through the heavy cloud cover.

Soldiers—which she had mistaken for part of the architecture—erupted from the edge of the stage, sweeping Alycia and Reid into a storm of black. They shoved past Colette, rushing with the brutal efficiency of ants in a disturbed hill, and she toppled in her ridiculously tight dress as a bullet smashed the lid of Simon's grand piano. She climbed to her feet and ran for the cover of the riser.

It was the wrong angle to see much of anything. She could move her head just slightly to see the tiny figures running out from the trees, the flapping blue and white flags, the machine guns like tiny sticks in their arms.

"Vive le Quebec libre!" rang like a page torn out of her tenth grade history textbook, and a grenade, the size of a potato, landed and rolled across the stage.

Simon's arm swept her down into the snow, his body shielding her own, as the riser exploded into aluminum shrapnel.

"We're under attack," Simon said, pointlessly.

She pressed into the ground. Even now, she clutched the rectangle of linen close to her chest.

"Where did Alycia go?" she hissed.

He cocked his head at the Train. It was distant—she ran every day, but there were city blocks between the rally site and the railroad, and men firing at each other from all sides. Simon, middle-aged and magic-drained, might as well have walked into the firefight with a white flag for all the chance he had of making the dash.

Colette hadn't seen much of the initial fighting after the Blight had receded. She lived in a good, safe neighbourhood. The Cleaners had established a perimeter early on, and while she'd hear distant gunfire at night, it seldom got close enough to see. Given where they were now, it had to be the separatists attacking, maybe Henri Vaillancourt himself. He'd been a banker, one of the faithful, right up until he'd betrayed Atherton and turned the province into a war zone.

She eyed the underside of the stage, bowed in the middle by the grenade's impact. Was that a bad idea? She should crawl towards shelter, that's what they always said during lockdown drills back in school, stay in the middle of the room, away from doors and windows, keep quiet on the floor and don't talk—

"Hey," Simon said. "It's under control. It'll be okay."

"Yes," she replied, as if terrorist attacks were a regular part of her life and not an infection of the war, of the Blight, past the blood-brain barrier of her universe. "Of course. It always is."

"We need to do our part." He took two long shaking breaths and began to hum, atonal at first, resolving into notes. His thin fingers wore white crescents into the flesh of his hand. The sound must have been too low for the fighters to hear, but she saw one of the separatists stop in his tracks, stand deer-in-the-headlights frozen before a sniper from the top of the stage took him down.

Colette stared at Simon, gaping.

"You thought you and Alycia were the only ones who figured out how to weaponize it?" he asked between measures."Can you carry a tune?"

"Did you tell Lucy about the prison?" Colette asked instead.

He nodded, hummed louder, cutting off any discussion. More men were running from the Train, now that they had the advantage.

"Why'd you do it?" Years of training her breathing paid off. She was calm. She was Zen. She could take responsibility for no one's actions beyond her own, and her own had been impeccably loyal. "Because he's an MAI?"

"This is hardly the time." Remarkable, that he could keep up the magic and the conversation all at once. But the music had taken on a life of its own, weaving through the firefight, independent of his voice. She elbowed out of the snow, her fancy dress ruined. "Am I going to end up one of your lab rats too?"

Simon was like Colette, apolitical, an MAI who knew both his value and his disposability. She'd never thought of him as a threat before. She clutched the square of linen, pressed her needle into it, as all around her, the soldiers turned their assailants in bloody splotches in the snow.

When it was over, she let Simon help her to the Train, but she didn't meet his eyes.

•   •   •

They were going to make her murder Simon, smash him open like a piñata and root through his secrets. Colette let herself into his room. It was narrow and simple, but well-appointed. The one light fixture cast a grid of shadows over the wall as it swayed with the Train's momentum.

She had never killed anyone. Not like this. The magic festered inside her volunteers until it rotted them from the inside and bloomed where their humanity had been. She might have killed them, but not intentionally, and it had taken them a long time to die.

(And there was the girl, little Celene with her recorder, but Colette didn't think about her outside of the last few bleary eyed moments every night before she yielded to sleep.)

None of those deaths had been murder, at least not in any way that counted. But Simon wasn't some terrorist whose fate would have been far worse if she hadn't swooped in to dredge some meaning from his death. He'd been nothing but polite to her. He'd saved her life. And though he might squeal, drenched in the unforgiving light of the Train's flood lamps, he was no mere lab rat either.

They wouldn't make Colette fire a gun. They had other people to do that. Besides, if he had run his use as a tool of the Dominion, he could at least take Ian Mallory's place at the facility.

As the Train at last was bearing back west, away from fractious, divided Quebec, she was increasingly convinced that her presence on it was meant to be some sort of test, one she hadn't studied for.

What was it, exactly, that Alycia wanted from her? She had been warm with Lucy Fletcher, treated her like a daughter, but Lucy had been weak, a traitor. She was no more than a moon, shining bright, but only when she was reflecting the rays of the sun. She had failed Alycia, and Reid, and all of the Dominion, and Alycia would have her hunted down and hanged, once she'd fulfilled her other priorities.

Colette would be stronger. This trip wasn't a test. It was an audition.

She gently tore the stitches of her embroidery, the needle still attached and sharp. She placed it in the dip in the mattress that his body had made, the thread snaking over the sheet like a drip of blood. She glanced only briefly at the framed picture of his teenaged son on the bedside table.

Like Sleeping Beauty. The tiniest prick of a spindle. He wouldn't even notice. She could be kind, when she needed to be.

Colette reached up and loosened the lightbulb before she let herself out.

• • •

Jasper was wailing. A tooth, maybe, or whatever small and furious injustice a toddler could rage against. "Nate, can you get Bear?"

"Which one is—"

"The grey one." These were the kinds of things a father should know about his son, but Nate was fumbling through the overnight bag, frowning. Their roomette was private, but it wasn't large enough to pace in, consisting only of a single chair, a folding bed for them and a cot for the boys, a washbasin, and a toilet. She had always cultivated mental stillness, but the needle on Simon's mattress had her on edge.

"Colette…"

"I have to see Alycia." The Train was stopped for the night, refuelling. She could get out, rent a car, and get them all home in two hours. If it were the Before Times, and the roads were safe, and Alycia Curtis wasn't breathing down her neck. "Just … do your best. I love you."

Nate wasn't going to drop Noah on his head. Jasper wasn't going to drown in a pool of his own endless tears. Everything would work out fine, and she was silly for giving in to his new-dad jitters. What was that saying? *Worry is like a rocking chair: it gives you something to do but never gets you anywhere.*

She slipped out into the hallway, Jasper's sobbing audible until she'd made it into the next compartment, and a tune, the burbling drone of the factory song, took over where it had left off.

Simon was waiting, the needle in his hand.

She could scream, if she screamed Nate might hear, someone might—

—a low centre of gravity was an advantage, according to the self-defence course she'd taken, she was younger and fitter and if she kneed him in the balls she could catch him off balance. But he was *humming.*

The air was sweet, heavy as thickening amber, and she moved in slow motion. The pressure bore down on her chest and squeezed the breath from her lungs. He had been so harmless and unassuming and she'd underestimated him, of course she had, you didn't make it to Alycia's table unless you were willing to murder to secure your seat there. She hadn't known he had the strength for it.

The thread was still in her pocket, in the coat that hung beside the door. All she needed to do was reach it. One good tug of the thread was all it would take; she had stopped Ian Mallory's heart with less. The car vibrated, in harmony with the notes. She couldn't move her hand. She couldn't breathe. Wetness spread between her legs and she had enough acuity to be humiliated.

"Looking for this?" He twirled the needle and the wisp of fraying red thread floating by its eye. It sparked with his magic, which bounced and fizzled against her own. "Did Alycia put you up to it? Or were you just *showing initiative?"*

She fought against the sludge of the air, uncontrolled, uncoordinated, nothing like the rehearsed simulations of violence in her class, the choreographed dance of dodge and swerve. None of those sparring partners had wanted to murder her; none of them were people she had tried to kill. He was closer to her, eyes wet and graceful hands shaking.

He slammed the needle into the side of her neck. The tip bit and bowed. She squirmed and it skipped across her skin, trailing spellwork that seared but lacked intention. She froze, heart stilled, throat collapsing around her breath.

Breathe. Centre. She found her heart chakra, focused on its radiance, its power. The needle was abandoned, a thin gleam in the line of dust where the wall met the floor. She had to live—the boys were a compartment away, Nate was, her family at the whim of a maddened wizard whose survival rested on her obliteration.

Her voice wouldn't come. Not even to whimper *please*.

Simon's face was a Halloween mask of bulging, glistening flesh. Bearing down on her, the death-song on his tongue, he took up her whole field of vision, his fear and his desperate desire to live filled her nostrils, her mouth, and the silvery whisper, *Simon Yamashita*, reverberated until it was a deafening drone.

The fist, millimetres from the bridge of her nose, unravelled.

Simon came apart in pieces. Splinter-thin fragments loosed themselves from his cheeks, his gleaming forehead, a membrane lifting from first one eye then the next hovering in mid-air before deliquescing. Globules of yellow fat split apart into smaller bubbles.

His magic unwound with him, a long, thin note like an oboe or the cry of a distant loon. It parted easier than his flesh; he hadn't turned every cell in his body into a war zone like Ian Mallory had.

He was striated, straining muscle. He was bone. He was blood. And then he wasn't anything at all.

Colette caught herself on the ridge of wainscotting. Alycia stood in front of her, where Simon had been a second ago, the poison of his name still dripping iridescent down her lips.

"You're welcome," Alycia said.

15

Adrenaline spiking through his veins, Jonah screwed his eyes tight and tried to calm down before he punched a hole through the car door. He focused on the dome of Maya's cheek and the jut of her crooked glasses, her lips falling open in barely contained horror as she craned her head to evaluate the pathetic huddle in the back seat.

She knew it as well as Jonah did. She was magic, down to her cells, and more to the point, she was Ian's apprentice. She must have felt the Ian-shaped absence in the universe as keenly as Jonah's ward tattoo did, the cruel joke of the body lying, breath issuing in pained wheezes, in his arms.

And yet, Ian *was* breathing. Unconscious, which, if Jonah were inclined to be charitable, might almost have been the mercy of a loving God who wasn't out to fuck them all. They'd done something worse than torture him, done something to his magic, but he was still alive. That was the only reason Jonah didn't demand that Maya turn the car around so that he could ram handfuls of live grenades up the asses of each and every one of those Dominion bastards.

Jonah forced long, slow breaths through his lips, hands shaking for a cigarette. Ian's hair spilled in seaweed tangles over a leather bench seat that was a shade or two darker grey. Desiccated skin clung to too-prominent bone, the last of the colour in his face so completely sapped that he looked like he'd been run several times through a bad copier. Jonah knew this, he'd known what was under the projection Maya had placed between Ian and the world. The cadaverous stranger before him had always been there, waiting for the sculptor's blade to reveal it.

Somehow the sight still came as a shock.

Ian had a beard, and normally Jonah would have ragged him for how it made him look like an old man, except it was then that Jonah saw his hands, one splayed out across his chest, the other dangling loosely over the side of the seat. His fingers were the bent and crooked branches of a dead tree, hands that would never grasp a pen and draw a labyrinth, would never cradle the neck and bow of his fiddle, ever again.

"He needs to go to a hospital," Jonah said, as if their nightmare clusterfuck of a world might rearrange itself into some less malicious configuration by sheer force of his will.

"The Cleaners would arrest us the moment we hit the parking lot."

"What, then?" The plan, which had failed to take into account just how badly the fuckers had worked Ian over, had been to switch cars outside of Scarborough and then take him to one of the many safe houses that dotted the Exclusion Zone. It still might work, but not if Ian died on a filthy floor in a strip mall indistinguishable from the cell they'd rescued him from.

"We can go to Cal's," Maya said. Jonah found himself nodding, because as much as he detested the senator, as bleakly as Cal's relationship with Ian must have ended, he couldn't imagine Cal turning them away. Cal would have food that wasn't scavenged from a dumpster, and running water, and a gigantic feather bed, and Ian needed all of those things.

Jonah, as softly as he could manage, placed his palm over Ian's bumpy ribcage. Stroked there, trying both to soothe him and assess the extent of his injuries, but Ian groaned and Jonah pulled his hand back as if stung.

He settled for rubbing his thumb over Ian's temple, which was tolerated, barely.

"What did they do to him?" he whispered. "They can't just—" But there were barely words for magic, for the thing that Ian had once been. There were none for the flensing of magic from bone, for the hollow husk they'd left in its place.

Ian stirred, blinked, and for a few minutes his grey-rimmed, sea-foam eyes seemed to focus entirely on Jonah. Jonah was, for the first time in his life, completely at a loss for words. He wanted nothing more than to cling to him, the absolute last thing he had in the entire world, and mumble all manner of sentimental bullshit that he'd never actually admit, even to himself, except that it had been such a long fucking night and Ian looked like he was dying.

"You stupid shit," Jonah said instead. "You're supposed to be the one flaying souls apart with your brain, not the other way around."

Ian's expression was unreadable, and Jonah pressed their foreheads together and shut his eyes to keep the tears in.

"Hey Joe." Ian's voice was rusted, buried under layers of sediment. Jonah was sure he'd imagined it until he heard it again. "Whaddya call a magician who's lost his magic?"

Maya made a small, pained noise. "I don't know," Jonah said, like a surrender.

"Ian," he said, and wheezed laughter until he passed out.

•   •   •

They switched cars just outside of Toronto. Jonah kept watch, revolver in hand, while Maya hot-wired a Kia in a snow-dusted parking lot drenched in the blue light before dawn.

When had he slept last? He must have nodded off a few times driving east, but he couldn't remember. Would he wake up in the church basement on a mattress that sank into the cold tiled floor? He watched Maya slide her hand through the car door and flick the lock open like she'd been stealing cars all her life.

"Time to move," she said. She'd been Ian's intern, once, and now she got to order Jonah around. She was some kind of big-shot general in the resistance army. There was little softness left in her round face. Only her oversized glasses and the rubber duck remained of the girl she'd been.

Ian weighed nothing. Jonah settled him in the seat with his head cradled in his lap and circled his hand around a wrist as thick as two of his fingers. He folded himself into what could charitably be called a stress position, convinced that if he broke contact, Ian would evaporate into the ghost he'd been since before the Dominion's bloody rise to power.

The cemetery lines of neglected high rises gave way to the highway. Maya drove on back roads to avoid Cleaner patrols. Jonah wasn't convinced they'd lost anyone hunting them, but as dawn washed over broken streets, overgrown with shriekgrass, the few cars on the road looked different each time they passed one. The shimmer of Maya's magic prickled his tattoo, more a vague annoyance than any tangible sensation.

They were driving into a pure fantasy of stately oak and elm. Though the branches were still winter-bare, they caught the early pinks and gold of dawn. Behind rows of conical junipers that guarded them from the road, he caught glimpses of a turret here, a row of Grecian columns there. The mansions were set back from the street, behind wrought-iron gates. Not a blade of shriekgrass pierced its way through the snow. Where the road had split in the Blight, it had been filled with new asphalt that glistened like a hidden vein of obsidian.

In all the devastation that the Blight had brought, in the last, desperate spell that Ian had aimed at places like this, it had somehow survived. It had emerged, intact, from some period drama, with flighty debutantes and their tutting servants and a self-absorbed heir hiding a heart of gold. It was absurd, grotesque in its placidity, its symmetry. It was all Jonah could do not to pry a cobblestone out of a driveway as wide as his last apartment and lob it through a double-glazed window of the nearest McMansion.

The gate at the foot of the road—Jonah refused to call it a

driveway—was locked. "Do we hop it?" he asked. Jonah could, easily, though maybe not carrying Ian, or without getting shot by whatever private security the senator had on staff.

Maya rolled her eyes and hit the buzzer. It was several long, tense minutes before he heard Cal's voice through a sea of static.

"It's me," Maya said. Someone could be listening—her nom de guerre was no less dangerous than her buried name. "From the Broom Closet. I brought company. Get decent. Please."

Jonah could only just make out a sigh, but there was a click and the gate swung open.

Senator Cal Harrison's ancestral home had its own circle driveway in front of a grand arch. At the centre of the circle was some kind of modern sculpture, planes of gleaming metal, edged in frost, that might have looked like two entwined human bodies if you'd just ingested a significant quantity of mushrooms. It was anodyne, bloodless, and no doubt hideously expensive—just like its owner. A brick arch concealed the garage—which already held a glossy Jaguar—from the street.

"No valet?" Jonah asked. At Maya's wince, he added, "Are you sure this is a good idea?"

Maya's earlier assertiveness was flagging. "He'll help us," she said. "He has to."

Cal met them at the door, bleary-eyed, in a monogrammed housecoat, only just able to move aside as Jonah hauled his unconscious burden over the threshold, where Ian suddenly and violently jerked back to life in his arms and slid to the ground.

Jonah stumbled after Ian, tracking mud over the Italian marble floor. Ian, for his part, had the good grace to make it to the powder room before curling over the rim of the toilet and splattering vomit into the bowl.

Jonah dropped beside him, reached a hand to touch Ian's upper arm only to have it slapped away. Ian snarled, eyes crazed, and backed up, half folded into the space between the toilet and the wall in an attempt to get as far away from Jonah as possible.

"Fuck off." His voice was so strained that Jonah's immediate reaction was to lean in closer, except that this was the wrong thing to do because Ian flinched further back, hugging his knees to his chest with shaking hands. A feral thing, flickering between fight, flight, and bloody dismemberment.

"Ian."

"Get. Out."

Any fantasy Jonah might have entertained that the starved, magic-stripped wretch would be grateful for the rescue, that the broken edges of the world might just slot themselves back together, evaporated on the spot. Ian was still pissed off at Jonah from the way they'd left things off, or the Dominion had tortured him into insanity, or both, and how would Jonah even tell the difference?

Jonah raised his hands and backed off, closing the door behind him, to find Maya there, looking every bit as tired as he felt, with Cal watching them both from the foyer.

From behind the closed bathroom door, came the sound of water running and something that might have been a fist slamming into porcelain, again and again.

"I'm going back in there," Jonah said. Maya grabbed his arm, half-turned to the foyer, her body a barrier between him on one side, Cal on the other.

To Cal, she said, "Can you leave us for a sec?" There was no venom in her words, just pure desolation. She wrapped her arms around Jonah and buried her face against his collarbone.

His arms were too stiff to hug her back properly. He settled for pushing his chin into her hair.

Jonah mumbled, "He could let me, at least..."

Maya reached for his hand and threaded her fingers through his. The sounds from the other side of the door were muffled, but not nearly muffled enough.

"I think," Maya said, "he doesn't want either of us to see him like that."

"I don't care," Jonah said. "I just want—" Not that he could finish that sentence, not that he needed to, Maya being the only person in the world who loved Ian as much as he did.

She squeezed his hand, the quick one-two rhythm she used on her stress-toys. "There's like, a thousand bathrooms in this place. Go get yourself cleaned up. We both smell like shit."

"He's—"

"I know." She dragged the back of her knuckles across her eyes. "I'm dealing with it. There's still—you have blood on you, Jonah."

He broke away from her grip, stared down at his own hand. There were lines of rust under each fingernail. "Good." But he moved stiff limbs in the direction Cal indicated, towards #24 of the thousand bathrooms, aware of every ache and strain in his body. He wasn't getting any younger, and it had been years since he'd been in a fight.

The shower's water dripped pink into the drain. He realized belatedly that he'd split his knuckles open at some point, and came up just short of deciding that listening to Maya hadn't been the worst idea.

A hundred years later when he finally emerged, he took a certain petty pleasure into tugging on his filthy, bloody clothes and wandering the near-empty halls of Cal Harrison's mansion, leaving wisps of grime in his wake. His entire hometown could have fit within the walls. Atherton's portrait hung in the lobby, a photo of Simon Yamashita in a suit above the grand piano, incongruous amid the modern art. Jonah took in the sweeping staircase, the suit of armour that he knew without asking had been passed through generations of proud, aristocratic Harrison men, and only briefly fantasized about flinging himself, dirty clothes and all, across every white-upholstered surface he could find.

He found Maya, hair wrapped in a towel, on the second floor. "They're inside," she said. He clasped his hands together, one thumb skimming over the broken surface of his knuckles. He'd beaten a man to death, hours ago. He should have felt something, grief, guilt, but he'd always known that if he was going to hell, it was going to be because of Ian and not for any actual sin he'd committed.

If they'd been a little later, if they'd found Ian dead, he'd have slaughtered every single one of them.

"Are you okay?" Maya asked.

"Are you?"

Inside the bedroom, Cal kept watch over Ian, who they'd wrapped in a silk dressing gown that might have made for excellent blackmail material a lifetime ago. Cal must have given him something to sleep. Jonah hated Cal but he might have kissed him if it meant that Ian got a few hours of respite. They'd have to cut his hair off, and that fucking beard, but maybe in the morning. If any of them lived that long.

"Why don't you stay with him for a bit?" Maya spoke to Jonah's hands, not his face. It was a measure of how pathetic he was, how *desperate*, that he nodded eagerly and dragged the armchair from the window to the bedside. If the adults were determined to have whatever discussion they were planning without him, the least he could do was guard Ian while he slept.

Experimentally, Jonah traced a finger over the maimed hand, so gently that he was sure Ian wouldn't have felt it even if he'd been conscious. The injury looked old, the bones shattered and never properly set, and Jonah's eyes darted around the bedroom in search of something that he could smash in retaliation. Patience had never been his strong suit. He might have been Maya's first call when prisons needed to be raided and skulls smashed, but he was no one's first choice for a caregiver.

More than anything, he needed Ian to wake up and be Ian again, derisive and arrogant and scowling and in possession of a cunning plan to drown every one of the Dominion's cut-rate jackbooted thieves and murderers in an ocean of cat piss. Heartless, like all of the fae, and unbroken. Three years ago, before the election, before Blight, before the Dominion, before Ian told him about the end of the world in an inked labyrinth on a crumpled piece of paper, Jonah would have sworn that nothing in this world or the next could have broken him.

Ian, or what was left of him, wheezed softly into the pillow, and didn't do Jonah the favour of stirring.

After the Blight, after Laura, it had been different. He'd needed Ian, and Ian was in prison, and then Ian was just *gone*. With no shortage of betrayals, vicious fights, losses and disappointments between them, and he still couldn't imagine a world in which Ian fucking Mallory wasn't the centre of his universe.

Jonah never prayed. He lived in the church, knelt, mumbled through confession, and filled his mind and heart with silence. Let those who still had something to lose delude themselves that God would keep it safe. He hadn't prayed since the night, three years ago, when Blythe had shown up on his doorstep, waterlogged and sobbing, and he'd understood at long last what God had in store for him.

Even now, he didn't so much pray as bargain. God owed him one. If Ian would just be okay, if Jonah could live long enough to fistfuck their enemies into submission, he would be the divine fucking sword of retribution, driven with righteous fury up the asses of the wicked until they choked on their own shit and blood. If only.

If only. He huffed, fingers reaching for a smoke. He leaned back in Cal's stupid ivory-brocaded armchair, lit up, and waited.

16

Cal kept contraband.

Maya had spent most of the last three years sleeping on old mattresses and dirty coat piles. She had ceased to believe in things like houseplants, and clean sheets, and chocolates. She hadn't seen real chocolate in at least three years, but here it was, dark chocolate, rich and bitter and melting on her tongue. Of course, Cal—whose wealth bought them fake IDs and who was a go-between for the Mac-Paps and the handful of spies they'd embedded in the low-to-middle ranks of the Dominion—had accumulated the odd personal benefit from the arrangement.

It was just that Maya hadn't seen chocolate in at least three years, and hadn't had real coffee in even longer.

She had eaten the first square too quickly for something bought in blood. She lifted the second one reverently from the porcelain tray. Maya held it between two barely-solid fingers and contemplated it with an intense focus born of fatigue as much as hunger, before taking the smallest bite possible and letting the chocolate dissolve on her tongue. Nothing she'd eaten in her entire life had ever tasted so good, and nothing would ever taste so good again.

Cal, ever polite, sat quietly until she'd finished the second square and was reaching, with somewhat less urgency, for a third, before gesturing for her to speak. She should save some to bring back to Shadi. "I'm sorry," she managed. *Maya Maya Maya* burned in flaming letters above Cal's head. "I can't even say I didn't have anywhere else to go. And I might have been followed."

Cal nodded, made a "hmm" noise, and sipped at his coffee. Maya did likewise, the liquid stinging her cracked lips.

"I might have fucked up," she added.

"I am not entirely defenceless," Cal said, and he cast an eye at the suit of armour, no doubt belonging to one of his illustrious ancestors, mounted in the corner. She had a sudden vision of him donning it and riding forth to battle with the Dominion's thugs, and she quickly coughed and covered her mouth. He must have realized, because he said, "I didn't mean—only that they respect the rule of law. To a point."

If Maya had any tears left, if she hadn't sobbed them out years ago in a cold parking lot, if she weren't wrung out like a filthy dishtowel, she might have wept. The rule of fucking law indeed. Cal, with his gentle voice and his sumptuous, treasonous chocolates, sat shielded in a mansion by the rule of law, the burnished grey oak dining room table, the tufted chairs, the slate accent wall with its Riopelle splashed in thick jewel tones, all bought with the wages of the rule of law. Every scar she carried, every corpse she'd stepped over, every *bhoot* that followed her and whispered in her ear with its high, nasally voice, had been slaughtered and dishonoured according to the rule of law.

"They'll respect it for a white man, anyway," Maya said, adding, graciously, "With the occasional notable exception."

"I am glad to see you, Maya," Cal said, his hesitation at her name only fleeting. "I hear things. I was worried."

That much she could believe. She hadn't known him well, before the

Blight, but the familiar was as priceless as what little good remained in the world. "It's good to see you too," Maya tried. Politeness sat uneasily on her tongue.

"You're not here to catch up," he said.

"Can you get someone out of the country?" Maya blurted.

Cal walked over to the sideboard and cabinet, returned holding a tray of glasses and a bottle of Glenlivet. Pouring, he said, "This conversation requires something a little stronger than chocolate, wouldn't you agree?"

She practically snatched the glass from under his hand, though she had the restraint to not drain it in one go. To his credit, he didn't so much as raise an eyebrow. It burned her throat on the way down. She'd kill to be drunk right now, and this was a horribly inefficient way to go about it.

"Someone?" Cal said, after a pause. "I can, and have. It isn't easy, as you know, but officials can be bribed. Ian Mallory, however? If his face hasn't already been indelibly printed in the minds of every one of the Dominion's enforcers, it certainly will be once they've discovered that they've misplaced him."

"They'll probably also notice the dead bodies."

"How *did* you manage to get him out?" Cal asked. "Not that I'm not relieved that you managed it, but—"

"Incorporeality and a high-powered rifle?" The chocolate and Scotch performed a threatening dance in the pit of her belly. She willed them all to stay put, at least until they had a plan. "Sorry, I'm a moron. Who is even taking in refugees these days?"

"Not very many countries. Does Ian have a plan, at least?"

Maya shook her head, bit her lip. It was too easy to let everything spill out of her, vomit, nightmares, the wilderness corrupted into white-eyed monstrosities. The peace that the aurora borealis had offered her, and the war she'd abandoned. Even if Ian was whole, undamaged, brilliant and brutal and the saviour she'd so desperately waited for, the scales couldn't possibly be balanced. "I don't think he's—" She couldn't say *sane*. "I mean, we didn't rescue him because he's useful to the cause."

Cal reached out and patted her hand, and she wouldn't cry, not in front of him, and certainly not with Ian upstairs. "Poor girl." She wished his voice wasn't so horribly kind. "I am well aware of that."

"He'd have seen it." Maya said. "Clearly, not the half-assed visions I get. He'd have known what to do." And worse, the Dominion had a plan. They always did, and they weren't swayed by emotion or nostalgia or compassion. "They must know where we've gone, somehow. I've put you in danger."

"You have," Cal agreed. "But I made my peace some time ago. There are far worse causes for which to die."

"You're not a revolutionary, Cal."

"No more than you. And yet here we are, a ragtag gang of dissidents sheltering an enemy of the state and waiting for the Dominion to kick down the door. You're all welcome to stay here until they do."

The corner of her lip twitched downwards. "I'm not staying," she said. "We can't risk drawing them here."

"At this hour? Get some rest, if you can. All of you."

Maya snorted. "We woke you up in the middle of the night and probably led the Dominion right to your doorstep and now you're letting us couch surf?"

"Sacrifices must be made," Cal said stoically. "And I would never make you sleep on the *couch*."

The guest bedroom—one of the guest bedrooms—had a mattress as tall as her forearm and a plush duvet that swallowed her in warmth. She wasn't even aware of drifting off, and she might have slept for hours if Jonah hadn't screamed.

• • •

Maya jerked awake, nearly falling over as she scrambled to her feet, one leg tangled in bedsheets. She grabbed for her pistol—which was gone—then for the duck that she'd at least thought to put under her pillow. It took long seconds to remember where she was, and to notice that there was a pile of towels and a clean t-shirt on a chair by the door. Her gun was neatly placed on top of it.

She hadn't dreamt the scream. Cal—who they had now woken twice—stood halfway up the staircase, head craned up at them.

It was Maya's place to go first. She pushed the bathroom door open.

It took her a split second to recognize the ink splatters pooling over the tiled floor and the sink as blood, to see the clumps of matted grey hair that floated in them as something that had been shorn, violently, from a human head. The entire bathroom was a B-movie horror as Jonah tried to wrestle a straight-razor out of Ian's hand.

Hyper-conscious of her position as the only person who was not in a complicated psychosexual relationship with anyone else present, Maya tried to make sense of the scene before Cal blundered in and made everything worse. "Jonah. What the fuck?"

Jonah made another swipe for the blade, but Ian was taller, a sharp object barely gripped in his broken hand, and radiating nightmare void energy. "Stay back," he growled, feinted to one side, then slammed into Ian with the full weight of his body, sending them both spilling across the bathtub and the razor skidding across the floor.

The immediate threat to life and limb on pause, Jonah, chest heaving, pinned Ian against the wall of the shower. "Stop it or I'm gonna finish what those Nazi bastards started."

Cal was behind her in the doorway. "The neighbours will hear," he said faintly.

The closest neighbours were a mile down the road. "Fuck the neighbours," Jonah snarled. He waited until Cal swept the razor off the ground to loosen his hold on Ian's wrists. Without the small, furious human vice grip holding him in place, Ian dropped. Jonah folded beside him, muttered, "You don't get off that easy," and pressed his head into Ian's shoulder.

There was so much blood. It slicked the front of Ian's borrowed dressing gown, now slashed beyond repair, dried to flakes of black under his nails, flicked in Jackson Pollock splashes across the side of his jaw.

"Um. Cal." Cal was already sidestepping her, rooting through the medicine cabinet for gauze and alcohol, oblivious to her guilt at dragging him into their ugly little melodrama.

"He did that to himself?"

Jonah's head snapped up. "Did you think I—never mind. He just went batshit. Thought he'd gotten up to take a piss or shave or—"

Ian had at least shaved, and cut off most of his tangled hair in an approximation of his old style. He looked almost human, but when he straightened, blinking as if seeing Maya for the first time, she saw a glimmer of violet and ruby under the bloody shreds of dressing gown.

The air was viscous around him, a sticky tar coating on her lungs. The magic in her recoiled at the empty thing he'd become. Maya's teeth clenched, and she edged towards him anyway. Fading into the Pattern or not, she still possessed a will of her own. "Can I?" she whispered.

Ian's mangled hands floated to his throat, then worked at the buttons. Maya's impulse to help, or to prevent him from revealing whatever it was that he was about to show them, was stopped only by Cal's hand on her arm.

The labyrinth was meticulously sewn into his skin in tight, shimmering stitches. It branched across his torso, blossomed curving tendrils over his sinewy biceps. Maya couldn't tell where it began or ended. Some of the threads had frayed, lashing livewires that sparked where they met air, cut free by the blade where he'd tried to dig them out. Each filament was animate, sentient, a living hive of malevolence woven into his flesh.

Maya choked. Every spike of pain from the spell carved into him jammed tiny needles into her eyes.

"What the shit is that?" Jonah demanded, and Maya glared. He'd *seen* spells before, they all had, no one who'd seen one of Ian's scrawled labyrinths could fail to recognize its cruel counterpart. But Jonah was already reaching for the razor. "Give that back—I'll cut it out of him."

"You'll kill him." Maya's voice came from a distance, a tiny, pitiful thing even in her own ears. The spell's bright hooks were caught in muscle and bone marrow, embedded in tissue. If she squeezed her eyes almost shut, she could see the map of it, twists of vibrating sparks that knotted around organs and ran through his colourless, magic-less body.

Cal, tenuous, asked, "What does it do?"

Maya shook her head. It was a net, or a blade, or a tripwire. It radiated heat, pain. She tested the remote intelligence at the other end of it. She swallowed blood from where she'd bitten her lip.

"It's a tracker—probably among other things. They knew they could find him again. And us." She had to get Ian free of it before it killed him and took the rest of them down with him. "Fuck. I need to think, I need—" Her hands were shaking too hard, she was fading too fast, she'd phase out completely, disappear through the floor...

She met Ian's eyes, searched for some recognition there. Whatever mad fight reflex that had possessed him earlier had fled along with the last of his strength. He slumped between the wall and Jonah, ragdoll-limp. He muttered something that might have been "Go on" or "G'wan wit' ye" but his nod, if nothing else, signalled consent.

She breathed in tightly and pushed her hands through his chest.

Ian made a small, choking sound. Tendrils of magic were coiled around his lungs, his heart, latched into bone and tissue with toothed barbs. She brushed up against the edges of the spell, followed each thread to its terminal, unspooled the coils from their anchors. The spell pushed back, tangled around her fingers, sliced razor wire across her palm, and Maya clenched her teeth and tugged back harder.

The spell thought it could hurt her when her own magic had done far worse. She'd ripped her name out of her own goddamned heart.

Thread by tangled thread, she unwound the labyrinth. At last, it floated, uprooted, a swaying mass of colour, in the air between them. Jonah swore, reached for it and whipped his hand back, stung.

"It's still alive," Maya said. She fumbled for something—a lighter, a knife—to obliterate it, but Cal snatched it from her first. "We have to destroy it."

It must have burned, but Cal remained impassive, a twitch at the corner of his lips the only indication that he held poison in his hands.

Stray threads flopped weakly, seeking purchase, butted up against his wrists like affectionate snakes. Given time, it would hollow him out, like it had Ian, but that was the least of Cal's problems. "You said it's a tracker?"

"Yeah." Her throat was dry. One breath and she'd crumble to ash. She searched for the blood on her lip, desperate for the slightest drop of moisture.

Cal crouched at Ian's side, tilted his jaw upwards. He was unconscious again, but the steady rise and fall of his chest told Maya that at least she hadn't killed him when she pulled the spell out of him. Cal's face remained inscrutable. Not for the first time, Maya wondered just how much Ian had told him. Whether what unfolded now came in any way as a surprise.

"Then," Cal said, "they've already found us. Go. Every second this ... *atrocity* is transmitting from my house is one more second you have to be as far away from it as possible."

Jonah was already tugging her up, alert while Maya's magic-addled brain worked its way around how Cal had said "you" and not "we."

"You're coming with us," Maya mumbled.

"Don't be absurd," Cal said. He'd climbed back up to his feet, the knot of threads clenched in his fist. "They won't drive me from my home."

Jonah rolled his eyes. "Bougie fuck." To Maya, he said, "Help me get him up."

Cal watched, entranced, the spell sliding over his hands, between his fingers, up the cuffs of his sleeves. As long as it remained intact, they would trace it to him, and it would buy the rest of them time. Maya might have argued with him, but he was the least volatile person in the room and she was more likely to convince him once he was well out of Jonah's blast radius.

"Go," Cal said.

"Five minutes," Maya said. "I'll meet you guys in the car."

Jonah, staggering under Ian's weight, didn't hesitate. He kicked the door shut behind them.

The spell wasn't meant to attach to a new host. It writhed and thrashed where Cal held it still, its threads trying in vain to slice skin.

Cal had to stoop to make eye contact with her. The creases around his eyes had deepened over the years, his hairline retreating across his scalp, but his smile was no less warm than it had been back in the days when he'd swooped in to rescue her from an awkward conversation or a Broom Closet shouting match.

"I can unmake it," she said. "At least, I think—" Her tongue was thick and heavy. "You don't have to."

"Dear girl," he said, far too gently, "I always had to."

"Cal—"

He disappeared into another one of the many rooms, returning with a thick file folder. "This is for Gaby," he said. "She'll know what to do with it."

Maya shifted from one foot to another. The walls, which had been so spacious, pressed inward. She couldn't breathe.

"I abandoned the work," she confessed. "I ran. I left Shadi and Martine." Pathetically, she stared up into the dead man's face. "It's not going to have been worth it."

"You ever hear that old story?" he said. "The old man, walking on a beach, throwing starfish back into the ocean after they washed up on the shore."

She finished the punchline before he could. "Am I the old man?" she asked him. "Or the starfish?"

"Maya," Cal said. "For fuck's sake. Run."

17

Cal added another log to the fire. He pushed at it, idly, with a poker, while the knocking continued. They had waited for three years to murder him; they could wait another five minutes while he finished composing one last text. He removed the phone's battery and tossed it into the flames, then the shell of the device along with it. He held his breath, the fire teasing the surface of the plastic, and for long seconds it refused to catch until at last it warped and buckled and funnelled inward.

He burned the spell last. It cried out, clinging to his fingers as he hurled it into the sparks. It screamed the entire time, spasming as its threads lit, incandescent, before crumbling to ash. The smell of it was foul, worse than the melting plastic of the phone, the toxic spew of the battery. Not that any of that mattered now.

He had never been a vindictive man. Still. He hoped it stung the caster on the other end.

The man at the door was RCMP, not a Cleaner. Another small courtesy, along with knocking rather than kicking down the door. He was young, lantern-jawed, could have starred in a *Due South* reboot if they still bothered to make TV shows these days.

Cal had finally committed a sin too grave for the Dominion to ignore, but there were still appearances to maintain. A bloody political assassination on the front steps would have ruffled the feathers of the Residents Association, and those people were all big donors.

"Senator Harrison?"

The title still technically belonged to him, though the Red Chamber lay in ruins inside the concrete sarcophagus that contained whatever inter-dimensional horrors the Blight had released on Parliament Hill. He smiled, and the officer, for his part, managed to keep a poker face at the sight of Cal, in his bathrobe, his sabre from his days on the UCC fencing team in one hand.

"So sorry to have disturbed you at this hour," the man said. Polite to the point of solicitousness, even now.

"Not a problem," Cal said. The blade did not so much as waver. "What can I do for you?"

The officer at least had the good manners to look uncomfortable. "We have reason to believe that you're sheltering a fugitive."

Cal looked past him, down his long driveway. The other cars would be arriving soon enough. They would have to send the Cleaners, those bright young thugs plucked out of a torchlit rally, devoid of any lip service to serving and protecting. "Do you?" he said. He stepped aside, levelling the point of the sabre at the officer, a quick jab away from his throat. He gestured, expansively, inside. "Feel free to present some form of documentation and you may search to your heart's content."

The officer muttered into his earpiece. Said, again, "I'm sorry."

"For all I know," Cal added. "You might have stolen that uniform. There's procedure, you understand."

The pretence of civility lifted, the officer reached for his sidearm. "Drop the sword," he said.

Cal listened. He couldn't hear the vehicles rolling up the driveway, not yet. His heart, sentimental organ that it was, beat a flutter of hope.

He took a long look at his foyer, the ancient suit of armour that stood watch over him.

"It's the great tragedy of our age," Cal said, "that it is no longer possible to live as a gentleman. And only some consolation that it's still possible to die as one."

The officer looked down at the blunted tip of Cal's sword. He made a noise that might have been a laugh. "You're kidding, right?"

"Alas, yes." Cal said, and squeezed the trigger of the tiny, 3D-printed gun in the pocket of his bathrobe.

Red blossomed at the bottom of the man's throat. The officer got off a single shot, but it went into the floor. Mother would be horrified, but she was in for a terrible discovery as it was.

The man staggered, swaying on his feet before stumbling and collapsing. Cal stood over him, watched him flop and wheeze on the threshold before hauling him inside and locking the door. The corpse wouldn't be much of a barrier, but every second counted.

He probably didn't have enough time for a shower, under the circumstances, but the cars were still distant, few and far between. There were stains on his bathrobe—Ian's black blood, at the cuffs, and the officer's arterial spray. He selected a dress shirt, eschewed a suit jacket for a cashmere sweater, forgoing a tie.

He spent longer than he should have settling on a pair of cufflinks. Unable to decide between the antique topaz-eyed ouroboros that had belonged to some distant ancestor, and the intricate gold maces that his father had given him on his appointment to the Senate, Cal frowned. Years of an on-and-off-again dalliance with a clairvoyant ought to have prepared him better for the inevitable, but knowing the future was not the same as altering it. That was the root of all tragedy, after all.

He decided, in the end, on the ridiculous little wizard hats Ian had given him as a joke. Let Atherton and Reid Curtis and the whole gaggle of sociopaths read into that whatever they chose. He loaded a last bullet into the chamber.

Cal poured himself a glass of 50-year-old Glenfiddich. The cars were definitely closer. He let himself out into the back. Snow hid the worst of the landscaping sins, shrouding the pool cover and the paving stones in a sparkling layer of white. Frost clung to the bare maples and the petrified bones of the rose bushes.

The gazebo's roof had kept the benches inside relatively dry, and Cal sat beneath it, watching the first spears of gold pierce through the heavy grey clouds.

By the time the Dominion's Cleaners smashed through the back door, boots falling heavily over the slippery paving stones, the tumbler in his hand was empty. The single shot sent a shower of snow from the branches and echoed over the courtyard before everything fell silent.

18

"I had this recurring dream," Maya was saying. "When first I moved to Ottawa. About my Ammappa. He died when I was eight? Nine?"

In the back seat, Ian pressed his face to the glass and breathed in sharp, ragged gasps. He watched the ravaged city and Jonah watched him. Maya wove an idiosyncratic route through uprooted streets. All three of them were lost in a private, unknowable grief, and Maya's monologue filled the empty space where connection or solidarity or simple human comfort should have grown.

"He was always so kind to me. He had a big grey moustache, I remember that, and the softest eyes. In my dream, we left him behind, we didn't mean to, but we thought he was dead. We'd had a funeral, we'd cried, and then we flew back to Canada, but he was still there, in the old apartment, waiting for us to come back. He didn't understand why we'd left him alone like that. He was starving to death, wondering where we'd gone. You could see his ribs though his shirt, the skin stripped away. Sometimes I'd make it back, but it was always too late to save him."

Jonah, world-renowned for his sensitivity and tact, said, "Cal could have come with us. You can't stop some moron dead set on becoming a martyr."

A knot at the base of Ian's throat constricted his breath. Cock-wobbling Christ, he was a physical and emotional wreck, Cal's clothes hanging off him like he was a kid dressing up in his dad's suit, Jonah watching him like he was the last plane out of Afghanistan. And Maya's hand kept moving to the file folder tucked into the sun visor as she drove. As ill-suited as she was to their brave not-so-new-anymore world, she at least had the fortitude not to burst into tears at the loss of a man whose death was Ian's to mourn, if it was anyone's at all.

Mourning would have felt better than the tight knot at the base of his throat. They could send him the whole butcher's bill, everyone he'd ever worked with or threatened or fucked or fucked over, all of them drowned and worked to death and lined up against a wall and shot, and it would only scratch the surface. He still couldn't cry for them.

He'd been sure there was no part of him left that could be damaged, that he'd been consumed with pain and terror for so long that he was somehow inured to it. The constant throb of his badly set bones became so much white noise, the tremor, the ache in his ravaged lungs less surprising with every inhale. The scooped-out shell of the city was Maya's home, not his, but his memories of it overlaid the skeletal husks of high-rises, an afterimage like the one that hovered above her, a faint echo of the girl she'd been when she'd had another name. There were more buildings bombed than intact, their windows gouged out, empty lots like broken teeth between them, entire city blocks buried under shriekrass and shattered by earthquakes. The snow had transmuted into freezing rain, which pissed down in torrents, slicked the roads black, and turned potholes to gaping mouths.

"He didn't have to die," Maya insisted. She wiped a sleeve across her eyes and straightened in her seat, hands clenched white-knuckled on the wheel. If she was waiting for consolation, for someone to tell her that it wasn't her fault, that Cal had made his own choices, it didn't come. The first victim of the Dominion's reign had been pity.

"So what's the plan?" Jonah asked. "We prostrate ourselves before your Glorious Leader, and hope that high powered weaponry and an ex-MAI is enough to make her forget you ran away?"

Ian heard himself speak, his voice flat, corroded. "How long has it been?"

"Thank fuck," Jonah said. "I thought..."

"You thought what, Joe?"

"I thought they'd tortured you into even further senility," Jonah said. "But I see I was wrong."

Ian barked a short, joyless laugh. "How long."

"Three years," Maya said. "We didn't stop looking, I didn't stop looking, I never stopped."

"Meanwhile," Ian waved a broken hand towards the snow-draped ruins. "The chuds managed to do all this."

"A lot was the Blight," Maya cut in. "They just didn't help."

"You're back now," Jonah said. "We'll hang them all from telephone poles. Upside down. By their entrails."

"Promises, promises," Ian said. "Joe?"

"Yeah?" Jonah sounded hopeful. Fuck hope.

"You looks like a Mormon with that haircut. Like you're gonna knock on my door and tell me the good news. It's a fuckin' disgrace." Maya smirked. His eyes bored into the rearview mirror, and she ducked his gaze. "And Gaby Abel? Really? Is this a rebellion or a Grade 8 assembly?"

"She's changed," Maya said.

"Lord blue galling fuckin' Jesus. Don't suppose you can turn around and put me back in that cell."

Jonah smiled thinly, and Maya said, "Don't even," and kept driving into the thick curtain of rain.

• • •

Fort Utopia, when they pulled into its parking lot, was as abandoned as the rest of the city. Jonah looked immediately tense, on the lookout for bullet holes and broken glass, for blood. But Maya's attention was fixed on a spot in a filth-smudged snowbank, her eyes paled with magic, and she nodded, as if in a silent conversation with it. She was a magic junkie now, like he'd been, and the absence curdled, threatening to rise in his throat.

The rebellion, she explained, had moved on to a near-identical strip mall a fifteen minute drive past near-identical tract housing. From the highway, it showed no signs of life, and the blue-tinted glass on the office building beside it was bashed in, racist graffiti left to drip over Sichuan restaurants and the herbal medicine shop. The caravan of cars in the delivery bays and the flicker of light in the windows of the pharmacy and one of the restaurants were the only indication that the Mac-Paps had set up residence there.

For long minutes, Maya froze behind the wheel of the car, catatonic.

Jonah said, "We going in, or—"

"Yeah," Maya said. "Yeah." She didn't meet either of their eyes.

A row of solar stills, propped up on cinderblocks, dripped into large gallon jugs beside the delivery doors. Wards blanketed the stills, the doors, spiderwebbed from the dumpsters and pylons and overhangs.

Maya evaporated the moment she'd gotten out of the car, leaving Jonah the only person brave or foolish enough to make awkward non-conversation with Ian in what had been a carpet store. There was nowhere else in the new Fort Utopia's strip mall where a person could be alone. A cluster of rebels slept downstairs, the main advantage of which, as far as Ian could tell, was that if the Dominion did bomb them, they wouldn't see their deaths coming. He saw the appeal in that.

Jonah had washed the blood from his skin and hair, but it had dried on his parka and boots. He worried at it, pointlessly, rubbing at the ends of a sleeve with drops of filtered rainwater retrieved from the still outside, but that only succeeded in smearing it around. He staked out the gaps between the carpets that blocked out the windows and provided, if not protection from a stray bullet or drone strike, at least the pretence of privacy. Finally, he tried to sit still, turning the fucking crucifix necklace over in his fingers and muttering bullshit to himself.

Ian eyed the pile of carpets that someone, at some point, must have been using as a bed. He could sleep, but he'd just wake up back in his cell, heart hammering, lungs too constricted to issue a scream. He forced his eyes open. He'd been asleep for three years, anyway. And in the meantime, the list of atrocities, the list of murdered, wasn't getting any shorter.

And Jonah had had hours, practically half a day, to grow out his ugly haircut, so Ian could only assume he was walking around looking like a townie choirboy out of spite.

"Is it a switch?" he asked.

"Huh?" Even if Ian couldn't hear how weak he sounded, the look of pity—pity, *fuck*—on Jonah's face would have told him everything he needed to know.

"The church bullshit. One minute you're a serious activist, the next you're hiding in some pew prostratin' yourself before the Sacred Heart of the bald-headed dancin' Jesus and forgiving centuries of colonialism? So. Is it a switch you flip?"

"We're not gonna talk about this right now."

"Oh," Ian said, "we are fuckin' talkin' about it right now, b'y."

"I'm not in church now, am I?" That was mild. The Jonah he'd known, the unrepentant sinner, would have bitten back. This one was focused on a stain on the concrete by his feet. Ian liked that development even less than he'd liked finding out Jonah had returned to the bosom of the Holy Mother Church. "Why do you care?"

"I needs to know how much of a problem this is gonna be. Are you gone all Hail Mary sanctifying Mother Macree or wha? Do you even believe in God?"

The muscles in Jonah's jaw, the corded tendons in a hand braced against the rack of carpets, visibly tensed. He might have literally carried Ian out of the jaws of hell but that didn't mean he wouldn't throw a punch at a crippled man if Ian pissed him off enough.

"What?"

"It's a simple fuckin' question."

"I don't see what—"

"Do you believe in the lord blue cross-eyed Jesus and his curly-headed father and all that benevolent bulls—"

"—which is none of your business anyway—"

"—after everything that's happened, after the Great Fuckening and the Dominion and all of it."

"I'm going for a smoke." Jonah moved, first for the front door, barricaded with another rack and the broken remains of an office desk, then stalked past Ian for the back exit.

"After Laura? Joe!"

"Go fuck yourself, Ian."

Ian moved too slowly to stop him, and it was only by chance that he caught a glimpse of Jonah's face, unguarded and furious. He gave it another minute, forcing deep breaths through an upper respiratory system in open revolt, and then went to find him.

Jonah had only made it as far as the overhang. The rain came in sheets, a veil between their little square of reality and the thing that lay beyond. He moved away as Ian approached, but a step farther would have doused his cigarette.

"When were you gonna tell me?" Ian asked.

"Shouldn't I be asking you that?"

Ian couldn't stop himself. The impulse to reach for a piece of paper and a pen was still there, even though his hand couldn't wrap around it, even though the labyrinth would never spark again. The branching pathways of the future lay in front of him, blackened and hollowed and foreshortened. He felt their presence even now, a vestigial organ that served no purpose and did him no good.

"I tolds ya, b'y," he said. "I never looked into your future."

"Bullshit."

"How'd it happen?"

Jonah looked up, and Ian would have personally gutted every single Dominion soldier and Cleaner if it would have taken the despair from his eyes.

"What were the options?"

"The camps," Ian said. "Typhoid. Earthquake. Caught a stray bullet during the unencumberances. I don't fuckin' know."

"You don't. You don't—Ian, you *see everything*. Every possible future and. What? She didn't have a single one?"

"You're the smartest guy I've ever met, and you're walkin' around with a ward tattoo, and you still haven't figured it out. Maya gets it—she can't even be in the same room as me, shoulda promoted her and never bothered dragging you out of the woods..."

"You could have told me."

"And then what? You drive yourself mad trying to stop it, you and Blythe and whatever time Laura had left, when there was never any way, when the entire future is just a black pit of void and carnage—"

"Fuck you," Jonah said, but there was less fire in it this time.

"So which one was it?"

"The SVAR hit the ship she was on, just off the coast. I sent them away." Jonah stabbed the butt of his cigarette into the brick wall and tossed it into the brown water pooling in a dip of pavement. "Blythe got away, though we don't—it would have fucked their chances, if I'd been with them." It wouldn't have. Jonah died with Laura, in all of those realities. It was a cruelty to tell him.

"Jesus. Fuck."

Jonah visibly recoiled from the same sympathy with which he'd earlier assaulted Ian. "You don't get to say you're sorry. You don't have that *right*." He lit a new cigarette, the flame catching the shine in his eyes. Ian moved, quickly, to block that particular maudlin view from anyone who might pass by the delivery bay.

"Joe," Ian said. "You only needed to watch her die once."

He'd known Jonah for twenty years, and had never seen him cry. Only the hitch of his breathing and the almost undetectable shudder of his shoulders gave away that anything was wrong.

It would have been better if Jonah had just thrown a punch.

"Did it hurt?" Jonah asked, still looking down.

"The hands?"

Jonah wiped tears and snot away with his sleeve. Laura's tiny baby handprint, inked on his wrist, had faded after fourteen years. His eyes were reddened but at least no longer leaking. "Drowning," he said.

Ian, never known for his compassion, said, "No."

"Liar."

"Not nearly as much as what I'll do to them when I get a chance." The words fell flat, dripped into the space between them. He wouldn't bridge it. His own wounds were far too raw, and he didn't trust himself to pull away afterwards.

As if a has-been sorcerer, the well of his powers long dried up, had any chance of toppling the Dominion, avenging little Laura Augustine, and restoring peace, order, and good government.

Jonah finished his smoke, long inhales broken by only the occasional hiccup. "In answer to your earlier question," he said. "Yeah. I do. And it makes it that much worse."

19

Two rebels in a safe house, Maya had learned, was a movement. Three was a mutiny.

"You do that," Captain Felipe Pereira was saying, "and I pull my people out of Gatineau." Maya had missed what *that* was, but the Mackenzie-Papineaus' Coordinating Committee visited the Scarborough cell more or less weekly, and at least half of those times, Felipe threatened to take his tin soldiers and leave the sandbox.

Gaby Abel stood, arms crossed, in the middle of the cell phone outlet store that functioned as an impromptu town hall, flanked by both of her daughters.

The substance of her had fallen away like decay in a time lapse film, winnowing flesh to bone, stripping more of her away each time Maya saw her. The outlines of her skull were visible at her temples, below a head wrap only slightly less faded than her khaki fatigues. Her combat pants were belted twice around, billowing out where they were tucked into high rubber boots. Ian would have thrown something at the screen if she'd made that face on camera.

"And what about the workers at the Midland plant?" Anton Yannick asked. He was a good foot shorter than Felipe, a barrel-chested ex-steelworker who filled out Gaby's small collection of anyone who had any experience building a mass movement at all. "Or are they not as glamorous as taking potshots at Cleaners? And *you*." Maya hadn't bothered to throw a glamour over herself, and Anton's sudden scrutiny smashed down on her like a hammer. "Just where the fuck have you been?"

Maya, or the girl she'd been before, had always been *good*.

She had done well in school. She'd sat through Tamil classes in what was her math classroom the rest of the day, faithfully copying the abugida characters into her notebook, and never complained that she was probably never going to use the language. She hadn't snuck out of the house like Anoj did. She barely dated, fundraised for the Environmental Alliance to make her volunteer hours. She'd blocked the Gardiner Expressway as a tiny child, but that had been a family affair, a *community* affair, and even with the headlines and the handful of arrests, her elementary school teacher had smiled kindly at her and commended her on peacefully standing up for her beliefs.

Until she'd blown up her alarm clock and her cellphone typing out emoji spells in her bedroom, the girl Maya had been had never managed to accomplish anything actually *forbidden*. She was accustomed to disappointing her elders, but never enraging them.

Shadi, always the peacekeeper, swiftly intervened, wrapping Maya in his long arms, his mutterings of relief outrunning Gaby's whipcord, "Jesus Christ, Maya," by a split second.

"I had to," Maya said, muffled by Shadi's forearm.

The Abel women plus Anton presented, for the first time since Maya had met any of them, a united front. There was nothing like enacting revolutionary discipline on a rogue wizard to bring a family together. Monique was stoic but for the tremor in one hand, while Martine vibrated with fury.

"You *left*," the girl spat.

"It was the right call." The void lingered as an afterimage, even away from Ian's presence, a reminder that her treason had all been for nothing. Well, a man's life, and one she had loved in the brittle, codependent way that MAI got to love each other, but what was that compared to the rebellion, the slow but inevitable rumbling of the Train? She leaned into Shadi's chest long enough for a heartbeat of reassurance before breaking away. "Gaby, we can't just keep running and hiding, we need a strategy, we need—"

"Which is why we need to be moving aggressively now," Felipe broke in.

"We need to be organized," Anton said.

"Organize who?" Felipe fired back. "The people who run the camps, or the people who build them?"

The thing about Gaby, now, was that she didn't raise her voice. A resistance movement wasn't the House of Commons. Desperate people didn't need someone who was good at winning arguments, they needed someone to project the appearance of being a calm, competent grownup. And while she had never been able to deliver a soundbite on *The National* without stumbling into a fuckup, Gaby could now at least manage to sound like she was in charge.

Most of the time, Maya even appreciated that about her.

"We need to be on the same page." Gaby's voice had an edge that would have cost votes, back when it had mattered. Sharply, towards Shadi, she said, "Did you know?"

"You need to not be a fucking *deserter*." Martine rescued Shadi from answering. "I was calling you."

Maya clutched the file folder to her chest. Her fingers slid and dampened it despite the cold. Shakily, she held it out for Gaby to take. "Cal wanted you to have this." With everything that had happened in the past 24 hours, she'd barely glanced at it. Tiny rows of numbers that had blurred under her exhausted vision.

Shadi said, "Maya, they're saying on Dominion channels that Harrison is dead. Is that true?" His hand on her back was supportive even as he joined Gaby in flaying her alive.

The walls were closing in on her. Stripped bare of their offerings, the faded signage and posters were the only remnants of the store's original purpose, their empty hooks beckoning fingers. She reached for the duck in her coat pocket, fingers closing around its grimy surface.

"I think so," Maya managed. "He could have left. He could have run. I don't know why he didn't."

"And all for what?"

"For me, seems like," Ian said.

He had moved into the doorway so quietly that Gaby visibly started. A sense of *wrongness* slouched behind him, spilled beneath his feet as he walked, a resinous shadow in his wake.

Standing in the sickly remains of daylight in a badly-fitted suit, he was more apparition than human. The flickering overhead fluorescents lit the ridges that age and starvation had gouged in his face, cast black shadows beneath his sharp cheekbones. His broken hands shook with the palsy of an old man.

"The rest of you, out, please now." Gaby's order was echoed by Monique, who shooed the still bickering Committee out the door. "Not you, Maya."

Maya cast a pleading glance at Shadi, who stayed, elbow against the doorframe lest the others try to get back in.

"I thought you were dead," Gaby told Ian, as if Martine hadn't spilled the reason for Maya's disappearance the second she'd left, as if that wasn't why Gaby had rushed back to Scarborough.

"Yeah, well, I'm fuckin' Gandalf the White." He shambled to the closest empty rack, leaned his elbow on it in what might have been a sprawl or might have been all that was keeping him from collapse.

Just ghosts, all of them, in the ruins of a suburban cellphone outlet, the wind screaming through the gaps where the seal around the doors and windows had worn away.

Ian let the standoff continue seconds longer than it needed to, and then, head bowed, said, "You look good, Gaby. The army gear—it suits ya."

"Enough," Gaby said. "Is this a coup?"

He laughed. It turned into a choking, tubercular cough halfway through.

"You'll wanna watch that one." He waved one white hand at Maya, fingers bent at cruel, unnatural angles. It was a mockery of a familiar gesture, but nothing changed, no light sparked between his maimed fingers. "I'm here for asylum."

Gaby sniffed. "Not if I know you."

"Nice revolution you've made here."

"We're doing fine."

"You're not doin' fine. The country's in the hands of the same deviant bastards who give hockey stick enemas at St. Mike's, who're treatin' the Geneva Conventions like a checklist, and you're so skinny I can sees the sin on your soul. That's the definition of not at all fuckin' fine."

"Ian, that's disgust—"

"Enough!" He lunged forward, void energy bristling from his grey skin, then caught himself, slouched back into the rack. He clasped one trembling hand over the other, but neither stilled. "*Fuck.*" He collapsed inwards like a controlled demolition and Maya flushed with shame, moved between him and Gaby as if, as in the old days, she could hide the horror of what he was.

"Ian," she said, softly, which wouldn't help.

His attention snapped to Shadi. "And who the fuck are you supposed to be?"

"This is Shadi Al-Abdallah," Maya said. "My husband."

"Your—we're havin' words about this later."

Gaby managed, "You don't just get to sweep in here and take charge. This isn't the Broom Closet, or the House. I've built something. *We've* built something. We've kept everyone alive, kept the Cleaners away."

Ian was silent for a long, tense spell. "But you're not winning."

"Remind me again where listening to you led us?"

"You'd do better," he replied. It was almost conciliatory, almost kind. "With me whispering in your ear."

"Jesus. Are you propositioning me, Ian?"

"You'd fuckin' wish, b'y."

Gaby whistled through her teeth.

"Gaby," Maya tried, in the event that Gaby remembered that she had infinitely more reasons to be pissed off at Ian than she had to be pissed off at her.

"I'm not your sock-puppet," Gaby said. "I can't function with your fist up my ass."

"Attractive as that prospect might be—" Ian waved one mangled hand in her direction. "—I don't thinks it'll work." He managed a paler copy of the charming, gap-toothed smile that must have saved him from getting punched on more than one occasion.

It didn't fool Maya. She recognized pure, animal terror concealed beneath bluster when she saw it. She saw it in Gaby, surrounded by her army of neighbourhood warlords, and she saw it every time she looked in the mirror.

And she saw it, undeniably, in Ian.

What the fuck had they *done* to him?

"Maybe I will join your little revolution, Gaby," Ian said. "It's time to blow up the Train, hang Atherton upside down from the Peace Tower, restore democracy and the rule of law, and once that's done, we can talks about puttin' someone in charge who's less of a stunned arse. Deal?"

"Outside of the Dominion," Gaby said, "you're the most evil person I know. I suppose if anyone has a shot at taking them down, it's the devil himself."

"I knew I liked ya."

"I've kept these people safe for three years." She glanced sharply at Maya. It would have been a convenient time for the Pattern to swallow her, dissolve her back into it, but magic had never come to her aid when the alternative was fucking her around. "When the entire country was out to murder us. When no one was there to save us but us."

"And the nation is appropriately grateful." He closed the space between them, just short of putting a condescending hand on her shoulder. Instead, he snatched the folder from Gaby's hand. "Now, are we gonna take a look at what Cal really died for?"

. . .

This strip mall was ill-equipped for a war council.

Gaby hadn't arrived alone. Martine referred to Felipe and Anton flippantly as the grownups in the room. Felipe was a career army officer who'd taken half his regiment with him when he'd been ordered to fire on a group of resistors in Montreal. Anton had reportedly been the one to name the Mac-Paps in the first place, after the Canadian volunteer soldiers who had fought in the Spanish Civil War, but he was still stuck in the old world, before passes and DEC and the outlawing of labour unions. A few of the local gang leaders were present, as was Devi, who'd been part of the Sheppard East Village Business Improvement Area before the unencumbrances, and was decidedly uncomfortable being around the criminal element even now. Besides the patchwork attempt at uniforms, they were barely distinguishable from the rest of Monique's cell, which was less an organized armed resistance than a shivering jumble of shit-scared refugees.

An afterimage of what the restaurant had once been still lingered. The tables in the restaurant, pushed together into a blobby circle, were tea-stained and crusted with the residue of spilled sauces. A cracked aquarium sat against the far wall, the water bled out from it, nothing remaining of its lobsters but dry bits of shell. A grubby scatter of plastic toys peeked out from behind the counter. A framed Canadian two-dollar bill, too worthless to steal, on the back wall. Red knot ornaments for the Lunar New Year dangled above the cash register. Someone had taken care with this place, carved out a home from the beige mall architecture. There were still little pots of Lao Gan Ma sauce on some of the tables, and these had miraculously survived the end of the world. Maya pushed back the urge to dip the tiny spoon into one and take a taste.

Maya was allowed a seat at the table. She was a deserter, but that didn't diminish her usefulness to the cause. She bridged the space between Ian, sprawled across a backwards chair, Jonah, who hovered tense at his side, and Gaby and her daughters and her ragtag army. At least she was short—if bullets started flying, it would be easier to duck.

Gaby worried at the surface of the table, probing it for stickiness before coming to a decision and placing the folder down where everyone could, theoretically, read it.

"The first page is an expense report," she declared. "Payments, certainly, through Alycia Curtis' foundation. But Cal had been sending these documents to us for years, and they prove nothing beyond that the Dominion hasn't let the apocalypse get to the funders."

"This is pointless," Anton said. "Forensic accounting isn't going to save us. Remember what happened to Tobias Fletcher when he leaked Alycia Curtis' MAI status? No one gives a shit."

"There are 15 pages." Gaby traced one slender finger down a column of tiny type. "It can't all be useless. Expenses, but not just expenses." She cocked her head at Devi, who shifted closer to read it.

"I can't make sense of it. This isn't normal procurement."

Felipe swiped it from under her. "This is redacted as shit. Equipment maybe, weapons? He didn't do a good job decrypting this." In the old days, Ian might have reduced Felipe to a wibbling puddle on the floor. Instead, he just scratched at the edge of the table until a nail caught on it, drawing blood.

"Shag it." Ian made what should have been a snapping gesture, if his fingers hadn't been knocked out of alignment. "I knows what it fuckin' is. Shoot it here."

He made only the barest pretence of reading the pages in front of him. "C. is a biologist named Colette. She's reporting to the Curtises and the big guy, that's Quinn Atherton, on three projects. The equipment she's askin' after is people. Human subjects. The red numbers are MAI, of which she'd had one when she sent this. The blue numbers are volunteers. The grey number is a second MAI, deceased. None of the three projects showed results she's ready for Atherton to hear about."

"Ian—" Gaby started, and Jonah shook his head. Maya shifted, the plastic seat squeaking too loudly under her.

"What are the projects?" Felipe didn't know any of them well, wasn't a science guy, wasn't anything more than a military man who wasn't enough of a piece of shit to fire on civilians.

"She's trying to transfer magic," Ian said. "To the deserving, from the miserable skeets cursed with it by chance."

From underneath the table, Shadi's knee pressed into Maya's, bobbing against the side of her jeans. What was she supposed to say to him, anyway? *Don't worry, I'm basically a massive axe trapped in a box that says "break glass in case of glorious people's uprising?" I'm just as likely to catch a stray bullet than fall into the grip of an evil scientist, and besides, I'm turning invisible. They'll never find me.*

"And the other ones?"

"No fuckin' clue, b'y. But you won't like it."

"We need someone with expertise," Gaby said. "Someone who might recognize the data, pick up on the bigger picture from context."

"Yeah." Jonah, at last, spoke, tugging fingers through his too-short hair. "I might know someone who could do that. But you won't like what she has to say either."

. . .

Not a single cell in Maya's body wanted to be in Ian's presence. Higher brain functions attempted to convince the rest of her that it would be better to talk to him than to be scolded by Gaby or worried at by Shadi, but even with several metres and a glass window separating her from where he sat, hunched, amid flapping rows of torn dry cleaning plastic, every hair on her arm was electrified, and her stomach, though empty, threatened revolt.

She sucked in a deep breath and pushed the door open anyway.

"It's not gonna catch," he said. "It took months, equipment that cost more than I ever made in a year, and a spell that you don't gots the fuckery in ya to cast. It took—" He stopped himself, his face a pallid, death's head grimace.

"I know," Maya said. "That isn't—"

He motioned for her to come closer. Shuddering, bile rising in her throat, Maya tried. The counter was between them—not a real barrier, but it was enough of a separation to keep her feeling safe, or safe enough. She ran her hand over the dusty surface, envious of its solidity.

"You got married," Ian said.

"There's a war on."

"That doesn't excuse it."

Her snort lifted dust off the counter. "You really want to talk about *that*?" Maya clenched and unclenched the fist jammed in her pocket, brushed up against the duck there and stopped herself before she could catch a rhythm. Magic had gotten all of them into this. She pushed through a swinging door in the counter and fumbled through the forest of empty plastic bags to find a second stool. "There was the Blight, and my parents, Anoj. Jamila. Everyone. You." She lifted her head, watched him through her eyelashes. He wasn't looking at her, which helped. "Shadi was the first person to make me laugh, after that."

"Ah yeah," Ian said. "A great fuckin' reason to shackle yourself to the patriarchy. Was it romantic, ducky? Did one of them b'ys in there walk you down the aisle at the Food Basics?"

"We don't—that's not even a thing for us. You know that, right? Even if we had a priest. And Shadi isn't even Hindu, so that wouldn't have—we just said it. Who the fuck is checking anyway?" She kicked at the legs of the stool.

"He's Muslim? What would your folks say?"

"He was studying to be an engineer. And a guy. Anyway. They're dead. So they don't get a say."

"You can't go spillin' your life story like that or you might as well not have buried your name. Was it a nice wedding, at least?"

There was a brief tug at her chest, where her name had once lived, as if someone had sewn through her skin and tugged, ever so slightly, at the other end of the thread. "We did it at the auto shop. Not the one here—like, three Fort Utopias ago. It's a pile of rubble now."

"Jesus lord lamp-lightin' fuck, Maya."

"I don't need you to approve. It's none of your business."

She didn't see him move. There was a flash of grey, and then he was in front of her, one bent hand on the side of her arm, the other lifting her chin to look in his face. His fingers were as cold as the superwinter, a chill that penetrated skin and fat and muscle, that sunk into her bones and stayed there.

For a split second, she remembered to be a little afraid of him.

"Oh Maya," he said. "Rubble. You should have had flowers."

He stepped back, useless hands floating at his sides. A taut cable, just short of snapping. He'd been the only person to understand her, once.

"I'm not going to ask," she said. "The experiments. When you're ready, if you're ever ready..."

His lips parted, revealing grey gums, missing teeth, a grotesquery of a smile. "Burn faster," he said. "It's not enough, never gonna be enough to save any of youse. The shit we do, the thing we are, it's got an expiry date."

"That doesn't matter. I just have to last long enough to take them down." The expression on his face couldn't be pity, if only because he was constitutionally incapable of feeling pity, let alone expressing it. "It's not a habit you can kick. How do you stop doing the thing that you *are*?"

The air around him was dead, motionless. Nothing moved, nothing lived, where he stood, eroded to bone and despair. The world was alive, awake, and shuddered in his presence.

"You ever find out, love," Ian said, "you let me know."

20

Simon Yamashita was dead, and, most disappointedly from Jonah's perspective, no one on their side was responsible.

"Are we sure?" Gaby asked.

"My sources," Felipe started, to which Anton snapped back, "Oh, well, your *sources*," and Maya let out a long huff and Monique picked at her nails, which were already bleeding.

"We're sure," Felipe said, and flashed his phone around the cluster of tables. Lucy, catching the headline, immediately started crying, and no one went to comfort her.

"Ya got less sense than your husband," Ian told her. "He'd be rollin' in his grave if he saw ya cryin' over a dead charmer."

"Do we believe natural causes?" Gaby neatly sidestepped him, patting Lucy's arm.

Ian said, "He betrays the Dominion, convinces Lucy to defect, and you're all wonderin' if he mighta been murdered?"

"You need to put out a statement, Gaby," Anton said. "Soon. We can workshop it.”

“Workshop it.” Martine was in the corner, braiding cornrows that sparked with magic into her little brother’s hair. A protection spell. Smart kid. Jonah tugged at his own hair, which wasn’t nearly long enough.

“We needs to hit ’em back,” Ian said. “Now.” His voice came through wheezes, a thin needle scratching words into rust.

It hurt to listen to him. Jonah noted who stopped talking anyway, and who glossed over his words as if he hadn’t been the one to make half of them important in the first place. Of course it was a wild suggestion, acting like they had an army at all and that he was in charge of it. Maya was tense, alert, but it was Gaby who spoke.

“Why is it so important?” Gaby asked.

“Traitor or not, he’s a fuckin’ wizard, and he was Alycia’s boy. If he’s dead—publicly dead, not disappeared into Colette’s black site to be vivisected—something’s gone wrong.”

“We don’t know that he’s not disappeared,” Maya pointed out. “They could lie.”

“Well,” Jonah said. “There’s a funeral next week. We could flip over the coffin and find out.”

“She doesn’t need Simon to do magic. She’s a way more powerful magician than he was.”

The conversation stopped. Lucy Fletcher had that effect on people.

She was beautiful even without her makeup, without her thousand dollar dresses, in a worn, shapeless peacoat with moth-eaten holes in the sleeves. When she decided to stop crying and mumbling, she commanded the room, even folded into a chair in the corner like a child up past her bed-time. Jonah wasn’t sure who had let her in—she couldn’t have been trusted so easily, so quickly, not with her face still adorning the Dominion’s propaganda posters. Then again, where else was there to put her?

“Alycia, I mean,” Lucy went on. “Have you been to Ottawa? Have you seen what happened to it? She did all that, herself. She threw a benefit concert for the unemployed, and I sang for her, and—”

How traumatic that must have been for you, Jonah managed, at the last possible moment, not to say.

"—some of those stones came from outside of the city. They dragged them in on trucks, and when they ran out of power, they carried them. She doesn't let on how powerful she is ..." Because she valued her life, she didn't say *more powerful than Ian used to be*.

"The music," Maya said. She flickered like a dying fluorescent bulb. Her pupils were blown wide. "At the factory—Shadi, do you remember? They were piping it in. If she could record him, she wouldn't need him at all."

"Doesn't matter," Jonah said, and much as it stung to say it, added, "Ian's right. Something went wrong and we need to know what."

"We need defectors," Anton said. "We tell them they can come in, that they can have a better life with us, on the right side of history."

"We've tried that," Maya said. "There's no one left but desperate people and white supremacist fuckweasels." She swept her arm at the restaurant, the split aquarium, the layers of dust and blood. "Why would either give it up for all of *this*?"

"Because they have pressure points like anyone else." Here, Ian acknowledged Anton with the tiniest of nods. When had they been talking? Jonah had barely left his side since their return. "See how long their ideology lasts when the fuckers are starvin' to death."

.   .   .

If it could have all just been meetings, Ian unleashing what remained of his once-legendary ferocity on Gaby's Coordinating Committee, spinning bluster and chaos as if his government had never fallen, Jonah might have been able to bear it.

Ian was a good liar. Even ash grey, even without his magic, even if Jonah and anyone else who'd ever met him could see him coming apart like wet toilet paper, he could conjure an illusion that everyone wanted to believe. Even if his voice gave out mid-shout and Jonah, or Maya, had to carry on for him, they could all pretend together that he just had better things to do.

And in the end, what was more magical than shared belief?

The Coordinating Committee's main task was logistical, managing the flow of refugees and food and clean drinking water across the truncated cities, war and revolution both distant priorities secondary to keeping people alive. Amidst that, Jonah did not allow himself to think that he'd been forgiven. Not for leaving Ottawa when he did—he wasn't remotely sorry for that, even now—nor for his life since, which they did not discuss, lest Jonah be subjected to the full force of Ian's Thoughts About Religion in General and Roman Catholicism In Particular. But a truce was definitely in order.

Whatever else you could say about Ian and his ability to hold a grudge, he did have a sense of priorities. And besides, Jonah had always been one of the few people who actually noticed when he was being funny.

And if no one in the Mac-Paps, Ian included, had needed to sleep, Jonah might have been able to tolerate it.

Instead, there was the office building across from the mall, its mirrored windows only a Potemkin shield against a Dominion drone strike. There were desks with grey melamine tops and steel legs, under which people slept, and grey tight-weave carpeting that scratched at his skin when he tossed on its cold, unforgiving surface. Ian had found the farthest possible desk in the farthest possible cubicle and claimed it for his own, a prison within a prison guarded by rows of grey office chairs.

The same Fort Utopia that once operated out of a used car dealership was now the vanguard of a movement. There were twenty or so people in the Scarborough cell, making it one of the larger ones scattered around the province. Monique had picked them for their loyalty to Gaby, the chosen few trusted with knowing her name and the degree to which she ran the Mac-Paps on her own. The degree to which the whole resistance was a shitshow and a facade. It was only a matter of time before someone got picked up by a Cleaner and gave away everything. The Dominion had broken Ian, and it would break weaker spirits for less. It wasn't the nineteen other revolutionaries that kept him up at night, though.

Jonah wasn't good with sharing space, as Blythe had never failed to inform him, but he'd have preferred her kicking at his feet at 2 am until he stopped snoring to curling on a pile of yellowed newspapers in the next cubicle. Through the gap in the chairs, illuminated by the faint, flickering jaundice of the emergency fluorescents, Ian was in the grip of some nightmare. He'd have committed a murder-suicide if he knew that he was making pained little noises in his sleep and Jonah could hear all of it.

He was carved from granite, every crease and hollow outlined in the thin, dead light. The blood that ran through his veins, that still pooled in bruises across his cheekbone, was pitch. He had no right to be so embarrassingly human. He had a face that belonged to a saint, a martyr, not to some Centre Block ratfucker, and not for the first time in his life Jonah wondered how other people managed to not die simply from looking at him.

His restlessness metastasizing into irritation, he reached for his smokes. Ian wasn't moving, so Jonah slid out from under the desk and picked his way through sleeping bodies, down a narrow corridor and out into the hall.

Something—a blur of black, a shadow cast by something he hadn't seen—flashed in the stairwell. He moved after it fast enough to hear the echo of footfalls on the floor below, fixing his mask as he clambered down the stairs.

There was a stillness to the Exclusion Zones, to the suburbs at night that had been there long before first the Blight and then the Dominion had ravaged them. They were not meant for people—that human life had somehow thrived in these places at all was down to the tenacity of the species. When it came down to it, people were as stubborn and difficult to uproot as shriekgrass.

Without the rush of cars, the stuttering of buses, only the limp little wind through bare branches and the low, ever-present moan of shriekgrass filled the silence. There was more highway than building, a stretch of useless pavement that had given way to craters and copses of winter-dead weeds.

The snow was no more than a gloss on the sidewalk. There was no power for blocks, and the streetlights were out, but in the starlight, fresh footprints creased the snow. He followed them, his own boots widening the prints but not creating a new set of tracks. At the end of the block, the footprints veered off into a ruined maze of tract houses, near-identical except in the specificity of their damage.

He hadn't brought a gun. Parts of the street were still intact, maybe enough that someone might risk living next to an Exclusion Zone. They were nice houses, nice enough to be deemed too exposed by the Mac-Pap cells. He could imagine a Cleaner or two, resentful at being deprived a shot at middle class home ownership, sweeping out the families that lived there and squatting. But there was no spark of life in any of the windows. The few cars left in the driveways were shot up beyond repair, fuel doors and hoods torn open for gasoline and parts.

Jonah gave up walking over the footprints and stepped into the shelter of a roof overhang. Something up ahead was moving again. This time he could see a small figure, masked and underdressed for the chill. The gait was familiar, as was the teenage slouch and the buzz across his tattoo.

Well. *Fuck.*

Martine Abel turned to run and he grabbed her, crooking an arm around her mouth before she could scream. She squirmed and hissed like a scalded cat, but he'd been in his share of Winnipeg bar fights and a pissed off teenage girl was easy enough to manhandle into the shadow between two houses, even if she tried to bite his arm.

"Let go of me, you piece of shit."

Jonah loosened his grip, enough that she could twist around but not enough that he couldn't pin her down again if she tried to knee him in the balls and run.

"I *know* you."

"Yeah," he said. "Back to Fort Utopia with you. Your mom'll be worried."

"Fuck you," Martine said.

He waved at a poster on a telephone pole, recruiting young men to join the Cleaners. "You think this is a fucking joke? Move."

Martine's eyes narrowed, and the mask did as piss-poor of a job of disguising her scowl as the hood did of concealing her hair. "I can't breathe in there."

He'd come outside for a reason, and it hadn't been hunting down wayward teenagers. He lit a smoke and puffed it into the night air. "I know."

She tugged at his arm. "Can I have one?"

"What are you, twelve? No. Fuck no."

"Sixteen. My mom wouldn't care," Martine said. "She's too busy with the *revolution*."

"She'd care." The nicotine caught in his lungs, stilled the tremble in his freezing fingers. It was an effort not to resent Gaby for her fortune, her small brood of still-living children, even if the middle one was a piece of shit.

Martine sucked her teeth. She was half his size but she stood her ground. There was a burning in the back of his skull, in his shoulder. The kid was lousy with magic. "You don't know what she's like."

"Of course I do. She was never around and every time your dad got caught with his dick in the cookie jar or your mom did one—*one*—shady little deal with the Venezuelans, the bitches at school talked shit about you and put nooses in your locker. And now you're trapped in a goddamned strip mall with her, with no running water and fascists breathing down your neck, and she still doesn't have time for you."

Martine pushed her hands into the pockets of her coat and slumped into the wall. "So?"

"So she cares, you brat. She can't help it if she's bad at it." He took another drag, smoke eddying and dissipating as it reached the skeletal rooflines, the gashes where the earth's spasms had torn loose shingles and crashed trees into bedrooms. "You go any further into the Exclusion Zone and there's demons waiting to eat you alive, MAI or not. And you go farther from it and there's an army of Cleaners ready to smear you into red paste. That shitty office tower's your best bet right now."

She stared hard at him, like she *knew* that he carried around his grief like a dry drunk carries his rage. And then her head jerked to one side and she shrieked.

"*Martine.*"

"Am I high?" she cried, "Are *you* high?"

The massive beast snorting smoke in the middle of the empty street was too incongruous for his mind to process. Maybe they were both high. But the thing that loped across the deserted four-lane highway with its rug of curled hair like a cloak and its ancient, amber eyes was not a hallucination born of days without sleep.

He tightened his grip on Martine's wrist. "Are you doing this?" There was nothing, beyond the background ping of Martine's presence, that reeked of illusion magic.

The buffalo stopped. Jonah forgot how to breathe. Even far away, it was huge, a distant potential of violent death that might be on them in seconds. He marvelled at the size of it, the way it settled into a space never meant to hold something so feral. Its breath shook the ruff of beard at its jaw. A pale blue tongue flicked out from between its black lips, before the mouth stretched into a wide yawn.

"Is it a demon?" she asked, though she must have known as well as he did—better—that it wasn't—its movements were far too natural. It had every bit of confidence that it, not the slumping skyscrapers, was what belonged here.

"It must have escaped from the zoo." And survived, as all of them had, in the gaps in the cement and the moments where the boot was lifted. He might have prayed for it, that it would keep moving, keep dodging, stay itself even in an Exclusion Zone.

A smaller, darker form emerged and picked its way across the street. Jonah only let himself exhale when the buffalo and her calf had finished crossing the road and disappeared, once again, behind the row of houses.

"Nature is healing." Martine laughed, abruptly, hysterically. There were tears frozen in the corner of her eyes.

"Come back in," he said. "There has to be tea...something. Fewer wild animals."

At last, she shook herself loose from the wall and started walking.

"Gaby needs you," he said. "She can't love you properly, not in this hell of ours. You're old enough to understand that. But she needs the *idea* of you, and the rest of us need her."

As wary as the beasts had been, she followed him through the graveyard neighbourhood, the snow filling in their steps behind them.

.   .   .

Jonah installed Martine in Gaby's section of the office tower with a solemn promise to feed her into a blender if she so much as imagined the outside of Fort Utopia without permission, then tramped down a flight of stairs to find Ian, awake and doomscrolling through a borrowed tablet. His marble skin stole colour from the screen, a blue light that reminded Jonah, like an aching scar in winter, of the magic he'd once cast.

Ian barely looked at him. "If you weren't homeless and living in an industrial park, b'y, I'd look in your attic for ugly fuckin' portraits. It's a sin." It was the closest to a kind word he'd heard from anyone—let alone Ian—in years, and Jonah's treacherous heart, which had never been sensible where Ian was concerned, backed up like a misfired engine.

Jonah slid down the side of the cubical wall across from him, legs stretched out over the tight weave carpet. He'd sated his nicotine urge but his hands were still shaking.

"You left," Ian said, too flatly for it to be an accusation.

"Had places to be," Jonah said. "Gaby's brat to rescue. I like her, by the way. She's an absolute terror." This, for some reason, was interesting enough to get Ian to put the tablet down. He moved, each long limb seemingly autonomous, resisting, to clamber over to Jonah's side.

"Gaby's a problem," Ian said. "They all are. None of them knows what the fuck they're doin'."

"Oh, and you do?"

"Don't need prognostication to see what's in front of me, Joe. The first whiff of success and it's time for a circular firing squad with them b'ys she's assembled. Felipe smells blood. What's it like out there?"

He didn't mean the buffalo, though he had half a mind to drag Ian outside in hopes that they were still wandering around. "People are scared," he offered. "And starving."

"Good."

"We're into starving civilians now?"

Ian's glare was white phosphorus. More powerful men than Jonah had withered and died under those cold eyes.

"You thinks there are any civilians left? The Blight brought the Dominion to power but who'd you think kept them there?" The void sat between them, nearly tangible. "Why didn't they kill you?"

"Rude."

"They rounded up all them poor bastards, shot them in the streets, herded them into camps, dumped them into the ocean...not you, though."

Violence was the answer in so many circumstances, and it was the utmost tragedy that this wasn't one of them. "If you're asking if I'm a collaborator, Ian, you've spent the last three years turning into even more of a raging asshole." The taste of the cigarette he'd smoked earlier lay on his tongue like a corpse. "I hid." He tapped his shoulder, where the ward tattoo squirmed uneasily under three layers of clothing. "I have you to thank for that, I guess."

"At least I did somethin' right."

"You used to give a shit about people."

"Y'think so? I chose some sleeveen as the voice of my conscience, huh?" He rubbed at the swollen joints of his fingers. "So Jiminy fuckin' Cricket, what would you have me do?"

"The supply lines are a good idea. That's Gaby's strength, feeding people, keeping everyone safe. And it'll always be the Dominion's weakness. But you're all stick, no carrot. There's little pockets of resistance, there are people who just want to live their lives, and if they don't know the Dominion can be beaten, they'll never lift their heads above ground."

Ian snorted. "When'd you get to be an optimist, Joe?"

"Molotov cocktails and barricades aren't the work of an optimist."

Ian's rasps filled the spaces where, for some time, his words weren't. "Gaby can't win a war. Not even a guerrilla war."

"Since when did you ever think about winning?" Jonah shot back. "We need a situation they can't control."

"Become ungovernable?"

Jonah wanted to smile. Instead he played with the crucifix at his throat, tugged at the chain so that it bit into the back of his neck. "Be the pack of meth-addled monkeys that you want to see in the world."

Ian nodded, finally. His crooked fingers tapped, in sequence, over one skinny knee.

"I'll head out tomorrow," Jonah said. "Take a few of the Mac-Paps who want to get their hands dirty."

"Not you. I need you here."

"You have Maya."

The tablet, abandoned, winked out, throwing the room into deeper shadow. He was aware of Ian's proximity only by the short, quick wisps of his breath, the restless micro movements of his broken hands, the glint of some borrowed light striking a colourless iris. "She's tough as a gad and loyal, and she'll do exactly what I says. So." His leg bobbed into the side of Jonah's, too close for deniability, and every bit as constructed as his rare media appearance back in the day. "I needs *you.*"

"We'll talk about it later," Jonah said. "After you've convinced Gaby that I'm a strategic genius."

"You're a merry-begot and a right maniac, but playin' nice with the politicos got us a world on fire and the fuckin' Dominion." He kicked at Jonah's boot. "Okay, b'y. We do it your way this time."

21

There was no self-help guide for what to do when the world ends and your existence doesn't do you the polite courtesy of ending along with it. There wasn't even a listicle or a meme. When the world ends, if you survive its death spasms, you keep going. Your body doesn't know it's dying, let alone that the planet is. Absurdity piles on absurdity. You still show up to the office every day. You are invited to dinner parties with fascists and you smile politely, knowing they'll slit your throat the moment you cease to be useful. You talk to your family, when your schedule allows it, when the internet does, and you speak in euphemisms about your week while your mother speaks plainly about hers with a liberty paid for in blood.

The urge towards normalcy is powerful, and it outlasts most things: 60% of insect life, two degrees Celsius of average global temperatures, and liberal democracy.

Senator Cal Harrison's funeral was a command performance with stakes no lower than those of Patrice Abel's show trial. Cal, traitor or not, still had friends in high places, and the Dominion, never one to waste a death, had attributed his murder to the terrorists. An honour, really, instead of the insulting heart attack and the quiet removal of portraits that had befallen Simon Yamashita. And so, while he was denied the pageantry of a state funeral, the Dominion upper brass, surrounded by security, had allowed a burial in the Toronto Necropolis in the family plot, and expected everyone, down to NPCs like Eric, to attend.

He did his best to focus, to contain even the slightest twitch of emotion, the sweat bleeding out between his shoulder blades, slicking his palms despite the chapel's shoddy heating. He did not warrant the front row, with Cal's ancient parents bent like willows in the pews, with Reid and Alycia Curtis in solemn mourning black. He was relegated to the rear of the chapel, thumbing the worn cover of a Bible, the eyes of the massive security detail burning into his back.

Eric wasn't sure if Cal had been religious, but he would have surely had something cutting to say about the ponderous Yamashita score, the minister's invocation of martyrdom in the service of the nation. He picked at the waxed wood with a fingernail, tracing a long groove in the back of the pew in front of him before remembering that it was more rebellion than he should have dared. He turned the fingernail inward instead, digging into the meat of his palm to the point of pain, the minister's words transformed into a davening of *Jakie and mom and dad and Jakie and mom and dad.* He fixed his attention on the warm wood of the high vaulted roof beams, the winter light shimmering through the stained glass behind the minister's head. Cal, if nothing else, would have appreciated the pomp of it all.

A flock of drones formed a net above them as they left the chapel for the grounds. The machines' shadows flitted over the snow, slunk up the faces of headstones and disappeared in their lee. Their presence wouldn't deter a gunman, and Eric wasn't confident that the Mac-Paps' intelligence dossiers could distinguish between target and double agent. Still, Reid Curtis projected fortitude, a sharp angled black silhouette against the snow and worn grey headstones. Alycia and Cal's mother were arm-and-arm, heads bowed together, steps behind their husbands.

The shot wouldn't come from the Mac-Paps anyway. They didn't have enough snipers, for one. When it came, it would be one of the hulking security guards, or a whistle from the overhead drones as he broke off from the gathering for where his car was parked on a side street. It would come when his back was turned, now that he no longer had Cal Harrison to protect him. He was alone in the cold.

"Sorry to see him go," Abbott said beside him.

"You were friends?"

His manager gave a non-committal noise in response. "We played squash together. He had a hell of a serve."

When they finally got around to offing Eric, he doubted he'd get even that much of a tribute. He shuddered through the remainder of the service, hands stuffed in the pockets of his coat, spine seized into rigidity.

Eric hunched down the concrete path, towards Sumach. Snow had melted in circles around the graves, around the roots of the ironwoods and elms. He watched the banks of white on either side for shadows. He fumbled at the bottom of his pocket for his keys, catching a glimpse of his watch. Three missed calls. His mother must have known he was at Cal's funeral.

It was the Call. The one that said her time had run out, there were Cleaners at the house, Eric had been too incautious and doomed them in his double-dealing, and he reached for his phone.

From behind him, like some demented Tory vampire that cast no shadow and made no footsteps, Reid Curtis said, "So he was mortal after all. Who would have guessed?"

Eric yelped.

"Your hands are shaking," Reid said. "A drink will steady them."

He turned, forcing slow breaths through tightened lips. "I'm driving."

"What's the point of running the country if you do your own driving?" Reid clapped a hand on his shoulder. He was well into his seventies, plagued with a cough that sat under his speaking voice, but his grip was iron. "We'll have your car brought to your parents'. You are staying with them, are you not?"

Eric wasn't sure if he was slouching to be closer to eye level with the old man or presenting his neck for the guillotine, but he shuffled after him, to where Reid's limo waited. Alycia was nowhere to be seen.

"How *are* your parents, Eric?" As if Reid didn't know, as if he hadn't kept careful tabs on them, on Jakie, as if Eric's obedience wasn't the precondition for his family's survival.

"My mother was complaining about the lack of fresh fruit in the grocery store this morning," Eric said, too brightly. "I don't think it's really sunk in about the apocalypse yet."

There was a thick pane of Plexiglass between the driver and the expansive passenger compartment, where Eric sat across from Reid. He was offered scotch, or did he prefer champagne? The limo was well-appointed. What was left of the EU had sanctions on what was left of North America, even if the ocean didn't swallow up as many ships as it allowed to pass. There were reasons people sold out their families for DEC.

Well, if he was going to get shot anyway, he was going to get absolutely blasted first.

"Isn't hoarding illegal?" The scotch, already filling his nostrils with peat and warmth, swirled in his glass.

"What thing worth doing isn't?" Reid reached across the aisle to clink Eric's glass. "To the spoils of victory." He had poured from the same bottle, so at least the method of execution wouldn't be poison.

Reid, casually, pulled an articulated screen from the armrest of his seat. It sprang to life with staticky surveillance footage. The camera flitted between several positions—a forest, an overhead view of a campus of squat buildings, a long hallway of prison cells. Sometimes there was movement, guards, in pairs, moving from one end of the frame to another, but most of the shots were still beyond the flickering noise.

"What is this?" Eric asked. It paid to play the innocent, the guy absolutely too dumb to betray the Dominion, though he couldn't have been fooling Reid.

"You've been surrounded by death lately, haven't you?" Reid's tone was pleasant, even kind. "Cal and Simon both in the space of a week. One might suspect you were angling for a promotion."

"I don't—" Eric started, and Reid laughed.

"Relax. You don't have the cunning." His hand stilled over the remote. It was a shot inside the prison, the lines of the corridor converging at the door at the very end. "Watch. This is the best part."

The two figures whisked across the frame so fleetingly he might have missed them altogether, had the black-and-white footage not sparked colour, cracked into bottle-green fractals that chased each other across the screen. His tattoo briefly sizzled, entirely unnecessarily. At the top of the frame, something black roiled, like burned film, like a hole scorched in the screen, in the world.

Reid rewound, paused, until the two invaders, liberators, were frozen in one corner. "They murdered a guard. A boy, really, a young father of three. And then they stole Ian Mallory, but I'm sure you've guessed that much already, if your contacts haven't told you."

"I'm not in charge of any secret prisons," Eric managed. His heart thrummed a 180 bpm protest. Reid wouldn't shoot him in his limo and ruin the leather seats. Reid wouldn't, personally, shoot him at all. "Maybe you should have a talk with whoever is. They're clearly not very good at keeping secrets."

"They had help," Reid said. "From the late Mr. Yamashita and a technician less concerned with lab security than she should be. Perhaps another source—but we can keep that between us for now. At least until she's found."

"Is he alive?" Eric asked. Because he was concerned about Ian, his lunatic tyrant of an old boss, and not his friend, not the bravest woman he'd ever met. "Ian, I mean."

"He's not of any use. Though I suppose that won't matter to the terrorists if they can parade him around. Symbolism matters to them nearly as much as it matters to us. What I'm interested in, Eric, are those two." He lifted a long, bony finger towards the screen.

"Blob and—" Eric pushed his glasses up the bridge of his nose. "Another blob."

"The terrorists have an army at their disposal, but they didn't send it."

"Sounds like they didn't need to."

"They had to identify the soldier by his dog tags. This was personal. *Brutal*. And that's an MAI distortion field. More scotch?"

Eric said, "Huh?"

Reid scoffed, and tipped the bottle towards him so that he had the choice of accepting or letting it splash all over his pants and the expensive leather seats. "Who's the MAI, Eric?"

They were driving perilously close to an Exclusion Zone, to the crushed bridge over the Don where hundreds of drivers had plummeted to their deaths in the first quivers of the Blight. The shells of cars, bright beetles streaked in mud and snow, still littered the sloping shores. It would be easy to disappear out here, to never know if his silence had killed Jakie as well.

"I can't recognize them." As if, even warped and glitching, there was any mistaking the small, squat form, or the violence Reid had described. Transmutation of a human body into a corpse was its own kind of magic. *Whickity whacky alakazaam, I cast the curse of humanberry jam.* Carefully, he said, "They probably didn't send an army because rumour has it that the leader of the terrorists doesn't care much for Mallory."

"That doesn't narrow it down much," Reid said. "Who does care—enough to balk orders and kill for him? You worked with him for years, Eric. You know him best of any of us. As well as you know your own *family*."

He did try, for Jakie's sake, for his parents. He could see the young woman, hunched over her old CRT monitor, playing with her stress balls, writing her fanfic on department time and acting like everyone else didn't know about it. Her black glasses, her hair messy except for when she'd glamoured it to perfection. Ian saying that if she made it a year, he was going to get her a name plate that read—

Funny. What was the name plate supposed to say?

Fucker in charge of all you fucking fucks. She'd laughed at that, but Ian said he was being serious, maybe they'd bother *her* for a change.

"She can't have been so below your standards of fuckability that you'd forget her name," Reid said.

"I didn't," Eric said. "Forget. It's just. Not there anymore." A quick twitch of his head failed to shake the name loose from his brain.

Reid's clever, wrinkled face folded inward, gathering downwards at his thin lips. "Interesting." Frame by frame, the attack advancing in slow, inevitable increments, the two tiny figures moved forward, flitting in and out of focus. "The other one. Is he causing you the same kind of memory trouble?"

He couldn't be sure. The girl—her name a persistent itch on the membrane of his memory—had done a decent job of concealing their raid. The glitches disguised the way he moved, knife-quick and precise. But not enough.

Eric must have been quiet for too long. "I had a meeting with your father the other day," Reid said, so his parents couldn't be dead. Likely his mother calling to complain about Jakie's latest nurse, or the shrinking DEC allowance. He tried to breathe. "He must be thinking about retirement by now. I imagine your brother's care puts certain stresses on him, and he's hardly a young man. Not to mention the finances. There's less and less that you can buy for cash these days."

On the screen, the taller, slimmer figure smashed against the door, slammed it with his rifle before the image cracked in another shower of green sparks. "His name is Jonah Augustine," Eric blurted. He hadn't been sure on the first watch, but something about the snap from controlled calm to berserker rage was unmistakable, brought to mind Jonah kicking at the leg of a conference table, throwing crumpled paper balls at him from across the office. Turning into a snarling bear for no good reason. Well. He'd betrayed better men than Jonah. "He was Ian's right-hand man—well, I don't know what he was supposed to be doing there, to be honest. I think he was some kind of consultant. He was an anarchist before, why in *fuck* would you put an anarchist in the government..."

Reid sat back, contemplating his drink. "Oh, we're all anarchists here." He made eye contact with the driver, and the limo slowed. "I'm familiar with Mr. Augustine and his background."

"Then you know," Eric said. "He's pure chaos."

They took a corner, the limo's turn ungainly. Not that anyone gave a shit if it bashed up into a cracked curb or knocked over a mailbox. He was doomed, they all were, his family and Lucy and the whole shitshow of a revolution.

"I'm looking forward to the challenge," Reid said lightly. "I'll have the driver drop you off at your place. And finish your scotch. There's no sense in selling your soul if you can't enjoy what you purchased with it."

22

The chatter over the comms was sporadic as the *Love Craft* sank. A fluttering of discontent, cursing, a bleak joke about madwomen at the bottom of the ocean, broken by static and the sonar whoosh of the water above her. Blythe fell, and the static metastasized, cannibalized syllables and turned the sound into formless void.

Thirty metres down, the walkie died.

Blythe was too tall to stand or stretch her legs in the observation sphere. She lifted her hands from the controls, flipped the walkie over. How much know-how did it really take to sink to the bottom of the ocean, anyway? For awhile she sat in the darkness, the silence. Her head was never quiet, not surrounded by ocean, a tiny bubble in the vastness of the cosmos, and she could tell herself that the white noise that infiltrated the cabin was her own compromised soul, the hum of the submersible's instruments and not the buckling of the hull under the ocean's pressure and years of neglect.

She slammed the switch for the flood lamp.

The *Love Craft*'s single beam turned the black of the ocean a murky green, speckled with stray dregs of dead seaweed. The printed maps Blythe had taken from the lab, meant to demonstrate the urgency of the ocean situation to Mitch's company, lay scattered and crumpled over the console. Blythe was chasing shadows, and there was no guarantee that the bathyscaphe could catch the tail of one before the creature had moved on.

The *Love Craft* moved in lurching fits and starts. She'd trained on it, a half-afternoon nearly four years ago, when the mission was merely speculative. The training had been a just-in-case box-ticking exercise that she'd promptly shoved into a metaphorical filing cabinet. Her actual experience was a panicked flight to the surface, braced over the prone body of a dying pilot, with the sea turned feral and hungry and her skull searing. Her hands remembered how the controls worked—not that different than driving a car, if the car operated along a hyperplane and was several strips of duct tape away from falling apart. But her brain resisted, urging caution as the bathyscaphe's air tanks filled with water and the ship dove deeper and further from the coast. At the bottom it bobbed and scraped, dragging itself along the seabed like a hobbled spider, its legs torn off by a sadistic child.

The charge indicator was at the quarter mark; if she aimed for the current, the ship could drift along without much intervention, and if she vented the water tanks, the ship would rise whether the engine worked or not. It wasn't, whatever Kenny had implied, as much a suicide mission as it seemed at first glance.

Even if she didn't exactly know what she was doing.

Wreckage dotted the coastal waters, ship-corpses of at least three nations that lay buried together like spent lovers. The Blight had done more damage to the SVAR's pirates than the archipelago's defenders had ever managed with their hijacked sailboats and motorboats. It didn't matter. They'd still lost everything that mattered.

Somewhere in the dark, Laura's murderers slept too, their bones picked clean by sharks and hagfish. Their flesh fed the ocean's ecosystem and their ribcages sheltered tiny worms and isopods from predators. It gave her no comfort to think about it.

The ocean's fury was visited indiscriminately on itself, catching its own denizens in its magic as much as it had the invaders. Vast swathes of the seafloor, from fronds of seaweed to rocks to fish, had been turned to glass. The beam of the floodlight scattered refracted light across the frozen branches of coral, over an unlucky fish flattened against a rock, its heart, blue-black, pulsing sluggishly in its exposed ribcage. The flash of magic that had cut across the ocean three years ago had carved a jagged brinicle of doomed, crystalline statues. Blythe's breath caught in her throat, bent over the dusty console, her head fell into her bent arms and she sobbed. She wept for the coral, of course, and the nudibranches and sea slugs, and the salmon and rockfish, and for the shore, for open mic nights and garlic bread and Laura with her dramatic preteen sighs and her grass-stained knees.

She followed the streak of glass. It was a straight path that branched into a Lichtenberg figure where the blast had ensnared a patch of sand, a cluster of anemones, a piece of debris. The din of the ocean's song kept her company. Whatever was out there, it wanted her to find it. She let it guide her. Resisting fate had never gotten her anywhere. She would kneel before the Faerie Queen in hopes that she would be granted a boon and not be turned into a small colony of ants.

The charge ticked lower, from yellow into red.

Where the glass road narrowed and split into chthonian fractals, a dead submarine lay half-buried in silt.

Blythe's heart beat a snare drum pattern. The ship was a SVAR design, as sleek and eyeless as a lamprey. Its blackened hull stretched past the spotlight into nothingness, abutted by shards of glass frozen into the shape of the current. She couldn't tell her racing pulse or her churning stomach that it had gone dark, that it wouldn't unleash a torpedo at her and dash the *Love Craft* to pieces. She knew as well as anyone that just because something had died, it didn't cease to be dangerous.

But nothing moved, neither the *Love Craft*, suspended in the brume of the current, nor the submarine, placid in its grave. The indicator slid lower, and she pushed the bathyscaphe closer on propellor power, waiting for it to react.

It didn't.

Some pitch material webbed across its hull, gleaming against the ship's matte finish. There wasn't obvious damage beyond that, and the glass didn't look strong enough to have trapped it.

Blythe knew better. She could hear Kenny quoting schlocky B movie horror lines at her even as she maneuvered the bathyscaphe to dock with the submarine. She'd assumed design compatibility, and as metal scraped metal, not quite aligning, she cursed engineers and libertarians and the lucrative trade in adaptors, and herself in equal measure.

The temperature in the *Love Craft* dropped another few degrees. She fiddled with the joystick.

She needn't have worried. The black webbing lifted from the side of the sub's hatch and slid onto the *Love Craft*, enveloping the bathyscaphe's hull until the camera by the hatch blinked out.

It was as good an invitation as any.

As cold as the bathyscaphe was, it was nothing compared to the crushing chill that shot through her palms when she grasped the handle of the hatch. Her skin prickled with pins and needles, the paralyzing numbness of frostbite that gave way just as quickly to a searing burn.

Blythe stepped into the corridor.

The strip of emergency lights still worked, washing the corridor in pulsing blue. Warm vegetable rot flooded her senses. A sticky substance on the floor gummed each step as she made her way down the narrow passageway. The black substance streaked the walls, a void that cut into the hull's surface, teasing a glimpse of the vast emptiness of space. It hummed softly, an atonal murmur just barely above a breath.

She was so entranced by it that she nearly stumbled over the bent leg of a corpse melted into the bulkhead.

Blythe screamed and immediately jammed her gloved hands against her mouth, biting down on her knuckles. The man was half in and out of the wall, incorporated into its aerodynamic lines and curves. He was contorted, head thrown back, Adam's apple still faintly bobbing though, from the bridge of his nose upwards, his skull had disintegrated into a maze of black, mossy ridges spreading over the wall.

The rounded door at the end of the passageway was open. Past it, the corridor was a living, writhing thing, constricting and expanding with the kicks and shivers of the bodies embedded from the floor to ceiling. She was staring down the entrance of a massive digestive tract liquifying, in convulsive spasms, what had been the stalwart evangelists of voluntary association and economic liberty.

The scent of rot edged into cloying, almost sweet. She should have brought sample containers from the lab. The substance coating the walls was, on closer inspection, composed of fine hairs, each branching off like miniature fronds of shriekgrass, waving lazily despite the submarine's dead air. She moved past a man whose mouth was crystallized in a scream, tongue colonized by a forest of obsidian structures. He'd died horribly, they all had, to the degree that they were dead at all, that they weren't kept in a state of barely-living suspended animation to feed the entity that had captured them in its web.

Gusts of breath whistled from the dead crew's open mouths, and it felt like an apology.

"Not fucking accepted," Blythe muttered, pulling her shoulders in tight as she made her way down the corridor. Her voice caught on the fuzzy hairs of the moss and died there. But the ship itself seemed alive, sighing and heaving as one single organism.

The bodies sang as she passed them by, not just from their mouths but from the rustling of their limbs against the growths on the wall, the bubbling of something liquid under their flesh.

The control room was an expansive necrobiome, a pulsating nervous centre that had devoured both machinery and man in its maw. Her shoes squelched in something thick and pulpy. She didn't dare look down at them.

Magic was magic because it defied explanation, physics, biology. Because it couldn't be governed. She could study heat maps and current patterns and ocean salinity for a thousand years, and she would never come close to understanding why sometimes the sea turned to glass, why the voices it contained had wormed its way into every cell of her being, why it protected her even against the extremities of her own recklessness. It could no more be shoved in a sample jar and analyzed than you could study fire by looking at ashes.

She knew, realistically, if she somehow managed to extract a circle of the chyme sliding over the walls, if she escaped from the doomed submarine and navigated the bathyscaphe to shore, if she brought the goop to the lab and broke it down into its smallest parts under a microscope—all the magic would do was fuck up her equipment. What was the point of a scientist in a world that so fervently rejected reason? She could neither manipulate magic nor quantify it; her only hope was to survive it.

Blythe forced herself to get closer. Amid the gobbets of repurposed flesh dripping over the console was a glass dome housing a copper coil. The surface was smudged with the same ichor that splattered the bulkheads, but within the sphere, an unmistakable bright spark crackled and shone.

Blythe watched it, transfixed. The ever-present tingle on her shoulder deepened, the roots of the labyrinth seeking bone.

The spark was the size of her fingernail, but even at a distance it was unmistakable. Its heart was mother-of-pearl, an iridescent flame with shades of blue and green and violet skittering across its skin. She'd never been to a wellspring herself, but she wouldn't have even needed to *hear* about a wellspring to understand what she was seeing. There was a buried ancestral memory in every human that recognized it. The sliver of imprisoned magic mirrored the void black of the room, a precise knife-cut that had excised a piece of the world she'd known before.

The SVAR didn't have magic, or MAI who could control it. They had tech that approximated miracles, a legion of big-brained genius boys unconstrained by safety regulations, red tape, or a basic ethical framework. But magic avoided the seasteads and skyscrapers with the same certainty that it haunted the forests and mountains. The crew of the submarine must have stolen it, which was madness. Or they had traded for it, which was worse.

Had Blythe not been trapped hundreds of metres below the surface of the ocean, imperiled by her own self-destructive instincts, with no easy way back up to sunlight, she might have scoffed at their hubris. Of course their ill-fated little invention had drawn unwanted attention. Nothing amused the gods so much as a modern-day Icarus. Still, she was here too, a marked woman standing alongside the corpses of fools.

Bought was more likely than stolen, and a trade relationship opened the door to a military alliance. Mitch, to his dubious credit, benefited from a simmering conflict with the Dominion, but there were other cartels that didn't. Blythe and her friends survived only so long as their enemies hated each other as much as they hated them. Unlike the sub's occupants, she didn't have the luxury of an anonymous death. Not yet.

Someone needed to know. If not what passed for a resistance on the archipelago, then the scattered cells across the country, the Mac-Paps in the east, the separatists, the Iron Alliance. Her mother. Jonah. Because as bad as the SVAR was now, a SVAR unified in cause and strengthened by access to Dominion magic was the genocide of the world.

"Well," she said to the console. It would have required a crew to operate, half a dozen skilled people who knew what they were doing. The same crew, she imagined, that formed some of the globules on the control panel. "What do you and I do now?"

The sea, or the ship, or whatever incomprehensible intelligence was driving, allowed her a few long minutes to contemplate the absurdity of her position. And then it stirred.

The movement began as a shiver, not yet distinguishable from the swaying of the deconstructed crew. Blythe backed away from the console to the centre of the control room and stood glued to the least-squishy patch of floor. The trapped magic shuddered in its cage. The ship rocked back and forth.

"I don't know how to work you," she said. Even if she could have cleaned off the controls, she wouldn't know the first thing about operating a vessel of this size, let alone shaking it loose from its cradle of glass and guiding it up from the depths. Judging by the tendrils of black that seeped under buttons and dials, she doubted it was operational in the traditional sense. It needed a wizard, not a sailor, and Blythe wasn't either.

She'd made contact of sorts before. Her mind had brushed up against its alien consciousness and let it lead her through the mountains to safety. It wasn't unreasonable to attribute intelligence to it, or to equate the singing to language. It had saved her twice now.

"I don't know what you want. This is fucking stupid."

Ian would have argued with her about that. She'd asked him once how he did it, what the process was. Whether the results were repeatable and predictable. He'd smirked that gap-toothed grin and told her that magic wasn't tame. You had to just go with it.

She rushed forward and, grabbing a screwdriver that one of the dead sailors had dropped on the floor, smashed at the console until the glass shattered.

The blast threw her off her feet. She landed hard, but her forearm and shin caught the worst of it, squashing into the inky lumps of moss and flesh. She allowed herself the brief indulgence of curling up in a ball and wishing that when she opened her eyes she'd wake up in her apartment in time to get Laura to school.

Pathways of light arced through the control room, glancing off the panels and bulkheads, scrolling into the ancient, inscrutable Pattern that had been carved into the dead god's bones.

The compartment seized and the light expanded. It jolted upwards, straining at the bounds of its prison until something broke loose and the ship shuddered. Blythe crawled up on her hands and knees, black liquid sluicing through her fingers. The smell of the gunk on the floor was overbearing.

But the ship was, at last, rising.

It had its own mind, its own agenda. The tendrils of its consciousness reached out to hers, brief, splintering visions of a cold, distant planet hurtling through darkness, of lashing tentacles and mouths that could swallow stars. The tension in her skull was all but unbearable. She begged, sobbed for it to stop, to release her as it had released the submarine from its prison, to let her slide into unconsciousness. But it seemed intent on one-way communication, assuming that what it was doing could be called communication at all. And it had a purpose for her. She felt the ship as it splintered free of the glass and pushed upwards, the water flowing around and under its streamlined body, the arc of its trajectory towards the surface. Her skin was its metal shell, her mind its circuits, her heart the nuclear reaction in its engine.

Just as quickly, it was over. The ship breached with a splash, and the pain receded. The tendrils didn't exactly retreat from her mind, but they quieted, letting the tide of her own thoughts back in.

Every limb bruised and stiffened, Blythe shambled back down the corridor, up the hatchway to stand and gasp mouthfuls of cold air. The archipelago was a series of pale blue smears at the horizon, dwarfed by the expanse of ocean. She gripped the guardrail and blinked in the sunlight.

"I guess you're mine now," she said. "Or I'm yours. Fuck it, I'm talking to a ship. I'm losing it and we're stuck with each other." She patted the rail, as if it were the machine itself and not the cosmic horror that had animated it that had responded to her distress.

A ship needed a name. Knowing those SVAR bastards, they'd probably called it after whatever crypto-get-rich-quick grift had sponsored it. Or it was one of several boats called the *John Galt*.

"Assuming we can ever get to shore," Blythe said. "I think I'll name you *Retribution*."

23

The cold was back, a knife of a wind that slashed across the road between the squat brick factories. Lucy shivered in line, warmed more by the people in front and behind her than by her fraying coat. She'd tried to shower before leaving, a complicated arrangement that involved a bucket and sheets of plastic to keep what little warmth there was in the melted snow they hauled in from outside. As much as she'd scrubbed, a thin layer of grime clung stubbornly to her skin like stigmata. She'd never be clean, or warm, again.

For a week now, Maya had moved from factory to factory as a day labourer until she'd landed on this one, a target that both she and Anton—and thus, reluctantly, Gaby—could agree was worth their time.

Lucy could handle it. Hadn't she already proven herself? Maya's description of the factory was unmistakably that of a place gripped by one of Simon's spells, and as his former instrument, she very well might be uniquely poised to break it.

"Your soul goes out your body after half an hour in there," Maya was saying. "You won't feel it, and then it'll seem like it's okay, but it's not, you have to stay awake no matter what."

Maya didn't look like Maya, and if Lucy had a mirror, she knew that the reflection wouldn't have been her own. Her new appearance sat uneasily on her; her body moved the same, but her shadow was taller, broader, having taken on a sinister independence as it deigned to follow her. She knew how people looked at her, men and women alike. Never in her life had she been below notice. It was good, it meant that Maya's spells worked, but she felt the loss nonetheless.

"Talk to people," Maya continued. "It's loud but it keeps you alert."

"I can't imagine sleeping," Lucy said. "Ever again."

"You'd be surprised."

The queue inched forward. There were guards posted at the door. Maya was twitchy, playing with her respirator, bobbing in and out of the line to check on its progress. Ahead, the guards questioned an old man, asking him to pull down his thin medical mask, inspecting his knobby, insufficient hands. Lucy stared down at her own, small and wrinkled in the cold. Maya had gone into detail, a single hair emerging from a mole below her ring finger, a crescent moon of black dirt under each nail. She strained to see her real body beneath the illusion, the way Tobias had been able to do, but her new flesh remained a stranger.

"You," the guard at the door said, "and you." He was pointing to Maya. "Not you."

"Why not?" Maya said. Lucy wanted to grab the girl and run. You didn't speak to guards like that, you never talked back, even if you held a blue pass, and neither Maya nor her forged identity even held a red one.

"Got enough."

"Please," Maya said, squeezing closer, and Lucy hated her, hated the guard, the ooze of desperation that roiled off him and how she kindled it in response. They spoke, heads bowed in quiet negotiations, and then the guard singled out one of the women he'd selected earlier, who started to cry.

She'd never held a green pass before; the colour alone was an assault, garish and undignified, a target for sport hunters. It was scanned and she was ushered in, shown to her station. A small woman, rendered incomprehensible by her mask and a thick accent, attempted to instruct her in the machine's operation. Lucy fumbled, apologized. For her entire life, she had been on display, a rare orchid misted and cultivated under glass. Her fingers had danced over ivory but turned swollen and unwieldy under the demanding hum of the machine.

"Again," the woman was saying. Lucy shrunk as small as her strange new body allowed, avoided the guard as he passed and winked at Maya. The machine beat a staccato rhythm, and she passed bits of metal beneath it, fed its unending hunger.

She didn't even know what she was building. No one talked about what they were building. It could have been anything—motherboards, GPS systems for cars, medical technology—something useful or lifesaving or even merely entertaining. It might have given meaning to the work.

Why did it smell so bad? She thought that the decaying strip malls, with their rot and fossilizing garbage bags, were as bad as it got, but the acid reek of piss was hard baked into the cement floor. She hadn't been paying attention when they talked about washroom breaks. Maybe she was expected to pee her pants. She moved the bits of metal forward, and there was always another one behind it.

She kept the belt moving, kept herself moving, even though her shoulders already protested. Maya had warned her. Hesitation was death, slowness was death, and whatever soft animal weakness existed in her, despite everything, cried out to live.

"You're doing great," the girl on the other side of her lied. Lucy was supposed to make conversation, that was the point, bootstrap into Gaby's uprising the very workers making the smallest components of the Dominion's killing machines. She couldn't talk and focus on the line simultaneously, and above the clack of the line, there was a sound like a thin needle piercing her skull.

Piped through a tinny speaker system came a piece she recognized immediately as one of Simon's, though radically different from the arias she had performed on stage. She didn't know the singer, and she felt a flush of gratitude that it hadn't been her. It was superficially harmless, a saccharine, inoffensive burble, like elevator music. How her gentle, erudite fellow prisoner had forged such a thing was beyond her; the only trace of him in it was that he'd been compassionate enough to set it out of her range.

She had been working for minutes. Hours. She had never not been working. Simon must have been so tired, composing endless fugue variations, worn from the toll that the spellwork extracted on him. It lacked the dynamism of the music that he had composed from love, but its hook was no less compelling. She traced its harmonies, tested its shape. She wasn't an MAI, wasn't anything but a singer in a world that barely needed them, but she'd been Simon's songbird long enough to understand how his magic functioned.

"What happens if you fuck it up?" Maya asked. How could she talk and work at the same time? The music visibly wore at her too, no less potent on her for all her own power. Still, she seemed to know everyone in her line. She'd been a different person last time, slipped through the guards' watch with a different green pass. But maybe friendship came that easily to her, or at least a camaraderie forged out of the drudgery of the line.

Lucy missed Simon, abruptly and fiercely. They hadn't been friends, not properly, not enough for him to have told her about his secret hypnosis music or whatever had made him turn against the Dominion. But tea, forced laughter, the things that passed for friendship—she missed that. To exorcise the ghost of him, filtered through a recording and terrible speakers though it might be, was a cruelty too far.

"Isn't that your area?"

"Just here to cover you. Any time now, by the way."

She felt out the structure of the song, hummed a few bars in harmony. The first notes emerged from her throat like smoke, thin and warbling. It began at the lowest end of her range, brooding and minor. The singer, her voice less rich than Lucy's own, was an octave lower.

Already, the workers were taking notice, as were the cluster of Cleaners slouching by the fire exits. You didn't sing in here; here the human was reduced to its bare physical functions, made only to serve a god of steel and silicone. Lucy's voice alone was a violation.

Plain though her illusory body was, she was at last attracting some attention.

Her diaphragm constricted, pushing against the song and its gold-spun spellwork. Maya thrummed with electricity, awaiting Lucy's cue.

She had once stood in front of Reid and Alycia Curtis and their entire invite list, the most wealthy and powerful people in the country, made to give voice to Alycia's magic, and she'd turned it into a weapon with a single wrong flourish. She had sung through stage fright before. This was no different just because the second the Cleaners realized what she was doing, she would be singing for her life. She tried to force her own will behind it, the quaver rests between notes, the way she'd once forced Alycia's, like a fat toddler in a pool imitating an Olympic swimmer.

She harmonized and then she pulled the spell sideways in a tritone that even Maya immediately recognized as a deviation from the resolution. The spell moved through her, Maya's and Simon's both, a clash that she felt in the pit of her stomach.

The note held suspended before the spell, and the factory, burst into chaos.

Three machines down from her, a young woman's hand dragged under the machinery, spraying blood as she shook herself and then struggled to get free. Lucy's poisoned note had ruptured the factory's circulatory system.

What followed was as much massacre as liberation, as the workers on the line jerked free of the spell, as disoriented and panicked as newly awakened coma victims.

"Grab any weapon you can," Maya said. For her part, she had her duck, vines of green light crackling and writhing around her clenched fists. If she'd expected a people's uprising once Lucy cracked open the spell, she was going to be disappointed. More people fled than fought, from the violence but also from Maya and her blazing spellcraft. Some crouched under the work tables, others fled for the barred doors.

The Cleaners moved in quickly from their positions by the doors, swinging batons at anyone too slow to get out of the way. The little woman in the mask knocked a garbage can over in the path of two of the men, shouting in a language Lucy didn't recognize, flailing with her small fists until a swipe of a stick across her cheek shut her up for good. Most of the workers around her were frozen, dazed, easy targets for the guards.

"Keep singing," Maya hissed, barely audible over the screech of metal grating against metal. There was nothing to harmonize with. A moon-faced girl, visible through the office window on the second floor, smashed the device playing the recording. Lucy sang anyway, a cappella, while around her, everything fell apart.

Her song barely stumbled. It was one that Yamashita had written for her, for the concert that both celebrated Atherton's first year in office and mourned the loss of his daughter Miriam, infused with the Director's heartbreak. The Cleaner closest to her jerked around at the sound of her voice. His hand moved towards his baton and faltered there.

The twist came in the third verse, from minor to major, the triumphant victory of life over death, of love and family and God. They never cried at the beginning, but she'd seen audiences moved to tears by the finale.

The Cleaner's lip trembled, mouth widening in what might have been awe at the song or at the unhinged mania of a woman in the middle of a factory riot who had, inexplicably, started singing at him.

She wove the song around him like a cocoon. He breathed long, startled breaths, as if he was inhaling her words.

The broken lord rose from the ashes of the empire, but only to his knees. Humbled, he lifted his face to the Light, to God, and begged, after all he'd lost, to take the burdens of the shattered nation on his back.

There were tears streaming down the boy's face. It was a beautiful song, wrapped around a single drop of spellcraft. He was young; perhaps he had never heard beautiful music before. She willed him to defect just like she had. It would be so easy for him to hand over his weapon, to surrender, to walk away from the Dominion. He could choose peace.

His throat opened in a seam of red, splashing hot blood across her face. Her brain caught up long seconds later, connecting the dead man to the jagged slice of sheet metal in Maya's hand.

"He was going to turn," Lucy gasped out.

"We need to move," Maya's voice was brittle, about to snap. There were a handful of women behind her; a few were still battling the Cleaners. More lay in heaps on the factory floor, or wandered shell-shocked over the blood-greased cement floor. "Otherwise I slit his throat for no good reason."

. . .

There was no place in Fort Utopia for falling apart amid the constant influx of refugees. In formerly bucolic towns, neighbours had turned on neighbours, or the Train had split open their isolation and left the passively apolitical forced to choose sides. Anton's quiet campaign in the factories and gutters brought in the disaffected and the hungry. Run by the leader's daughter, and currently housing the leader and her Coordinating Committee, Fort Utopia had tighter security and less capacity, but Lucy overheard other Mac-Pap cells on the radio, pleading for more rations, or for Fort Utopia to take in more defectors. Felipe's people grumbled about the additional bodies; Anton's faction complained about the secrecy.

Their cell housed the newcomers on office floors, which were never meant to be living spaces. Even the strip mall stores, which had served as meeting places and caches for food and clothing, were filling up with sleeping bags.

There was no time for grief either. When Lucy's parents died—her mother of an aneurism, her father, presumably, of a failure to manage preventative care without a woman to organize him—there had been months where her existence was suspended, liminal. The kitchen table had erupted in flowers and sympathy cards, and she'd had the luxury to dither on what was to be done when the flowers withered and the pile of cards became insurmountable. There had been relatives checking in on her. Tobias ordering in from her favourite Thai restaurant so that she wouldn't have to leave the house with her eyes red and puffy. But here, the loss of a husband barely registered amid an avalanche of mourning. The weight of loss was a slow rallentando unravelling what their lives had been before.

Lucy paced behind the loading bays, just inside of the ward line, until her boots pinched too badly for her to stand. She curled by a disused air conditioner and stared down at her hands.

A decomposing deer splayed in the middle of the road, outside of the ward, its head bent backwards and eyes plucked clean. Its belly was split in two by fronds of shriekgrass that had sprouted from its guts. The heads of the blades were near-translucent, sprouting growths that cried at their approach, a delicate lace against the deer's dark hide. The beast's ribs were prominent, the flesh sunken in the gaps between them. It must have been desperate; animals knew to avoid shriekgrass. She had heard of people who had died that way, during the first winter of famine, people who had refused the Voluntary Relocation in favour of starvation.

She reeked of the factory. Even in the cold, it clung to her clothing and settled there to live. She could smell it on her skin, between the constellations of blood.

She'd known they were terrorists when she cast her lot in with them.

"You did okay." Maya was still wearing her grungy jacket with a slash of brown across it, and from the look of it, hadn't availed herself of the not-quite-a-shower either. "With the song. I wasn't sure it would work."

"I didn't know either," Lucy said. "But it makes sense, right? Vasai Singh's buildings stayed up without her, once the spell was there, and I—I was under Alycia's spell, and Yamashita's. So I'm still—" She couldn't make herself say "enchanted." She was still a child of the last century. Even if the spell lingered like old perfume. "Anyway, what does it matter? It was a nightmare. I don't think any of those people survived."

"It'll take days for them to get that factory back up and running. And they'll think twice before they use Yamashita's songs on people." She stood up again. "Good talk."

"Maya." The sentence in her head wobbled and collapsed in a heap.

"Go clean yourself up," Maya said.

And what did she expect, really? She'd done one good thing—if it had even been a good thing—after faithfully serving the Dominion for three years. She wasn't going to get a cookie and a pat on the back for it. She wouldn't be handed a golden key to a secret door that, when unlocked, would lead out of the wreckage and back into paradise. The reward for surviving was just another dawn of grinding hell. And Maya could never give her back what she'd lost. No one in Fort Utopia was any closer to a good emotional place, no sympathy would be forthcoming. Lucy brushed off the ridiculous corduroy pants they'd given her—presumably out of spite—and paced the stretch of doors and dumpsters.

Where the driveway wrapped around the corner of the strip mall, leading out to the highway, Ian Mallory stood. He was so pale and so still that he might have been just another relic of the old invisible clockwork that had manifested bread and shoes and cellphones on the shelves inside. The sharp knife of a cheekbone was silvery in the dark. She had nearly bumped into him before she saw him, and he didn't so much as turn to acknowledge her.

She didn't see much of him, and when she did, he looked past her. She had spent her utility and they no longer existed to each other. They must be stashing him somewhere in the office tower lest he take morale below the ninth circle of hell.

The black bruises had faded to a paler grey, but he was otherwise as much a walking corpse as the thing that had rasped out its message to her in the Dominion's black site. He was a stone monument to the world that she'd known. Her enemy, once, or Tobias', but as her reality had shifted so abruptly, an enemy was at least something familiar.

"Lucy Fletcher," he drawled. "Heard you're a murderer now." Now he looked at her, his eyes battery acid that reduced her to a steaming puddle in the snow.

"I was the bait," she said. "Apparently."

"Didn't think you had it in ya." He coughed so hard that her own ribs ached in sympathy. The remnants of rations she'd swallowed before heading out jostled in her stomach. "You're not feelin' sorry for them skeets, wah? You wouldn't even make it to Atherton's little firing squad if they got their mitts on you."

"I thought it might help," she said.

"With the throbbin' hard-on for bloody revenge that you won't admit to? Nothing helps with that."

"You don't have to be crude about it." She slid her hands into the oversized sleeves of her coat, gripped her own elbows, but the skin there was just as cold as her hands. The warmth had fled from the world. "They were just kids."

"So were the b'ys who killed your husband," Ian said. "Sad little kids wantin' to live as bad as he did. They get 'em young and stupid, puff 'em up with nationalistic bullshit, tell 'em they'll get jobs and get fucked, and give 'em a gun. Nothing more vicious than a half-cut potato who's been given an important job to do."

He'd been with Tobias at the end. For all the years she'd spent with him, for all their lazy breakfasts and box seats at the ballet, all the times his mouth had traced the inside of her thigh, it had been Ian who was privy to his last words.

"Could you have saved him?" A ridiculous question to ask a man who wore his scars as openly as Ian did. But what else was she supposed to ask him? Had Tobias suffered? She'd seen the cell where Ian had been kept, the empty cell beside it. She would never know a good night's sleep again.

"He died alone and miserable in his own piss, just like everyone else," Ian said. She wouldn't let him take her apart like he did to Gaby and the others. She wouldn't cry anymore; she had wept enough for a hundred lifetimes. "What I did was I set him free. And I set you free too, yeah?"

"That's not going so well." It was ridiculous to pretend that she hadn't been better off at Alycia's side, and just as ridiculous to pretend that she hadn't felt the doubt growing in her like a cancer. How long could someone live with that kind of poison in them before it rotted them from the inside? "I'm useless here."

His lip curled into a smile the way that an animal curled before it died. "That makes two of us, ducky."

The way the temperature dropped around him, the pins-and-needles sensation on her skin. "They really—"

"Cut it out of me? Yeah." He made a snipping motion with his twisted fingers. "As normal as you are." Tobias hadn't lived to see his enemy stripped of all his power, reduced to a pillar of ash. She doubted, somehow, that he would have found it very satisfying.

"What does it feel like?" She immediately clapped her hands over her mouth. She hadn't been raised to ask the kinds of questions people didn't want to answer.

Nor did he answer, at least not right away. "You'd know, wouldn't you?" he said after a long pause, then, "The Dominion shat you out easily enough."

"Alycia doesn't *need* me." That shouldn't have hurt. It didn't hurt.

He made a noncommittal noise. "Not fragile like a flower," he said. "Fragile like a bomb. I hope I'm out of the blast radius when you go boom, Lucy Fletcher."

24

J onah turned the spit on the slow-roaster someone had installed in
the delivery bay. Thick, oily smoke caught in the wind and blew into
his eyes, conspiring with Maya to conceal her approach even as his ward
tattoo crackled at her presence.

"What are you doing out here?" she asked. She edged around the oil
drum, flickering, fluttering, as if caught in its heat haze. The radio hissed
and spat at her presence, then settled back into its drone of strings.

"People need to eat."

"I didn't think you could stand being away from Ian for so long." Now
she was just teasing, a ghost of a tease from a ghost of a girl.

"He likes you better anyway."

"Yeah," Maya said. "Sure." She wrinkled her nose at the smoke. "I'm
afraid to ask."

"Raccoon." They were skinny and the smell from the grill was greasy
without the evergreen astringency of rosemary to cut it. The raccoons
should have been half in hibernation, but the cold had gone on for too

long, and they'd reemerged out of desperation to pick over the bones of human civilization. He respected raccoons—like the Mac-Paps, they knew how to survive in the cracks left behind when the world shattered. That didn't change the fact that people were hungry and the .22 rifles someone had recovered from a Bass Pro Shop weren't good for shooting at anything that actually deserved it.

"Gross. If life ever goes back to normal, I'm going back to vegetarianism." She hoisted herself on the hood of a car that they'd cannibalized for parts. She was flickering on and off like a shorting lamp and hadn't cast even a half-assed glamour. There were lines of black dirt under her fingernails, which she picked at, her arms clasped around one knee.

"Make your decision after you've tried my trash-panda brisket. What are you doing here anyway?" He left the slow cooker to do its thing and hopped up beside her. She could have leaned into him, could even have cried if she hadn't committed whole hog to the heartless action-girl routine.

Just as well that she didn't. Grief was a wellspring—poke at it and it would go nuclear. He twisted the crucifix hanging from his neck between his fingers.

"Avoiding the Coordinating Committee." Maya twirled the radio dial, but Dominion radio always sounded the same, the bombastic Wagner-lite soundtrack to the razing of neighbourhoods, anthems to firing squads and murdered children.

"Felipe still at it?"

"Among other things."

"Well," Jonah said. "You wanted to get into politics." In lieu of emotional catharsis, he updated her on the rounds. "The Nanak House people say their wards are failing. Someone spotted them—not a big deal, they took care of it—but you or Martine should go fix it ASAP. And they want more guns."

"Everyone wants more guns," Maya sighed. "What the fuck are we doing, Jonah?"

It was the same problem the Mac-Paps always faced—too few people, spread over too much geography, under-resourced and restless and desperate. Her work in the factories had brought in newcomers, each one of them a new mouth to feed. For Jonah's part, he'd visited three different safehouses that afternoon, none as established as Fort Utopia, each of them with a laundry list of needs. He charmed them. He promised them things. Tech. Food. Some vague yet hopeful future.

He couldn't face Ian afterwards, and not because of the void he carried on his skinny shoulders. Unlike Maya, he'd gotten used to that. It was because Ian would tell him what absolute bullshit all of his efforts amounted to.

"You thought finding Ian would be the end of it?" he asked.

"I thought something. You're the super-religious one. Why don't you ask God how we get from eating raccoons to winning?"

"I don't think God's interested in what I have to say lately," Jonah said.

As if to underscore Maya's question, the radio buzzed to life with an actual human voice.

"*And we continue our retrospective of the work of the late composer Simon Yamashita, whose funeral will be held this Sunday...*"

Jonah and Maya stared at each other as the announcer continued, the world's slow breaking apart pausing to take note of the burial of one gullible, ill-fated stooge.

"Well," Maya said, "this is going to be an absolute shitshow."

. . .

Lucy had a fresh round of tears about it. It was one thing to be declared dead by the Dominion—more than a few people at the table had been—and another for them to have produced an actual corpse for a funeral.

"He was always kind to me."

"He was a collaborator," Martine said, with the certainty that no one could be both at the same time."

Martine," Jonah said, as gently as he could manage, "Shadi wants to talk to you about enchanting that drone."

She got up and went to find Shadi in the electronics store, leaving the rest of them to their impromptu conference. He hadn't thought the distraction would work. Laura wouldn't have fallen for that—she'd had an infallible ability to tell when he was lying. Martine wouldn't have listened to her mother or sister. But in the days since he'd accidentally saved her life, she'd shadowed him around Fort Utopia, constantly underfoot, a one-girl surveillance apparatus. She was still pissed off at Maya, and she'd been born pissed off at her family. Jonah, very much used to pissing off anyone he even slightly cared about, found himself in the very strange position of being the one person the girl apparently liked.

Without her commentary, the rest of them had to listen to Lucy weep, and act as though it wasn't the most pathetic display they could possibly be witnessing.

"This is all a distraction," Anton said. "The Dominion has a surplus of bodies and weapons to throw at the problem. They won't stop until their production is stopped. Tell them, Maya."

"I'm making progress?" Jonah hadn't heard her vocal fry that bad since the Broom Closet days. She must be nervous—not of Anton, Anton was harmless—but of the growing dissent in Gaby's ranks. Jonah found a scrap of cardboard, scrawled, *This meeting could have been a gunfight*, and passed it under the table to Ian.

"The Dominion's claim to power is their strength," Felipe said. "Their ability to maintain order. Take out enough of their centres, you shake their foundations."

Gaby, flanked on either side by representatives of factions that were jockeying for her thankless job, shrunk in on herself. *Bad move.* Ian had his *I'm not angry, I'm thirty seconds from a nuclear explosion that will level a small city* face on. "A direct attack will bring reprisals," Gaby said, returning her attention to the spreadsheet Monique had made of their current armoury. "That's a lot of explosives either way."

"It's a lot of dead fascists," Ian said.

"We're not trying to kill any—" Gaby started.

"I don't mean your little pyrotechnics display."

Jonah knew that riptide growl. Ian was, as usual, operating on a different wavelength. Back in the day when he'd do that, Jonah had at least been relatively assured that he wasn't completely batshit. "The Cleaners at the factory. Yamashita. Cal, as far as the public's concerned." He counted them off on his crooked fingers, changing the order so that Cal got the place of honour in the middle. He hadn't shed a tear for Cal, at least not that Jonah had seen. He just wavered between frenetic motion and catatonia. "They'll want to keep the rest quiet but Yamashita's been their boy forever. Did the Curtises realize it was him that betrayed them?"

Lucy's crying had settled into a low, steady drizzle. "I don't think he meant to betray them. He didn't care about politics at all. He just did it for the music. To write the kind of music that could touch people like that."

Jonah twisted his tone into something like sympathy, as if Lucy had more than skimmed her toe into the ocean of tribulation that a person could suffer. "Was he still in their good books when you—" *defected* "—left?"

"Do you think they blamed him?" Oh shit, he'd said the wrong thing and now she was about to unleash the waterworks again. "Simon just told me what he knew. I—I didn't know they'd come after him."

"And he's the one they trot out in front of the cameras when they have to prove to China or the Saudis that they're not the racist kind of genocidal fascists," Maya said. "We don't think it was Atherton's people?"

"Not unless he wants to fuck with Reid—or Alycia. And why would he? They are his patrons as surely as they were Yamashita's."

"He was sick," Lucy said. "The last few times I saw him, when he was working on *Egregore*. He looked, um." She glanced first at Ian, then at Maya. "A little like you both. Maybe they used him up."

Maya quickly slid her hands inside the sleeves of her parka, as if the

Devil's bargain she'd made with magic wasn't obvious in her face, the translucency in her cheeks. Ian, meanwhile wore his curse defiantly, like a facial scar from a knife fight that didn't end as badly as it might have.

Gaby muttered some stream of French expletives, then said, "About the attacks, Felipe."

"You couldn't cut a paragraph out of a draft policy statement back in the day, and now you're committing domestic terrorism?" Ian's smile—the grey gums, one canine chipped—was cruel, feral. "Never mind the towers. Not yet. Tin Soldier's right, you don't have the capacity. The funeral's the weak spot. They'll need boots on the ground to protect the dignitaries, more if there're crowds."

"No one gives a shit about some composer," the aforementioned Tin Soldier said. "I don't see what—"

Jonah did. There would be people on the streets, more than usual, and more emotional than usual. People who with slight prodding might be willing to unleash more chaos than the Cleaners could handle. Led by strategically placed cells, they might see, for the first time in years, a chance to resist. It wouldn't be the first time in history a state funeral for the lesser of a host of evils had turned into a rebellion. "I'll spread the word. And get Martine to do her thing to the north cells, see if they'll come down."

"What are you planning?" Anton asked, as though he still got input once Ian had come to a decision.

"Jonah likes drama." Ian—*who knew nothing about drama whatsoever*—laid out the plan.

Gaby spoke first, small and drained and weary. "People are going to die. Ordinary, innocent people."

"That doesn't make it a bad plan," Maya said, and when had she gotten so ruthless? "It's a safer one, anyway."

"And find out whether Eric's heard back from Blythe," Ian added.

"Who the fuck put the wizard in charge?" Felipe asked, just as one of his men was asking who Eric was, and who Blythe was. Jonah dug at the fabric of his jeans—useless, utterly fucking useless.

"I did," Gaby said. "He is the only person I know more ruthless than they are. Worse, maybe." She was watching Ian hopefully, as helpless as any of them. Everyone caught up in the same shared delusion that he was going to somehow swoop in and save the day, sparkling with his old magic. As if he wasn't more than halfway insane, as if he hadn't fallen apart back when the Dominion was still in its wriggling larval form of private members' bills and 4chan memes.

"How'm I supposed to keep up morale?" Felipe asked. "Magic got us into this shitshow. You gonna wave a wand and fix the world?"

"You gonna take your guns and go home?" Ian replied. "Or, wait, you don't have those either."

"I don't know if they can be fucked," Gaby replied. "But if there is any way at all to fuck them, he will find a way."

Ian nodded in Gaby's direction, the acknowledgment barely there, but Jonah saw it. The last thing anyone needed was a coup on the inside when they were trying to do a coup on the outside, but the end of the world wasn't going to suddenly change the left.

"Got it," Jonah said. "Know anywhere I can get a nice suit for a funeral?"

· · ·

Simon Yamashita's funeral was public, but closed casket. Whether that was because of the ambivalent position he'd occupied with the Dominion or because whatever was left of him was not fit to be seen by the plebeian hordes, Jonah didn't know.

Jonah had come like some Hudson's Bay Company lackey with the boys from Felipe's mutinous regiment a few blocks behind. Conspicuous on the barren streets, he pulled his toque lower around his ears, the respirator scratchy over the bridge of his nose. The thin line of spectators was slightly more diverse than he'd expected. The regime had stumbled at the two-thirds line on the way to creating a white ethnostate, tripped up on the whole part where they needed doctors and engineers and electricians to keep the Train running and the lights on, and they simply didn't have enough Old Stock warriors left to do it. It made for a precarious social order, with a class of workers labouring under the knowledge that, at any moment, the Dominion might want to fire up the engine of genocide again.

And also—at least in Ian's estimation—a populace ripe for a little rebellion.

Jonah didn't see any signs of it, and for a good half hour of walking along boarded-up St. Clair Avenue, was convinced that Ian had been wrong. A few clumps of sad-looking old people in worn windbreakers, sitting on lawn chairs with droopy little Dominion flags. The odd old Canadian flag among them, a weird symbol of defiance given its own murderous history. Yamashita, the model minority, the exceptional genius whose existence refuted the worst theories about the Dominion's plans, could still draw a small crowd. With his death, the iron fist would come out of the gold lamé glove.

Jonah had put the word out, Gaby had, Martine had, but Gaby's hold over the other cells was tenuous, and there was no way of knowing whether anyone else would answer the call.

And then he saw them.

They came from out of the subway, from tunnels that had sat empty for years, from the office towers and half-finished construction zones. They bore placards with Yamashita's name in kanji—Maya, an anime nerd, had made sure that Martine burned symbols in foot-high flames into everyone's minds. The signs were inoffensive, if awkwardly homemade, but when Jonah passed a heavyset Latina woman in a purple toque, he saw that the cardboard was lashed to a heavy wooden stake.

The crowd was a living beast, carnivorous, oppressive in the weight of its musculature. It pressed down on him from all sides. The last time he'd seen so many people was at the docks, where he'd broken Blythe's heart for the last time, where he'd doomed Laura to the sea.

A detachment of Cleaners milled around the corner. They could take down a layer of mourners before they had to reload. This was a terrible fucking idea. It was a great fucking idea.

Well. It was never going to be peaceful. The window on that had closed, if it had ever been open more than a crack. Protest worked when the government had a conscience. When your enemies were sociopaths, it wasn't about whether blood would be spilled or not, but whose.

Jonah weaved past a man still in a high-vis vest, a woman losing down from an overstuffed parka. He stood on his toes in hopes of sighting the convoy on the horizon. The frozen cement blasted through the soles of his boots. His childhood winters had been in Winnipeg, where the cold could kill you in minutes. But his years out West had spoiled him, left him unprepared for Toronto's damp, slushy misery, and his jacket and boots were splitting apart.

A cry rose up from the crowd, like the roar of an audience when the roadie got on stage and started tuning the guitars, only with the joy stripped out of it. A dull, wordless howl.

Blocks away came a growing din then, above the disused streetcar tracks, a shimmer of black, then the sea of Red Ensigns. The funeral procession was coming.

It was one of Yamashita's more bombastic pieces—not that Jonah counted himself an aficionado—butchered by the speakers mounted on either side of a truck. Between the rumble of the crowd and the shuddering of the engines and the wind corridor between the office buildings, the layers of instruments were a muddy blur.

Two motorcycles led the motorcade. The black glass of their helmets obscured the faces of the drivers, but one seemed to stutter for a moment before the driver regained control. They hadn't been prepared for the crowds. The Cleaners at the corner, too, snapped into alertness.

There was a moment where it might not have ended in bloodshed. The city's population was allowed its small catharsis, and the motorcade drove by unsettled, flags flapping in the dull wind.

Several in the crowd, dressed in black, stepped out into the street, arms linked. The driver who'd hesitated did so again, but the other gunned the engine. Someone had to break first. Someone did. A boy at the end of the chain dodged onto the sidewalk, just as the motorcycle plowed through two of the linked arms.

Jonah didn't throw the first brick, but that was only because he had a pistol.

A woman beside him screamed. He put a hand on her arm, guided her behind him as he drew the gun. He'd been in riots before, had been part of that living organism teetering between ecstasy and eruption.

This time there were no cheeky signs, no hastily exchanged grin with the stranger standing beside him, no one with bottles of water ready to spring into action against tear gas.

Yamashita's concerto was the soundtrack to a massacre. The placards were bludgeons—he saw a guy take a swing at one of the motorcycles, sending the driver careening into the sidewalk before he was swallowed up in a sea of roiling black. Someone in one of the cars opened fire. Blood and bone sprayed from the edge of the road, and Jonah dodged an eruption of cement shrapnel. Something hit his leg, hard enough to bite into his jeans, not hard enough to draw blood. He was thrown onto his hands and knees, fingers inches from a purple toque soaked in brain and bone shards.

He scrambled through a narrow gap in the bodies—some running towards the street, more running away from it, others converted, through leaden alchemy, to mere obstacles to be stumbled over. He managed to shoot two Cleaners before they redirected their rifles at him, and he ran back for the cover of the buildings.

He couldn't hear, between the explosion of his own pistol and the drumbeat of blood running through his ears. He ducked around the building to emerge a block ahead of the remaining Cleaners.

Everywhere, bodies lay in the streets. Blood ran into the gutters, splashed red across the little piles of slush that sloped over the curb. He hadn't seen so many corpses in one place since the days that had immediately followed the Blight. Jonah ran out into the middle of the road, dropped to his knees and fruitlessly, pointlessly rolled over a famine-thin man, checking for a pulse, but anything that couldn't get up and flee on its own was doomed anyway. Just like Gaby had warned, it was a fucking massacre.

But the cars that hadn't fled were surrounded, emptied. Someone was climbing up the scaffolding in front of one of the office towers, clawing for the Red Ensign jutting out from its porte-cochère. They were reaching for a match. He had enough time to think, *No, that won't work, they make them out of non-flammable material now* before he remembered that no, they didn't anymore, just as the flag went up in a burst of flames.

It was only the cheer of "Viva Mac-Paps! Viva Tkaronto!" that told him, for the first time in three years, they'd pushed Dominion forces back.

He tugged the burner phone out of his pocket and called Martine. "Do it now."

The street lit up with flaming letters. By the way the survivors stopped, and watched, he could tell that they weren't just in his own head this time.

Hold the streets.

We are winning.

25

The corridors of power were as dull as the offices at Laurier Ave. West had been, a maze of off-white walls and beige carpeting, the odd placid watercolour framed above cubicle-enclosed desks. It was one of those great glass buildings removed from time and space. Transplant it nearly anywhere in the world and there'd be no difference beyond the language spoken. Only the portraits of Atherton adorning every office reminded Eric of the type of future he was living in. No flying cars or hoverboards, just cameras recording every whisper, every movement, and soon enough, given sufficient advances in magitech, every thought.

His ringtone, a song nearly two decades old, broke the brutal efficiency around him. "Mom," Eric hissed into the phone. He ducked into his office, forcing himself to pull the door shut slowly, to avoid drawing any more attention than he already had.

She started in immediately. "Did you *hear*? They took over the whole downtown. Your father says there are riots downtown, the police had to retreat—"

Eric held the phone a few inches from his ear, his mother's voice retreating to a muddy din like a swarm of mosquitos. He pulled up the Institute's Slack and scanned rows and rows of messages. Food deliveries withdrawn, that was concerning.

Troops withdrawn. That was pantshittingly terrifying.

"—warning that they might spread—"

"Mom," he said. "You need to take Dad and Jakie and head up to the cottage." It wasn't winterized. The roads wouldn't be plowed, if they even counted as roads anymore. And they wouldn't be able to care for Jakie, not isolated from the rest of civilization, without the expensive, semi-legal network of aides they called upon when he was too much for two geriatrics to handle.

But it was better than being in the middle of what was coming. He'd worked for this, spied for this, but he hadn't imagined his parents stuck on the wrong side when all hell broke loose. Bureaucrats, collaborators, and quislings didn't fare well when the Molotovs flew and the barricades went up.

"Eric—"

"I'll try to meet you," he said. His side of the conversation came in jagged splutters. Every silence on his mother's end was a Cleaner in the kitchen, come to drag Jakie away like they'd taken Abigail, or a brick through her window tossed by bloodthirsty rioters.

Norm walked past the glass wall of his office, the reflected fluorescent light slashing a bar over his face. Eric's stomach lurched, though the fact that the man bothered to knock told him that he wasn't getting murdered today. "Go," he hissed into the phone. "Leave today. *Please*." He motioned for the man to come inside as he hung up.

She wouldn't listen to him. He would always be a child to her, no matter how many promotions he garnered, no matter how many secrets he carried or how many innocents he'd buried in his work for Walsingham. He had nothing important to say.

"Alcott needs the polling numbers by noon," Norm was saying. The spreadsheet on the monitor in front of Eric was a blur. There had to be something useful in there, something more worthy of Blythe Augustine's time than the encrypted data he'd sent into the ether. Something that could help the Mac-Paps and take down the government and save his parents and Jakie and protect Lucy but without Cal to guide him, with his employers tracking his every move, there was no hope of teasing it out.

"I can tell you that now," he muttered. "90% of respondents with working phones disapprove of food riots and anarchy." He suspected Norm hadn't been so much hired as grown in a vat. "Noon. Got it."

"And Reid Curtis is here. He wants to speak to you."

. . .

Eric stepped into a boardroom full of the most powerful men in the Dominion, men who could kill him with a signature, and said, "I need to go to Toronto."

Reid looked amused. It was too early to be drinking, so he twirled a pen between his fingers instead, the movement faster and defter than a man of his years should have been able to manage. Alcott was there as well, so at least Eric had an excuse for being late with the data. And worst of all, Quinn Atherton flickered on a laptop monitor below his own portrait, soaking in an excess of gravitas, noblesse oblige without the oblige. He eyed Eric like something he'd caught on the underside of his shoe.

"The polls are still suggesting support for a strong hand." The sample size of respondents was too small to justify that statement, and you couldn't assume that people would feel the same way about a question when it was hypothetical versus blowing up the neighbourhood Starbucks. But you didn't correct Director Atherton. "The affected regions are scattered and mainly away from residential areas."

"Like St. Clair Ave.?" Eric muttered. Reid raised an eyebrow. Whatever else could be said about the man's insatiable lust for power and blood, he wasn't an idiot.

"This trip of yours," Reid said. "On the ground reconnaissance?"

"Family." He couldn't mention Jakie, and fuck oh fuck that had been the worst thing to say in front of the Director. There had to be some unmissable social occasion. When was his parents' anniversary?

Reid pursed his lips together, hummed in feigned concentration, and switched tracks, oblivious to Eric's barely concealed distress. "Do we believe the populace has an appetite for a heavier approach?"

"They'll tolerate troops on the street for a little security," Alcott said. "Not air strikes."

"A rebellion is an infection," Atherton said. "You would cut off a limb to save the rest of the patient."

"You can't amputate *Toronto*." Alcott had chosen a dangerous time to have one of his biannual attacks of conscience, and Eric clenched his jaw and averted his eyes. "If I'm allowed to be candid—"

"Of course, Alcott." Reid said indulgently. He wasn't a supervillain; certainly he couldn't slaughter his entire middle management.

"—this is a job for stronger messaging, not military might. We need to connect the story points and leverage the goodwill we've earned with the critical demographics."

"Do you think?" Atherton asked. "Because you just described these riots as *growing*. Which sounds to me like the terrorists gaining confidence."

"The riots will peter out," Eric said. "They don't have the people or the infrastructure to sustain them. People need to vent their frustrations every so often."

He was prey to these men, just a soft-bellied little thing to be torn asunder between two pairs of hyena jaws.

"We'll contain these disruptions in designated areas," Reid said. "As far out of the public's eye as possible. Let the fire burn itself out. If any of the leaders can be apprehended, so much the better. Reestablish public trust in our ability to keep the peace. Direct observation couldn't hurt."

"I'll—" Eric started.

"You're needed here," Reid said smoothly. He wasn't so crass as to smile. "Eric. Please stay a little while longer."

Alcott hesitated, edging up against the border of Reid's tolerance, before choosing self-preservation and fucking off. "Stronger messaging," Reid cheerfully called behind him. Alcott might have even recognized it for the taunt that it was.

"He's good at his job," Reid said. "Not a man who likes to get his hands dirty, though."

"Neither am I," Eric said. He pushed up his glasses. There was a streak on them. If he turned his head slightly to one side, the smudge caught the fluorescent light and slashed it across Reid's high forehead. He took them off, rubbed at the glass uselessly with the bottom of his tie.

Reid chuckled. "I suspect you'd find a way to cope, Eric." Not *son* or *my boy*—he was far from that level of Reid's confidence and affection. Important enough to be drawn into Reid's games, not important enough to be spared the axe should he fail to scramble fast enough and bow low enough. "Alcott will do what he's told. He'd suck dick for DEC—"

"*Reid*," Atherton said from the screen.

"—if you'll pardon my language, but he lacks conviction. Like a hagfish—all skull, no spine."

Eric kept his tone light. "I'm a data cruncher, Reid. If I work really hard, maybe I'll get to write a policy document or two. PR copy, if Alcott's guys are feeling uninspired. I'm not a military strategist."

"We can both leave the military strategists to their job. I have no doubt they'll wish to avoid unnecessary collateral damage." Here, he gave the laptop a sharp glance. It felt sordid, to watch the most powerful man in the country brought to heel by an old newspaper baron. "There are too few exterminators, too many rats."

"The rats don't have F-35s," Atherton grumbled.

Reid wasn't a supervillain, but he could monologue like the best of them. "And we barely do. Rats may occasionally forage downtown, but I don't suppose they nest there. We don't need to write off downtown. There are more effective targets." He stood up, straightened his tie despite it, to Eric's eyes, requiring no straightening. "Scurry along, Eric. I won't keep you from your data-crunching any longer."

. . .

There was no direct chain of evidence. Or maybe there was—Eric had been quietly scraping data from the Dominion's intranet for three years, but he'd leaned on Cal to make sense of it all, to keep him apprised of the latest contact point, to tell him what the fuck he was supposed to do. The line to UVic wasn't secure, and he had no way to know if the data he'd sent to Blythe had ever made it to her.

Somewhere, in some windowless corner in the building, or in his private car on the Train, Atherton was on the phone to the Minister of Defence, and the Minister of Defence would be on the phone with someone at CFB Trenton, and then it would be over. They used satellite phones with end-to-end encryption—none of it would pass through the Walsingham servers—but the shape of things to come was in the emails that weren't sent, the orders that weren't given.

In the corner office, Alcott was brainstorming a series of announcements.

Eric tried his mother again. It rang for an agonizingly long time before it went to voicemail. He paced the length of his fishbowl.

Of course the Dominion wouldn't bomb the rioters. The Mac-Paps were using the architecture of the city itself as their shield, the graceful dilapidation of the cemetery, the wide streets and the streetcar tracks that might be operational, one day, with a great deal of indentured labour and wishful thinking. So little of the world-that-had-been remained that the Dominion would hesitate before blasting it to pieces.

The inner suburbs, the ugly high-rises and strip malls that crosshatched the Exclusion Zones, the places fit for rats and demons and little else—that was another story.

Without Cal, the information copying to his USB was useless. He was useless. He couldn't protect Jakie, or Lucy, or the dying embers of resistance sparking on the winter-grey sidewalks 400 km away.

For whatever misguided reason, Lucy thought of him as something more than a human-shaped puddle of sludge and anxiety. He could sit with his churning conscience, and live, or he could do the other thing.

Eric sat down, and stood up again, at least four times. He must have looked suspicious. There were eyes on him at all times, from every angle. He pressed the soft, useless pad of a finger into the edge of the ID tag on his lanyard until the pain drew him to sharp alertness.

Maybe so many lives balancing upon the outcome of his choices was less a testament to his own failures of character than it was an unflinching barometer of just how *fucked* everything had gotten.

Goddamn it.

Eric stuffed the USB into his pocket. He yanked his coat off the rack and marched down the stairs, clearly in a hurry but not fleeing, never fleeing, just an important man with long strides and somewhere to be. A lunch meeting. A bit role in the theatre called Back to Normal.

He expected the shooting to start at any point down the corridor, in the endless descent of the elevator, at every jerk and shutter and ding for one floor after another. But, of course, if he were the murderous tool of a fascist government, he'd have probably waited until he reached the parking garage too.

"Mr. Greenglass." Always polite, respectful, as befitted someone who almost counted as one of their own. They'd be apologizing for barking his elbow as they shoved him into the back of a car with a bag over his head. A few hours ago, he probably could have gotten one of these men to bring him a coffee.

He squeezed his car keys, unlocked the door, backing away from the two slabs of Aryan übermensch. They wouldn't kill him right away. Reid would strip Eric for parts, squeeze out every bit of rumour and connection he might have, ensure that everyone he'd ever talked to was crushed just as thoroughly.

He wasn't Ian. No one was coming to rescue him.

"Just a sec," he said, and the show of civility was the split second he needed to throw open the door and slam it, brushing the fabric of one of the security guard's coat. It took an act of will to start the car through the shaking of his hands. This was how he was going to die, thrown into a ditch with the other degenerates with his hands tied behind his back, thirty-eight years old and having done exactly one good deed in his entire life.

He put the car in reverse and gunned the engine, backing into the second man, then swerved side to side, testing the Prius's ability to be an unstoppable force against the immovable object of the state's apparatus. He smashed through the barrier and kept driving. Better to die in a head-on collision with the garage door than get tortured to death by Reid's security. But it gave way, triggered automatically, and he was slammed, blinking, into the sunlight.

They were following him, radioing for backup, but they weren't shooting, that just happened in the movies, and he drove like a maniac. Why weren't there drones after him? It would have been easy to send drones.

"Call Dad," he told the console. It went to voicemail. "Get out of town." He sounded high-pitched and frantic even to his own ears. He could run, he could still turn north and find them, but no one was answering and they were probably dead already. "Things are going to explode if they haven't already, tell Mom, get Jakie, get *out*, please, just *trust me*."

His next call was to Jonah's latest burner phone. Jonah might have been an asshole, but miracle of miracles, he picked up. He could barely make out Jonah's voice from the screaming that surrounded him. Eric managed to squeeze out, "They're going to carpet bomb Scarborough," before the line went dead.

He tossed his phone out the window. They couldn't have started bombing. Five hours down the highway, if no one stopped him, if he got lucky, if he was unimportant enough. He could call a thousand times and neither of his parents would pick up. The snow was falling in earnest, turning the roads to a sea of grey slush. He faded into a sea of cars, all careening in the muck.

It was over. If his parents—if *Jakie*—ever had a chance, he'd doomed them with his stupid, desperate flight. But he'd been deluding himself if he'd ever thought they had a chance.

The tail lights in front of him were a sea of bloodshot, weary eyes. He turned the radio on, expecting to hear about a manhunt for him, but it was just another story about Yamashita's funeral, a brief mention that the riots were contained and its leaders identified.

He looked to see if they were following him. In the blinding white, one car looked the same as any other, tired commuters indistinguishable from state security forces. They might have tailed him all the way to Toronto.

But then again, why bother? He was driving himself into hell.

He could turn off the highway, head straight for his parents'. If they were still alive, he could force them into the car and keep driving until they hit Muskoka. He kept driving.

There were tanks on Eglinton, but as Eric pulled to the side the road was blocked off—he could see that they were abandoned. A barricade of detritus—felled trees, stray bricks—stood in between the vehicles and the crowds. He left the Prius and ran.

He shouldn't have been able to find anyone in the teeming waves of people holding the street. It was a crush of bodies, placards, banners, sandbags and wooden pallets. They had walled off the street, taken over the buildings, waved black flags from the top of bank buildings. It was loud and beautiful and absolutely *fucked*.

They were being *tolerated*. Meanwhile, Trenton's planes and drones must already be en route to Scarborough.

Jonah, when Eric miraculously found him, was predictably in the heart of it all, pistol held loosely in one hand and a cigarette in the other. Eric screamed out his name and he stubbed the cigarette, pulling his mask up.

"The fuck?"

"If they can't find the Mac-Paps they'll just flatten the neighbourhood. Maybe the whole thing. Wherever it is, wherever they're hiding—we need to warn them." There would be collateral, of course, shriekgrass spores spread from the Exclusion Zones to downtown, escaping containment. Reid didn't give a shit about any of it. Jonah was waving his phone in the air, trying to get a signal. How long would it take CFB Trenton to fuel up? However long it took, whatever roadblocks they met, it couldn't possibly be enough time for Jonah to get through to Fort Utopia, for anyone to organize an evacuation. All the wards in the world wouldn't keep out a drone strike.

Jonah hissed, "Where's your car? Is it still in one piece? Were you followed?"

"I—they must have..."

"Anyone gets too close, I'll shoot our way out. Come on." Eric pointed in the direction he'd come from and Jonah pushed his way through the crowd, Eric stumbling in his wake. By now, word had to have been spreading, and the street teetered on the precipice between occupation and riot. Some people insisted on holding the streets, others, convinced that the attack was coming for midtown, wanted to run for cover. A man screamed about his family trapped back in Scarborough.

Jonah, radiating waves of fury like a Silver Age comic villain, was unmoved by the panic they'd caused, fuelled by too much pure, visceral wrath to be contained within the mere cage of his skin. Reid had been frightening enough in his carefully worded death sentence. But Jonah had been wasted in the Broom Closet. The Dominion's brutality had granted him a sort of perverse, unchecked freedom. Eric suspected Jonah had always sort of *known* that a day would come when he would be called upon to visit epic violence on someone who richly deserved it. And, unlike Reid, he was the one standing next to Eric, gun in hand.

They reached the Prius. Eric unlocked the door from half a block away, lest Jonah tear the passenger door off its hinges. He drove, gunned the little engine as hard as it would go, drowning out the Greek chorus of possible scenarios. *What if someone jumps in front of the car? What if the assholes tailing me have guns? What if the battery fails? Are we really about to drive into an airstrike? What if the rioters tear us to pieces first?* Only the gear shift stood in the way of Eric being throttled by a rage-drunk madman. "Drive drive drive," as if Jonah could compel Eric's guilty white liberal-mobile to undergo some kind of magical-girl transformation into a fucking battle tank.

"Did you warn them?" Eric asked. "Did you get through?"

"Still trying." Jonah craned in his seat, unmoved by the car's pleas to fasten his seatbelt. He peeled off his mask, swiping a forearm over sweaty tangles of hair. He had the phone on speaker with nothing but dead air. Snow lashed the windshield, threatening hail. "They have to get out."

Somewhere above the thick onslaught of cloud cover, came the rumble of drones.

"Faster," Jonah said, unnecessarily. The car hydroplaned, veering in and out of the lane. The road was a river of sludge that tossed the car in its current.

They weren't going to make it. A better man wouldn't have felt relieved.

"Jonah—" he started.

"I know. Shut up, you absolute shitweasel. I'm trying to *think*." Jonah was *thinking* about jumping out of the car, right there on the highway, and booking it for Fort Utopia on foot, and Eric knew that because he was thinking it too.

The view ahead had gone white. Maybe the pilots wouldn't be able to see their targets and turn back, no matter how loudly the Defence Minister complained. He yelped as he barely missed swerving into the barrier on the exit ramp.

There was no one on the road. Why would there be? This was a sprawl built for cars at the best of times, let alone in a brewing snowstorm, let alone at the periphery of an Exclusion Zone. The high-rises were grim sentinels, the relics of a long-dead empire. Not a single window was lit. "Maybe they all left?" Eric managed.

Jonah's black eyes, reflected in the slate of the mirror, were devoid of emotion. "Where the fuck would they go?"

Hope would only make it worse, but he indulged himself by pretending that the rumble was getting quieter, farther away.

Through Jonah's tinny reception came Martine's voice, followed by Jonah barking orders at her like he was a general and not a human incendiary device.

And then Eric saw the fleet of drones as they dove, with the grace of synchronized swimmers, over the jagged roofline, spilling their black cargo against the white sky.

Oh, he thought. *That's where all the drones were.*

Eric slammed on the brakes and Jonah almost broke the door handle before he thought to unlock it, before he was staggering into the blizzard and the slush-drowned street. The wind's howl swallowed the whistle of the bombs, right up until the first of them cracked open the side of a tower.

Eric wrestled Jonah behind the Prius—as if the car would have been enough to shelter them—choking on ash and heat. The slick pavement buckled under them. Every window and cement slab shuddered and heaved and strained to break free of its moorings.

Jonah squirmed and screamed and thrashed in his arms, promised to tear Eric limb from limb if he didn't let go, until at last, as bursts of flame erupted from the buildings all around them, he clung boneless to the crumpled side of the car while the snow, impervious, fell all around them.

Book 3

The Maple Spring

This is a packed crowd, a very packed crowd. I haven't seen this many smiling faces since—

—Well, you understand. You were there too.

It can be hard to smile sometimes. I think of my wife, Elizabeth, who passed from cancer ten years ago. She was a proud mother, a doer, truly the head of the household. And I think to myself, how lucky I was to be able to mourn her, how lucky our daughter Miriam was to have a gravesite to visit. How the tragedies of these last few years have piled one on top of each other until none of us can mourn. The sacrifices that all of us have made. That *you* have made, hardworking Canadians, to achieve stability and safety in a world made volatile by magic. That we continue to make together, to secure a brighter future for our children.

—No, don't applaud for me. Give yourselves a round of applause.

There are, as always, naysayers. The worms eating a hollowness at the core of our country. Woke extremists who want to return to that chaos, to a country ruled by sorcerers and managed by degenerates, lurching from crisis to crisis.

I am here to tell you that we *will* maintain peace, order, and good government. Together, we will see these foreign-funded criminals in the streets put behind bars. We will enact common-sense measures to bring economic prosperity and moral decency.

I urge you to continue to do your part. To continue to work hard at your jobs, to obey the curfew, to cooperate with the authorities. Together, we will forge a better nation.

26

They were bickering like it was the early 2000s and nothing had real consequences when the call came. Maya, made of vapour and cobwebs, looked like some necromancer had managed to get a passable pulse going after several ill-fated lightning experiments. Gaby, as far as Ian could tell, was trying to get herself usurped, with all the aplomb of sin fucking a porcupine.

Felipe wanted to cripple the Dominion's cell network.

"They'll have it back operational in a week," Shadi argued. He was doing most of the talking as the representative of the faction that didn't require careful supervision when using scissors.

Gaby, resuming her role of reluctant Team-Mom-slash-project-manager, said. "Do we have the resources?"

"We would if we weren't wasting bullets." Anton shot a look at Felipe that he no doubt thought was withering.

"We wouldn't be wasting bullets if we had leadership who could prioritize objectives," Felipe replied.

Ian was tired of it. He'd bullied his way into the strategy meeting, appealing to Felipe's grossly inflated ego. He had, after all, extensive experience fucking up government infrastructure from both ends.

If he stopped talking, there remained the horrible possibility that someone might offer him sympathy in lieu of a viable course of action, and if that happened, he would have to unleash the Four Horsemen of Monumental Fuck on his own erstwhile allies. The sharp aches in his joints were made all the worse by a pressure front building across a sky that had been shrouded for days. "Where'd they put the mass graves?" he muttered, too quietly for anyone to respond. They'd killed so many people, they had to have put the corpses somewhere.

If Jonah were here, he'd have backup. But Jonah had appointed himself a general in the Maple Spring, proving to be just as much a festering wen on the ass of the Dominion as he'd been on Ian's. Without him, the politicking was glacial-slow, the best sniping amongst themselves while the worst ramped up their passionate intensity.

What was worse than *that* was that the Dominion was nearly as slow, its state apparatus even more lethargic than the bloated bureaucratic machinery they'd abolished in their crawl from the primordial muck of the *Post* to the Train.

In an even—if not fair, never fair—battle of politics, they wouldn't stand a chance against Ian. They had no right, no legitimacy. Even if they weren't torturers and murderers, they'd still have no place at all in a game like his. And yet there they were, the nation beaten into cowed submission beneath them, and the vast might of their military-industrial complex aimed straight at Jonah.

"We've taken the streets," Shadi said. "The Dominion hasn't been able to break through."

"It's not when the people takes the streets," Ian shot back, as if every block hadn't been painfully obtained with the blood of useful idiots. "It's when they stay there."

"And it's not when the army starts shooting," Felipe said, as if he had any idea, "but when the protest keeps going anyway. We need to claim the offensive. Keep them on their feet. Hence the towers."

"It's not the worst idea I have heard today," Gaby said, which meant that it fell to Ian to piss on everyone else's parade.

"And then what?" he asked. "They get the towers back up and running. And then they bombs the lord lamp lightin' fuck outta us. We're sittin' around with our dicks in our hands and nothing to show for it." Anton was nodding along as if he actually knew something, though Ian hadn't seen any evidence of that. His whole strategy had been tied up in the factories, and that had been a shitshow and a half. "You want to do propaganda by the deed, you gotta do the fuckin' deed."

He should have been focused on the next move, the way Felipe, for all his single-mindedness, had managed to be. Instead, he watched Maya flicker in and out, wondered, his chest tight for reasons beyond the scar tissue, where Jonah was sleeping at night.

The moment the Dominion moved in to clear the streets, the moment they made an example of Jonah and his ramshackle uprising, they'd make a production of it. They'd air it on state TV, blast it across the electronic billboards looming over the ruins of Sankofa Square.

Ian refused to imagine Jonah dead, Jonah still for more than thirty seconds. He'd know, the loss would be tangible in every parched, malnourished cell in his broken, crooked body, and that was the only reason he ever slept at night at all.

"I think what Ian is trying to say—" Felipe started, just as Martine smashed through the door, burner phone in hand, screaming that they needed to clear out, get everyone to the basement, because the bombs were coming any min—

.   .   .

For the longest time, the world was black and amorphous.

They must have blinded him. They'd been stripping pieces off him for years. Fingernails. Three teeth. The other thing, that he couldn't think about, the thing that had screamed and coiled and seared as they ripped it from his chest. Why *not blind him while they were at it?*

His eyes were there, intact, and the darkness blipped into deeper black as he pressed the lids down. Not blind. He found a bloody scrape just below his hairline. Staggered to his feet and crashed immediately into cold concrete that bled liquid, the walls oozing from a crack that ran along its length, a crack he knew by heart, the way he knew every inch of the cell by heart. The way he knew the lock wouldn't budge, the vent that had made a mockery of poor Tobias Fletcher in its intransigence. A foot farther and he'd bash over the bucket, not that it mattered, he already reeked of piss and vomit and blood—

—Not that he wasn't dying, had already died, buried somewhere no one would ever find him—

He ran a finger over the crevice, searching for the loose piece of concrete that lived there and pried it free and forced a breath past the nausea in his guts and the pain in his lungs.

He took the little piece of concrete and dragged it savagely across the wall. He couldn't see the mark it made but there was dust under his fingers and if he could make a mark, he could still affect the world, he was still in the world, he wasn't dead, and he fell to his knees, sobbing, scratched into the walls of the prison Ian Mallory was here.

The light as the door opened burned splinters into his eyes before he was slammed again into darkness and a hand closed around his wrist what the fuck are you doing *and the bit of rubble the last thing he had dropped from his fingers and* what do you think you are you little piece of shit you terrorist do you think you're allowed to write—

With the last of his strength he folded forward and smashed his elbow into the guard's balls.

Still, he didn't expect the blow until it came the crunch as the butt of the rifle pulverized bone over and over pain bright and sharp and something shrieked high and inhuman and it was him—

"Wake up, Ian," Gaby was saying.

In the movies, people returned to consciousness slowly, a merciful blur gradually coming into focus. Gaby's sharp features offered him no such on-ramp. The only light came from a crack in the ceiling several feet above her head, casting pointed shadows over her dusty cheeks and cracked lips.

His mouth was full of grit. It was everywhere, coating his skin; he tried to wipe at his face but managed only to deposit more dirt from his filthy hands.

"Oh good," she said, "you're alive," eliminating any possibility that he might just get to lie down and quietly expire.

Gaby was framed in crumpled rebar and frayed pink insulation. The basement ceiling had partially collapsed, bowing into a cave that, sitting up, his head barely cleared. She clutched at his wrist. A shock of pain arced up his arm, but at least it jolted him back into alertness and out of his prison cell. "Maya?"

She gestured at the pile of rubble behind her. "On the other side of that. She said she was going to find something to dig us out with." She was shaking, seconds away from going critical.

"The kids?"

"Safe." He remembered now—Martine rushing into the room with the walkie, the foot-high flaming letters warning everyone to get underground.

"How bad is it?" Ian asked, which was the only cue Gaby needed to start sobbing uncontrollably. "Sweet merciful fuckin' Jesus, keep it together, luh." He shook his wrist free of her grip. His bent bones whined in protest, but if he focused on the pain, he didn't think about how shitbaked he was, either.

Tears burrowed rivers through the dust on her face, collecting in the lines that he'd seen etch themselves deeper into her face over the years. "You don't need to be a prick about it. I'm claustrophobic, you know?"

He *did* know. There had been timelines where he'd been trapped in an elevator with her, or the office in a power failure, even timelines where it was Gaby, not Tobias, in the cell next to his. But in the spacious halls of the House, it had never seemed especially relevant.

"Yeah," he ground out. "That makes two of us. At least I have good reason to be."

Gaby wiped at her face with her sleeve and took a few shuddering breaths. Her eyes were still glassy, dripping, and she was watching him as if she'd exposed him, flayed flesh from bone and left him bleeding out his trauma on the concrete floor. It was a desperate ploy on his end, and under ordinary circumstances she'd have seen through it, but she was clearly too preoccupied with her own psychological and physical minefields to doubt his sincerity.

She sniffled, and edged closer to him.

"If you try to hug me, I'll bite you."

This, of all things, brought a shaky smile to her face, though it vanished just as quickly. "I fucked everything up," she said. "I sent those people out there—I practically *invited* them to bomb us."

"You didn't kill anyone, ducky."

"Didn't I?"

"Not unless you're a vastly better fifth column than I gives ya credit for."

Now the waterworks started again in earnest. She bent nearly in half, her narrow shoulder blades protruding from under her thin jersey. Her words squeezed out between hiccups. "They were right, all those journalists, all those years ago. I'm useless. Incompetent."

He could strangle her and then she'd have to stop crying, and even with two crippled hands and the lung capacity of a geriatric chain smoker, it probably wouldn't have been hard. Instead, in a hiss that had once turned ministers' bowels to liquid, he said, "You're the fuckin' *leader of the revolution*. Act like it."

"Felipe is gunning for my job."

Ian rolled his eyes towards the collapsed ceiling. "If Felipe was any good as a military leader, we wouldn't be here. But this isn't a military coup, b'y, it's asymmetrical warfare. If you get any troops he gets to lead them. If he's even still alive. You're the one that gets to bring back Medicare. The CBC. Whatever makes this sad sack sham of a country worth fighting for."

After a long string of ragged inhales and exhales, Gaby said, "And here I had you pegged as an incorrigible cynic." The tremble in her voice was muted now. His distraction was working.

"Why'd you think I ever did any of it? It wasn't to be loved." He jerked his head towards the scrabbling above them. "They're digging."

"Yeah." She wiped at her eyes again. "I hate just *sitting* here."

There wouldn't be any cameras to capture her hand breaking through the floor. But it had to be more than just Maya trying to get at them. Enough people to germinate a legend.

"Start digging," he said.

"With what?"

"Your hands, if you have to." He stared down at his own useless ones.

"It won't—"

"Of course it won't. But it's better than sittin' on them." Flinching in anticipation of the pain, swallowing past the dry desert of his throat, he gripped the edge of a chunk of concrete and pulled. Gaby moved in beside him, shoving at a piece of rubble nearly as big as her torso. Somehow, while he rotted away in a Dominion black site, she'd become something he'd never in a million futures have predicted for her—an actually decent politician. It was too late, it was always too late, but he was a little proud of her.

Well. Brick by fucking brick. The Sisyphusian task of moving one pile of ruins to a new pile went on forever, until—and it might have been a hallucination, the delusion of a dying mind—the first shards of light at last broke through.

· · ·

Ian emerged, caked in dust and asbestos fibres and coughing like a 19th century consumptive, into the watery afternoon sunlight. One face of the office tower had been sheared clean off by a bomb. The remaining structure had partially collapsed, wafting plumes of black, acrid smoke into the air. The parking garage, where he and the rest of Fort Utopia had sheltered, had been spared the worst of the damage, but he still saw Monique and Junior hauling something wrapped in a bloody drop sheet.

"Anton," Martine said. She stood, sallow, frowning, shovel in hand, then dropped it and rushed to Gaby, burying her face in against her mother's collarbone like a little child. Ian allowed them their reunion and went in search of Maya.

He found her with Shadi, digging out the remains of his gear and hauling anything that could be salvaged into the back of a pickup truck. She shuddered at his approach, the way everyone warded or MAI did. She had risked life, limb, and, worst of all, reputation to rescue him, and now his very presence repelled her. Still, disappointment was a privilege for people who didn't have revolutions to salvage.

After her initial flinch, she whispered something to Shadi and then picked her way over a landscape that had been lifted and crushed in a giant's fist. She brushed dust off the edge of a slab of concrete—as if that would make a difference—and sat down. She had been older in his memory, during long stretches in his cell when he replayed their card games, listened to her deranged *Night Beats* fan theories. As if he'd constructed the adult she'd never gotten to be, instead of the little girl playing soldier in front of him.

"You'd better not tell me I should have seen it coming," Maya said. "I've never been as good at prognostication as you were."

"*Gaby* saw it comin', ducky. They were always after glassing the opposition, whether we gave them a pretext or not." Scattered groups of Mac-Paps cleared rubble, and he was as pointless as a knitted condom, not even fit for grunt work, let alone to shield Gaby from the massive Aegis missile Felipe had aimed at her back. "At least we gave 'em a bloody nose before they bashed our balls in."

And poor Maya, gathering up the fragments of herself in her oversized army coat, still trying to disguise the degree to which she was fading away. She was a tough girl, though, and she wouldn't cry, not in front of the rebels still digging their comrades out from under a pancaked strip mall.

"Did you ever look backwards?" she asked. "I know you can't *go* backwards, that would fray the fabric of reality itself, I get that, but did you ever just look? At all the other possibilities?"

"Isn't the future maddening enough without all that?" He swatted at the rubber duck in her pocket. "You should help them."

"Me?"

"You're a fuckin' charmer, b'y. Go do some magic."

He might as well have asked her to throw herself on the revolution's smoldering pyre. "Oh," she said. "Yeah. Right. Fuck." She clenched her hand around the duck and squeezed.

Ian took a few steps back, gave her the space to mass the fronds of pale green around herself. The magic, where it sparked by him, hissed and extinguished. Maya raised an eyebrow, but kept vibrating, stuttering in and out with the rhythm of the Pattern.

Around her, the slabs of broken concrete shifted and split, a time-lapse of petals blooming and falling away. Here, a piece of sheet metal curled up to reveal an empty shoe, there, a shard of roof melted to release part of a solar still.

There were no miracles, no child curled alive under the ruins, no rescuers reunited with loved ones feared dead. But people stopped, watched in awe at Maya, the grimy fighter compelling the universe to dig them out. If there was any hope in it, Ian couldn't tell.

And then, after an eternity, Jonah emerged from drifting smoke as if Maya had summoned him, like one of the futures he'd never allowed to happen.

He was shrouded in ash that cracked around his mouth where he'd spoken or screamed, around the eyes where he'd wept. Nearly as spectral as Ian himself, but alive.

Jonah didn't run to him. Ian didn't collapse, exhausted, at his feet, despite having more justification than in anyone in the course of human history for doing so. It was enough that they could see each other over a sea of destruction, exchange an acknowledgment that *not now*, meant, unambiguously, *later*.

Jonah hiked his rifle over one shoulder and grabbed one of the bags to join the long procession of the walking dead. Ian watched him disappear behind the ruins of the gas station. He got up to follow, pausing only to give Maya the hug he'd wanted to give Jonah.

•   •   •

"We need to get back out there," Gaby said. They had sheltered in what had been an arena. If they were lucky, the Dominion would assume they'd killed everyone. "They've hit more areas than just us. There will be scared, desperate people looking for help."

"We can barely feed ourselves." Felipe's survival, amid so many dead, would never not be a disappointment. "Let alone rescue civilians."

The worst of it was that he wasn't wrong. They could rush out and look for survivors, and the snipers would be waiting, the drones, and the Dominion would rain more death on them all.

"It's optics," Ian replied. "All those b'ys occupying the streets downtown. They can give up or they can get pissed."

"Fuck this," Jonah said. "I'm going back out."

"Jonah," Gaby said. Jonah hadn't bothered to change his grubby clothes since appearing in the midst of the evacuation. He ignored her, grabbed his rifle from where it rested against the wall, and stormed out.

She turned to Ian in a silent plea.

"He's going to make it worse."

"No shit. I'll deal."

He caught up with Jonah by a ransacked pair of vending machines and hauled him, with a strength that no one would ever have suspected an angishore like him of possessing, into what had been a storage room.

"So?" Jonah put the rifle with surprising delicacy against the shelf, then rose, slowly, to face him.

"We needs an organized resistance, not a rory-eyed gommel making a last stand."

"Stop me," Jonah said.

There was no space in the storage room—a literal broom closet, and the irony didn't escape him—and he was close enough that he could smell the nicotine on Jonah's breath. Melted snow leaked in a steady drip from a sagging gap in the wall to plink off his shoulder, but he didn't seem to notice. "Eric says that Reid Curtis knows who you are. He's gunning for you. We're doing it your way, I promised, but you stay here, luh?"

Jonah said nothing for a long time. He watched Ian steadily. It was too dark to make out much beyond the whites of his eyes, but Ian was used to navigating shadows. "Are you done?"

"Not even warmed up, b'y."

"Good." Jonah was cornering him, to the extent that someone the size of an average domestic housecat was capable of cornering anyone. Ian took a step backwards, then yelped—there was a bulletin board riddled with pushpins behind him. He was scrambling around for a light switch when Jonah's face smashed into his own.

It wasn't anything that could be called a kiss. It was too clumsy, too feral and desperate, Jonah's mouth sour and his breath hot and ragged. His bitten fingernails found Ian's wrists and scraped a line down his skin just short of pain. He would have asphyxiated them both if Ian hadn't—with more reluctance than he'd ever admit to—shoved him off.

"What the fuck is wrong with you, b'y?"

"Thought you were dead under a pile of rubble, asshole. *Again.*"

"And you chose to celebrate this by gnawing my face off? Where'd you even learn to kiss, the Franklin expedition?"

Jonah responded with a lunge that just missed, catching the side of Ian's jaw instead; undeterred, he trailed a wet path along his neck. Ian shivered, reached for the mud-stiffened sleeve of Jonah's coat before the shock of pain reminded him not to reach for anything, for anyone.

"You're not even my type," he added.

"I'm *exactly* your type," Jonah replied, sliding a hand over Ian's bony hip. He hadn't been able to find a pair of pants that came close to fitting his emaciated frame; Jonah's palm slid easily under the belt that barely held them up. "You've wanted me for twenty years."

A strangled noise fought to get past his lips. Even if it wasn't true—and he wouldn't insult Jonah by denying it—three years of torture and isolation and the war raging outside and the general fuckery of a planet on fire would have broken anyone down.

And it was Jonah, grief-mad and deadly and the last beautiful thing in the desecrated ruins of the world, twitching like a live wire in his arms. Every joint in Ian's body had rusted stiff, but he managed to regain control of his spasming hand and lift Jonah's chin.

"Stupid cunt," he said, not without affection. "You've gots some timing on ya."

Jonah laughed. The cloud of his breath, thick with nicotine, should have been disgusting, not intoxicating. "Guess I do. Are we gonna dance around it or do I bend you over that shelf, pin you down, and fuck you into next week?"

Ian flinched. He recovered almost immediately, but Jonah, with one hand cupped around his balls and the other gripped around the back of his neck, Jonah who possessed the unerring instincts of a drug-sniffing dog when it came to other people's damage, definitely noticed.

"Ian." Jonah sounded dangerously like a man who'd gotten the wrong impression. And Ian would surrender to Director Atherton himself before he'd let Jonah—who had lost so much more than his hands, than his magic—pity him.

Ian traced, through the layers of fabric, the place on Jonah's shoulder where he'd tattooed a ward. It should have reacted to his presence, called out to him, but the link wasn't there. Only the anchor of twenty wasted years.

"Pin me down, b'y, *ever*, there's gonna be two smacks. Me hittin' you, you hittin' the ground." He bent down to kiss Jonah—properly, one of them wasn't a repressed Catholic closet case—and added, "The rest of it though."

Jonah, having taken more initiative than he'd ever managed in months working for the government, stared at him, stunned, so Ian maneuvered them both as far away from the rifle as possible in the tiny space and flipped over what he thought was probably an empty bucket. He'd fucked in some fousty places in his misspent youth but whatever Jonah thought was going to happen was severely limited by logistics.

This was no deterrent. Jonah pushed him down onto the bucket and sank to his knees in front of him on the filthy concrete floor. "You're the worst Catholic," he muttered, before Jonah's mouth closed over him and he forgot, momentarily, how to form words at all. He threaded his fingers through Jonah's too-short black hair, the sizzle of pain up his bones the only reminder that this wasn't some tendril of future possibility that he could cut short before it bloomed and fucked over both of them forever.

There was a war outside—there were *people* outside, people who depended on both of them—and he willed himself not to cry out, not to gasp or beg or flatter, even with Jonah determined to suck out his soul through his dick. He watched, vision settling into the darkness, Jonah wipe his lips clean with the back of his hand and grin. Fucking *repulsive*.

Jonah bent his head against Ian's knee, a penitent in confession. His breath was a whisper over Ian's skin. "You gonna return the favour?"

Ian's beleaguered libido was eager to do anything Jonah asked of him, but his brain wasn't about to give in. Gaby wanted Jonah out of the fighting, cooling his heels until they could work out a strategy more efficient than senseless flailing and violence. If a distraction was what it took...

He yanked up his pants, tightening the belt as best he could with his uncooperative fingers. "Nah. Not today."

Jonah scrambled up after him. "Fucking prick."

He leaned over and kissed Jonah fiercely on the mouth. "Guess you'll have to stick around for a bit."

"Ian—"

Cheerfully, Ian said, "We have a dictatorship to overthrow, Joe."

Jonah's spluttering protest followed him all the way down the corridor.

27

The ocean remembered every wound humanity had dealt it. Every oil spill, every drilling rig, every coral die-off and plastic island and acid strangulation. It howled its fury at Blythe through the cage of the submarine. Barely human herself, she was in no place to beg forgiveness for the sins of her species.

Her veins pumped seawater towards a heart of branching coral. Her bones were a shipwreck. Women contained oceans. She chided herself for gender essentialism. All humans contained oceans, water and salt, ancient aquatic memory encoded in their DNA. But she had carried Laura in water, gave birth to her in a flood so unlike the one that had killed her.

When she'd successfully defended her thesis her mother had straightened her sash and called her a water protector. Her face, pressed to Blythe's shoulder, was damp and smelled like the sea.

She hadn't meant it like *this*.

Blythe didn't know the first thing about piloting a sub, let alone an over-engineered SVAR monstrosity like the *Retribution*. She wandered the corridors, counted the bunks in the crew quarters. It must have taken dozens of men to crew the ship, working in shifts and sleeping too little. Not one grief-ravaged scientist alone and starving.

The ship's nuclear nervous system propelled it with an autopilot she was mostly sure its designers had not intended. It moved in a cloud of black ink, dancing with the ocean's current. She was afforded only the occasional glimpse through the periscope between bursts of greasy darkness.

How long had it waited for her on the sea bed? Capable of its own movement, its own will, what the *fuck* could it possibly need her for?

The ship drifted, suspended, a sleek shark in the blackest layer of ocean. She would not have presumed to guide it. There was a manual for each instrument, each of its deadly functions, and even if she memorized them all, one person could not have run from one control to the next, operating a complex system designed for a team of skilled sailors. It was Blythe who was a tool of the ship. It wanted something from her. It sought a mind, a spirit, a consciousness whose will and desires aligned with its own in whatever five-dimensional game of chess it was playing.

Without the ability to steer, she found a bunk that was empty of corpses or black fungal growth and lay on it, arms crossed over her chest. A woman whose life had shrunk to nothing, in a coffin within a coffin. There was a little reading lamp, and a built-in shelf. The dead sailor had few personal effects—no photos of his family, no tattered paperback, not even a pinup girl taped to the wall. Just a slick device that was password protected and looked like it belonged to some divergent sci-fi future where human ingenuity had triumphed over magic's raw chaos.

With the lid folded over her and the light switched off, she could make out only the faintest of forms. The slopes of the bunk were edged in a silvery-blue sheen, a nautilus outline that branched into fine dendrites before falling into shadow. Designed by an engineering genius, no doubt, to optimize space or productivity or anything other than the comfortable sleep of a human being. Still, she had been running on fumes for weeks.

In her first dream, Mitch laid out the budget for the upcoming quarter. It was a cruelty of her unconscious mind that, miles from anywhere in the grip of a haunted murder-submarine, she would still dream of sitting in a meeting with him. Edgar was wearing an old dress shirt, the one he'd worn to department meetings when they'd still had a department, now fraying at the elbow, and he had shrunk inside of it into something small and vulnerable. She reached for Edgar's shoulder, but her hand exploded like a soap bubble.

Further in, the images grew hazier. Her mother was a curving beam of cigarette ash in her wheelchair. Tiny children, none bigger than a pop can, crowded around her base and begged for the grey flakes that shook themselves free of her body.

Jonah was shining, bright veins of light that burst golden through his skin, and he was scrambling to cover the eruption with a tattered mummer's mask. From behind him, a hole shaped like a man moved with feline grace and spread its arms wide. Blythe screamed at Jonah to run, but he only turned to embrace the figure, tiny pieces flitting loose from his skin to be swallowed by its darkness.

She clawed up through water dense as the core of a star, towards the surface she could see in scattered dapples above her, but the dream, the ship's great consciousness, that construct of ruin and bones, pushed her deeper. Water filled her lungs. Her fingers grew webs, her skin paled and sprouted gills. Though her gills did well enough, she cried out for oxygen.

At the very bottom of the well, penetrated only by cold, distant stars that floated in the dark like specks of dust, there was a teenaged girl cowering in the void. Her black hair was hacked into a rigid bob and she was dressed in a blouse made of some stiff fabric and a skirt that bunched around her skinny knees. She cast no shadow. Her finger tapped on the divots between two knuckles in a rhythm that Blythe should have recognized. A song, maybe, from her childhood. The girl was crying and her thin shoulders trembled.

The sticky black striations of the ship's mind slid over her, found ingress in the corners of her eyes, her half-opened mouth. They rolled maple-sweet, with an undercurrent of salt, over her tongue. They travelled the blurring lines of her ward tattoo, lighting it up with warmth that was more welcome than feverish.

Even now, her mind tethered to it, she couldn't fathom what it wanted from her. Only that it wanted.

Blythe pushed against the dream's membrane, towards the girl, but every time she opened her mouth, more water flooded in. She called the girl's name, she knew her name, had been the first to utter that name into the seashell of the girl's ear, but her words were swallowed whole by the ocean.

And still, the girl moved. Her fingers twisted the folds of her skirt in a death grip, and she lifted her head, turned, excruciatingly slowly, towards Blythe, and there was something there beneath the black curtain of her hair, a horrifying blank, the mandibles of an arthropod, the hollowed out face of a dead girl beseeching her with weeping eyes. Blythe whipped her face away.

Her eyelids snapped open to the coffin's lid, stripped of the glowing labyrinth. "Hello?" she managed. Unimaginative, really, though there was a chance the ship actually *would* respond to voice commands if any of the SVAR programming was left uncorrupted by magic. The syllables echoed as they should have. She was breathing air; when she held up her hands, they were pale and blurry and material in a way that the dream hadn't been.

"You could just tell me what you want," she said, sliding open the lid. "You don't need to be *cruel*." Her joints ached. The space had been calculated for an average-sized man, and a scrawny woman should have fit in it comfortably, but she'd twisted her limbs into pretzel configurations and everything was either numb or hurt. She limped for the control room, the dead muttering from the walls in mockery.

The sub had risen while she'd slept. They were nearing shore.

The far-flung islands of the archipelago, some drowned, others reshaped, stood sentinel at their approach. She studied each one in detail. They had changed, bent and reshaped by storm and tide. Each erosion was a personal betrayal. She had left this place, repeatedly, and each time she had returned, her home had put on a new face.

She observed, coolly, as if she was a guide leading the cursed ship on a tourist cruise through the archipelago. *This is the territory of the Orcinus orca, the largest species of oceanic dolphin. It is known by many names: kakaw'in in Nuu-chah-nulth, sgáan in Haida, kéet in Tlingit, q̓ałtáləmačən in Lkwungen.* She reached for the Michif word. *Enn balayn, for whale. L'ork, from the French orques. Today, they are threatened by habitat destruction, prey depletion, persistent organic pollutants, the creature buried beneath the ocean floor that knows neither age nor entropy, that waits patiently for its cage to crack, for its time to arrive …*

Crouching off the truncated stub of the old naval base, suspended in the sickly green of the periscope's lens, was the massive SVAR seastead.

Blythe shut her eyes, the steel of the console undulating under her palms. Something feather-light brushed over her knuckles, a gesture she might have, under other circumstances, found comforting.

"You don't need me," she told the *Retribution*. "You can move on your own. You can murder people on your own. I don't need to see the fucking *massacre*." As if it would distinguish between their occupiers and the civilians who laboured inside a prison made of spreadsheets and stock options.

She looked anyway. She had never been so close before. The humped, Frankenstein behemoth was smaller than the privateering seastead that had attacked the *Empress Willow* and dragged Laura down in its death throes. It still dwarfed the *Retribution*, an array of cannons sprouting from its sides, the yellow-and-black hoisted proudly above its blocky silhouette. It was about half a kilometre out from what remained of Fisherman's Wharf, a distorted funhouse mirror of the tall ships dead in the sea like placid, doomed livestock.

She waited for her little black-haired daughter to drift past the circle, hair fanned out like she was swimming in the lake and not water-bloated and blue with seaweed choking her tongue. She waited for closure. She was not so naïve as to believe that the creature had brought her here for a reason, that alone of all humans it had chosen to spare her, to sing to her. She had a ward, an ouroboros that simultaneously protected her from whatever future that Ian had seen for her and served as a siren song to lure that future towards her. Its logic was not a puzzle to be solved with sufficient application of the scientific method. Maybe her suffering was reason enough.

Why would it have made it so that Laura was alive, even in a dream, even for one aching moment?

The *Retribution* dove lower, close enough to the seastead's cruel machinery that she could make out rivets on its hull through the blur of her own ship's motion. It speared through the water, veering away from the harbour through the maze of half-sunken islands, the drowning ferries, towards the shelter of a cove carved out of what had once been Beacon Hill Park.

The *Retribution*'s breach was violent and jarring, a loud jerk upwards as it broke the surface, a splash of seawater that felt like a scream. She lurched as the ship rocked to right itself and scrambled for the hatch to the outer hull.

Her last shred of self-preservation instinct warned her to stay below deck, where at least, some day far in the future, they'd be able to find and identify her body. She pushed through the hatch anyway.

Waves sloshed at the *Retribution*'s flanks, washing over the narrow space where Blythe crouched. The wind whipped over the frozen expanse of ocean, lashing at her damp cheeks. She clutched the railing.

Beyond the thrashing of the waves and the distant cry of gulls over the white crests, the shore was quiet. Above the steep wall of algae-stained cliffside, the highway was bowled in, the hotels and upscale apartments with their spectacular view collapsed under snowdrifts. A triad of gulls swirled, specks of white flitting in and out of the sullen clouds. She waved her arms but they barely regarded her. She had ceased to be a person, a part of the natural environment. The uncorrupted birds —too low in body mass to become demons—rejected her very presence.

Blythe straightened, shifting her balance as the boat swayed beneath her feet. She was unsteady, but the black film that stretched over the ship was tacky and clung to her boots, keeping her upright. The ocean recoiled from the *Retribution*'s oily hull, eddying and heaving in its wake as it drifted, slow and inevitable, for the docks.

The beach was empty, save for a few rotting fishing boats that butted like faithful dogs against the pier. She saw no trace of the men who had risked their lives to get her out to sea. Any footprints would be indistinguishable from the snow-dusted ridges and valleys of the pebbled shore. Though the shore looked abandoned, the occupiers had left their mark. A SVAR drone, broken from its patrol, skittered over the rocks before making its jerky flight back towards the city.

She ignored it. They couldn't kill her in any way that mattered.

The *Retribution* came to a dead stop a few feet from the edge of the dock. Blythe braced herself against the railing and slowly, shaking, climbed over it and jumped the gap to the pier.

She paused to look back at the ship. Her eyes couldn't take in the full enormity of it at a glance; they kept moving in and out of focus. The spill of light over its side suggested something smooth, but if she focused on a fin or the seam of the hatch, each detail contained fractal multitudes.

Blythe shuddered and pulled the sleeves of her parka past her hands. The ground was pockmarked with muddy craters, already filling in with snow. She slipped and stumbled up the hill and ran for the city. She dripped seawater behind her, a long liquid trail that sprouted black branches from the earth as she fled across it. The ocean seethed, shadowing her footsteps. The air, clean and crisp after the fetid swamp of the sub, was a thousand tiny knives in her lungs.

She had Rip Van Winkled herself into a dead world. Even in a superwinter, even in an occupation, the downtown should have been bustling in the afternoon. There would have been shriekgrass patrols, couriers dashing through the broken streets on bicycles, risking their lives for a few dollars and a rare cell phone, there would have been sallow, starving people crawling out of their tents with hands outstretched towards her. The city, crawling over its own rotting corpse.

Instead, only a handful of private security forces milled around the boarded-up buildings. More of the downtown had receded into the water, the bridges and walkways thin sutures knitting together the bleeding earth. The SVAR had conquered and subdued the archipelago, but no amount of techno-optimism would let them hold it.

It wasn't spore season, but she checked anyway. A few blades of shriekgrass, frost-dusted, squeezed through the ice, but the blackened swathes of ash meant a patrol had come through. A bloom hadn't carried off the population into madness. There were lights, electricity. It was a more human-made premonition that kept everyone inside.

The Last Call was boarded-up, with a heavy padlock on the door. Her frozen knuckles barely made a sound when she rapped on it, the sound squeezed from the air along with the street life. Around the back, though, the trap door to the cellar still opened to her knock.

Kenny rushed into her arms with a soft, solid thud, before her eyes adjusted to the lone candle's light. It took Blythe a second to remember that her arms could move, could bend at the elbows and wrists to enfold him, that each of her limbs existed as both part of herself and separate from the *Retribution*'s heaving consciousness. There was a scent to him, something earthy and human and, at first, as alien as the words that sat half-formed on her tongue.

Someone coughed. He wasn't alone; there were a dozen or so people crowded into the basement, Bailey, Edgar, the two ex-grad students, Kitty and Omid. One of the fishermen who'd helped tow the *Love Craft* from the shore. A few regular drunks and a few regular troublemakers, some of them the same individuals.

"There's a storm coming," Edgar said.

"Literal or metaphorical?" Blythe found the limits of the room in the thin slats of light leaking from the gaps in the trapdoor. The fermentation buckets and kegs and carefully hoarded bottles of wine that lined the far wall, the old milk crates stacked and lashed together for shelving, the friends and strangers gathered on the floor, cleaning and loading their meagre supply of pistols.

"Maybe both." Kenny broke away from her, watched her a little too long, a little too skeptically. A ward would have lit up at her presence now, at the ropes of black ink that wove over her. Human and untouched by magic, he only watched her with a lover's wistfulness, knowing that he had already lost her. "There's intel from the Mac-Paps. It could be old—I don't even know how they managed to get it this far. But there's a whole mess of stuff. They wanted you to look at it."

He had a laptop pillaged from the university, which she dutifully bent over. The encryption was trivial. One of the students had been working on them for days, but the documents were inscrutable. There was a business case for a trade agreement between the Dominion and the SVAR, the suggestion that they might carve up the West Coast between them. Nothing that the glowing shard in the control room hadn't led her to conclude, sickeningly, on her own.

But it didn't end there. There were massive shipments of tech pouring into Toronto from the SVAR via an intermediary in the Free States. Lead-lined containers of raw magic drawn from wellsprings in Alberta. Prisoners, from everywhere. It was all headed for the Rogers Centre—her brain still wanted to call it the Skydome—under the direct supervision of Reid Curtis. She couldn't fathom what a man who'd built his reputation buying up local media outlets for a right-wing propaganda machine would want with any of it, beyond that it had to be something like the sub, a high-tech weapon powered by unimaginable magic.

"We have to warn them," she said, after she'd explained. "Whatever revolution they're planning, this thing will devour it. It'll make what happened to Parliament look like Disneyland."

The kids were on it immediately, securing a channel out. Blythe kept reading. There were more files, after the project they kept calling *Egregore*, and at first she thought that Omid had just given up decrypting it until the text jittered and glitched before her eyes. It wasn't a standard encryption. Magic had touched it, corrupted it so thoroughly that she slammed the laptop shut, afraid it might brick the hard drive.

Kenny squeezed her arm. She slid away from him. Her skin was liquid over muscle and bone. She would slip into the floor, leech into the cement searching for a subterranean current that led to the sea. When she looked down, her hands were still there, with the same number of digits, the bargain neither struck nor official.

The part of her heart that was still muscle and blood thrashed in her chest. There wasn't the capacity to take out a fraction of the occupier's drone fleet, let alone drive them off the archipelago. There was barely enough for the would-be revolutionaries to ensure themselves a dignified death.

Edgar could be decisive in department meetings, but he was too much of a scientist to not admit when he was out of his depth. "You know the mountain passes. Your mother has Iron Alliance contacts."

She had never stopped running, not in three years, not since well before the Blight, when the bars of her marriage had broken open, when her hometown had been too small to keep her. They'd last longer out in the bush—she had her defences against demons.

But she was so tired. Just as in the first bloody conquest of Turtle Island, there was nowhere so remote that would escape the occupiers' notice, or their hunger.

"Does anyone here want to run?" she asked.

In the cellar's darkness, Edgar was a crooked, whittled knight-errant who'd foregone sleep and food in favour of tilting at some new windmill. "We can't take the labs with us. No antibiotics, no insulin—we would just be more mouths for the Iron Alliance to feed. If the demons didn't get us first."

The archipelago was full of refugees from the Dominion who'd been smart enough to stay put when they reached the edge of the world. People who hadn't thrown their children into the ocean's maw. "I don't think anyone can run anymore," Kenny said. "And there's more news from the Mac-Paps. They say they're holding parts of Toronto. So people want to fight."

Blythe felt like she'd been fighting her entire life. It was everything she could do to not just collapse on the bare concrete floor with the dirt and the pillbugs. "So," she said. "I have something to show you."

28

There was nothing left of the neighbourhood. Jonah had thought the block around the safe house, with its crumpled office towers, had been the worst of it, but that sight didn't prepare him for the endless stretch of grey, a thick, omnipresent haze that turned the night into perpetual twilight, dust that got into his respirator and eyes and lungs despite the seal.

It was a city of ash, a ghost city, populated by charred corpses and eyeless high-rises. Nothing moved; a strong breeze would have swept the towers into dust in its wake. There had been no precision to the bombing—not that Jonah expected the Dominion to live up to its own hype—just an endless stretch of destruction. Why should the drones have targeted Fort Utopia specifically when they could carpet-bomb everything east of Vic Park?

They moved haltingly. Every dash from the cover of one crumbling city block to the next was run with a prayer caught in his throat. The straggling convoy of cars and trucks, straining under the weight of everything they'd managed to salvage from Fort Utopia, kept being blocked by the craters left by the strikes. The same low-lying cloud cover that concealed them from the Dominion's watchful eyes made it impossible to spot anything else up there gunning for survivors. Maya's veil hovered above them, washed out by the dust, the green of the ward faded to almost nothing. The spell was a bright nervous system that sat parallel to the road and branched out in spirals and thin canals, arcing a kilometre over the procession.

No one spoke. Jonah stayed on the periphery of their band, farthest from the core where they covered the weakest, the children and the injured. By all rights, Ian should have been among them, but he insisted on being in Jonah's line of sight at all times. He might have been yet another wisp of smoke. But they were all grey, cocooned in fine particles of soot. Martine straggled behind him, but even her usual stream of invective was muted, as if sound, like colour, had been burned out of the world.

The heat still lingered, shuddering where it met the freezing air and collecting above the broken pavement. Fires dotted the rubble; survivors huddled among them, moving like hants through the shroud of dust. Sometimes, they were close enough that someone could duck out from under the mantle and pull them in, to relative safety, but they saved few people that way. Most were too far away, or too shellshocked, to join the staggering procession.

An hour into their evacuation, one of the trucks broke down, and then Shadi broke down, falling to his knees. He tugged at a slab of upturned concrete, first deliberately, then with desperation, his arms too skinny to pry its weight loose. Jonah caught himself moving forward—had Shadi heard someone cry out from under the debris? Thick streaks of blood striped through the dust and stained his cracked hands. Jonah was ready to help him when Maya abruptly stopped, her ward faltering, and ran to his side.

"There's no one under there," she said, and he wept. Jonah didn't know him, barely knew this pale copy of Maya. He stood over them both, pistol at the ready, guarding the shameful display from bombs and prying eyes.

Shadi and Maya were both soldiers now, as heavily fortified as any of Felipe's men. Shadi trembled for long minutes, then straightened, held upright by one of Maya's arms, and brushed ash from his coat and jeans. Maya, for her part, flickered like a dying fluorescent bulb. Jonah pushed down the cruel impulse to compare suffering—this was their neighbourhood in ruins, their pasts threatening to burst free from the gouges the bombs had carved in the pavement.

"I miss my Teta," Shadi said quietly, and moved what he could from the back of the dead truck onto one of the others. People swarmed to scavenge it, siphon gas and free batteries and arm themselves with scraps of metal.

Jonah exchanged glances with Ian. It was too cold for much conversation. The respirator muffled his speech, and lifting it invited ice crystals into his lungs. Even with its protection, his nose hair was freezing together, his eyes frozen at the corners. If the bombs had fallen silent, it was because the Dominion hadn't expected anything to survive out here. Fuckers, all of them, and Ian most of all.

The factories that Maya had tried to organize into a revolt had been spared the worst of the bombardment. A small crowd had gathered—some of the workers, who Maya and Lucy ran to talk to—and the usual band of grifters and vultures that swooped down in the wake of any disaster, promising bottled water and ration cards and DEC and sparkling magical unicorns. They had salvaged what they could from the collapsed buildings, piles of junk, old tables and mirrors and melted plastic chairs, musty yellow books for fuel, the spoils of the old world laid bare in their useless impotence, all the shit they'd burned the planet for sat in useless old garbage bags in the dust.

"Passes! Passes! Dominion sealed, guaranteed to hold up under inspection!" Maya had let the mantle slide enough to admit newcomers and they came rushing, the bereft and predatory alike.

"Tickets to Mexico." Another man grabbed at Jonah's arm, pinch-faced and sallow. "Hey. You're dark enough to pass." He waved papers that might have resembled train tickets to someone too young to remember train rides. Jonah brushed him off. There was about as much chance of getting to Mexico as getting to the moon, and from everything he'd heard, it was as much a wasteland there as anywhere else.

"Fuck all the way off," Ian told the guy, inserting himself between Jonah and the interloper. Foolishly mistaking it for affection, or even just basic human kindness, Jonah reached for him, but he was swatted away with just as little regard as Ian caught up with Maya. It couldn't just be Maya left on her own, holding up all of them, carrying the entire doomed revolution on her back. Now it was Shadi holding her up, forcing her to keep moving, Martine moving in with a second pulsing ward to cover Maya's failures.

"We need to keep going," Shadi said, whatever anguish he'd pulled out earlier now neatly folded and locked away. "Stay on the road."

Like everything else, the road had fallen to ruin in patches, crumbling and pierced through with shriekgrass, a hunched spines exposed beneath drifts of snow. Felipe, ahead of them, called out to watch for downed power lines and debris. Where the snow had melted in the flames and trickled in runoff through the streets, it had turned into root systems of ice that caught the boots of the people trying to flee.

They weren't going to make it. Jonah scanned the crowd, swelling in number as refugees limped out from sagging buildings. Between the dust and blood and the shrouds of blankets and old coats it was hard to tell young from old, who was injured and who was likely to reach the relative safety of downtown in one piece. Too many children, he thought, not just Martine and little Junior, who he watched for signs of faltering, but smaller ones still, toddlers and babies carried in flagging arms. It was nearly a full day's walk to the closest Mac-Pap held region of the downtown, and the wind tore at their faces.

And there was Ian, who had looked nearly dead when he'd crawled out of a bombed-out office tower, had looked like that before the bombing, before even the large-scale clusterfucking of the world they'd known. Ian, who had made Jonah kill for him, who had wielded him as a weapon against the world, who not hours ago had, after twenty years of Machiavellian cruelties, at last involved him in a sin worth burning for.

So he had to keep moving, because the second he didn't, it all fell apart and Martine was dead and Maya was dead and Ian was dead, and his heart was a smoking ruin but he was too weak a man to relinquish its beat. His feet were solid blocks of ice in his boots and the cold crept up his legs, stiffened the denim to his skin. He trudged forward, racing nightfall.

. . .

The Bloor Viaduct had stood for a hundred years, weathered the shifts and sighs of the earth as it aged and eroded. Only the shuddering aftershock of the Blight was enough to undermine the structure. The bridge hadn't collapsed, but it sagged in sections, vertebrae shattered, dragging its dying corpse across the steep face of the Don River Valley. The river itself had dried to a trickle, a thin rope of ice that wove between the rocks and disappeared into tangled, overgrown forest.

They'd followed the road until it became impassable, a thick seam of wellspring energy lanced with shriekgrass, and had to walk single file across the thinnest point, carrying the children over it. The vehicles wouldn't make it, and he watched Maya and Martine lace wards over them while the drivers parked them sideways to block off the road.

Below the lattice of steel arches and crumbling concrete columns was a tiny city of blue tarp and oil drum fires. Jonah didn't see it, not right away. Instead, an absence like the squeal of feedback from a microphone alerted him that something should be there. His ward tattoo burned, and he turned his head to look at it sideways, narrowed his eyes so that the valley was in the periphery of his vision. The spell draped over the tents, echoing the Luminous Veil at the top of the bridge that had once redirected would-be suicides to a less public location.

"Did you do this?" he asked Maya.

She nodded. "Ages ago. I can't believe it's still holding."

Now that he was aware of it, and of the midnight scavengers shuffling between tents with flashlights and paper lanterns, the rents in the ward were obvious, the threadbare rot of an old t-shirt too beloved to throw out. Maya, too, was scrutinizing it, her fingers outstretched as if testing it by touch.

"Are you sure about going down there?" Jonah asked. Felipe's plan, such that it was, involved walking all the way downtown, but that hadn't accounted for the weaker refugees, and Gaby had vetoed it. They'd have to stop somewhere, and the valley, which Maya had warded as a hideout, was the closest to safety they could find.

She twisted one hand behind the other, an oddly girlish gesture. He could see the outline of her zygomatic bone though her skin, the frantic pumping of a blood vessel below the translucent flesh. "They don't hate me any less than the Dominion does."

"Yeah," Jonah said. "Well. Welcome to the fucking club."

Ian had always been private about his work. When they'd been young and the world had been several degrees less fucked, Jonah had considered it some kind of privilege to watch him at it, performing arcane rituals to keep the cops away, and on the Hill, once they'd no longer been young, charming the mouths of recalcitrant politicians shut or befuddling the press corps.

It was different with Maya. Times were different. There had been purges after the Blight, literal witch-hunts, before cooler—or at least more pragmatic—heads in the Dominion had prevailed over Atherton's anti-magic stance. If anything, MAI were feared more than they had been, both by the Dominion and by those ostensibly opposed to it. There was no telling what they'd find down in the valley.

Nevertheless, exhausted, she led the procession of refugees behind a ragged witch hazel, where a trail of bricks and wooden palettes led down into the valley. Between the shriekgrass and the ice, the route was steep and slippery. Jonah tested the edge of the decline with the side of his boot and reached out a hand to Ian, which was promptly refused. He skittered over exhausted and eroded ground nailed into place by weathered wood, to where the land and the veil enfolded the survivors in its shroud.

There were still predators in the valley, carrying bundles of old papers sold at a premium to kindle the oil drum fires. One glare from Felipe warned them away. There were rulers in the tent city, petty warlords who staked their claim to melted ice and rows of vinyl, but the arriving Mac-Paps were the ones with the guns.

He left Felipe to bully his way into supplies for the refugees and took his place at one of the oil drums with Ian, Maya, and Shadi. The valley was too crowded for them to find a tent for shelter. They huddled under the corner of a snow-laden tarp on the smokey side. A row of caged pigeons cooed at their back. Poor fuckers, dragged over from Europe to be messengers and then cast to the streets, living fat and happy off civilization's scraps but abandoned by their gods.

They were mostly avoided—the Central Committee for their guns, Ian and Maya for the push-pull play of magic and its opposition that whistled in the air between them—but a girl pushed her way through the crush, calling Maya's name.

Maya lifted her head from Shadi's shoulder. "Taz?"

The girl was wearing one of the paper-thin factory uniforms. She seemed to know Maya, judging from her sour expression. She looked shell-shocked, a massive cut across her scalp dripping thick blood into one eye. "You were right," Taz said.

"What happened at the factory?" Maya asked.

"They moved everything out before the bombing. I don't know where they took it." The girl staggered to the ground beside her. Shadi rubbed his hands together, skin spiderwebbed with red cracks. Maya had her arm encircled through his, her hand on his knee, and Jonah envied them their easy, public intimacy, their private language. "Did you see where?" he asked.

Taz shook her head. She'd been crying too, and she curled into a ball, sharp little glances at the menacing shadows of people passing between the flames. "Towards downtown, I think."

Jonah should have been able to get more out of her. He'd been good at talking to people once, before the words had rusted in his throat. He should have been watching Maya, ensuring that the Mac-Pap's MVP didn't get taken out by one of the many lunatics who skulked in the demimonde, too broken or brown or queer to make themselves useful to the regime but too scared or too stubborn to take up arms and fight back directly.

As cowardly as he'd been, before Maya had found him and dragged him back into the land of the living.

Instead, he had his eyes on Ian.

"We needs to find them, then," Ian said.

It was a laughable prospect, given the brutal reprisal with which their tiny rebellion had been met, after everything, to still believe in him.

"Tell me this all isn't stupid," Maya said. "You wouldn't let this happen if there was no hope."

"I can't see forward anymore. You knows that." Ian sighed heavily. "But I'm never after bein' the most righteous corpse on the barricade. I'm here to win."

. . .

Maya was spinning out. The Mac-Paps were all spinning out. He'd seen it happen a million times with the million minuscule activist groups that chewed people up and shat them out again, talking a good game about mutual aid until someone had to watch the kids, someone couldn't make a meeting because they'd taken on a second job, someone's heart broke or their brain broke and they were left a dried up husk. Back then there had always been a fresh crop of young uni kids, grist for the mill. Now there was only one Maya.

"All we ever do is wait," she said

"I'm dying to kick some ass too," Jonah admitted. Never mind the lightning shock of panic every time he'd had to, the sleepless nights where he'd seen the gory face of the man he'd beaten to death. Real tough guys, both of them. One moment of calm and he drifted into fantasies of taking out the regime single handedly like he was The Man With No Name and not a coward with his name buried.

"Were you safe? Before?"

"I was a birth-alert baby," he said. "I was *born* unsafe."

"I mean, before I came to find you. When you were in hiding."

"I had a pass." Fake, of course, but he'd been living with his name buried for over two decades. Even if he didn't have half a dozen reasons for the Dominion to want him dead, a real pass was hardly an option. "They never checked. For all that you Toronto folks used to go on about the rural vote no one really gave a shit there. They didn't want the Dominion stepping on their toes anymore than they wanted our guys doing it."

"I'm sorry," she said.

"Yeah, you should be." She had the decency to look crestfallen. "I'm fucking with you. You used to have a sense of humour." Ian was pretending to sleep a few metres away, and in exchange, Jonah pretended that he wasn't watching. "I don't have anything left to lose anymore."

"I want to *do* something."

"You did. We wouldn't have made it out of the blast zone without you."

"It's not enough." She stared down at her hands, swollen with chilblain. "I'm not enough."

"Who is it you think you have to burn yourself out for? Gaby? Your husband? Ian?"

"Yes," she admitted, then, "you're trying to kill yourself for the cause too. Or for him."

"Ian and I are complicated. Besides, I was giving you shit. Because the second you let your guard down, the second you let yourself be truly powerful, the rest comes flooding back. All that loss and grief and pain and rage. And you don't trust yourself with it."

"Are we still talking about me?"

He rooted around in his pockets for one of the cigarettes. He'd done a terrible job of rolling them, packing the papers with sprinkles of sage to stretch out the too-small stash of tobacco that he'd been able to scrounge up or trade for. It tasted sweet and faintly dry, not unpleasant, but hardly the drug he needed to calm his nerves.

He felt the prickle of Martine's approach before the girl said his name. "Mom wanted you to see this."

The files that Eric had stolen and Blythe's team had decrypted and annotated were prefaced with a note from her.

Dear Jonah. We are all completely fucked. And I can't figure out what the last bit means.

Crackling with magic, Maya squeezed next to him to read over his shoulder.

"Rogers Centre, huh?"

"Skydome," he corrected, though he wasn't from Toronto and barely had a stake in it, and it was hardly as if any of it mattered anymore. "What are they doing in there?"

He sought out the crucifix around his neck. Ian would mock him for it, but he'd hedge his bets. Her eyes radiated white, streaks of lightning that split her face like broken china, following Blythe's projections into some nebulous future.

The possibilities surged to the surface, unbidden. Another black site? A Chilean-style mass execution? Gladiator matches under the thumb of a jeering Director Atherton? The prison where they had Ian was too small to hold every person who'd gone missing under the Dominion's rule. They'd need a bigger space, either to hold captives or bury them in mass graves. But then, why the factory equipment?

And then the light blinked out. She swayed, then slumped into his arms. He could see the folds of his parka sleeve through her neck. "Maya!"

She curled in on herself like a dying leaf.

"I couldn't see inside," she said. "Too bright. It was like... back in the wellspring. Like being *devoured*."

He shouldn't have let her do this. What were they thinking, blundering into some grotesque turducken of Dominion malfeasance? Her round face, too soft and sweet for the butchery she'd had to commit, tightened. "Jonah?"

Right, be useful, be a fucking soldier for the cause.

"So we know they're doing something fucky with magic. Probably magitech, if the SVAR is involved. They'd have to be getting it from a wellspring," he said. "Even if they were ripping the magic out of MAIs, they just don't have enough."

"It's a weapon," she said. "What else would they want?"

Jonah nodded. Prisoners made a sick kind of sense, either as a workforce or test subjects or both. More pathetic little shrivelled people, ground up in the maw of the great Frankenstein engine that fuelled the Dominion. He twisted the chain of the crucifix between his fingers. "We need to get them out of there."

It took her long seconds to speak. She was dappled with the dying embers of her magic, a vitiligo of light and glass. "Us and what army?"

A series of absurd scenarios presented themselves in glorious technicolour, all of them ending with both of them bukkake'd across the stadium walls. Beside him, she'd stiffened into something cold and unbending, the weapon Ian had promised to make of her. "We can't just let this happen. You—you did it for him."

"And where's that gotten us? He's fucked, we're all fucked, just biding our time until the Dominion gets a bead on us and takes us all out. I'm sorry, Jonah. I know you—" *Would feel better if you could go out in an uncomplicated blaze of glory.* "—I want revenge as much as you do, but like. I'm sorry. I'm not brave." She gripped his wrist. Aftershocks of magic rippled over his skin. "But we're not giving up."

"This *feels* a lot like giving up."

She squared her shoulders, suddenly every bit the commander she'd been when she had dragged him out of a church and into a revolution. "There's no scenario in which we bust any of these people out with just the two of us. We need to talk to everyone."

Empires fall when they extend themselves. Ian had been, at best, a distracted student of history and only an accidental politician. But that was the Party line, that desire to hold on to what pitiful gains they'd managed to win, lest everything be lost. Patrice Abel had never wanted to rule the world. The same couldn't be said of Quinn Atherton.

What the *fuck* was the Dominion up to?

"What good does a warning do?" Where was Maya's fucking fire? Where was her urge to keep kicking out at the world until it finally broke her? Where was his?

"This isn't the kind of fight we win," Maya said. "It's the kind of fight we fight."

29

Sage wafted astringent smoke through Colette's office like a weighted blanket. She already felt cleaner, more grounded. She luxuriated in it, guiding the smoke over her face, through her hair, over the nooks and crannies where her predecessors had worked and wept and finally acquiesced to the inevitable march of change.

The paint was still drying on the newly reopened facilities at what was now called the Ansel Graves Memorial Institute. On her first visit with Alycia, it had been like opening a portal into a past that she barely remembered. The commons was bright and open, the windows an invitation to entropy, the electricity a miracle. She had been picking scraps from the world's bones for so long. Had UVic looked like this, so pristine, so big and white and polished, all those years ago?

It was also isolated and heavily guarded, and despite Alycia's assurance that there would, eventually, be a whole team, it seemed like the entire complex belonged to her and the guards. Colette's lab had been intended for automotive engineering, or small aircraft repair, and while the heavy equipment had been removed, enough of the infra-structure remained to make it look austere. Science-y. Colette needed an operating table, a thread, and a needle to do her research, but perversely, Alycia didn't seem know or care about that. The look was right.

Colette purged her office of its resentment, of the lingering energies of some instructor who'd failed to make tenure, some department deemed redundant, some thwarted mind whose breakthrough would never come to fruition in a future where the survivors fought for crumbs. At least the sage smelled good. Alycia hadn't wanted her to have a window for security reasons, but the office was otherwise cheery. She'd put framed photos of Nate and the kids on her desk, hung an array of inspi-rational quotes on the door and the wall next to her medical diagrams. It was a step up from the repurposed POW camp, but it wasn't right.

Alycia coughed as politely and gracefully as she did anything else. Maybe it was to get Colette's attention; maybe it was just a bad reaction to the sage smoke. "Come in," Colette said, unnecessarily.

Alycia sniffed at the air. "You're making yourself at home," she observed. Colette wasn't going to think about Simon unwinding into gore and vapour. She wasn't going to think about how Alycia also knew *her* true name.

"It's almost there," Colette said. "I am—doing other things. Not just decorating."

Alycia's nails raked the freshly painted doorjamb, inches from the explosion of watercolour and its looping script that read, "Just breathe." Colette was going to take the poster's advice if it killed her.

"You've done remarkably. Considering." She left the rest unsaid. *Considering you're not a real scientist, just a dropout we scrounged up from an extremely limited talent pool. Considering we've kept you in the dark about what you're actually doing.*

"The mice arrived yesterday," Colette said. "So thanks for that." A hysterical giggle threatened to burst from her throat as she imagined one of the mice somehow picking up the shreds of Ian Mallory's magic, shooting little blue sparks out of its tiny claws. In truth the mice were useless—their brains weren't complicated enough to control magic, and their body mass was too low to turn them into demons. At best, she could sew bright thread under their fur, blast them with sensation that, more often than not, caused heart failure even without magic. She'd ordered pigs, but they kept getting intercepted.

"Does it work?" Alycia asked. "Reaching out, waiting for the magic to tell you what to do?"

Colette considered lying, and then considered Simon's skin sloughing off his flesh. The cheery posters mocked her, undulated in pastel watercolour ecstasy while she sweated. Cool patches materialized under her arms, the small of her back. "Not yet."

Alycia said, "Come with me."

Their destination was on the top floor, at the far end of campus. The tight, neat clack of Alycia's heels filled the cavernous lobby.

The room, like every room here, was larger than it needed to be, intended for some purpose that the Blight had rendered obsolete. There was a mural, a swirling scene of pink mermaids dancing in aqua waves. Piles of soft toys, some mostly complete, others shredded to ruin, were stacked in the corners.

She saw the nurse first, a nervous little brown mouse in pale scrubs whose mass of black hair escaped her tight bun. The monster registered in stages. Something failed along Colette's optic nerve; she saw it, but the thing she saw failed to resolve into meaning.

The demon was an ice sculpture in the shape of a child. Sunlight trickled through the window, shattering in rainbows over the linoleum floor and igniting its pulsating red heart into glowing coal. It did not move at Colette's approach. Were it not for the heart's steady beat, it could have been a beautiful, if unnerving, piece of art.

Slowly, the neck crackling like breaking ice, its head turned towards her and cocked to one side.

Colette's magic reacted before her body could, a roiling, violent force that threatened to burst out of her chest. The needle was in her coat pocket, thread still attached—she could sew it through her own finger if need be, if that was what it took to throw a ward between herself and the demon.

"Relax." Alycia said. "She can't turn you into a demon. It doesn't affect us. And she's really quite docile most of the time, so I'm told."

The nurse wouldn't meet Colette's eyes. Not an MAI, if she had to guess.

"How—" she started. As far as she knew, demons couldn't be killed, or stopped, or trapped. Against her better instinct, she took a step towards the demon.

In one fluid movement, it—she—lunged from her chair and strained, elongated, towards Colette and Alycia. Her jaw dislocated, revealing sharp, transparent teeth, and a long rolling tongue. Colette shrieked, and Alycia laughed, soft and musical. The nurse rushed to the demon's side, her hands on the glass shoulders, stroking her crystal hair, shushing her.

"You're perfectly safe, my dear," Alycia said.

"Where did you find her?"

"That much is classified, I'm afraid. As is most of the information about how she came to be here."

"But she's different than the rest of them," Colette said. Or she'd have devoured them, MAI or not. Ian had confirmed what Alycia had claimed—MAI couldn't be demons—but there was more than one way to be consumed.

"Yes," Alycia said. "She's important."

The demon—the child—was calm now. Colette picked out details in the facets of her skin. Eight or nine years old, if she had to guess. It would have been a remarkable thing, if a carver had made it. As a living creature, malformed bone and glass exoskeleton, it was a horror.

"How long have you had her?"

"Since the beginning. Since the first day of the Blight."

"And you didn't—"

"As I've said," Alycia said. "Classified. Only four people know. Five, now."

"Why?" Colette asked, unsure if she was asking why Alycia had withheld the demon from her, why she had somehow captured it in the first place, why she was finding out about this only now.

"Isn't it obvious?" Alycia asked. "I believe you have code names for your projects, do you not?"

How had she found out about that? "Eat, Pray, and Love."

"You know what Eat is. The transfer of magical ability from the undeserving to the deserving."

"Which has been a miserable failure."

"Not for lack of trying. And you'll find out about Pray in good time. Reid is—unwilling— to disclose details at the moment."

"So this is Love."

Alycia smiled. "You could call it that."

The demon, under the nurse's care, had settled back into her chair, though the odd burst of tension still rippled over her glass skin. She might have been any ordinary child, restless at being confined, desperate for the world outside.

It wouldn't have made sense for an adult, or an animal, to have lost mass and age. This had been a real flesh-and-blood child, someone's beloved daughter transformed into this abomination.

"Who is she?" Colette asked.

"You really don't follow politics very closely, do you?" Alycia kept a wary distance from the demon, but she hadn't taken her eyes off the creature's mouth, not for an instant. "You are not to harm her in any way, or conduct experiments unless they pass my approval first. Any physical contact also must pass my approval. As tragic as her condition may be, we are acutely aware that it can still, theoretically, get worse."

"What am I supposed to *do*, then?"

"I believe you already know," Alycia said. "You're going to make her human again."

. . .

The nurse, Amelia, didn't talk much. Alycia hadn't even seemed to know her name. She had barely acknowledged the young woman before leaving, the clack of her shoes trailing after her like a penumbra. She had hastily introduced herself, but only when Colette had asked, and then scooched to a corner of the room, head bowed and hands clasped in front of her. The girl didn't talk either, and her eyes, carved from milky quartz, stared straight past Colette.

"I have two boys," Colette said to the demon. "Noah and Jasper. They're twins. A little younger than you—well, a lot younger than you." How old was the girl? Demons grew larger than the humans they'd been, not smaller, accumulating matter as they fed. Her build was slight, but there was a grief in those stone eyes that made Colette second guess herself. "They're not mine—I mean. I can't. We can't. They're adopted."

Amelia raised an eyebrow at this.

"MAI. We can't have kids. They did a study after it happened a few times, I guess. They come out, like..." Though the girl did not react, Colette flushed at the faux pas. Maybe she didn't know that anything was wrong with her—maybe Colette was the first to break that grim news. "Is that what happened to her?"

"That's way above my pay grade. I guess the usual. Stepped in the wrong place, maybe. She's been here a long time, longer than me. But she wasn't born like that, considering—"

There were cameras in the ceiling, as new as the rest of the renovations. No one—not Colette, not Amelia, certainly not the small monster that stared blankly ahead—could be trusted to behave themselves unsupervised. Colette had earned herself some favour, or else she wouldn't have been here, and the nurse must have as well, but it wasn't as though either of them had choices. A person couldn't quit working for Alycia. Even if Alycia wouldn't turn her inside out for what she knew, Colette was registered. The job market for wizards was exceptionally limited.

Lucy Fletcher had been a coward, and a fool, and a traitor, and wherever she was now, if she still lived, she remained all of those things. But she'd fled for a reason. The Dominion was a pressure cooker, not meant for those who lacked resiliency.

"And what am I supposed to do with you?" she asked the girl-creature. "Can't touch you, can't even get a needle through your ski—"

It happened too fast for her to scream.

The statue lashed out so quickly that the movement was almost imperceptible. The tiny glass hand, with its corkscrew nails, whipped around Colette's wrist and stayed there. One claw opened a bright slash across her flesh.

Colette gasped and fought the instinct to kick out and twist her arm, the way her Women's Self Defence teacher had instructed, the weird twist of the ulna and radius that she'd worried she would never remember in an emergency. But she couldn't hurt the demon—even touch was forbidden—and she was on thin enough ice with Alycia as it was.

"Just stay still," Amelia said. "She can't change you."

Even pinned in place by the glass hand, Colette craned in Amelia's direction. The nurse shuffled rather than walked. Her slippers—how could she manage in slippers when the room was so cold?—barely made a sound on the floor. She knelt by the girl's side and whispered something in her ear.

"Does she have a name?" Colette asked. "You have to call her something."

"Don't ask so many questions, please." Amelia bent her head to the girl's again. Surely her voice, inaudible even inches from where Colette was pinned, was too low for the girl to hear. But little by little, the pressure on her wrist eased, and Colette wriggled her hand free.

"I'm a scientist," Colette, the imposter, said. "How am I supposed to fix her if I don't know anything about her?"

Amelia stared at her, then snorted a laugh. There was some life left in her after all.

"You think they brought you here to fix her? This is where people come to be forgotten. Alycia Curtis doesn't care about fixing her."

"*Someone* does." *Or they would have killed her.* Alycia was as interested as anyone else in figuring out how demons worked, either to make them a weapon or stop them from being a threat. Even if it was true that you couldn't kill demons, Alycia could have had her buried in a sarcophagus like they had done with Parliament Hill. Alycia had resources—she was perhaps the only one in the country left who did.

"Someone does," Amelia agreed. She stroked the girl's hair.

She had said too much, and they both knew it. Amelia shook her head, like an Etch-a-Sketch resetting itself. As if she could unwind the whole conversation, go back to being a silent, ghostly presence in the corner.

"You don't think there's a cure?" Colette asked.

"Do you?"

Colette believed in many things. She believed that the universe, despite all indication to the contrary, was a benevolent place. That if you put positive energy out, you would receive positive results. That God had a plan for her, and every other human on the planet. She believed that with enough force of will, she could do anything she set her mind to.

But she did not believe magic followed the same rules as everything else. No matter how much she manipulated and contorted it, magic from one person would devour another from the inside out. It would gnaw like a caged animal at bone and viscera until it was free, a bleeding nub of a thing writhing on the floor, never returning to its original host, never settling in new blood, new bone. She had sought to transform the world, and had only managed to mutilate it.

"No," she whispered. "Magic is magic. We're lucky if we get to control it a little."

Amelia nodded. "That's what—" She stopped, clicked her tongue around an absence that sat there. "That's what I thought too."

. . .

As a privilege of her new station, she was to give a command performance on the Train when it stopped, briefly, to celebrate the reopening of the facility. She was to report on her progress—or, rather, report that she was *making* progress—perhaps, Alycia suggested, even give a demonstration of why magic remained vital to the Dominion's strategy. Atherton himself had joined the Curtises and a handful of military commanders in one of the conference rooms, which could accommodate more people than his personal carriage. There were nearly as many security guards as attendees.

Colette hadn't seen Director Atherton up close in years. He had taken office with a grim, battle-hardened competence, the most senior member of the government to survive the attack on Parliament. Since then, he'd developed a tremor in his hands. Living under the Blight had aged them all, even her. She had been a third-year university student, and now she was somehow among the Dominion's top researchers, a wife, a mother, a person to be respected. A person with a stake, trusted and exalted.

Reid Curtis had tacked a large paper map to the wall that delineated the occupied sections of downtown Toronto, the remaining Dominion positions, the wide swathes of suburban sprawl decimated by aerial bombardment. Pinned around it were the identifiable photos of the terrorists. The two extant photos of Jonah Augustine were pinned by the top. One was cut out from a family portrait with him smiling stiffly into the camera as if he were unsure whether to pose for it or bite it. His arms looped around a small girl with a gap-toothed grin. The other was a still lifted from a drone surveillance video, in which he was calmly putting a bullet through the head of a fallen soldier.

Beside him, the blurry photo of his accomplice, whose name had reportedly slipped from the memory of the one witness who could identify her. "An MAI," Colette noted, though they had to have figured that out already.

Below them were the traitors, Lucy Fletcher and Eric Greenglass, and crossed out, Cal Harrison. A silhouette, standing in for the still-unknown leader. At the centre of the web, improbably, was Ian Mallory. Not the shattered, starving wretch whose heart Colette had stopped, whose magic she'd wrenched from his wasted body, but a man she had never met, sneering at a scrum of reporters, the power behind the throne.

Atherton had given a speech earlier in the day. It was Reid's speech, and it had sounded better on paper. Now he sat, atrophied, in place, and the weariness showed, the gravity tugging at his jowls, the corners of his eyes.

"We need to make a decision here." It was clear that one particular commander wasn't happy with the conspiracy board. He moved some of the pins around. "We can turn it to rubble, or we can retreat. But we don't have the manpower to hold it long-term."

"That's not acceptable." Reid spoke before Atherton could make a pronouncement. "We are not surrendering the most populous city in the country to the hordes." He looked to his wife, then, for a longer time, at Colette. He wasn't an MAI, but something in her curdled. "Certainly, there are other options to subdue them."

"I don't know," Colette said quickly. Alycia's attention was on her hands, her lips pursed in concentration. Expecting some big show of magic, as if she was anywhere near the level Ian had been. Her magic was subtle, intimate. Not the sort of thing you used for crowd control. "I can't, I don't think."

"Nonsense," Alycia said. She was no longer speaking out loud; her words were meant for Colette alone. A command. "We have no need for restraint."

The commander who was standing frowned. "As I was saying. We need practical solutions, not whatever *this* is."

As if they all hadn't feared magic when Ian Mallory was running the show. Back then, magic was newsworthy, threatening, paradigm-shifting. Now, with shriekgrass claiming more and more landmass each year, with the demons stalking closer to civilization, with the superwinter promising famine if their relationship with the Free States faltered any harder—now the man was choosing to play the skeptic.

Well, that wouldn't do.

Colette twined the thread she'd been working on around her finger, tighter. The tip went white, strangled of blood. The pressure was a distraction that fell short of pain.

She seethed. The room pressed in on her, these small-minded, incurious men, with their cruel, superior wives, and she could destroy them all, with a thought, with a name—

There was a last name embroidered neatly on his uniform. Crowder.

She held it in her mind, savoured it. Only half a name, but she had only been asked for a proof of concept. She threaded it carefully, hooked it through the shape of him.

He was a spaghetti tangle of strings, veins and arteries and capillaries, looping quantum particles that reached back into some distant essence of being. He vibrated. She traced the trajectory of him. The intersections of his self and the selves of the other bodies in the room, the military brass and even Reid and Atherton, even Alycia herself. She snagged them in her web, unravelled them, wove them back into order.

"Colette," Reid said, a warning.

"Stick out your tongues," Colette said.

One of the commanders was cogent enough to look at the man next to him; the rest did it immediately. A few looked like big dogs with their tongues lolling out of their jaws; others, like cheeky children pulling a rude gesture. Atherton's lips moved, gapping, but Reid slapped a hand over his wrist, nails digging into the skin below the cuff of his shirt, and he pulled himself out of it.

Alycia was going to fire her. Alycia watched, unruffled and amused.

"Choose a weapon," Colette said, softly. "Remove the tongue of the man to your left."

The moment hung, suspended in amber, swollen to bursting. And then the room exploded.

Men scrambled over each other like rats, snatching at scissors, staplers, even the thumbtacks on Reid's conspiracy board. Some, barehanded, pried the mouths of their fellows open, grasping at slippery flesh with clawed fingers. One man slapped staple after staple into another's mouth, while another, sliding between the two, stabbed at his eyes with a ballpoint pen.

Colette caught Alycia's eyes. Had she read her right? They both needed a show of force, a demonstration of potential, but these were important men. The Curtises needed them—*Atherton* needed them—they were the last line of defence between civilization and the terrorists. She couldn't flay them on a pin like she had Mallory. Surely Alycia wouldn't let it go that far, surely she'd misread—

A man flew past her, his uniform dishevelled, blood seeping from his mouth. Another, by the wall, had no one close enough to target, raised both of his hands to his face and began to scratch.

"Enough," Alycia said, and her anxiety spiked again.

Colette let go, covering her mouth with her hands. The strings connecting her to each man went first taut, then slack as she released them.

The madness had passed. No one looked up—no one looked at her, or at Alycia. None looked at the man they had just been assaulting.

A blood-drenched hand softened, letting a pair of scissors fall to the ground with a clatter.

"I think you'll find our methods, while not inseparable from a prudent military strategy, *entirely* practical," Alycia said. She slid her pale, thin hand along the surface of the table to uncharacteristically take that of her husband. Colette exhaled. She wasn't losing her job today. "Please, go on."

30

On the eve of the uprising, visions of every possible outcome in light-leaked Super 8 film strips dancing before her eyes, Maya didn't sleep.

She sat awake, pistol over her knees, and listened. The valley was cold and damp, the tarps blooming black mold. People slept on mattresses salvaged from the ruined buildings, on piles of old newspapers and plastic bags, or they paced in despair.

More and more refugees from the world above joined them by the hour. It was no longer just the poor and brown and Black and gay who had been the first to join the Mac-Paps, but increasingly, the people who had thought that if they kept their heads down and did their jobs, the Dominion's excesses would spare them. They came with stories of ever more brutal neighbourhood patrols, confiscated passes, food shortages, workplace purges. The slow, simmering cold war had taken two days to heat up.

And there wasn't enough food to keep everyone alive. There wasn't enough in the generators to run the lights or the heat.

Maya's joints protested and popped as she hoisted herself to her feet. She was supposed to be on the move, checking for incursions or, as was far more frequent, heart attacks or overflowing latrines. Dust, blown in the polar vortex from the shattered high-rises to the east, had drifted west-wards across the city, blotting out the stars and moon. Amongst the tents, someone snored. Someone farted. A thick soup of sulfur squatted in the dead air.

Some of the others were gathered in a clearing by a shrivelled crook in the frozen river. A pair of puppeteers reenacted an old *Night Beats* episode with sock puppets they'd assembled for each of the characters. They were doing the one where Jordan teamed up with Titania to stop a vampire with presidential aspirations. The Queen of the Fae was resplendent in scraps of yellow yarn and a dress of garbage bags. Jordan, predictably, was *just* a garbage bag. The two puppeteers managed to squeeze considerable expression from a flick of the wrist, a sinuous motion of the forearm and elbow, and the cavorting flames concealed a multitude of aesthetic sins.

Martine stood at the far edge of the little crowd, watching. Maya pushed down the unhappy murmur of guilt and approached.

"Weren't you keeping watch all day?" They were the only two who could fix one of the wards if it went down. Gaby kept them at different ends of the valley, running different shifts, better to make use of her scarce resources and all that.

"Couldn't sleep," Martine said. "Came to watch this shit instead."

"It's not shit," Maya said. There was something comforting about the puppet shows. They had been running through the entire series, one episode a night, beginning back in Fort Utopia. "This was one of my favourite episodes."

"Oh my *God*." Martine's huff of teenage despair earned them both several unhappy glares. "I can't believe I was ever intimidated by you. You're such a nerd."

Intimidated? "Shhh," Maya hissed. "Learn a thing."

Titania's puppeteer tossed a small shower of torn paper above her head, lit by the quick flash of Jordan's lighter. "I have never trusted humanity either." The puppeteer had a high falsetto for Titania's voice, but they'd managed to get the weird cadence of the original actor's delivery dead on. "But President Cassius will reign on a throne of blood. We can go back to quarrelling when we've ended this threat."

It took Maya a moment to spot Ian and Lucy at the other end of a patch of dead shrubs. Taut, drowning in an overcoat that swallowed her little hands, Lucy was watching the performance, enraptured, while Ian loomed over her like a stone gargoyle. Her magic still recoiled at his presence, but her uneasiness was no greater now than that from her sleep deprivation.

He caught her eye. He was past enjoying dumb kids reenacting dumb TV shows, the warmth and humour and joy leached out of him along with his magic, but he'd always known how to fake it for a crowd, even before she'd first walked into the Broom Closet and cast her illusions for him.

"C'mon," Maya said, nudging Martine over.

This was also well below Lucy's taste, but at least the other woman had the performance skills to act polite about it. She clapped in all the right places.

"You're no less a killer than Cassius himself," Puppet Jordan said.

"Better the devil you know," Puppet Titania replied.

Ian smirked at this. There was an episode, two seasons later, where it turned out that Titania *was* the Devil, or was at least standing in for him while he took a thousand-year sabbatical, and she had no doubt Ian had seen it.

She bent her head to Lucy's. "Wanna see something cool?"

Lucy's eyes widened, but she nodded. Maya squeezed the rubber duck, gathering the Pattern around her. The wisp light that danced around her flickered, as if she was a human battery with only so much power. But it was enough. Titania's yarn became her white-blond hair, her face a porcelain doll's. The air hissed and sparkled around her, trailing swirls where the puppeteer moved her like the dear, terrible CGI that Maya had once lovingly mocked. Jordan kept his garbage bag leather jacket—it was just too funny—but from it emerged his bland, square-jawed face, lined with stubble. His puppeteer blinked but didn't skip a beat of the script.

There was a smattering of applause, Lucy's being the loudest. The puppeteers moved on, to the scene where Jordan walked through the archway into the Shadowrealm. Martine coiled living vines up the bent coat hangers at the edge of the stage. Beyond the archway, smoke roiled and the dark, fey inhabitants of Titania's kingdom stalked between bursts of flame.

"Oh," Maya said to Martine. "So you *did* watch the show."

"Maya," Ian said. "Look at your hands."

She did. They were wreathed in magic. Her own, the green of new shoots pushing through the snow, and Martine's, a shaky, spluttering flame.

And they were solid.

"I don't al—" Maya started, but he'd picked up on something. Her magic and Martine's had met somewhere between their hands and the stage, and each spell reinforced the other. It wasn't just not draining her, her magic was stronger somehow, as if it was feeding off Martine's and not from Maya's own body.

She'd felt that only once before, in the Alberta wilderness with demons closing in and the universe whispering at her to surrender. Then, it had been Ian's magic that kept her own aloft.

She turned to Martine. The girl was alight, her customary scowl replaced with a wide grin. Her slender fingers danced in rapid motion, spinning the stale air of the valley into wisps of light that settled over the puppets and the janky set.

It wasn't just that magic wasn't draining her either. Maya had never seen her have *fun*.

Jordan's puppet vanished through the threshold and Martine first dimmed the fire, then sent a shower of fairy lights bouncing through the darkness. Some of the older people were already humming the *Night Beats* theme song. Both of the puppeteers stood and gave brief, ironic bows, first with their puppets, then their full bodies, before indicating Maya and Martine.

"What should we do now?" Martine asked.

Maya looked from one face to the other, desperate and luminous in the fading lights.

"We should talk," Ian said.

. . .

"You said Yamashita seemed like he was fading before he died," Maya said.

They were huddled around her ghost-light, on overturned milk crates. It cast a cold gleam, spiking black shadows up the branches of dead trees. She leaned in closer anyway, as if playing along convincingly enough would turn her illusion to heat.

"He looked sick," Lucy confirmed. "Thinner, like he was collapsing inward. But everyone looks sick. And Alycia didn't look any worse, and she uses magic all the time."

"What about—" Maya stopped herself. She hadn't asked Ian about his time in a Dominion black site, not more than he'd volunteered.

"Colette," he said softly. The name came through a tight jaw, squeezed through the gap between his front teeth. "No, she was fine. She never let you forget for a moment how fine she was."

"Because she was drawing your power from you," Lucy said. "Like a battery. Same as Alycia, with Simon, and probably me as well. But all three of you, you draw it from yourselves. I don't think Simon would have known how to do it the other way. He—he wasn't cruel. Not like that. And you're not either."

Ian snorted. "Look at you. It's like watching a baby learn to walk. Except by "baby," I means "adult woman" and by "walk," I means learnin' basic human decency."

"This is big, though, isn't it?" Martine said. "It means Maya doesn't have to ration." As if Maya could have rationed, as if magic wasn't ready to burst from each cell in her body at a moment's notice, even if it killed her. Even now it vibrated, skin and muscle and bone longing to burst into shards of light.

No. Not now. Not yet.

"How come you didn't know?" Maya asked Ian. "Why didn't anyone know?"

"You've met charmers," Ian said. "We don't exactly play well with others."

"You and I did," Maya said. "I thought."

"Yeah," Ian replied. "I guess we did." He reached a crumpled finger into the dancing will-o'-the-wisp. It recoiled from his touch, bouncing off Martine's shoulder. Anything to avoid him. "Look at all of us, b'y. Atomized. Forced into competition. Lucky if we meets someone else like us even once in a lifetime. But I shoulda guessed, shoulda known, when I saw what you an' I could do. The two of you, you'll be fuckin' unstoppable."

"Really?" Martine's facade dropped.

"No," Ian said. "They've got F-35s. But we can make 'em bleed for every block. We can make sure those fuckers never sleep again."

She needed to get him alone somehow, and never mind the roiling anxiety that his presence provoked in her. There was so much she should have asked him, would have if she'd known what was going to happen. He had been ready to die, expected it, prepared her as best he could for the day that she would have to continue without him. He'd interpreted a future that had gone sideways, but it was still death of a sorts, and he'd met it not with dignity but with blood and shit and pain.

She would have asked him, had there been time, if he'd only been pretending to accept it.

She wanted to live. She wanted that elusive future she'd glimpsed in the lights. She wanted to see the sun again, the thaw of spring. She wanted to wrestle the space to grieve and mourn from the onslaught of the Dominion's advance.

"When do we attack?" she asked.

"Ridiculous girl," Ian said. "They're only waiting for your call."

. . .

Maya, when she had a different name and a better life, would rather have died than give a speech.

She had Shadi and Ian and Jonah on her side, and Martine, for the drama, and the puppeteers, who could rally a crowd. She hadn't talked it over with Gaby, let alone Felipe or Devi or any of the dissenting voices in the Coordinating Committee's ranks. No longer the loyal general, she started talking, first quietly to Taz, then to a handful of girls from the factory.

"Right now," she said. "There are whole city blocks downtown that are ours. And there's a stadium full of prisoners building something magical and terrible. We can't wait for the right moment—they need every single one of us here to flood the streets and show them that we can win. Cover your faces, disguise yourselves, and here's what we're gonna do."

Three years ago, the Blight burning holes in the asphalt, she had stumbled behind a procession of the walking wounded, of orphans and refugees. She had fled the interstitial rest stops and charging stations as the world spasmed, then crumbled. She had come home to find her home in ruins and her family dead.

This time—she pretended, as if playing a game to distract the child she'd been—would be different.

"This is the darkest night of the year," she said. "Maybe some of you still remember how we used to celebrate it. We used to welcome back the sun. With costumes, and revelry, and fire. The Dominion won't be expecting this many of us all at once. They won't be expecting what Martine and I can do. So. Um. I'm going to start walking. Like, now. And I think you should start walking too. Fourscore, fight them on the beaches, throw open the gates of the Shadowrealm, that kind of stuff."

It was a shitty speech, and she knew it, but Ian boomed, "You fuckin' heard her," and Jonah was already on the move and she sent a will-o'-the-wisp burst of light ahead of them, winding up the steep pathways out of the valley and across the ribs of the great sunken bridge.

The wind whipped at her cheeks, each snowflake a tiny bite of glass. It lashed against her legs, a tangible force that pressed into each step she took. It sliced through the spell that she and Martine had woven in the air to conceal their approach towards the city.

The DVP, once a major artery, hadn't been used for cars in years, and the few vehicles they had moved gingerly, over the icy gouges the raging earth had worn in the pavement.

She walked anyway. Running towards was different than running from.

Ian had found, somewhere, a shabby charcoal greatcoat long enough to fit him. Everyone in the crowd had dressed for the occasion, aware of the meat grinder that waited for them. Gaby in her army fatigues, Martine in layers of torn fishnet. Others in drag, in sequins, in torn tarps. Ian was a scrap of old newspaper that had somehow, accidentally drifted onto a vibrant collage.

Maya shrugged. "It feels exposed."

"No one's ever said the left are cowards," Ian said. "Never said we were smart either."

She had been alone on that first march, in the company of the dead and the soon-to-be-dead, and this was different, because it *had* to be. The chorus of boots crunching newly fallen snow, the coughs, the rumblings of fatigue and frustration and someone's fainthearted attempt to start up a chant, all of it was a scream of desperation.

But she wasn't alone now. Shadi was there, a steady presence at her side. Martine and Gaby were up ahead. Ian's loping steps first outpaced her, then slowed down. Every so often she caught Eric's overgrown mop of hair, Lucy's stupid black coat, Jonah dashing ahead of them, disappearing into the crowd, as the sliver of new moon rose low above the withered skyline.

. . .

Toronto, the old Toronto, the quaintly provincial clusters of red brick duplexes and neighbourhood names invented by real-estate agents—all that had passed for a city, hadn't existed in years. Its mythical past of dive bars and used bookstores had been overtaken by chain stores and shining towers and tourist attractions, hollowed out in the centre, well before the Blight had crumpled it in a giant's fist. But something of the ancient city remained, as if the earthquakes that had brought down much of the downtown and bowed the CN Tower precariously towards the lake had also cut away the layers of gentrification, revealing its vulnerable, molten heart.

The girl Maya had been had lived in Scarborough and crawled back to die there. She'd lived at home, commuted to York, skirted the edge of the metropolis, flirted with urbanity.

In second year she'd briefly dated a girl who lived downtown and those had been two months of debauchery, indie film festivals run by an old pervert out of his living room, cheap red wine in an illegal basement apartment, and best of all, the moments when the city would stop, breathe, and unfurl some street festival like the worship of an ancient god.

Amber had told her about the Festival of Lights, but their relationship had only made it to the first week of December. She had ended up back at home that night, and the ones that followed, with Jamila, binging *Night Beats* and cursing the fickleness of downtown hipsters.

The scene that greeted them at the mouth of the Market, spilling from Augusta onto College, was larger and louder and angrier than Amber's descriptions of those old parades. But it was still a riot of lanterns and giant puppets and torches. Music blared from somewhere, an off-key, off-beat symphony of drums and vuvuzelas and old guitars and nasal, clumsy singing, and somewhere, below the joyful din, a low blast of a tuba that she felt in her belly.

Maya knew the stakes. The Mac-Paps had been permitted the city in patchwork pieces as the Dominion focused its limited fuel and weapons on the suburbs where the true threat lived. That stalemate wouldn't hold. The Cleaners would be on them with guns and batons, and the cops with horses would come, and then the shooting would start.

But she still wanted to run towards it. She wanted to grasp this one perfect night, to lose herself in the crowd and sing and scream and dance in all the ways she hadn't in years. The drumbeat was a pulse through the fat, squirming, living animal of the gathering. Her magic danced with it, skittering fireworks over the drooping power lines.

Ian was recognized before Gaby was, even though she was mere feet away from him. He made a show of slinking into the shadows and pulling up his hood, adjusting the mask over the bridge of his nose, but he was too tall, too incongruous for anonymity, and the scattered light from the homemade lanterns splashed streaks of orange and red over the grey of his skin.

"I was expectin' an uprising, not a block party," he muttered. Louder, he grabbed the first person to approach him with a shit-eating grin and a cloud of pot smoke. "Anyone seen Jonah? Yea high, hair that's a war crime, cheekbones that could cut glass?"

"I'm here." Jonah grinned brightly at Maya and Shadi, and held Ian's gaze for a second longer than was, strictly speaking, normal. "Well. You're not exactly low profile."

"What's happening?" Shadi asked.

"It's solstice," Jonah said, as if that were an answer. "Eat, drink, and be merry, and all that." He moved closer, his head almost colliding with Ian's arm before he stopped abruptly. "You think we're fucked."

Ian huffed deeply, then clapped a hand on both of their arms. "C'mon. Don't bother just standin' there like you expect to live forever."

The crowd was a Narnian forest of coats. The further in she pushed, the less she could see. The black nest of parkas slid over her vision, and she was almost brained by the butt of someone's flag stick. Lanterns, like fireflies, like a sea of stars, glittered between the movement of bodies. She'd already lost sight of Martine and Gaby. She would see a familiar face, open her mouth to call out, and before she could speak they had transformed into a grinning mask, the head of a raccoon or a pigeon, something feral and monstrous.

Towards Dundas, the crowd thinned enough that there was breathing room but there was no end in sight. The people who'd climbed on top of burned-out police SUVs or shimmied up telephone poles might have been able to tell her where the streets emptied, but from where she stood, it seemed to go on forever. It wasn't enough. Mere drops in a bucket already too shallow to do more than annoy the regime. Even if the entire city—the Mac-Paps and the others, the ones who had been too frightened or soft to fight back, the ones who'd bet their lives on a return to normal—even if it had emptied out at the call of the marching samba bands, it couldn't stand up to one Dominion fighter jet, let alone the dozens it had at its disposal.

Still, she breathed through it. The thousands of paper lanterns fashioned from old newspapers and scraps of fabric swelled with luminescence and pierced constellations through the darkest night of the superwinter. Clasped in freezing hands and hoisted on bamboo rods and sticks, they were magic in their own way, a bright defiance that shone harder than spells.

One of the samba bands was behind them, belting out a raucous version of "Bella Ciao," surrounded by dancers with diaphanous shawls whirling in a storm around them. A few people in the crowd knew the words, shouted lyrics in Italian and Spanish and Persian, syllables shoving and stumbling over one another. It was cold, and the snow was coming down in thin, sharp blades, and people were laughing and clapping and stomping along.

"What're we doin' here?" Ian asked.

Jonah, enough ahead of them that he had to turn back, and even in the sliver of his face visible above the mask, Maya saw how pale he looked, how tired.

"Dancing, you miserable fucker. Like it's the end of the world."

31

The city was on fire.

Rioters had set up barricades throughout the downtown. The cars from the caravan blocked off sections of Bloor. Jonah had led a small mob in uprooting the streetcar tracks along Dundas and Queen to create an impenetrable maze of warped metal and shattered concrete.

"Under permanent construction. Just like how it used to be," Maya said, her arm still linked with Shadi's, and with something in the neighbourhood as a smile.

With the streets dammed with rebar, the four of them had to walk, past the revelry of the Market and further, where the riots had lit up the ruins of Chinatown. 52 Division was a smoldering shell, ACAB sprayed in bright red across the cracked glass.

Three blocks from the periphery of the fighting was a strange oasis of calm. Cradling the portable radio in his arms, Jonah stopped in the middle of the street and looked up. A few flakes of snow caught and evaporated metres from the ground. It was long past midnight, but the smoke had turned the sky to dull orange, swimming with bright sparks.

It was a carbon emission nightmare of a revolt, but it wasn't like they hadn't already trashed the planet to hell. The air tasted of teargas and campfire. Phantom pins and needles rippled over his skin.

A group of revellers dashed past, shrieking, dressed in shimmering robes and animal masks. Maya uttered a startled, muffled laugh. Ian's face was inscrutable, still mainly hidden beneath his mask. The grit that thickened the air and reddened eyes was only another shade of grey in Ian's.

Felipe's voice crackled over the radio. "Spread out. They can surround one big march, but not a thousand little ones." That had been Ian's idea and it was working, but Jonah bristled. It should have been Gaby's moment to shine, and she was using it as always, to ensure that supply lines and communications moved along with their forces.

Still, Jonah hadn't seen any of the Dominion's forces since they'd routed a battalion of cops from the Market. The radio crackled with reports, sometimes gunfire, but the Mac-Paps were still holding blocks of the downtown. Shielded in a warded veil and the cover of night, they evaded more than clashed, the onrush of a river that would wear down the Dominion's stone.

Ian took a break from looking haunted long enough to slap Jonah's upper arm. "So, are we gonna stand around with our dicks out all night—no offence, Maya—or go back and help?"

They had only planned this briefly, in whispered exchanges when saner minds in the camp were sleeping. What Jonah had proposed was just short of a mutiny, but if Ian was right about Felipe's agenda, there was going to be a mutiny regardless. Like takeout from a roach coach, it was tempting but left a lot of room for tragedy.

He expected to lose the others again, but Ian trailed him through the crowd until he reached Felipe, ensconced in what had been the Bell Media building. It could be worse—while Jonah had burned a trail of chaos across the city, Ian had been watching the Central Committee at its work, increasingly convinced that Felipe had designs on Gaby's position.

It hadn't taken long for Felipe to establish a tiny fiefdom, his throne room a sound stage with torn red curtains. There were soldiers at the doors. Jonah raised his hands, but didn't relinquish his pistol. Ian merely glared, and even without the force of magic behind him, his presence was unsettling enough to make at least some of them back away.

"I need volunteers," Jonah announced. "We've spotted more troop carriers headed for the Skydome. Gaby's headed there next."

"I thought you were coordinating a street festival." That was no more Jonah's role than it was Felipe's.

"It's cover," Ian said. "They're busy, they're distracted, if there's any time we have a chance at gettin' in that stadium, it's now."

There would have been a time when just those few words from Ian would have had Felipe and his men on the move. Even now, with his bent, useless hands and starvation-eroded frame, he was still very much the vindictive scarecrow who'd ruled Parliament with an iron fist.

"Gaby doesn't have the firepower to engage directly," Felipe said. "Why isn't she coming to me herself?"

"Don't know if you've looked outside lately, b'y, but Gaby's got a people's uprising on her hands."

"We need to take the stadium," Jonah said. "We can't let the Dominion keep access to the waterfront. And the thing they're building in there— it's not a nuke, Felipe, but it might as well be. It could end all of this in a heartbeat." He didn't have the slightest idea *what* the Dominion was building in there. Only the roiling unease that jerked him away in the early hours of the morning, fingers and toes stiff with cold, fumbling for his rosary.

"Gaby's mind's made up," Ian said. "'Sides, if there's anything the Blue Jays have shown, the place is completely indefensible."

One of Felipe's commanders actually laughed, and Felipe shot him a stern look. "Tell her to hold off," Felipe said. "I'll go there myself."

Ian couldn't have made Jonah's cue more obvious. He was, at heart, a trickster god, ready to beg Felipe to not throw him into the briar patch. "The fuck you are," Jonah said. "Gaby sent me."

Felipe's gaze went right over him to settle on Ian. "You can talk her out of sending a bunch of amateurs," he said.

"I can try." It was hard for Ian to infuse anything that sounded like doubt into his voice, but he made a gallant attempt. "Alls I can say is if you're gonna go, b'y, go quickly."

· · ·

Hordes of civilians had poured out into the streets at the first suggestion that they might not get shot over it but none were prepared for genuine urban warfare. They had spent years learning the furtive scuttling of pillbugs under logs and, unused to their newfound freedom, some ran while others sat on curbs and rusted benches, frozen in indecision.

It wasn't his first riot, or Ian's. The thing that always tripped him up was that you had no idea how things were going beyond a block or two in either direction. If he could get up on a roof, or even a balcony—but an uprising the size of a city wasn't the same as hurling water bottles at riot cops or throwing down with fascists. It *felt* like they were winning but that didn't mean that they were.

Either way, they had to keep moving. Maya was a target, Ian even more so. He shouldn't have been out at all.

"Horses!" someone shouted, and the word echoed through the crowd, carried on waves of enthusiasm and panic. Jonah jogged to the source, amid the squat, ugly towers on University Ave.

From where he stood, he made out eight horses and a mixed contingent of Cleaners, cops, and soldiers. Some had managed to get into one of the buildings and were sniping down at the crowd, while others were less organized, swinging batons wildly at whatever body they could reach. The horses were the most destructive; he could already see people lying on the pavement, trampled, while others threw chunks of concrete and bottles at the wild, terrified animals and their riders.

It was pure chaos. A horse reared and snorted, maddened by the tear gas and smoke. Even one horse, driven into a frenzy, could do as much damage as a gun.

Someone bashed into him, pushed backwards by the horses. Maya was on the pavement, fumbling for her glasses. Jonah fought his way over to her, taking an elbow to the face for his troubles. Shadi grabbed one of her arms and Jonah grabbed the other and pushed all of them behind an overturned mailbox, the radio tucked under one arm.

Maya wiped at her bleeding lip. "Fucking *horses*."

"You're a wizard," Ian said. "Do something about them."

She moved her hands together, light unwinding from her fists and spilling over the ground. The pavement flooded with bioluminescence, sinuous coils of vine and serpents twining at the horses' hooves.

Jonah aimed at the rider, breathed in, and fired. Between the teargas and the illusion, he couldn't see if he'd hit, but the horse was tearing through the crowd, scattering people before it.

With an apologetic glance back at the others, he handed the radio to Shadi, hoisted himself up on the mailbox and scaled part way up the telephone pole. Shivering, his breath was short and swift under his mask. The rider was slumped in the saddle, the horse stamping in tight circles, its nostrils widening in Guernica horror. It tore a path through the crowd and he didn't think, didn't hesitate, just swung from the pole down and onto the horse's back behind the dead cop and slid the corpse off and onto the ground.

The horse bucked, the muscles of its back flexing and contracting to throw him off. He clung to the saddle and reins and tried to get a foot in the stirrups. His whispers wouldn't be audible between the mask and the shouting, but he promised it nonsense anyway, green fields and fat carrots, as it tried to dislodge him.

He'd grown up riding but it had been decades, and he was a stranger to the animal, a threat. He guided the reins but the horse fought him, as wild and chaotic as Maya's serpents. A violent pitch forward smashed him into the saddle and he yanked on one rein, trying to encourage it into a circle, to move it away from the crowd. The smoke was thicker than ever, and the horse screamed and bolted. He was thrown sideways and clung to the side of the saddle before losing purchase, his fall broken only by the sheer density of the crowd as the animal galloped free.

The crowd moved like a surging wave. The block was a mass of bodies, hooves, batons, and lead. Gunfire ripped from the building. Jonah threw himself to the ground, crawled back to where the others had ducked behind a bullet-riddled wall.

Maya had both of her hands over her ears. He pried one away. "Time for a real illusion."

If she spoke at all, it was buried under the rap of gunfire. Her fingers twitched towards the rubber duck, first, as if in slow motion, then seized it like a lifeline. The spell, wrenched loose from the rhythm of her hands, flittered uneasily to life.

Cobwebs of light burst from her fingers, weaving their way through the clash. Where they touched one of the protesters, they caught and exploded in bright explosions. A split second earlier, humans had stood, fresh from the street parade, in patchwork costumes. There were now fierce chimeras, giants with the heads of raccoons and pigeons and sunflowers, great antlered monsters, beings of fire and light. They swooped across the streets on incandescent wings, shrieked wild, animal cries. Maya's flame lilies, woven from the air, spilled over the gutters, writhed in tripwires at the feet of the attackers. She crossed her arms, keeping her distance even as the revellers adjusted to the spaces of their illusions and turned, in fury, on the Dominion forces.

"Demons!" one of the soldiers was shouting, "They have fucking *demons*." Gunfire punctuated the cries, and Jonah rubbed the tragi of his ears, willing them to stop echoing.

Ian wrapped an arm around Maya and kissed the top of her head. "Fuckin' brilliant girl. Let's keep moving."

. . .

At City Hall, climbers had scaled the flagpoles and were tearing down the Red Ensigns. It was all purely symbolic. Years ago, a thin tendril of magic had ripped through the buildings during the Blight, rendering them mostly unusable, and what now passed for a municipal government mainly existed to enforce whatever madness the Dominion conjured from the Train.

Still, symbols mattered.

Gaby Abel stood amid the vast sea of light-creatures, Martine at her side, the threads of her magic now connected to Maya's, darting through an army of minotaurs and garuda and sun gods. A flame-crowned, red-robed king banged a burning staff on the concrete and breathed out a gout of phantasmagoric fire around her.

Gaby herself was unchanged, thin and small and wearing a respirator over most of her face. It didn't disguise her crow's feet, or the heavy bags under her eyes. Her head wrap was a bright speck of red, visible from Jonah's position on the periphery.

"I can't hear her," Maya said.

"You've heard a politician prattle on before," Ian said. "Sentimental bullshit about hardworking families and our children's future. Did ya think it's gonna be any different come the revolution?"

"I want to get closer." She pushed through the crowd. Jonah hesitated—every second Felipe and his army of chucklefucks were advancing on the stadium was an opportunity for them to fuck it up—but Ian was also moving forward, clearly keen to see the politician that had emerged, phoenix-like, from the forge of his abuse and manipulation.

He only caught the end of her speech. She was boosted by a portable sound system and some of the microdrones that Shadi had refurbished haloed her head, capturing the speech for posterity. Years from now, when the Dominion had ground the remnants of human civilization into radioactive ash, maybe sentient cockroach archaeologists could dig it up and laugh at it.

"The Dominion wants to believe that it cannot be beaten. That it alone holds the monopoly on peace, order, and good government. That the suffering you endure—the passes, the curfews, the starvation—is inevitable, the spoils of a fallen world. That to keep us safe against the Blight, the shriekgrass, the demons, we must turn on our neighbours and surrender our freedom. And if we disagree, it doesn't matter. They have the drones, and the guns, and the country."

"Did you write this?" he whispered to Ian.

"Eric," Ian hissed back. "My version had more fucks in it."

"They would have you believe all hope is lost—" Gaby's strained voice threatened to crack. A needle on a turntable, staticky, but not without warmth. She raised a rifle in her left hand, and all around Jonah, fists echoed the gesture, a sea of black flags and sticks and lanterns.

"—So let them see what it looks like when we fight without hope."

32

Lucy was singing and dancing along with the rest of the parade when the first shouts of, "Cops! Cops!" rolled in like a cloud of piss over a summer picnic. The crowd had long since swallowed most of the people she recognized, except Eric, who stuck close to her side. Maya and Martine couldn't have been far off. Their magic crackled and whipped over a night sky turned oxblood in the light of the fires and lanterns.

She couldn't see the police, or even hear the sirens over the smashing drums. Lucy had never been in a crowd this size before—not on the crowd side, anyway. She quickened her steps to keep up with Eric's pace. People died in stampeding hordes all the time, or at least they had before the Dominion had stepped in and assured that, whatever else the nation had become, it would remain polite and orderly.

But there was no panic. That was the most surprising thing. Her heart fluttered, a hummingbird thrum against her ribcage, but she braced her feet into the snow and stiffened her spine. They had rained bombs down on her and she hadn't known she should panic then, it had been so fast, and the only difference now was that death, if it came, would have a face attached to it.

The drummers, the ones beating skins and trashcan lids, were still louder than the mechanical thunk of batons striking riot shields. She still had time.

A group of people in ski masks and floor-length, satiny skirts were handing out respirators and stakes, forming a barricade of car doors and wooden pallets. Even before the influx of refugees they hadn't had enough guns to go around. Eric gripped a steel pole in white-knuckled hands. The stake she'd found, unwieldy, still riddled with staples from a placard that had been broken off, ground against her palm.

"You should get into one of the houses," Eric said. "It'll be safer."

The market was a maze of houses and old shops, brick buildings huddled up into each other, braced for earthquakes and insurrections. Some windows had been punched out, others boarded. In the closest three-storey house, a hurried dash of shadow past a curtain suggested someone inside.

"I don't think anything is safe out here," she replied. "I could have stayed back in the valley. But if you're scared—"

He laughed, a weird, tight little sound muffled by his mask. "I'm guessing you've never been in a riot before."

"Have *you*?" The thwack of the approaching riot police was definitely louder now, but she still couldn't tell which way they were coming from. One by one, the paraders' lanterns went out.

"Stay close," Eric said, uselessly.

Lucy had just determined that the invaders were coming from the empty lot when a small object sailed with a whistle over their heads and landed a few metres away. One of the rioters rushed forward, hockey stick in hand, and swung, sending it flying back into the line of cops in a puff of grey. A second, then a third, and they were raining too quickly to be tossed back. She tried to see through the legs and feet of the people in front of her—a can of some kind? A water bottle?

It exploded.

The smoke was everywhere, all at once, swampy, almost sweet. She had enough time to think, *oh, this isn't so bad.*

And then her eyes were on fire. Everything was fire, stinging her skin, her nostrils, her throat—*fuck*, her throat, she couldn't sing if she couldn't breathe—a blinding incandescence, a hundred thousand needles spiking at her vision.

Now there was panic, the blind stumbling of the bodies around her, flailing in search of the oxygen that had to be just outside of the cloud of gas. She couldn't get a deep breath, couldn't cough out the smoke she'd inhaled no matter how hard she tried. It burned where it was trapped under her mask and shriekgrass spores be damned, she ripped it off and gasped like a dying fish. She was leaking tears and snot. She wouldn't have guessed that there was so much mucus in her. Her face was coated in sludgy goo, and wiping at it only intensified the pain.

Eric tugged at her arm. "This way." She could barely hear him past the blood pumping in her ears. Was she gushing snot from her eardrums too? She pitched after him, convinced she was somehow walking upwards, into the air, sometimes that she was being buried alive. Her world swayed.

Another whistle, this time closer, louder, and Eric was wrapping something over her face that pinched the nails driving into her eyeballs even harder. Someone shoved into her and he all but carried her across the ridge of a threshold.

The wind died, though she could still smell the sweet, acrid smoke. She unwrapped her face and wiped at her eyes, wincing and swearing. Off in the distance, a series of tiny pops echoed over the screaming.

The house's floorboards were lifted up to the cement underpinnings. Eric, shallowly puffing from the floor beside her, was a thin Impressionist streak in her blurred vision.

"You okay?" His tongue lolled at his lips, thickening the syllables. His breathing was shallow and rapid, words stolen between huffs.

For her part, Lucy couldn't summon enough breath to form words. She coughed, strove to push down the terror that she would never sing again, and managed a faint squeak. "Where—what?"

"Tear gas. And—the first house I could find." He coughed too. He was faring better than she was, whether because of his height or his glasses or maybe he'd built up immunity to tear gas in a youth more reckless than she'd given him credit for. The interior of the house was taking solid shape through her squinting, swollen eyes. It had been a modest structure, old and sturdy and practical, but there were hints of grace in its now-chipped wood. Even gutted and graffitied, it held strong against the war outside. Old newspapers taped to the boarded-up window fluttered in the cold gusts that burst through the gaps between planks, the gas drifting in a sickly fog that turned the air to grain and the inside of her mouth to sandpaper.

"Can you walk?" Eric asked. He extended a hand. His fingers were pleasantly cool. For a moment the floor teetered, lurched, and if her throat hadn't been so constricted she'd have vomited, but then she was upright again.

They picked their way up the broken stairs, half-climbing, half-crawling every time a burst of gunfire bellowed outside. The upstairs walls had been savaged to the studs, spouting cotton-candy tufts of pink insulation and electrical wires. None of the doors remained on their hinges. Barricade material.

The top floor of the three-storey was a cramped garret out of a Victorian novel. In a room that looked down over the street, a sniper in a gas mask huddled against the windowsill. They were practically on top of the sniper before Lucy understood that this was a real person and not some dummy posed in the window with a Nerf gun.

"We come in peace," Eric said, quietly, and the pause was long enough to convince her that they were both about to get shot.

The sniper grunted and turned to look to the street below. A real sniper. War, for real. She was always ready for the world to slide back into normal, for the grim rollercoaster of their days to recover its gentle upward slope. To wake up in bed beside Tobias, the last three years a febrile nightmare. Nothing could go on like this forever. No one could.

Lucy re-adjusted her respirator, but it failed to stop the sting of the tear gas, which stuck to everything—her clothes, her skin, the old chipped hardwood floor.

Safe, she thought, and then laughed, vicious and bitter. Eric blinked at her through his glasses, streaked with chemical residue. Almost miraculously, he produced a bottle from somewhere in his bag, and poured out water into a bandana.

"It'll help," he told her, and when she didn't move, squeezed it over her eyes. Lucy yelped, but the initial pain eased up a notch after a second or two of cold.

"You've done this before?" She kept her voice low, wary of spooking the sniper, or of somehow drawing attention to their location over the sounds of shouting and gunfire below.

"Uni was a weird time for me," he said, a little sheepishly. The sniper leaned out the window and squeezed off a shot, impossibly loud, impossibly close, before throwing themself back against the wall. Their breathing was laboured through the gas mask, and the echo of the gunshots turned over in her ears like ocean waves. Would she have hearing loss if she lived?

Eric was on the burner phone, his words an incomprehensible mumble beneath the gunfire, even as close as they were sitting. Lucy huddled on the floor, helpless, her eyes and nose swimming in resin. She was no use in this situation, any more than she'd been when they had arrested Tobias, over the long days of his absence and the lies she'd swallowed about his death.

"We just have to hole up here for a bit," he said. "As soon as things die down we can get out the back door and meet back up with Jonah."

She wasn't sure what good that would accomplish, besides all of them dying together. Through the small rectangle of sky at the bottom of the window, bright specks of snow lit up with the flashes from fireworks and gunfire beneath them.

What had she been thinking, coming here? Just the same drifting through life that she'd always done. First she'd followed her mother's trajectory, and then Tobias', and she'd become unmoored after his death, waiting for something else to catch her in its wake. She'd believed Alycia's lies, at least enough to justify the executions, until she couldn't anymore. But she wasn't a fighter, wasn't a revolutionary, didn't even know how to treat tear gas like Eric did. Just a silly little woman watching the Dominion roll over their silly little uprising.

She wasn't imagining it. The shooting was definitely closer now.

The sniper turned around again, said, "Keep down," just as the whole house quaked on one side and the wall by the window exploded into pinholes of light.

Something black burst from the corner of the room and she shrieked, but it was only a cat, startled by the gunfire. It arched in the opposite corner, corpse-stiff in its hissing terror.

She forced herself to look at the rest.

The closest bullet was by her outstretched foot, just sitting there, inches from blasting a hole. Eric wrapped his arms around her and pulled her back, farther from the window where the sniper hung with one arm over the sill, blood splattered over the wall and floor where, a moment ago, they'd been moving.

She'd seen dead bodies before. Both of her parents, wax mannequins at their funerals. The amorphous shapes that dotted the countryside from the windows of the Train, or hanging off bridges, no one sure who was in charge of removing them. The victims of the drone strikes. This person was definitely dead, blood dripping from their fingers, down their neck where the gas mask ended.

"Fuck it," Eric said. "I'm not waiting for Jonah."

"Hold on." Lucy broke away from him and crawled across the floor. Her clothes were already filthy and covered in sticky residue.

It was only a body. Gingerly, she lifted the mask. It was strapped tight to the sniper's head and didn't come loose. She worried at it before finding a clasp that she could loosen enough to tug it off and toss it across the room to Eric. Beneath the mask, the sniper's face was young—but they were all young, weren't they, everyone who was left standing—pale and splotched with drying blood. Maybe something in a pocket would have given her a clue to who they'd been, who to tell, but she was already robbing the dead, and how could she ever find out who out there was missing them?

The rifle had fallen by their leg. She picked it up, cradled it between her hands like a newborn.

"Lucy," Eric said.

"I can do this," she said, as much to herself as to him. Her own voice was wobbly in her ears. "Martine taught me." She lined up the barrel of the rifle, staying low so that her eyes only barely cleared the edge of the window. The street had emptied out, lit by burning oil drums that caught the thinning drifts of gas and abandoned lanterns. The shadows themselves were alive and stirring.

There was a small group coming around the corner, the same armoured riot cops who had swept through earlier, smashing on their shields with their batons. They weren't so organized now, and one of them was limping. There was a vicarious satisfaction in knowing that someone, somewhere, had gotten a hit in.

She lined up the shot. Were there even bullets in it? There wasn't time to think about it or question her judgment or even whether she knew what she was doing before she was squeezing the trigger.

Her first shot hit the road in front of the men, and she fired again, the wave of adrenaline smashing into her so hard that she forgot to aim, wasn't even sure what she was hitting. Hatred like acid scorched her burning skin and eyes, rage and vengeance for the dead kid slumped beside her, for Tobias, sweet, stupid, beautiful Tobias, for her own small and curtailed life. It was only Eric's hand on her shoulder that told her that she was out of bullets. On his knees, he pulled her away from the window and the body and she leaned into his chest, breathed in sweat and chemicals and the salt of her own tears dribbling under her nose and over her lips.

She grasped fistfuls of his coat, and he was kissing the top of her head, shaking as hard as she was, stroking her hair, her swollen cheek, the top of her shoulders. She looked up. His face was awash in orange light from the window and the bullet holes in the wall, damp and glistening. There was blood up the side of his jaw, from the dead sniper or because he'd scraped himself in the flight from the riot. He took off his glasses, smeared with gunk from the chemicals and the mud. His eyes were bloodshot, red-rimmed, the kindest eyes she'd ever seen.

"Lucy," he started. His voice was scratchy from the tear gas, oddly tentative.

"Oh," she said. "Shut up."

She wasn't sure if she moved first or he did. His nose bumped hers and she'd misjudged, caught the side of his mouth. His lips were dry and chapped, coated with the same sticky substance that seemed to cover the entire world. Her skin vibrated like it was marinated in chili peppers. It hurt, everything hurt, but she laughed into his mouth, a shuddering sob of a laugh, kissing him in the ruins of a crumbling house while the streets burned outside. For the first time in three years, she was alive.

• • •

She curled in Eric's arms for hours, both of them little more than dried-up crusts of snot, mud, and blood, shaking until her tears abated and she breathed a shuddering gasp into his shoulder.

"Do you think it's over?" Lucy asked.

"I think it's just started," he said. "It'll be purges and firing squads next if we're lucky, pogroms if we're not."

She didn't peer through the bullet holes in the boards to hazard a guess as to which one it was more likely to be. The time before, Lucy knew, had been the easy years, peaceful years, when she could pretend she was a patriot and Tobias a hero. Years of a warm apartment and a steady stream of DEC in her account, over now in favour of bloody struggles for a city block.

"I think they've moved on," Eric added. "For now."

Lucy needed to be sure. She wriggled out of his lap and moved the gun out of the way and nudged the dead body out of the way, draping it in her coat.

"There're a few people out," she said. She shouldn't stand so close to what was left of the window—it would only take one stray bullet, one unlucky shot. "I think—ours? Or normal people."

The cat hissed. She'd forgotten it was there. The door had blown shut, trapping it in the room with them. It was brown, nearly black, and blended in with the shadows.

"Poor thing." Lucy drew away from the window and crouched, offering it two outstretched fingers. "Do you think it belonged to—" she gestured at the dead sniper.

The cat was a starved goblin of a creature but it was interested in them, watching them as it paced by the door. Its patchwork fur hung in listless clumps, outlining prominent ribs and spine, its yellow eyes squinting like a boxer sizing up an opponent in the ring. It attempted a second, less committal hiss, and then approached, fur still on end, to sniff at Lucy's fingers.

"It's okay," she told it. "Did you breathe in the gas? It's okay, it's over now, it's over..."

It pushed its face into her hand, and she scratched behind its ears.

"I wouldn't have guessed you were a cat person," Eric admitted.

"I wanted a dog," she replied. "My parents hated animals. Thought they were dirty."

"They *are* dirty," Eric said, as if either of them was one to talk.

"I guess I could have gotten one," she said. "But with Tobias' schedule..." Lucy bit her bottom lip. "Sorry." Dog person or not, she'd charmed the cat. It butted its head against her hand, her bony knee. "We have to take him back with us."

"What?"

"We can't leave him here." She sat two feet from the dead sniper, the pool of blood stilling by the tip of her boot. All of her emotional well-being, all of her sudden, violent fervour was invested in the animal. "He'll starve, or, or someone will eat him."

"*Are* we going back?" he asked.

She sank down on her knees, folded one leg under the other. The cat circled her. She picked him up and put him in her lap. He didn't resist. He must have been someone's pet, if not the sniper's.

"Where would we go?"

"I couldn't run with Jakie or my parents," he admitted. "BC maybe—the SVAR isn't as bad, I don't think, or what's left of America. Israel? Cash in every speck of privilege we still have."

"We're defectors."

"We could disappear here," Eric said. "It was good enough for my ancestors. Pick rags, raise chickens, build the new world from scratch." She laughed at that. "We should regroup with the others. The Dominion will drone bomb this place once they realize what happened here."

"I'm taking the cat."

"Okay."

"And the gun. Can you take the gun? See if there's more bullets?"

She shifted the cat in her arms as she stood, cradling him like a baby. He yowled and dug his claws into her neck. She hushed him. He squirmed, a half-wild thing, but didn't try to spring away. However long he had been skulking around the old house, he must have carried some memory of warmth and tuna, of soft beds and mammalian solidarity.

"Someone's going to eat it," he warned.

She squared her shoulders, clutching the cat tighter, stroking the patchy fur on his skull. Blood trickled from a hole that his claw had punctured in her neck. "Well," Lucy said. "I've shot a man for less."

She opened the front door, into whatever new future had asserted itself.

• • •

The downtown was a festival and a war zone. Long stretches of familiar streets—this had been Spadina, this was Dundas—were reflected back through a shattered funhouse mirror, reassembled into something new in the way that demons sometimes resembled bits of the human they'd sprung from. Eric was her tour guide, pointing out the cool coffeeshop where he'd peered over the top of a book of Neruda poems he'd scored from Seekers, trying to impress a girl with clear-rimmed glasses and blunt-cut bangs, the Chinese restaurant that let him and his friends drink tea until one in the morning after a night of canvassing. All in ruins now, reclaimed in stalagmites of shattered glass and flash-frozen weeds and neon graffiti.

The city, in the blue hour before dawn, had roused from its long slumber. Traces of magic hung in the air as persistently as the tear gas did, transforming the human into the animal, the monstrous, the schizophrenic architecture into alien landscapes. Fires, contained in barrels or abandoned construction sites overgrown with shriekgrass, lit the overcoat of smog above the streets. Sometimes, she saw another person, or a small group. Liberated from the Dominion, it was as if they didn't know what to make of their newfound freedom. All they could do was run in the streets at civil twilight, no longer under curfew, without purpose or plan.

The rebels' main force was at City Hall, and they headed there, Eric's arm around her and the cat bundled in her jacket.

That sterile monument to mid-century social democratic modernism, draped in banners and dripping magic, gave her a momentary shiver. The Blight seam through the buildings glowed menacingly, fenced off by another impromptu barricade. The square itself was alive with people, painting murals over the ramp and pavement, drinking and singing and making out, riding the wheel of revolution before its inevitable downturn.

Inside was just as chaotic. It was some time before Eric found anyone they knew, and unfortunately the people he knew were Ian and Jonah, both of them standing on the observation deck on the 27th floor. Jonah was smoking a cigarette against the wall while Ian leaned over the edge, his long arms draped over the railing, looking down on the inferno of a city.

"You took your time," Jonah said. Smoke drifted around him, dissolved high above the skyline. "Thought you'd died."

Lucy wasn't convinced that she hadn't.

"Where's Gaby?" Eric asked

"Holding court in Council Chambers," Ian replied. "LARPing at a real government. What the fuck is that supposed to be?"

He was gesturing at Lucy. She released the cat. He prowled a few metres along the walkway before returning first to her, then butting up against Ian's ankles.

"His name is Bastien," Lucy declared.

Ian bent down and offered his crooked fingers for the cat to sniff. He seemed to find him acceptable. "He's a she," he observed.

Eric asked, "Did we win?"

Ian snorted. "You Toronto b'ys. Always gotta be the centre of the universe. Of course we didn't win." He gestured expansively at the city below, the teeming crowds gathered in the square, the fires lit for blocks. "But for one glorious sweet second, they lost."

. . .

Morning found them in one of the offices, kept awake by adrenaline and fear. She still hadn't gotten used to the Mac-Pap tendency to catch sleep whenever and wherever one could, under desks on the floor, a weapon in arm's reach. The industrial carpet left a pattern of reddened dents in the side of Eric's face.

"What are you thinking about?" she asked.

"My brother's dead. They kept him alive to control me and my parents, but now—I mean, I don't think—they don't keep people like him alive without a reason."

"I'm sorry."

"My parents, too. Reid can't exactly use them as hostages for my good behaviour. Jakie was my only real friend for the longest time. Maybe ever. I told myself everything I did, everyone I betrayed, it was to protect him. And now he's gone."

Bastien complained piteously, robbed of Lucy's sole focus. Apologetically, she scratched at his—her—ears.

"No one's gonna give a shit," he continued. "They should be buried right away. No one is going to do that. They're all ashes, or in a mass grave somewhere. No one's gonna sit shiva for them. What the fuck is left?"

Lucy trailed her fingers through the cat's fur. "Revenge," she said.

"I miss pizza," Eric said abruptly. "I don't know how long it's been since I had a pizza. I didn't even like pizza that much, but Jakie did."

"Ice skating," Lucy said.

"Really?"

She nodded. "Here, sometimes. And on the Rideau, before it stopped icing over."

"You'd have looked cute in ice skates."

"Play the game, Eric." But she leaned into him and kissed his cheek.

The world before was vapour, an old, half-remembered dream. The water had long boiled, and she had forgotten what it was like to feel the cool air against her skin.

"Hockey Night in Canada," he said.

"You're lying."

Wasn't that the point? To lie about how the old world had been, to pretend that the shadow of this one hadn't always loomed long over it.

"Play the game, Lucy."

"Tobias," she said, softly. An apology. "Every second of every day."

"Do you want to—"

"No. Yes. Is it weird? Obviously it's weird."

"I don't mind weird," Eric said.

"They said they were searching for weeks," Lucy said. "It made sense, at the time. People went missing every day. They had Tobias hunting demons—things could go wrong. I just didn't think. I mean. He was so strong." Her voice threatened to splinter. "It didn't occur to me that he could die. When they told me, they said the rebels did it. An IED, like in Syria. His worst nightmare. They said it took so long just to identify his body."

She drew in a long breath, and he waited.

"I think he would have feared that the most, after what he saw over there. Being blown to little bits, obliterated. Forgotten. He was always taking pictures of me, at the stupidest moments, like when I was trying to eat dinner or get through a new piece. As if he needed an image to remember what was real."

He folded his hand over hers, traced the indents between her knuckles.

"I believed them for years. We went to the same parties, do you remember back then?" As if the gulf of ideology between the Party and its Opposition, yet to fill with blood, was nothing more than a gentlemen's disagreement.

"How could I not imagine your side as murderers," Lucy said, "when we always had our reasons, too? And I never saw it, they never let me anywhere near it." She scratched the cat idly. "It's funny. Tobias hated Ian. He was everything that was wrong with this country, with everything that the Cascade did to us. And there he was, just a sick old man in the end. But he could still end my entire world with a single sentence."

"I'm sorry," Eric said.

"I'm not," Lucy lied. "It's better to know, isn't it? It has to be."

She would have been happier not knowing, secure in her belief that the garbage would always be taken out, the roads always paved, a livable ration card always delivered to her digital wallet at the beginning of the month.

Her fingers closed around his wrist, the bone there more prominent than it had been, hunger wearing them both down into something small and hard and sharp, like the little cat scratching at the underside of the desk.

"I sold people out to save Jakie," Eric said, "And my parents, and now they're dead, and Cal's dead, and they deserve to have it mean something. Guess I have to see this through."

She rescued him from his own self-loathing. "I didn't think you'd really run."

"Bet," he said.

"You're braver than that," Lucy insisted. "We both are. Or we wouldn't be here at all. You know, when we first met, you told me there was no escaping politics. Not even in strawberry daiquiris."

"That wasn't the first time we—never mind. I want to promise that you'll get to drink strawberry daiquiris in some overpriced bar again. That there'll be music again, and ice skating, and life."

She pulled her knees up under her chin, a child telling stories in the dark. Around them, the sounds of movement, life, even in the ruins.

"Promise, then," Lucy said.

33

The shore was iridescent, swirling oil-slick rainbows that danced over its glassy surface. Scores of glass fish crackled over the shore, smashing showers of glittering scales against the frozen veins that spread from the water's edge. The *Retribution* was where Blythe had left it, writhing at the fractured surface. Only when she reached it, did she really believe that it had, like an obedient dog, stayed put.

They were clustered at the base of the dock: Edgar, their students, Kenny and his staff of two, Bailey, the fisherman, the drunks, the foundations of a conspiracy they'd always been too exhausted, too broken, to build. She shouldn't have been surprised that the nascent rebellion had at last stirred. They had buried their dead here and the SVAR would zone a toll highway over their graves.

Blythe could just make out the lump of the invader above the bend of the coastline, its stumpy bulk and its stupid little flag. She could reach it, if the *Retribution* wanted to play along. There were SVAR people, SVAR security, SVAR weapons, all over the city, but the seastead was the occupation's heart.

"I'm going to fuck up their ship," she said.

"With that?" Edgar was enraptured by it, as any scientist would be. The oil slick that coated it moved of its own volition, its movement too fluid, its sheen too dark, for it to follow the same laws of physics as its surroundings.

"It's a bastard of a ship," Blythe said.

"Blythe," Kenny said. "Walk with me a sec?"

They followed the seam where the ridge of glass met the stoney shore in a grim echo of a tide. Kenny kicked at it with the scuffed toe of his boot, the way you'd tap at ice after the first frost in anticipation of its satisfying crunch. Laura used to do that, but then, every kid did that, Blythe had done it when she was a kid and Jonah had never stopped. Still, it all but summoned their presence, and she kept turning her head, convinced she'd see them running just behind her along the beach.

"I know you. What you've lost." He stopped before she could make him. There was one rule in their relationship. They drank, and they fucked, and they made fun of Mitch, but they didn't talk about what had happened. She bore scars, like cicatrization around a broken tree limb, armour to protect them both. "I want to fight them as much as you do. So does every single person here. But we're not revolutionaries. We're not sailors or pirates. I don't think we can make a dent in that with one ship, and even if we do, they'll massacre us on land in revenge."

"And if demons don't kill us, if the SVAR or the Dominion don't drone bomb us, all it takes is one cold snap. Where're you gonna get T in the mountains, anyway?"

"Not the mountains, then. But somewhere hidden. Just to regroup." He wouldn't meet her eyes."It won't work," he conceded. His boots, even after a year without a summer, the deepest cold any West Coaster had ever known, were meant for a normal BC winter, not the November of the second superwinter in a row. "I don't wanna die."

She didn't bother lying, not about that. "That ship isn't invulnerable," she said. "I've seen one destroyed. They'll keep pushing, into more remote places, until they find the Iron Alliance and everyone else who's hidden. Until they have the whole country, or the Dominion does, or they join together in the Great Merger of the Assholes. If it's true about the Mac-Paps getting some wins, maybe it's time now."

"So you're going to—"

"You don't need to come. But look." She stopped walking. The tide, halted by the glass plates, heaved and smashed against the barrier in frustration. A jagged section ran ahead of them, almost to the scrubby tree line, where the Blight had arrested it mid-wave. Little shells and bits of driftwood were trapped in the crystal like insects in amber. Branching, mushroom forms, bones and starfish and anemones, all turned translucent and glittering in the afternoon light. "I think Laura is alive."

She had never spoken her daughter's name to Kenny, not out loud, not since. He'd known of her, of course, even met her a few times in the days after the Blight, but he'd done her the courtesy of forgetting about Laura's existence.

"Blythe—"

"It was trying to show me something, when I was out there. It was trying to speak to me, only we don't share a language, we don't even share the same sort of sentience but. I don't think it was a dream. She was older, and she'd cut her hair, but she looked like her, Kenny, like she would have if they'd let her grow up."

"All the more reason not to go down fighting."

"So that there's not a world left for her? For all I know, she could be on the other side of the country—how am I ever going to find her in a million years?"

"Isn't it better to hope?" Kenny asked.

"No," Blythe answered. "It really isn't. But. If I can't. For whatever reason. Find Jonah, okay? Find him and tell him. He won't believe you at first, but he should know."

•   •   •

The uprising took its cue from the rumours filtering from the east, that the Mac-Paps had taken over parts of Toronto through a series of fast, fluid occupations. Victoria's rebellion was smaller and shorter.

As Blythe crouched behind a wall that had seen better days, a pistol in hand and smoke in her throat, she thought that the problem was institutional memory. The people who knew how to organize, who were willing to run into the streets and throw a brick at a SVAR security guard, had all died in the first feeble spluttering of a resistance three years ago. All of their bravery, their history, their fucking *idiocy*, wiped out in one sweep of drones and semiautomatic fire. The people blindly flailing at the walls of the university were the cowards, the homeless and the hungry, the ones who were as tired as she was. They were loud and disorganized and barely a distraction from the considered acts of sabotage that Blythe and her friends had carefully orchestrated —equipment smuggled out of labs, viruses unleashed on the LAN, jamming signals coordinated to drive the drones into wild, futile spirals.

It didn't change the fact that the university was a fortress, the downtown tiny and easy to corral. Or that the SVAR, for all their cruelty, weren't the Dominion—they were agile and had recruited half the archipelago, the very people they'd starved, to work as their security apparatus. Each well-equipped mercenary had half a dozen skinny recruits armed with knives, baseball bats, and a burning desire to avoid hunger.

She hadn't been inside the lab when it fell. She, along with her department, had moved everyone they could outside, to the shriekgrass-ravaged neighbourhoods where the SVAR was hesitant to invade. They'd done so over the protests of the engineering department, who had insisted their work was too vital to the occupiers for them to be in any danger. They had probably still thought that, right until the shooting started.

Kenny was hunched over the bar, stuffing strips of fabric into bottles. The people outside, still trying to appeal to the hearts and minds of their occupiers with homemade signs and banners, would understand the necessity soon enough.

Edgar had jury-rigged his own surveillance apparatus with what he'd liberated from the university. Video cameras mounted on the Last Call roof fed into a laptop, while a second laptop monitored several company Slack channels. "They're sweeping the neighbourhood," he reported to no one in particular.

The pistol was slick in Blythe's hand. It wouldn't do much good against a private army. Almost no one on the archipelago was armed. Kitty had found some bows and arrows from the university archery club and distributed them to anyone who said they could use one, or knew someone who could.

"We should start moving the equipment," Bailey said.

"Get to PKOLS," Blythe said. "Mount Douglas. You know." She waved, aimlessly. It was high ground; they wouldn't be able to miss it. The irony didn't escape her; a W̱SÁNEĆ Elder had brought her to a ceremony there when she'd started at UVic, told her the history of the place, as beautiful and bloody as all of their histories, and at the heart of it, a promise that they might roam free and unbothered by settlers. Of course, the SVAR had plans to log it.

They hadn't, yet. And the locals still had the advantage in the forest.

She tucked the pistol back into its holster and broke the inertia, started tossing everything they'd liberated from the lab into milk crates, loading them onto the creaky dolly that Kenny used to haul empty kegs. The drones were close enough to be visible. The ruins of the neighbourhood, reshaped by earthquakes and floods, the old cedars holding strong against shriekgrass and masses of kudzu that coiled over telephone poles and rusted-out cars, made for tricky flying. It made loading what they could into the trucks just as much of a challenge, but it would buy them precious minutes.

"Edgar," she said, pulling him aside while the others were occupied.

He was running on fumes. Had been as long as she'd known him, but the brutal pace of the SVAR's schedule and the double life he'd been forced to live had taken its toll.

"You'll get everyone to the mountain, right?"

Wearily, he said, "I'm going with you."

"The fuck you are."

"Me and Bailey. We talked about it earlier. Kenny can get everyone hidden. He's good at leading people."

"So are you. You led the department for a decade." She closed a hand around his wrist, felt the sharp jut of bone under her fingertips. "I'm not coming back."

"You discovered the Blight," Edgar said. "You warned the world. You found a life form that no one could identify, something that changed our understanding of biology. You have decades of papers in front of you. What makes you think that this is the end?"

She shook her head. Words wouldn't come. Her breath stuck to her throat, weighed down her tongue. She hadn't cried, wouldn't cry, but her eyes burned, pinpricked by thousands of tiny needles. Her ward tattoo was a searing brand.

"They're here," Bailey said.

It wasn't Mitch's company, just some private security contractors. The laptop showed several black vans parked up the street. The crowds were thick enough that they didn't need to give chase; they could just reach for the nearest person and slam them into the pavement.

People fought back. They were armed with whatever was available—kitchen knives, pots and pans. She never would have guessed that stately, staid Victoria was capable of it.

The first shots were non-lethal rounds. Rubber bullets, pepper spray. They weren't the Dominion, and they needed the workforce.

A group of men approached the door.

"Out the back," Kenny hissed. The truck started up. She should have gone to him, at least said goodbye—

—The light, when the door smashed open, was blinding.

A man stood, framed by the broken door, square-jawed and well-fed the way SVAR goons tended to be, a guy who woke up at 4 am to grind like the Blight had never happened. He had killed Laura. No, not him, but a man exactly like him, and maybe Laura wasn't even dead if the thing beneath the ocean was to be believed, and there were equations to be made, disparate realities to be untangled and woven together, and maybe he wasn't a murderer but he was still guilty.

They would lose but he could still die.

Blythe didn't see who threw the first punch, whether it was someone from her lab group or from Kenny's bar or one of the strays they'd collected. It didn't matter. They had all lost someone. They all knew what a SVAR-Dominion alliance meant, what happened when giant powers divided other people's land and homes amongst themselves.

They all had different stories but in that one beautiful moment, in the split second of a brick flying overhead across the room, they were all of one mind.

Her legs had turned to stone. She should have fought, or fled, but she was fixed in place, the room turned to thick mush. Her own body, frozen in terror, thwarted her revenge.

The SVAR's non-aggression principle held out as long as it took for the first guard through the door to get clipped in the side of his head, and then the firing started.

Edgar was tugging her away from the fray, towards the door, and her limbs at last answered her wildly cycling brain. There was nothing but the din of gunfire in her ears, nothing but heat and light and panic. She scrambled over a clump of bodies like wet leaves in autumn, searching for Omid and Kitty and Bailey and anyone she knew, as if her presence, her recognition, would save them from an anonymous death on a filthy floor.

It was both a miracle and cruelty that, in the avalanche of gunfire, she caught Edgar's eye from the other side of the bar. He was screaming at the men to hold their fire. She pushed through a sea of bodies, living and half-living, a zombie nightmare unlike any of Kenny's rehearsals for the apocalypse.

Edgar was crouched on the ground, cradling Omid's head in his hands. Kitty had a coat balled up against his chest, but his eyes, fixed open and glassy, told Blythe all she needed to know.

This was how the world ended, not all in one spasm like the Blight, but piece by piece, flesh ripped from bone by a starving dog. The way her world had ended before, and would again until there was nothing left.

She hadn't gotten to say goodbye to Laura, and so she seized Edgar's hand, hissed, "Run," like it was a plea or a prayer and then she was pushing him away, she was running, not for the truck or for the mountain but down to the harbour, a knot of black tar squeezing her chest. There was another crowd battling it out with another company, and she fired the pistol, recklessly and uselessly, used the distraction to stumble towards the boats.

The *Retribution* was gone. She could sense it, an itch in the back of her head that wouldn't quiet. But she couldn't see it.

The unseasonal, bitter snow turned to rain. The stones of the beach were dark, glistening, alive and sentient. They welcomed the sky back from under its oppressive cloak.

What was she supposed to do? Somewhere beneath the churning waves lay the archipelago's salvation, and Blythe's revenge. It was a test of faith. She would have to wade out into the storm, let the sea take her. Drown if she needed to.

The waves crashed into the rocks along the shore, spume stinging her eyes. Somewhere in those depths were the answers. Where Laura was. What the entity wanted from her. Why no matter how hard she'd worked, how fiercely she'd loved, how far she'd run, she never belonged anywhere but at the bottom of the ocean.

Carefully, she put one foot forward. The tide was higher now, up to her knee between one step and the next. The cold was barely a shock. She had been cold for so long that she didn't remember what warmth felt like.

Another step. The water was up to her waist. Her breath was clarified, austere, her physical form taking up no more space than it had to, ceding its excesses to the sea.

The ocean should have screamed. She was surrounded by water—now her chest, now her neck, brushing like a lover's hand below her chin—and yet she could hear no direction from it, none of the commanding rage that had been the soundtrack to her sleepless days and nights. The wind and the explosion of wave on stone was deafening.

Maybe she'd been mad the whole time. Maybe she would just walk into the sea, drown like Ophelia, like so many madwomen before her, husband gone, daughter gone, career irreparably fucked by an invasion of libertarian tech nerds, and not a single person would be surprised.

She turned for the shore and a wave crashed over her head, saltwater in her nose, in her mouth, and for a moment she was drowning again, her ward aflame. She thrashed, fighting for the surface, caught in the wave's onslaught.

Not in years had she felt so small. So pitifully human.

Another wave—they were closer, the heartbeat of the ocean racing, plunging her under. She choked, unable to scream. Somewhere above her there was land, warmth, human contact and empathy. And she would give anything to reach it again.

She could see the shore when she breached the surface and took a shuddering lungful of air. The roar of the ocean was louder now. No. Not the ocean—a motorboat, skimming across the choppy roof of the waves.

There was Edgar. And Bailey. And what looked like several massive crates of explosives.

Blythe pushed up and waved her arms, but she wasn't far from shore. They'd seen her walk out, seen her try to drown herself, seen her suddenly and belatedly cave to the stubborn human impulse to keep breathing. The boat swerved and slowed, and they were pulling her over its side, soggy and freezing and retching seawater onto the deck.

Maybe it wouldn't be the end after all.

The *Retribution* was gone, but they could still fuck up the seastead. They might be in the belly of the beast, but they didn't need to be digestible.

She put her hand over Edgar's where it white-knuckled the steering wheel. The seastead, unmoved by the storm, was dead ahead.

34

Jonah left Maya with Shadi and Martine and Gaby, all of them busy securing City Hall. Felipe had been quiet on the burner phone for too long, so whether he was fighting the Dominion or planning to turn on Gaby, Jonah was reluctant to leave him to it. There would be no magic once Jonah headed south, no ruses of demons, no carnival of beautiful tricksters. The same strategy that had the Dominion playing a game of Whack-A-Mole against their forces had left the movement's leader an open target. He'd have to go on alone, and hope that the others could keep Gaby from fucking it up too badly.

He sensed Ian's presence before he heard his footsteps, a cold spot on his tattoo.

"You shouldn't be here," Jonah said.

"Tryin' to sneak off again?"

"You want to leave Felipe in charge of liberating a prison? By himself?" Jonah forced himself to turn. Ian was alone, standing in the middle of the street with snowdrift ghosting at his ankles, his fists crumpled in fingerless gloves at his side, braced for the world's most anti-climatic gunfight.

Whatever the fuck was going on with him, whatever this new, tenuous chapter in their dysfunctional relationship was going to be, Ian wasn't going to make it less of a pain in the ass than the preceding few decades had been.

"I ordered out the Charge of the Shite Brigade, not you. You're not cannon fodder. Felipe is. Wait until he's cleared it out."

"Are we ever gonna talk about—"

He might as well have suggested that Ian slide on a pair of fishnets and stand in front of the Train with a fuck-off rainbow flag belting the Internationale at the top of his withered lungs. That scenario was far more likely than Ian ever talking about his feelings.

"Mind now I does that. One halfhearted blowjob and I'm the next Mrs. Augustine?"

"Go to hell, Ian."

He had a terrible sense that under the mask, Ian was grinning at him. The knot above his lungs didn't loosen as such, but he could breathe through it. "Wasn't halfhearted," he muttered, though his own mask would muffle it.

Ian slung an arm around his shoulder, the way he might have done back before everything had become a fractal clusterfuck. His middle finger landed on the top of Jonah's still freezing tattoo and sent a shiver across it through layers of parka and army surplus gear. The void energy he was bringing wasn't *worse* than it had been earlier, but proximity and attention made Jonah more conscious of it. "What does it feel like?"

"Like someone walking over my grave." The inconvenience of the ward tattoo wasn't his fault, but a better man might have apologized anyway. "You don't even have a gun," Jonah said. "City Hall's safer."

"When the fuck have you ever known me to be safe, b'y?"

You'll slow me down, Jonah almost said. *I'll get shot because I'm watching your back instead of my own.* Not that Ian would care about his life. "I'm actually useful. I can't rescue people if I'm carrying your busted ass."

Ian glared at him over the rim of his mask. For a moment they both stood, waging some kind of mutually assured scowl-based destruction. "Run away, then. It's what you do best, isn't it?"

Jonah wrenched away and started walking again. The chill across his skin didn't cease, nor did the footsteps. Eventually he fell into pace with Ian's longer strides.

. . .

At the dome, Felipe's assault had already started, but the bursts of machine gun fire sounded more controlled than they had in the mess of the riot. Cleaners were thugs, used to mowing down unarmed civilians huddled in apartment buildings, and the revellers-turned-rioters weren't any more organized or methodical in their violence. This was something different: two groups of trained soldiers going to war.

What the *fuck* were they doing in the middle of it?

He couldn't tell who had the upper hand. Without the torches and lanterns, he couldn't see much of anything at all. The stadium lights were a blinding glare, sodium-yellow, cats' eyes in a night still dense with gas and smoke grenades. He hid and let his vision adjust to the darkness, Ian's Darth Vader rasp next to his ear.

Below the gunfire there was another sound, the screaming of a chorus of the damned. Father Morin, when he was growing up, used to talk of Hell in such a vivid way, of unending, unceasing torment. Jonah had always known where he was headed.

Magic writhed from the stadium, leeching white filaments from the cracks in the ice-crumbled concrete. It scorched afterimages into his vision when he closed his eyes.

He moved closer. His arm ached. He could handle pain. He'd alternated between on fire and dead inside since Laura had drowned, and it couldn't hurt worse than that. Ian at least had the foresight to tattoo his non-dominant hand; the right one could still hold a gun. He could still take a few of the fuckers down with him.

343

Ian stepped out in front of him, into the mantle of radiance pouring from the stadium. Jonah could have sworn the temperature had dropped by ten degrees, but the pain also retreated, the ambient magic shivering back from Ian's presence.

"Okay, yeah, but there's no way you could have *known* you'd be useful." This earned him another string of barely comprehensible ancestral curses.

He saw their chance around the back of the stadium. The guards had moved from the door to engage a cluster of Felipe's guys, and they passed into the deeper darkness in the heart of the building.

It had been some kind of delivery entrance. He pressed up against something that might have been a pile of stacked risers, willing his breath to be as quiet as possible. Petal-pale rivers of magic seeped around the corner, throwing ropes of shadows across the risers.

Jonah reached for his gun.

The corridor wound through the back of the stadium. As he entered the arena, the light thickened, cutting a jagged line across the rows of seats. From there—the fighting strangely distant, almost an afterthought—he looked down onto the playing field.

The arena had been converted into a factory floor. Rows of long tables held troughs through which magic flowed, so blinding-bright that someone might have taken a pin to scrape lines in the surface of reality itself. They formed a great circulatory system, channeled the unearthly glimmer towards a construction in the middle of the stadium that looked like nothing so much as a slowly pulsating heart. Scaffolding and weathered tarp concealed a structure that might have been fifteen feet high, something that pulsed in a languid rhythm like a slowed-down version of Maya's Pattern. Slashes of silver criss-crossed the floor under the seats, interrupted by a scuttling movement.

The smell came before his eyes adjusted, a seething, roiling onslaught of sweat and piss. He gagged and backed into Ian, who—fucking useless or not—caught him before he could slam into the edge of the aisle.

It took him another second to recognize the sound: snuffling, choking gags coalescing into sobs.

The thing that crawled out of the mouth of the aisle was barely human, all shrivelled flesh and protruding bone. He couldn't differentiate where grey skin ended and grey uniform began. The folds and creases in the creature's face and hands, in the fabric, would tear like paper at the slightest tension.

Just as the initial shock faded first into revulsion, then searing, visceral rage, a second face, as hollow-eyed and bent-wood twisted as the first, shuffled into the light. And another. They were packed, half-living and half-dead, into the stadium, splashed in their own shit. A few at a time, they picked their way from the risers or from the floor, mouths gasping like asphyxiating, flopping fish at their first breath of cold fresh air. Insect limbs at sharp points above a sharp ridge of vertebrae. The tangled rat king of human misery had no end point, no separation between one writhing corpse and the next. They coughed and staggered and retched their way into a line before he could fall back, a piteous column of ghosts marching into the bleak afterlife.

One of the corpses pulled away from the others, crawled towards them on limbs charred and fragile as charcoal. Jonah steadied his pistol. Breathe. Aim.

It lifted its head. She. She lifted her head. Her sunken eyes, deep brown, and all-too-human, met Jonah's. She indicated the guards and raised a finger to her lips. They kept the wretched parade moving, pausing occasionally to shout an order at one of the prisoners still strong enough to stand.

"What are you building?" he whispered. There was no comprehension in the woman's face, eyes glazed, mouth cracked and caked with grime. Her tongue clacked against broken teeth.

Jonah's fingers tightened over the trigger. The gun was an impatient toddler, demanding attention, release.

"Isn't it obvious?" Ian hissed back, and of course it was, of course in this stadium was everything the Dominion had ever wanted. Magic, quantified, tamed, commodified. Channelled into the tall metal scaffold at the arena's centre line, which encased a shrouded, beating magic heart.

They'd hauled in truckloads of prisoners, the missing, the un-en-fucking-cumbered, to build an abomination their own people wouldn't touch.

Bloodied fingerprints trailed streaks through the layer of filth that crusted the underside of the seats. By Jonah's foot, a gash caught the light where a fingernail had fought steel and lost. He gagged at the smears of shit, the ammonia stench of piss that congealed below the grates in the floor. His tattoo thrummed with looted magic, more than could be repelled by Ian's presence.

The fighting had reached the arena. A group of soldiers emerged from one of the other entrances, using the seats for cover, blasting away through the door. Jonah crept along the perimeter, stealing through the rows of seats towards the fighting. At some point the terror had to subside, the hammering of his heart had to slow into a steady trance of violence. He would forget to flinch at the sound of gunfire, forget even Ian's presence at his side, unarmed and hapless and already half a corpse himself.

Jonah waited, and when that didn't happen, he opened fire anyway.

Through the smoke and darkness he couldn't see what he hit or whether anyone was shooting back at him. He knew only that he kept firing, that Ian was still alive, a cold, spectral presence keeping the storm of feral magic at bay, that as long as the soldiers were occupied, they couldn't turn their guns on the starved, screaming inmates in the work camp.

In the periphery of his vision, Ian herded the prisoners through the entrance they'd come through, away from the fighting. Dragging them, where he could, with his forearms braced through a bent limb. The dying clung to him like drowning men on a life raft, and they would bury him alive in their desperation if they could, but he kept moving them forward anyway. Kept ensuring that whatever sins Jonah committed tonight would be against their enemies and not the human wreckage on the arena floor.

It took him long seconds to notice it when, at last, Felipe's forces broke through. In the muddy gloom of the stadium, they were barely differentiated from the Dominion soldiers, dressed in the same dusty uniforms as the government forces.

"I'm on your side, asshole," Jonah shouted back. Holding his gun in the air, he stepped out from his position behind the seats. The floor was littered with dead and wounded, soldiers, rebels, prisoners. He spotted Felipe ducking out from behind an entrance and dashed over to him.

"Thought you were keeping Gaby under control." Felipe leaned out to take a potshot at a group of soldiers.

"Gaby needs eyes and ears down here. She's too busy liberating City Hall for the Glorious People's Republic of Fucktopia to babysit you."

"And she sent you two?" Ian had reemerged, a shambling train wreck only slightly more ambulatory than the doomed prisoners. "What're we supposed to do with these people? Gaby give you any orders about *that*? We can't feed them."

Jonah had seen the Mac-Pap storerooms, or what was left of them after the bombings. In a sane world, there would have been saline IVs, tube feeding, months of rehab. They could probably get some of the prisoners out in the carriers brought by the men they'd just slaughtered, but they'd only make more work for themselves digging graves afterwards. The Dominion had already done most of the work of killing these people, but burying the bodies was left to them.

"Better start getting them on the trucks," Ian said, and then took up his old policy of shouting at someone until they were sufficiently cowed to do the impossible for him.

Felipe looked disgusted, but he motioned his men forwards, his boots squelching in a lake of gore.

Another one of the fighters, whose name Jonah wouldn't learn until much later, said, "This is some fucked-up shit," and lifted up one of the cracked troughs from the table.

The rest of it happened very fast.

Jonah had never seen someone transform into a demon, not outside of Tobias Fletcher's grainy footage from the illegal SVAR camp a lifetime ago. He'd thought it would be smoother, like Jane's werewolf transformation on *Night Beats*. A whisk of budget CGI and the creature was standing where a man had been. He hadn't imagined the cracking of joints as they reversed angles, the lengthening of bone, the stretching and parting of flesh to reveal new monstrous geometries. He hadn't imagined feeling it, a dizzying turn of gut acids, a haloed double vision that must have been his optic nerve protecting his brain from revealing entirely the spectacle before it.

The demon lunged for the closest person to it, a second rebel who hadn't moved back quickly enough. Jonah had been standing right beside him. Luck and a quick dodge to the left meant that the demon fixed its yellow eyes on the other man instead.

Jonah still expected him to run. Instead, the demon stopped at arm's length and whispered, "Asssh. Bahh-ree." Long seconds paused before the mantra formed into a name, and the man took a step forward, gun clattering to the ground.

Private Ash Barry went to his death with the placid, stunned expression of a cow on a slaughterhouse conveyer belt. Long, pointed jaws lined with layers of sharp teeth seized around the man's neck, nearly beheading him, as several of the hairy limbs gripped his torso.

"We need to evacuate!" Felipe shouted, but his men were so drunk with violence that they'd forgotten the basics of demon engagement —which was that the only way to survive an encounter was to run like hell in the opposite direction. They fired on it, which served only to piss the thing off further. Its segmented body whipped three of the fighters off their feet before it slid for a man standing two feet away from Jonah.

The man blasted at it. Shell casings clattered in a circle by his boots. The demon reared, and brought its head close to the man's ear.

There were words—a name—in the sibilant gush of air, woven in the rotting-meat smell of the creature's breath. The man deflated, the flesh of his cheeks sunken in, a stop-motion animation of a corpse decaying. He shuddered to collapse, thinning and darkening, until a husk stood in his place, wrist splintering under the weight of his gun.

Jonah had never considered himself a brave man. He broke from the line of fighters, grabbed Ian's arm, and ran.

The demon was on top of both of them in seconds, a giant fuck-you to the law of conservation of mass, tendrils spilling over the seats and the arena floor and the pillar behind him. There was nowhere to run, and the last real conversation he'd had with Ian was both of them sniping back and forth, each trying to inflict the most damage. When he thought about it, he'd kind of figured that was always how he was going to go out.

The demon's eyes, centimetres from his own, were still human. Warm and brown and terrified, the last refuge of a spirit hijacked by magic. They were both closer than they should have been able to get to a demon without it shredding them to pieces.

Its jaws parted, and it whispered to him. There was an emptiness on its tongue where the names of its other victims had sat. Its hiss danced like it belonged in his brain but couldn't find anything to attach to in there. Instead, the sounds floated, disconnected, irrelevant, incapable of resolving into words.

Gripping the pistol in both hands, Jonah edged in front of Ian, shoved him backward, aimed squarely into the demon's mouth, and fired.

The blood that splattered him, in the gaps where his skin was exposed, burned like battery acid and for a moment, he still thought he was dying.

He observed, as if from a great distance, the slow process of the demon's death. He owed that much to whatever was left of the soul it had consumed. It thrashed, its bottom jaw dislocated by the gunshot, leaking ichor in thick streaks over the concrete floor. It made noises, great sobbing heaves that grew ever more ragged and reedy.

It was as if his flesh was parted, his ribcage cracked open to pour the demon's truth into him. A toddler learned to walk, his mother's face a shining sun before him; a boy skated on a frozen pond. A teenager, the age Laura would have been, breathed pot smoke into a girl's mouth. A young soldier traced the maple leaf flag on his arm as he lowered his rifle, refusing to fire on a crowd of protestors. The magic infecting him, infesting him, gnawing his soul to splinters in instants. Its bewilderment, metastasizing to rage.

Jonah waited for it to transform back to the unfortunate human it had been, but of course that didn't happen either. It remained stubbornly itself, lumpish and misshapen and very much dead.

"Move move *move*," Felipe shouted, shaking Jonah out of his trance. Only then did he notice he'd been crying.

"We can't leave," Jonah said. "We can't let them have this."

Felipe dragged him, trying to save his life despite Jonah's half-assed attempt at getting him killed. Maybe he hadn't noticed. Jonah stumbled, searching for Ian in the retreat. Ian was probably willing to cede the abomination to the Dominion, let whoever spawned it be devoured by their own creation.

The flight from the dome to relative safety in the lobby of one of the condos was a blur of blood and someone else's memories. Felipe's remaining men swarmed around Jonah, jocular parodies of camaraderie. He stood, stiff, numb to their fist-bumping, their stupid misplaced awe.

"Look at you," Felipe was saying. Jonah couldn't breathe. He was having a heart attack. "Fuckin' demon slayer. Didn't know they could be killed."

"No one did," Ian said. He was up in Felipe's face, using his height and his unearthly appearance to its full effect. "Get gone, b'y. All of youse. Give us a sec."

Jonah sank into the frayed leather couch, across from a long-dead palm tree planted squarely on a marble floor. He couldn't breathe. The reek of shit, blood, and ichor had come along for the ride, wrapped a bony fist around his throat. He placed the gun across his knees and bent over, digging the crucifix out from under his shirt collar, and willed the world to stop spinning.

"We'll have to come back with fire," Ian was saying. Maybe to him. "Colette, she wants a demon. Can't let her have one. Best to burn the whole place down, or smother it in lead."

"Uh huh," Jonah said, because he was expected to say *something*, and not just sit there like a shell-shocked WWI veteran.

"Joe." He'd never known Ian to speak softly. With the blood roaring in his ears, it was a minor miracle that he could be heard at all.

"I need a smoke."

Ian waited, until it must have become clear that this wouldn't happen on its own, and then dug into the pocket of Jonah's parka. There was half a hand-rolled cigarette left. Ian lit it, inhaling the smoke with a cough, lowered the top of Jonah's mask and then put it between Jonah's dry lips.

"Shit'll kill you."

"Pretty sure something else'll get me first. Was it talking?"

"Trying to."

"It tried to say my name," Jonah said. "Not my—I mean. The other one. The one you buried."

"At least we know the spell works now."

This, at last, broke Jonah out of his stupor. "You didn't know that would work? You didn't *tell* me what it meant?"

"In my defence, I was 25. I didn't knows if *anything* worked. And I wasn't gonna tell you to go out and shoot demons to test a theory."

"Is that how I killed it?" He had to think like Blythe, reason it out. Demons whispered your name before they killed you, he had no name, not in any meaningful sense, ergo—

"You can thank me when we're at City Hall," Ian offered. He slouched at the wall, close enough that he could take Jonah's hand if Ian were a normal person and not a trauma-addled wight. Jonah could just barely manage the cigarette, a slow inhale and exhale that filled his nostrils with something other than the stench of death. Beyond that, he couldn't make himself move.

"City Hall," he echoed dully.

"Those soldiers will follow you anywhere now. Into the fires of Hell itself or wherever Quinn Atherton makes his home. You'll be a fuckin' legend. You didn't think we were done here, b'y?"

I'm done, he almost said, as if that were an option, as if on the longest night there was anything he could do besides keep fighting, keep the watch, make sure that the wolf didn't devour the sun. "Of course not," he said, instead, the weariness etched in his voice. "We have a city to win."

35

One of the pigs had died in the night. Colette felt the thread that connected them abruptly sever, a tiny death like an electric shock, momentarily startling her out of her sleep. Heart failure, like the others. She tightened her mask, sucking in a breath and holding it before sliding the bottom of the cage open to retrieve the body. The smell of them, earth and straw and the sharp acid of animal terror, burned through. The pig had partially turned demon before dying, pearlescent tumours, like inlaid gems, sprouting in labyrinthine patterns from where she'd sewn through the skin. The teeth had changed too, rows and rows of sharp shark incisors lining its mouth. It was still recognizably piglike, and it had lasted longer, and shown more promise, than the mice had.

She'd have to see about getting some lab assistants, if Alycia decided that this line of research might bear fruit. Colette had managed the mouse autopsies by herself, but the pig was unwieldy. Dense with newly formed muscle, it sagged dangerously as she tried to extract it from its cage.

She called Nate. "I might be a bit late," she said. The boys shrieked in the background. She rolled the pig's thick eyelid back. Two dark pupils fought for space on the glistening wet sclera. "Can you handle dinner?"

"They hate my cooking."

"There's lasagne in the fridge," Colette countered. "They like that."

"Not when I reheat it." Nate's tone skirted the edge of a whine. Men could be such children sometimes.

"I'll be home when I can."

"Jasper, can you—" Something broke, and he stifled a curse. "Hon," he started. The words fell to a hush. "That broadcast, the things they're saying about what's happening in Toronto..."

"It's nothing," Colette said quickly. "Terrorist psyops stuff. And it's nowhere near here. I asked Alycia—she said our neighbourhood is really safe, and you've seen the patrols."

"You don't think you're a target?"

"They have no idea who I am," she assured him. Which was almost the truth. Nate didn't know about Ian Mallory—that part of her work was geased, even if she'd wanted to share the gory details with her husband—but how much of a threat could Ian Mallory be now? "Babe, you're safe. We're safe, the kids are safe. The work I do, it's all about keeping us safe."

He was still talking, his attention split between the kids causing chaos in the living room and her own soft reassurances. She hiked the phone between shoulder and ear, sliding off her gloves. It was unhygienic, but she needed to feel.

The pig's skin was colder than it should have been, and unpleasantly hairy. She placed her hand over the animal's neck. Several of the caged pigs voiced their protest, grunting in distress.

"Yeah," she said into the phone. "As soon as I can. Love you."

The current moved under the pig's dead flesh, weaving together the organic and the demonic, a living, pulsing thing that reached for her, recognized in her some common purpose. The skin bulged, a muscle reflex pushed to near-bursting. The corpse was only a vessel for the thread, as Ian had been, as one day, she would be. It stretched out to something greater, across realities that smashed into one another like calving icebergs.

It was being drawn to something that swallowed her own small, bright spirit in its enormity. An all-encompassing galaxy of a thing, channeled into the lumpish, hairy body of the animal.

It was too much. Colette slid to the ground, the phone still clutched uselessly in one hand. Her magic wove strands of itself through the folds and crenellations in her brain, marking out a map for her to follow. She had breathed her intention into the universe and it, at long last, had given her an answer.

She knew what it was. More importantly, she knew *where* it was.

"Babe," Colette said into the phone, "Can you drive me somewhere tonight?"

• • •

The twins slept in the backseat. Every so often, Noah fussed; Jasper, after his rampage through the living room, made only soft, snuffling whispers. She had considered—slipping into old thinking patterns—conjuring some kind of babysitter in the middle of the night. She hadn't lied to Nate, not really. But leaving her children in the hands of an unknown entity seemed a greater risk than taking them towards the knot of magic in the heart of the city.

"But what is it?" Nate asked, for the thirtieth time.

"We are, as ever, united in our condemnation of these terrorist attacks, and resolve to stand strong against—"

"Fu—dge." Nate checked the rearview mirror, but the boys hadn't budged. "Can you at least turn that to something else?"

Colette played with the radio dial. There wasn't much, the Dominion having throttled most of the bandwidth, replacing it with its own channels. One spewed the address from Director Atherton on repeat—she didn't want to listen, *couldn't* listen—and so she settled for one of the other ones, playing soft, mesmerizing classical music. Post-curfew music, woven with minor magic to settle the populace into compliance. It would keep her boys calm. Her own energy answered it in turn.

"I can't describe it," she said. Literally—there was enough of Ian's magic in the thing that the geas applied—but besides that, the source itself felt too big for words. "Remember when you were a little kid, and you waited up all night for Santa, before you even knew that it was your parents sneaking presents under the tree." Christmas had been on her brain lately, their second one since the Blight and their first one with the boys. The balance had gone up in her DEC account, which meant beet sugar, maybe even imported chocolate. Some people on their street had put up decorations that they had carefully hoarded from the old days, silly plastic things that she nevertheless looked upon with warmth. They could have a normal Christmas, if she hurried, if she was as sharp as a scalpel.

"I think I always knew it was my parents," Nate said.

"I didn't," Colette said, sheepishly. "But you were excited, right? Too much to sleep."

"Sure."

"Like the excitement was better than whatever presents you might get, because it *contained* all possible presents."

"You think we should be doing more? For the boys?"

"It feels a bit like that," Colette continued. "The magic. Like a thing that's so big because it has everything else inside of it. And somehow, somehow I helped make it happen."

Pray. The project Alycia would tell her nothing about, had expected her to stumble into by faith. Eat and Love had failed, lay in crumpled skeleton-men and carbuncle-encrusted dead pigs, in the dead-alive glass child that locked her tongue into silence. But Pray was alive, and it called to her.

She recognized her mistake even as they approached. Nate had been scared, and rightly so, of the fighting, and she'd forced him to drive right towards it. There was an overturned army truck across the highway lanes, in flames, the driver burnt to charcoal trying to crawl out of the window. She jerked her head to the backseat, but the boys were both still sleeping soundly.

"Shit," Nate said. "I'm turning back."

This couldn't be happening. She had taken the murmurs of revolt as a distraction, nothing more than the selfish, hotheaded grumbling from the usual kinds of rabble-rousers. They posed a threat, of course, but that was what the Cleaners were for, to keep everything orderly and safe. Atherton had assured them that the situation was under control.

"Pull over for a sec," she said. There was no one on the highway, the highway disappeared into thick fog ahead, demon-fog, and she had to *think*.

"Colette, the *kids*."

"Right," she said. "You're right, this was a mistake." And leaned across the SUV's gear selector to prick his arm with the needle she kept in her pocket.

She couldn't look at his face, her poor, sweet Nate who barely understood what the thread could do at the instant of their connection. He would have been conscious long enough to know he'd been betrayed.

"I'm sorry," Colette whimpered. To Nate, to the boys. To her perfect little family, who she might never see again. It was all for them, it always had been, but they weren't MAI and they could never understand why she would have to leave them here, helpless and vulnerable. "I'm so sorry."

She pressed two fingers under his ear. He was still breathing, slumped against the wheel. She'd performed enough experiments to be confident in her ability to channel magic into him without harming him permanently. He'd be conscious in minutes. Probably. He would forgive her, once he understood. She placed a soft kiss on his temple.

Then she pushed the door open and stepped out onto the highway.

• • •

The ramp was deserted, mist-shrouded. Colette had foolishly expected a checkpoint and had retrieved her purse and checked her wallet for her pass, since her cell had dropped to 3% battery. When she at last came upon the place where the checkpoint should have been, there were six dead guards, littered unceremoniously where they'd fallen in the snow. Some had bullet wounds. Others, from their bloated faces and orbital fractures, collapsed parietal bones, had been beaten to death. A kid with sandy brown hair and freckles who looked like he should be playing minor league hockey draped over the edge of the ramp, neck bent at an impossible angle. Several feet away, one of the terrorists lay face-down, bright blood pooled under his chest, mouth half-open with the snow drift collecting between his blue lips.

She kept moving. She would be brave. Halfway down the exit ramp, the concrete had split, the ramp dropping off abruptly into darkness. What remained of the condo towers were likewise blackened. In some windows she saw small, bright flickers of light, fires set in the hearts of the cold giants. They looked no brighter than the spray of distant stars over the skyline.

Colette slung her purse across her chest and over her back to free her hands, then climbed downwards, her sneakers—comfortable enough for the lab—sliding over the gap of broken concrete and exposed rebar. It was a feat of sheer athleticism to reach the highway below, and she shivered under the ravaged support beams beneath the Gardiner. She might have been the last person in the world.

Magic in lazy, iridescent aurorae whorled from between the crumbling pillars. There were wordless voices in them, patterns in a rush of current, like a distant chorus in a foreign language. She thought she recognized Ian Mallory's rasp amid the murmuration but it disappeared before she could be sure. She followed the stream through the rubble and uprooted streetcar tracks.

A convoy of army trucks rushed past along Spadina, spraying slush and snow across her legs, the magic backsplash enough to paralyze her for long minutes. They were coming and going from the Rogers Centre. She picked up her pace when she could move again. Her only weapon, the needle she clutched in cold fingers, seemed absurdly insufficient to take on any threat that lurked there.

Her first instinct was to run back for the car, to beg Nate to forgive her mad impulses. There was still fighting around the stadium. She had almost made up her mind to bolt when Reid's car, with its distinct old gasoline aura, rolled up at the end of the block.

He crouched in the back, curiously small, watching the soldiers. Had the Train made an emergency stop? He was ostensibly running communication for Atherton, though that hardly meant reporting live from a war zone.

"What are you doing here?" Her words came out breathless, childish.

"I could ask you the same. No, don't look away, it's good you're here, in fact." The car circled the stadium, turned on Simcoe, then Front, the trucks parting way for him.

"Is Alycia here too?"

"She's somewhere," Reid said, the syllables clipped. "Or half the men in there would be demons by now. There's been an accident."

Even at a distance, there was more magic in the stadium than Colette had ever seen in her life. It felt much more purposeful than the fey, capricious miasma that had seethed across the world since the Blight.

"Tell me about your projects," Reid said.

"You want a progress report *now*?"

"I would rather hear it directly from you than from my wife."

"You can't transfer magic from an MAI to an ordinary person," Colette said. This one, she could be decisive about. "It devours them from inside." In the end, *Eat* was a more appropriate name than she'd intended.

"One could say the same about what it does to an MAI," he replied, and where *was* Alycia, was she being eroded as steadily as Ian had been? She had always seemed so vital, despite her age. "Go on."

"That was Alycia's project, wasn't it?"

He offered a slight smile that wasn't quite a confirmation.

"And the demons. That's Ath—"

Reid raised one thin finger to his lips. In front of his driver, as discreet as the man would have to be, he couldn't admit what he knew Colette had already guessed. The demon, the glass child, was Miriam Atherton, the Director's daughter.

"It's not possible either," Colette said. "The changes are structural, at the DNA level. They shouldn't even be *alive*, and I'm not sure they are, in the strictest sense. Given time—years, decades—someone might be able to develop gene therapies. Maybe."

"*Love* is a no-go."

She shook her head. She had wanted so badly not to disappoint him. Even now, his wrinkled face was kindly, expectant.

"You will, I'm sure, understand the necessity to continue the pretence that it is."

Or Atherton, staunch opponent of magic that he was, had no use for MAI. For Colette, or for Alycia Curtis. There was nowhere in the Dominion they would be safe if they couldn't be useful.

"And *Pray*." She let herself feel, at long last, the magic emanating from the stadium. This was where the labyrinth had been leading her. This was the heart of something, damaged, but beating. Blood, yes, but also power, such immense power that it was all she could do to not rush headfirst into it, drink in exhilaration. "That one's yours."

"Yes," Reid said. "You can feel it, can't you? The bloody bastards destroyed everything they could lay hands on, but it chased them out."

"What is it? I never understood how I was meant to solve a problem when I wasn't given the parameters."

"And you found it anyway. Mrs. Greene, are you familiar with the concept of an Egregore? No, I can see by your face you are not, why would you be? Simply put, it is an entity, a being of immense power, brought forth from collective thought."

Ah, so that was it. He's been a madman this whole time.

"Like an angel?" she asked.

"Like a god. Such a thing wouldn't have been possible before the Cascade—pure foolishness, the territory of occultists and conmen—but look around. This is what the wrong sorts of beliefs can do. Our enemies, they are savages, terrorists, but they do believe in something beyond destruction. And so they have risen from the darkest places of the earth to put their beliefs into action. So must we." He smiled again, this time with more teeth. "You look distressed, my dear. Are you a Christian?"

She hadn't gone to church since before the move east away from her parents, hadn't found the time, had been far too busy with the job and the kids, had made every possible excuse, but she nodded anyway.

"I believe in—something," she said. "Spiritual, anyway. That the universe has good plans for us."

Reid laughed. "Do demons and shriekgrass seem to you to be the work of a benevolent god? Does Ian Mallory?"

"I don't know."

"I do," Reid said. "Atherton is a man of simple beliefs, but he is a moral man. A good leader, with good foundations to build on. It's why Alycia and I chose him in the first place. He can give shape to something strong, solid. An Egregore that will keep us all safe forever."

And Alycia's spells, backed by the overflow of magic that they'd assembled inside the dome, could convince large numbers of people to believe in it.

"Why?" she asked.

"There is a terrible threat out there," Reid replied. "Not just the terrorists—though given tonight, they're bad enough. Something deeper and darker, based on intelligence from our SVAR allies. Only a god can ensure men behave morally, and only a god can save us from the darkness that is coming. I know how this sounds. You're an intelligent woman, but that isn't why Alycia hired you. You've never shied away from doing the necessary work."

The boy she'd left at the black site, tearing out his flesh with his fingernails as the stolen power within him consumed him. Ian, splayed out on her table, his heart stopped by her thread and the magic leaking free from his emaciated body. The girl Celene, gripping her plastic recorder until her tiny hands slackened around it, and no matter how hard Colette pumped her chest and gasped into her mouth, her breath would not return as Ian's had.

All because it had to be done. Not because Alycia said so, or Reid, or even Atherton himself, but because it was necessary to keep her family safe from the monsters outside.

"What if I walked away?" Colette asked. "My husband and sons—they're up there, up on the bridge. What if I just quit?"

He patted her hand, lightly, but there was strength in him still.

"You and I both know a hundred reasons why you won't. Cheer up, Mrs. Greene. We all have a brighter future ahead because of your work. Because magic has chosen you, out of everyone else in the world, for its gifts."

The cold knot in her lungs loosened a bit. He couldn't *truly* be insane, after all. Whatever he had done here had amassed a power like nothing she'd felt in her life. And hadn't his decisions brought stability and safety to the country after the worst disaster it had ever experienced? Hadn't he provided for her, for all of them?

"Are you really trying to make a god?" she asked.

"I play Pascal's Wager to win." He winked, then opened the laptop wedged beside the seat. "I have one other thing to show you."

He opened a video file. Digital artifacts resolved themselves into what looked like surveillance footage. Some kind of nanny cam—she had a similar one in the boys' room, disguised as a teddy bear.

"My apologies," he said. "To have kept you in the dark for so long. It was necessary, especially after Lucy Fletcher's defection, and you've more than proved yourself loyal and trustworthy. And my apologies, too, for the lack of resources. I hope to change that very soon."

A teenage girl paced in a bedroom. The resolution wasn't good enough to make out much of her features beyond chin-length dark hair and a slight, angular build. She tried the window, which had security bars on it, and when it didn't budge, slammed her palms hard into it.

Her hands moved too quickly to be seen, and the video glitched again, this time violently, with a flash that split Colette's skull. When it cleared, the girl had moved to the bed, shaking, and the bars on the window, while intact, were twined with leaves.

"An MAI," Colette said, unnecessarily.

"Meet your new test subject," Reid said. "Her name is Laura."

36

Maya and Shadi stood in the burning ruins of the city, for an instant just a woman with her husband at the end of a long nightmare. Their cell had left behind a few mobile affinity groups to defend the territory they had claimed, but there were too few weapons, too few people who knew what the fuck they were doing, and if they still outnumbered the army and the cops and the Cleaners, they didn't outgun them, and that was what mattered.

"You okay?" Shadi asked. He pressed his lips into her hair, greasy and tangled from days without showers or a comb, and she was too tired to be ashamed.

"Fuck you," she said, a flutter of hysterical laughter in her voice. "I can't start crying in front of these people." He'd have offered to go somewhere quieter with her, but she preempted him with a head shake. "We need to get supplies. Make sure everyone's fed, make sure the radio network is running smoothly. We can't just rely on Martine—she'll need to sleep eventually."

He broke from her and held her at a distance, his hands around her wrists. She could pretend to be solid, if she worked hard at it. "You will too."

"Sounds fake."

The distant eruptions of gunfire could be new street battles or just echoes in her ears. Her veil obscured the city blocks they'd claimed downtown, though it wouldn't spare them from the kind of aerial bombardment that the Dominion had unleashed on Scarborough. It wouldn't change the fact that below the barbed wire No Man's Land of the old GO train tracks, no more than a half-hour's walk away, the Dominion had an unfathomable cosmic horror capable of obliterating the entire city. She would have to find Martine, exhausted or not, shore up some more assertive kind of diversion...

"Maya," Shadi said. The name was grafted onto her in a way that had never quite fit. "Come with me, please."

She took his hand, and he led her across the street, to the Sheraton. It had survived longer than most of the high rises, a tribute to 60s Brutalism and dumb luck. The front doors were smashed in and she stepped over a pile of broken glass into the lobby. Moss had overtaken the carpet and furniture, the relics of a bird's nest in a couch.

After the bombing, everything in her resisted being in any kind of tall building, cognizant of its fragility. When she had slept, in the hours following their capture of City Hall, she'd slept in an office on one of the lower floors, under a desk, like a kid in an old civil defence film. The hotel room that Shadi jimmied open, overlooking the emptied pool, with its too-large glass windows and opulent bed, was as secure as a password-protected PDF.

Still. "Fuck. Is there a shower?"

He tried the taps. Not even a drip. "Should have gone into plumbing instead of computer engineering," he muttered. "Sorry. I promise you don't smell worse than anyone else."

"Liar." Maya conjured a ghost light, flowing the bedroom and the bathroom with phosphorescent green. Shadi reemerged, a tall, lanky silhouette, haloed in the unearthly glow.

In the streets below, people were singing. It had to be three, four in the morning. She had never felt so old, so bone-weary.

"They need me," Maya said.

"Yeah," Shadi said. The pale light caught the sharp edges of his cheekbones and cast shadows into his eyes, glinted in sparks where his beard, neglected for weeks, had grown bushier. His hair curled to his shoulders now. She stood for long minutes watching him, categorizing the changes in him, studying the new angles that hunger had carved, committing his image to memory in advance of their next long separation. He took off his glasses and placed them on the bedside table, then reached for hers. "They always will. And so will I."

"I should be—"

He placed a finger to her lips. He smelled like gasoline—which, admittedly, was better than she smelled—and his skin was fever hot, soft against her own. His beard tickled where he kissed her neck.

"Don't disappear," he murmured, fumbling with her bulky, oversized sweater. No one had touched her, looked on her as anything other than a weapon, in such a long time. "Don't burn yourself up, Maya. I need you too."

She tumbled with him onto the big rich-person bed, the duvet draped in dust and ash but still incredibly plush. He rolled over and under her, both of them tugging off clothing, stealing breathless kisses, seeking the familiar heat of the other's skin.

After, she lay with her head on his chest and her leg thrown over one of his, poking mountain peaks from the silky underside of the duvet. The winter cold settled over the room like a curse; his breath misted, then evaporated, with each exhale.

"You did all that," Shadi said. "The parade, the demons..."

"Martine helped, too. It won't keep them out forever. I don't know if it'll keep them out the rest of the week. And they can probably just glass us from a plane."

"It's still incredible."

"Sure," Maya replied. "I'm all about going out in style."

"It's given them hope."

Hope had died on the parquet floor with her parents and brother, bled out in a house-to-house raid as the Cleaners scoured for anything with a pulse to liquidate. What was left was the cold fire of her false name, the monsters she'd raised from the Pattern that wouldn't let her die.

"I'm glad you think so," she said instead, and if it sounded as bitter as she felt, he had the grace not to point it out.

. . .

The second morning in the liberated city came as a mild shock. Dawn, bleeding through the frosted window, unfurled a spray-painted Black mermaid in the empty swimming pool, bonfires on the deck circled by little groups debating, dancing, playing makeshift instruments, melting snow and ice in barrels to supply the occupation with water. For another night, the Dominion hadn't obliterated them all while she slept.

Reluctantly relinquishing the fluffy white bathrobe, Maya and Shadi put on their frozen-stiff clothes and walked across to City Hall. They stood in the middle of the square and stared up at the sky, waiting for a bomber to burst through the heavy cloud cover. She crossed the ice rink where she'd skated on school field trips, her falls padded by heavy snow pants and childhood invulnerability. Fragments of her magic hung in the air, glinting over the grey concrete.

Gaby hadn't claimed the Mayor's seat at the front of the Council Chamber—the entire desk, splintered by the Blight or the looting that followed, had been colonized by flags and graffiti, and Jonah and Martine were sitting on it. Gaby was instead in one of the councillors' seats, dwarfed by the dome of the chamber. Maps scattered the floor. Her inner circle was too small to fill even the seat of civil government. Felipe paced, his troops diminished.

Ian was the only one who immediately took notice of her. "Glad you decided to join us."

"Nothing's been decided yet," Gaby said.

Had they actually been waiting for her? She too looked at the map, red pooling in the places they'd conquered. Even compared to the city limits, it seemed inconsequential, even if it represented tens of thousands of people who may have abruptly decided that they weren't sure they wanted to be ruled over by a gang of kleptocrat fascists after all.

At the bottom of it, spreading like a melanoma across the grid of streets, was the black zone denoting the Dominion's magitech weapon. They hadn't been able to approach it since they disrupted the engineering processes at the work camp. The perimeter alone threatened to turn anyone who approached—well, anyone but an MAI or someone warded to hell like Jonah—into the mother of all demons. The only good news was that the Dominion troops couldn't get near it either. They were trying to salvage what they could, and the scouts reported that every so often, they threw a Cleaner or two into the meatgrinder to see if it had calmed down.

It hadn't.

Even with the loss of the Entertainment District, it was more of a victory than anyone had seen in years. Naturally, everyone was fighting. Felipe's faction wanted to go on the offensive, seizing the momentum to take out the Rogers Centre and push east to crush the enemy between the Mac-Paps and Vaillancourt's separatists. Gaby wanted to shore up their defences, ensure that they had popular support lest they overreach. Jonah suggested a campaign of sabotage, taking out the railroad tracks in multiple places, cornering the Train, maybe blowing it up, which Felipe called a juvenile fantasy, as if he were one to talk.

"You're being quiet," Gaby said to Ian. "I have never once known you to not have an opinion."

"Oh, you wants it now?" He bent over the map, the Train's tracks cutting through the top of the city like a scar. "Toronto's not the centre of the universe, whatever Maya thinks." She rolled her eyes at this. "We gots a long ways to go before we can take a swing at the head of the beast."

"Okay, but that would buy time," Shadi said. Always the peacemaker, the connector, sliding in with a big case of Engineering Brain and no understanding of how sectarian politics worked. "If we want people to feel like this is something that they can build on, we need to make sure that the Dominion can't just storm in."

Jonah kicked a boot against the desk he was sitting on. "What we need to worry about is the highways. We can stop the Train for a day or two, but they have tanks and carriers."

"And drones and planes," Felipe pointed out acidly. Pointless to worry about highways when the Dominion could decide to carpet bomb them at any time.

This kickstarted another round of arguments, and Maya slipped out of the room, down the hall, and out the door. She climbed up on the ramp that overlooked the square. Even in the morning, it was more alive than she'd seen in years. Two days of hangover hadn't diminished the joy of the downtown's liberation.

A cluster of children had discovered the rink. It hadn't been in use in years, but it had iced over anyway, accumulating layers in lumps and tides. Nor did they have skates, but they slid across it anyway, worn soles providing no traction, bashing into each other and giggling. The girl Maya had been was terrible at skating, but learning how to fall was a talent too.

Everyone was busy, distracted with arguing about how they would meet their deaths, and she was threadbare, immaterial. It would take one spell, barely a breath of magic, and then she'd be free of it all.

Maya stretched over the edge of the ramp and, charging the duck between her palms, cast a spill of moon-bright flowers down the concrete pillar, winding around the rink's perimeter and lacing up the crumbling concrete arches. One of the kids noticed, and then they all noticed, pointing in awe at the tiny blossoms erupting in emerald and azure and violet amid the snow.

Without Martine's magic at her back, tired and overextended, she was already unspooling, dissolving into the spell. The Pattern wrapped its shimmering arms around her, eroded skin into ethereal petals, substance into mist. As it had once before, it whispered a name to her that her mind had buried but that lived in her body, her cells, that slept uneasily under a concrete parking lot.

This time, it didn't tempt her with visions. She knew what it offered, the dance between worlds, the freedom from her stone-heavy body, liberation from the burdens and vulnerabilities of fallible flesh. A home amid endless possibilities, beyond winter and death.

And hadn't she done what she had set out to do? The city, or enough of it, was free. Martine was confident in her magic, far more than Maya had ever been. She could carry on where Maya would leave off.

She drifted, past her body, across the council chambers. Shadi holding court now, outlining his strategy for restoring communications, digging into their occupation and fortifying the city against a reprisal. He talked with his hands as much as with words, animated about a solar array that they could build, how they could resurrect the four water filtration plants. Always so resourceful, from the day he had found her in the ruins of her old life, always with an eye towards fixing what could never be repaired.

She wanted to keep him here, in this brief stutter of optimism, before the bombs fell.

She was looking out over the city now, at its myriad transformations, at the rations depots turned into communal kitchens, the fences and checkpoints dismantled. The Red Ensigns and Atherton portraits burned in a massive bonfire. Somewhere people were hauling food from abandoned houses and hunting squirrels to feed their neighbours, somewhere people were furtively fucking in doorways and derelict cars. She could leave them here, and evaporate into the Pattern, the last trills of her consciousness a ward spell over the fragile and temporary peace. She could encase this glittering victory in amber with one last act of will.

But she wasn't alone.

Something black and viscous wound into the bliss of obliteration, and she blinked back into her tired, leaden body, the flowers she had spun afterimages behind her eyes. In front of her was a thin rip in the world, a void in the shape of a man.

"The fuck're you doing, b'y?"

Half-starlight, she saw him as magic did, a negation, a rejection of itself, a shrivelled, empty, dead thing roping her to earth. He pulled her back into the world of cement and ice and the weight of her own fatigue. His shattered, knotted hands gripped her shoulders, and the pain it must have caused him was plain on his face, but he didn't let go until reality, remorseless and knife-edged, resolved his features into the grim mockery of the human he'd been.

She just shook her head. Her own illusory flowers glowed bright behind her skin.

"You wouldn't understand," she managed finally.

"The fuck I don't. You don't think I heard it too, for *years*, until—" He let go, wringing out his hands. "You think I wouldn't give anything to feel it again?"

She was too exhausted to feel shame. "They all died," Maya said. "I walked in and they were dead and *you weren't there*, you fuck, you were dead and you *knew* and you *left me* and I couldn't clean up the blood, I couldn't have a funeral, I couldn't mourn, I've been running ever since and I'm *tired*, Ian. I'm so. Fucking. Tired."

She folded onto the ramp, welcoming the sting of cold, her back to the wall of the ramp and the rubber duck sitting primly in the snowdrift beside her. The smile cracked his face like a broken phone screen.

"I know, ducky."

"I didn't ask for this." Which was a lie, she'd practiced, she'd *dared* magic to choose her, but he nodded anyway. He was too close, her magic shrinking back inside of her at his presence, smashing her back into the earth like a fucking meteor.

He'd tried to tell her, tried to show her, back when futures had seemed infinite, when it had been a matter of finding the right combination, like a video game puzzle, dying over and over again in her mind until she found the way forward. She could have looked directly into their fates, played the torturous game that he'd lost. Instead, she had looked away, unable to witness—as he must have done—the deaths of everyone she loved. He'd tried, and she found she could still resent him for it anyway.

The tears were an afterthought. She huddled, tiny and spent amid the miracles she'd made.

He wrapped an arm around her shoulders and she stiffened. "We're not gonna hug it out, are we?"

"I'd rather rail a line of asbestos." He kicked at the snow with the worn toe of a boot. "You love them, yeah? That rawny husband of yours and Gaby's little nightmare hellbeast child and the whole fucked revolution."

"What's the point?" She waved an arm towards the sky, clouds pregnant with foreboding. "They're all dead."

"They are," Ian agreed. "And what do we owe the dead, b'y? A kind word and a funeral? Bullshit. What we owe the dead is to burn down the world that murdered them. You don't gets to rest 'til that's done."

She pressed her head into his bony shoulder and took a deep, shuddering breath. "When did you know? About my family."

"Before I met you. Same as the Blight. There's nothing you could have done."

"Or you?"

"I was only put in this world to do one thing," he said. "Hold off the flood as long as I could. Murder the least amount of people when the shit monsoon hit the fan. That's all it's ever been. All my life, I thought it was gonna be the only important thing I ever did."

"Was it?" Her own voice sounded faint in her ears, like it was coming from the bottom of a deep well.

"No." He took her hand, still crackling with magic, her fingers small and blunt in the rotted tree of his. The void coiled around him, twined across her arms like a skittish but persistent cat. Her skin prickled beneath her puffy coat, but the absence of magic no longer sickened her. She could coexist with the monster he had become, just as she could live in the wreckage of the planet. "This is. Right now. Pinning you to your life like a butterfly to a card. The most important thing in the fuckin' world."

.   .   .

Two nights after the uprising, with street battles still raging, the temperature plummeted below -30°C. Even in the old days, the times everyone swore were better, Toronto winters were deadly, with stories of homeless people scraped off the sidewalk, frostbitten flesh fused to the metal grates of exhaust vents. Maya, coming off evening patrol, tucked her gloved hands under her armpits and huffed into her mask. It didn't help.

Despite the cold, the rebels and the newly liberated alike gathered in the square. Beneath the open hands of the curving City Hall towers and the unblinking eye that they cupped between them, they were closed in by a perimeter of fire barrels. On the sidewalks and the ramps that gated the assembly, Felipe's tin soldiers patrolled with a paltry hodgepodge of stolen guns. A hundred yellow eyes poured out their light from the top floors of the high-rises at their back.

"There is a spectre haunting the dead malls of Scarborough," Gaby was saying. The sentences that followed were buried under an onslaught of chatter. Thawed from the Dominion's control, the Party's beloved masses cared little for its revolutionary fervour. The conversations around her, louder than Gaby's barely amplified speech, were about missing friends and relatives, the locations and relative qualities of intact food depots, nostalgia for Blue Jays games and block parties. Without fuel for the loudspeakers, Martine's magic splashed the words in flaming letters superimposed over the knot of restless, impatient humanity.

Maya couldn't see. Everyone who had showed up was apparently six feet tall and built like a brick shithouse, a massive wall of undifferentiated obstacles. She knew none of them. She pushed through a sea of tattered coats in search of Shadi, or Ian or Jonah or anyone else she recognized.

"We have done the impossible." Maya saw the words more than she heard them, absorbed them in quick, violent bursts faster than she could physically read. "We have stood up. We have said, no more. No more disappearances, no more secret prisons, no more hangings, no more mass graves, no more cities made of bones. We have driven them out."

There was more talking than cheering, even with Martine's dramatic flourishes. Gaby didn't need to try so hard. Their liberation of the stadium, the festival atmosphere that had turned the world upside down, the sight of Dominion soldiers slinking back along the highway in their convoy—all of that was enough for Gaby to command the people, at least for now.

It might have been the crowds—what business did everyone have being so tall, anyway?—or the hunger and sleep deprivation, the giddiness of unleashed power and near-obliteration. Her stomach roiled, her breath thorns in her chest. She should find somewhere quiet, cast into the murky future. After years of practice, she was barely better at it than when Ian had made her try, over and over again in the Broom Closet, but she was the best they had now. And every victory against the darkness was temporary. More than reading the future, Ian had taught her that much.

Premonition, that was what it was. Sometimes you searched the Pattern for the future; sometimes, the future came knocking at your door.

Where the fuck was Shadi?

Gaby was still talking, but Maya paid her no more mind than anyone else in the crowd. A vice tightened around her temples. Even with the fire and so many people, all bumping up against her, breathing heat in wisps above her head, she had never been so cold in her life.

Thunder, the clench of dread, came before the lightning.

Behind the blackened silhouette of skyscrapers to the south of the square, a pure white flash, echoed and amplified by the low, lazy cover of clouds. Fire belched upwards into a mushroom. Smoke billowed. You weren't supposed to look at explosions, or was that eclipses? Maya watched in mute horror, oblivious to the panic sparking around her.

A second explosion echoed the first, and now the crowd was an injured animal, screaming about nukes, the Dominion had nukes, there was no point in running because they were all already dead. People dropped to the ground with their arms over their heads; others ran for shelter under the arches or inside the dome. Maya zigzagged through colliding bodies until she caught a glimpse of Shadi by Gaby's podium, shielding her from the chaos. She ran, the concrete in front of her brightening in the false sun of another explosion.

Smoke rolled over the square, great clouds of ash that smelled like someone had dropped a chip wrapper in a campfire. She would keep moving. She had no choice. She had run since that night, three years ago, and she hadn't stopped running since. The explosions had to be at least a few blocks south of the square but the rally had to be visible from the planes—everyone was running, certain of another massacre...

Maya froze, metres from where Shadi bent over Gaby, his coat thrown uselessly over her. The kids huddled behind the podium, Martine etching ward spells in the air as Monique covered Junior's eyes. All of them were covered in grey ash, broken only by the rivulets of tears down Junior's cheeks. They were still moving though, still alive.

Maya looked up.

One by one, banks of light in the towers blinked out. Spreading as far as she could see, the city went dark.

"Maya!" Gaby reached her before she could move again. Gaby was shaking her, gently at first, then hard until she snapped out of her trance. "What is happening? Is it a bomb?"

She reached for the duck. Her hands were too cold, the rubber too stiffened and frozen, but she somehow found the right rhythm. In the murk, only seconds ahead of her present moment, the highway was flooded with retreating army trucks, smoke hazing in their wake.

"The substations," she managed.

Shadi filled in the rest for her. "They're pulling out of the city but there are tons of residential substations between us and their retreat," he said. "That's what they blew up."

"Can we use the generators?" Gaby asked. They had lived without power for years in the abandoned strip malls—but they had been hundreds then, not the tens of thousands who had poured into the streets to throw off the Dominion and welcome the Mac-Paps as liberators.

"They won't be enough," Shadi said.

Gaby took a tight, shallow breath. Straightened and stood out from under Shadi's coat. The flames in the fire barrel beside her, still inexplicably alight, turned her skin to gold and emphasized every groove and crease in her face.

"So they have left us a city," Gaby said. "But it is a city in rubble."

"You need to call for calm," Maya said. She reached out for Martine's hand, encrusted in grit, the lit fuse of her last spell still sparking off her palm. The girl clambered to her feet and squeezed back, the magic a wavering thread between them. "They'll still listen to you, they'll do what you say but you need to talk to them, get them to stop panicking."

"I am panicking."

Maya's pulse was about to burst through her throat, but she kept her voice steady. Every political non-instinct she had ever possessed scrambled to write out a script. "You can't," she said. "You're their leader. You don't get the luxury. Monique, can you get Junior somewhere safe?"

Monique and Junior would know that there was nowhere safe if the bombing started. Gaby knew it too, if she would let herself think about it, but there was no time for it. This was the inheritance Maya had been left—this was what Ian had saved her for.

"The PATH," Shadi suggested. "Or the subway, if it's not blocked off."

"Martine," Gaby said. "Go with them."

Martine, instead, looked at Maya who shook her head. "I'm sorry," she whispered, pointlessly. *Sorry you're a wizard, sorry that you don't get to flee to safety, that instead of a childhood you get a never-ending nightmare. Welcome to the saddest club on Earth.* Their magic twined and twisted into a loose braid that encircled their small group. Gaby stood, straightened, Shadi's coat draped over her narrow shoulders like a cape.

"What am I supposed to say?" Gaby asked, her voice so tiny that Maya was convinced that no amount of magic could project it.

Maya smiled grimly. "You're a politician," she said. "Lie to them."

37

The collection of oil drums and ramshackle masonry ovens in the smoke-drenched kitchen of what had once been a China Wok would have been enough for a five-alarm fire. Worse, Jonah was convinced that Maya was laughing at him.

"You could help," he told her.

"I'm on inventory tonight," she replied. "Besides, this is funny as fuck."

Okay, she was laughing at Ian, not him, which was *fine*. Watching him perform culinary necromancy with near-expired military rations, scraps of raccoon meat, instant ramen, and packs of ketchup and hot sauce was genuinely fascinating. Jonah paused in his chopping to appreciate the scent wafting from the simmering pot, which despite Ian's violent separation from magic and his mangled hands, must have been conjured via some occult pact because it actually smelled edible.

"Did you two lose a bet or something?" Maya asked, "What's with the sad girl dinner?"

"I won't stand for my culinary prowess being insulted," Jonah said haughtily, and offered her a swig from a bottle of home-brew that one of the newcomers had donated to the cause. She looked like she needed it. "An army marches on its stomach."

"It's also fucking Christmas," Ian muttered, as if he gave even the slightest of shits about it. Jonah would have given anything in the world to be celebrating it with Blythe and Laura, divorce be damned.

After the bombings, the Mac-Pap cells had evaporated from the downtown, claiming neighbourhoods or patches of forest, leaving Gaby's Central Committee behind. It wasn't safe to gather in one place—if she was killed, someone else would have to take up the cause. But she'd kept her children close, and skirted the edge of their Malthusian deadline by bringing the cell together for one last gathering.

The food supply was going to be the least of their problems. They'd scavenged the Dominion's depots for all they were worth, and the closest untouched ones were well outside of the territory they held. But the cold would get them first. The Dominion didn't need aerial assaults or tanks or soldiers. It just needed time.

But this was what people always did, in the darkest season—huddle together for warmth and convince themselves that the dawn would come again.

Beneath the downtown, the PATH underground mall was lit by candles and the glow of their infernal kitchen. The rebels were more shadow than solid, flickering ghosts with gaunt, hopeful faces.

"It's like mummering back home, lookin' at them b'ys," Ian said. "Creepy as shit."

Jonah tossed the last chopping board full of burdock into the pot, bumping against Ian's elbow and jogging his cup of cedar tea. Ian had given up drinking anything else after half a cup of home-brew, which he claimed gave him a headache and a temper. It was a testament to their desperate circumstances that, at the end of the world, Jonah had at last convinced Ian to have a drink with him.

Ian held a spoon to Maya's lips. She looked nonplussed, but dutifully tried it. "That's actually not bad. Absolutely insane, but not bad."

"Could use a hand with it," Jonah said, loath as he was to leave the kitchen for the colder environs of the food court. They carried out bowls and mugs of chimeric instant noodle monstrosities, a paltry feast for the starving. The food court was too loud, too crowded—he didn't know how to shroud himself in illusion like Maya did, or to bluster and intimidate his way into confidence like Ian. It was Christmas and Laura would have been a teenager, might have checked her phone all through the obligatory family dinner and the stilted silences as he and Blythe tried to get along for her sake. Might have relented and gone with him to Midnight Mass like they both did when she'd been little.

"Thank you," someone said as he dropped a bowl on the table in front of them and avoided their eyes.

"Yeah."

"Joe," Ian said. "You gotta eat something too." Which was rich, given that Ian hadn't sat down to a meal since the last time the Leafs won a series. "You first," Jonah fired back, but the three of them, the Broom Closet, ended up huddled around a plastic mall table. They'd never done anything like that, not even a lunch break in a food court, in all the time they'd worked together. It was ridiculous, wistfully longing for some kind of TV office camaraderie in the midst of a viper pit.

At the far side of the food court, there was music. Thin at first, so faint that Jonah thought it was his overtired imagination, then building in confidence and volume until it filled the space from the brown-tiled floors to the crumbling ceiling. A single voice couldn't contain such depth and heights simultaneously; it was as if Lucy Fletcher had a chorus behind her, filling in the harmonies of an operatic rendition of "Hallelujah."

"You know that's not a Christmas song," Eric muttered at the table next to them, though he watched Lucy with big, lovesick eyes that nearly brought the questionable noodles back up Jonah's throat.

It wasn't a dancing song either, but it didn't stop one of the teenage kids from grabbing another and with the parodic gestures of a spasming mime, whirling her into a slow dance. They were joined by others, the rage of the last few days transfigured into tenderness by some obscure and pointless miracle.

Ian stood, and for a moment Jonah's traitor heart wanted to follow him, but he moved to Gaby's table instead, extending a crumpled hand. She blinked, but accepted, and he folded her into a surprisingly graceful dance.

Still, it was never a good sign when Ian was nice. He bent his head to whisper something in Gaby's ear, and Jonah strained to decipher it.

"Maya," Jonah said, "Can you go listen in?"

"Oh my *God*," she replied, but she was up and moving, and then flitted out of his perception. She'd cast another glamour, relegating herself and Shadi to the margins of anyone's interest.

Someone had found a guitar and Lucy switched to a more upbeat song as Maya released her glamour and returned, Shadi in tow, to the table.

"Well?"

"You'd better ask him yourself."

"Fuck this." The home-brew was hitting harder than he'd initially thought, though objectively he understood that no amount of alcohol was enough to turn Ian even a little bisexual. It was courage enough that he could swagger up to the two of them and use his inch of so of height advantage to stare Gaby down. "Could you excuse us for a second?" he asked her.

Ian growled a warning, but Gaby moved off to let Jonah cut in. Freeze won out briefly over fight and flight, and Ian was braced as if to attack. "Not here, Joe."

"Just shut the fuck up." One stupid inch forward, then the slightest movement closer, a Zeno's Paradox of ill-considered intimacy. Lucy was still singing. Was that "Home For a Rest"? She'd seemed too bougie to know that one, but it was already a strange evening. "You owe me."

He folded his arms around Ian's narrow back and waited for the flinch, or the shove away, and instead felt the pressure of Ian's cheekbone on the top of his head. He swayed, unsteady, as if Jonah was the only thing keeping him upright.

"What was that about?" Jonah asked. "With Gaby."

"Morale," Ian said. "You know. If we had enough guns for everyone here we'd still lose. But she's gots ta think otherwise, eh?"

"Don't fuck her."

Ian snorted. "I'm not fuckin' Gaby, ya stunned arse. Jesus, are you jealous?"

"Seriously, Ian?"

Ian angled them around with none of the languid poise he'd managed with Gaby, a demented St. Vitus dance. "Over there," he murmured. "By the wall. Don't stare."

There was a woman, one of the newcomers, holding a shivering child swaddled in a mass of blankets. "What about them?"

"Wait." Jonah didn't want to. He was tired, and more than a little drunk, and he knew better than to imagine that they got to have some big romantic moment together, swaying like besotted adolescents at the world's most awkward junior high slow dance. Just for once, it could lack an ulterior motive, it could be about something other than manipulation. He let the turn happen, glancing over Lucy, who dangled a piece of Spam above her mangy little cat, and when he saw the newcomer woman again, she was concealing a cough that rattled her entire thin body.

"The plague," Ian said. The flu, maybe something worse. The scarce medical supplies they'd amassed over three years were buried under the rubble of an office tower; the downtown hospitals had long since been stripped and pillaged. And for the first time, they could boast of more refugees than hardened revolutionaries. "I told Gaby to circulate, and not shake anyone's hand. Find out who's sick and quietly isolate them."

"What the fuck—how long? Were you just going to sit through dinner and not tell anyone?" It was the Blight all over again, the plotting and the secrecy and the stupid, pointless conspiracies that had dirtied Jonah's hands just to push the disaster a little farther down the road.

"What'ddya take me for, Joe? I noticed her ten minutes ago. The whole group she came in with is sick."

"Shit."

"An entire tsunami of spraying liquid shit, and we're livin' in a mud hut on the coast. Not a metaphor, Joe, that's literally what's gonna happen once we overload the plumbing."

It wouldn't be the cold after all, or the starvation or the drones or the guns. It wouldn't even be an apocalyptic spell from the Dominion's tame wizard. Jonah strained, expecting to catch a telltale cough amongst the conversation. He knew better than to expect the finale to come all at once.

It was never the end times. You had to live through whatever happened next.

"Do you want—" But there was no good answer to that. Lucy's song petered out, and he stood there among the dust-draped plastic tables like he'd lost a game of musical chairs. Ian *wanted*, certainly; as spectral as he was, his broken hands clutched desperate fistfuls of fabric at the small of Jonah's back.

"I wants you to stay the fuck away from it, b'y. Someone has to go off to reason with the Iron Alliance and you're the man for that job."

It sounded like an excuse. He wouldn't delude himself into thinking that Ian cared enough to send him away from the plague just to keep him alive.

"We didn't drive the Dominion out of Toronto just to die of something stupid."

"Yeah, well." Ian broke away from him. "Here's to the revolution: forged in fire and drowned in shit."

. . .

"*Out of the ashes,*" Director Atherton said over a tinny, hand-cranked radio. "*We will, together, build a bright future of peace, prosperity, and the rule of law. We are a proud country, with proud traditions, and a history for which we do not and shall not apologize.*"

"Did you have *rule of law* on your bingo?" Shadi leaned over and checked Maya's card.

"This I can promise you: By next Christmas, we will have tripled production in the oilsands. We will have a roof over the head of every family. We will have cracked down on the crime and chaos that anarchists have brought to our streets. We will continue our transition to managed democracy. I see, for all of us, a beautiful future, of families that sit on their front porch as their children play hockey on their well-paved street. Of security for our nation's most important asset—our children."

"Bingo!" Martine shouted out. "For the *children.*"

Maybe it was just the home-brew making the room spin, tightening the air like a noose around Jonah's neck. "I'm going," he announced.

"Where?" Shadi asked. "Party's just getting started."

"To find out whatever Atherton loves most and fistfuck it to death."

Focused on finding somewhere he could breathe, it was only the ghost-creep over his tattoo that alerted him to Ian's presence. He had no scent; magic had robbed him of all physical substance, just an empty shell draped in musty castoffs.

He stopped in front of a utility room with a bashed in door. Inside, a disused electrical panel hung open, its guts stripped for their copper and hanging out over a brick wall. The meek had inherited the earth, or at least the city, but it was a shit inheritance.

Ian leaned against a bare metal shelf, looking every bit as dishevelled and disreputable as the day they'd met. Jonah was about to ask him what he had in mind exactly when Ian was pressing him up against the door of the panel, all stubble and sharp angles and a wisp of moonshine.

He wasn't naïve. He knew a distraction when it mashed its face into his, and Ian sent up more red flags than a May Day rally, but he wasn't made of steel and it wasn't like his dick had ever come with an off-switch. Besides, the alternative was spending Christmas wallowing in grief and self-pity. He'd take what he could get.

It would have taken Ian forever to maneuver out of a button-up shirt, so Jonah did it for him, and he stood a bone-pale smudge in the darkness, thin and grey as a marker in a mass grave. It was a mercy that Jonah could barely decipher the scars, the dent of a broken rib that hadn't healed right, the knobs and valleys of his too-prominent spine. The tattoo on his shoulder blade in elaborate script across a banner, which he hadn't had back when he'd done Jonah's shitty stick-and-poke labyrinth. It was a line from a Dennis Lee poem: *And best of all is finding a place to be / in the early days of a better civilization.*

Jonah fell upon him like an avalanche.

. . .

Jonah dreamt of drowning.

The SVAR gunship loomed over the thrashing ocean. Salt-sting in his eyes, he drowned in ice and fire beneath the wounded wreckage of the ship. With every stuttering breath he screamed that he wasn't there, that he hadn't been there, and each time his head broke the surface his blistered eyes searched for Laura. Machine-gun fire strafed the swells and he fought, though the ocean was too vast to yield up the small body it had devoured.

He was wrapped in seaweed, in abyssal tendrils that squeezed a cold fist around his throat and plunged him under. At the bottom was Laura, her small hands outlined in pinpricks of light, but when he reached for her, the hand that dragged him across the jagged rocks was as dry and weathered as driftwood.

He looked up from where he lay sprawled on his belly, dripping seawater and blood, at Ian, his grey skin mottled and peeling, as still as the dead.

And he cried out, spitting ink and bile, did you fucking rescue me, what the fuck would you save me for—

—and woke up, staring into Ian's open eyes with the scream a shrivelled thing in his mouth and his skull pounding. Ian pressed a finger to his lips. "You were dreaming," as though he didn't have nightmares every night, as if it even made sense for him to be curled in a nest of old coats instead of having just fucked off, as if it even made sense for him to care about Jonah's fucked-up *dreams.*

"I don't wanna talk about it," he mumbled around uncooperative lips, fused together by cold and drool. He placed a hand over Ian's chest—tentative, testing if this was allowed, and apparently it was. The dead spell was etched over his skin and he was as much of a frozen corpse as he'd been in the dream but he had a heartbeat nonetheless, frantic.

"Yeah," Ian said. "Look, Joe—" he started, and looked acutely relieved at the knock on the door even as Jonah scrambled to cover himself with the coat. "Fuck off, you Santa's ballsack friggin' *prick.*"

Gaby opened the door anyway. "I need to talk to you." Her schoolteacher frown was indication enough that either she disapproved deeply of their life choices, or that whatever she had to say wasn't good news.

"Me?" Jonah asked.

"Both of you. All of you."

They risked running one generator for the computers, which were kept out of the view of all but Gaby's most loyal cadre. Even three years after the Blight, the temptation to connect with the outside world would have been too strong for most people to resist. Shadi monitored it, and he was halfway through explaining what he'd found to Maya when Jonah and Ian squeezed into the tiny computer hub.

"I think it's authentic," he said.

"How did they even find us?" Gaby said. "Did you create an email address for the uprising?"

"Nothing like that," Shadi said. "But your old riding office email still works. Apparently it was beyond the capabilities of the Dominion to purge that at the time. And these are government accounts. They're not trying to reach you personally. There's one in Patrice's as well. They just want someone in the resistance and I don't think they know who that is."

"And *they* are?" Gaby asked.

Shadi's Adam's apple bobbed in his skinny throat. "Two messages," he said. "On repeat, both of them. One's from Luther Sears. Defender of the Faith and President of the American Free States, greeting the Mac-Paps in the spirit of Christian brotherhood. He, uh. Wants to open up negotiations."

"The fuck he does," Ian said.

"Gaby, tell me you're not considering that," Maya said.

"I am not ruling out options."

"It's nice to be asked to the dance," Jonah said, and Maya elbowed him in the ribs.

"Yeah well," Shadi replied, "You're all gonna like the other one even less. They're specifically looking for Ian, so I guess it's out that he's still alive."

"Who in the moose nuts fuck is trying to email me?"

"It's a Russian IP and if I had to guess, it's President Surkov's office. Maybe even the man himself. There's an attachment, though. Dominion green ID, looks pretty authentic but who the fuck knows." It was a scan, poor quality, but the name was legible. Amelia Fatimatou, aged 26, a nurse on a non-citizen work permit. Her employer, whatever fascist bastard had deemed her so necessary to the Dominion's operations that she hadn't been murdered or deported, wasn't listed, but there was a hand-scrawled phone number at the bottom of the pass.

"I did some digging," Shadi said. "An infant son, probably deported or killed, and a massive family that didn't make it through the unencumberances."

"But not her," Gaby said.

"Not her," Shadi agreed. "So what's she doing walking free?"

Ian uncoiled his hand, motioning with his crooked fingers, and grinned a vulpine smile as Shadi tossed him one of their scarce cellphones.

"Let's find out."

38

Blythe knew the language of the ocean, but not its desire. It stretched her until she was a taut protective membrane shielding her companions from the water that hungered for them. It was so much bigger, and she couldn't answer it, no one had ever told her the rules for communion with something so much greater than herself.

"It never used to get cold here," Blythe said.

The SVAR, champions of the free market and free association and all things free, had surveillance cameras and blinding LEDs set up in every makeshift harbour. Out on the Inner Harbour, Blythe watched a drone, flying too, low get caught in the sweep of a wave and pulled under.

Bailey, barely audible over the crash of waves, shouted back, "Huh?"

"Microclimate," Blythe explained. Her head was full of corroded metal, sharp, rusting edges. "We're in a rain shadow from the mountains. A gift from the Juan de Fuca Strait drives the worst of the weather systems elsewhere. It was never summer, never winter. Just its own little oasis, safe and protected from the rest of the world. Outside of time."

"And people say the weather is boring," Edgar said.

"It's not anymore," Blythe said. Her teeth chattered. The searchlights were concentrated on the Inner Harbour and Ogden Point. Only a little south, where the ocean had devoured the long stretch of Dallas Road and turned the low rises and luxury homes to soggy ruins, there was too much shriekgrass for the patrols and the lights to be worth it. The road and bike path were frozen in the violent paroxysms that had rendered them useless three years ago. Jewel-bright facets of transformed coastline jutted up between the black lacunae where the road had been. Past the uprooted railing and the drowned ruins of a park, a lost ferry, unmoored from the terminal, had drifted south by the breakwater.

Beneath the surface, the *Retribution* moved of its own volition. If she strained, she could catch it moving parallel with them, shark-sleek. She could breathe in time with it, its black fruiting bodies coiling through her lungs. The ocean surged, unsettled. It had a pulse under the wooden floor of the boat and it resisted the spear of the motor. She murmured quiet promises to it, lost under the drone of the waves. The water crunched like tinfoil before ceding to the propellor.

They pushed through the sludge, in the shadow of the dead ferry. Next to their rickety little boat, the ferry looked impossibly large. A ghost ship, it had torn itself free from the dock a year or so ago, settling amid a crystalline glass formation. Rust and deep green rot crept over its flanks, a crust of barnacles colonizing the tourism ad's sweeping portrait of the Rockies. She reached a hand towards the rust-crinkled railing as they passed by.

She hadn't noticed how drenched she had been when Edgar and Bailey had pulled her into the boat, but now, crouched in the motorboat's belly with the wind lashing above them, her jeans plastered stiff to her legs, the chill hit her with its full force.

The SVAR ship was visible, as it was from every point along the shore, a hulking island city dotted with searchlights. Drifting snowflakes caught in its beams and dissipated before they touched the surface of the waves.

"Thank you," Blythe shouted above the waves and the spluttering of the overwhelmed motor. The wind was picking up, too. The waves rocked the ship from side to side. "For being here, for lending your expertise and...well, for risking your lives. I was going to do this alone, somehow—Edgar can tell you."

"She was," he said. "If that's what you were trying. Completely insane."

"I hate them," she said. "With everything I have left. I would swim over and board them in a suicide vest if that's what it came down to. But that's not how we do things. We are scientists and engineers and healers and gardeners and community-builders. And they can burn our city to the ground but they can't—they won't—change what we had here. What we were before they came. The land will remember. The sea will."

The SVAR seastead was closer. Or, more accurately, they were closer to it, a sardine swimming in the wake of a humpbacked whale. The ship would eat the whole sky. Its searchlights streaked blinding white over the ocean's surface. Cannons, trained on the coastline and ready to fire on whatever nascent rebellion boiled there, encircled its sides.

The wind raged even as the ocean thinned the snowfall to a heavy fog. She was past cold now, the numbness welcome. Her clothing was a frozen exoskeleton. She should have been working with Edgar, lending whatever vague technical expertise she could to guide the motorboat through the seething, infected oceans. She should have been checking and rechecking the explosives with Bailey, ensuring that they wouldn't go off too early, that they would go off at all. She should have been praying, the prayers that her mother had taught her, half-Catholic, half-nehiyaw, all Otipemisiwak, more demand than plea. For strength, and pride, and most of all for solidarity.

She did none of those things. She was a column of ice. The peaks of the waves smashing into the motorboat's prow were child's hands, stumpy fingers reaching for hers, never connecting. The sea wailed for her. A nail of pain pierced her eye socket, the barometer of an oncoming storm.

Part of her wanted to scream to the others that they needed to turn back, wait for the squall to pass. Instead, she yelled to Edgar, "Can they see us?"

She couldn't be sure if he was shaking his head because he hadn't heard her, or because he'd heard her and they were merely a tiny speck in the vast ocean, inconsequential to the SVAR's vast machinery of conquest and occupation. The wind lobbed spears of sleet, turning the railing and the deck to slippery rime. The ferry lurched.

The sky, the ocean, had turned to white. The crests of the waves frothed, rabid, above thick fog. The searchlights, which had been a beacon from the shore, splintered and refracted into a thousand points. Hand over hand, Blythe crawled her way over to Edgar.

"Can you call it?" he yelled.

The *Retribution* was in her every nerve and synapse. It was in her mouth, forcing its way down her throat; she would choke on it. She bowed under its weight. Parts of her cracked, split apart.

"Yeah," she said, and screwed her eyes shut.

The *Retribution* answered.

It rose from a sea of glass, breaching the mist, a stygian blot on the white spume. It thrashed tendrils that had calcified to bone. It came up near the motorboat, rocking them violently aside before Edgar pulled around its nose cone to right them. A rush of water crashed over the side, the ocean closing its fist around her. She spluttered free, gasping.

The ocean ignited.

The seastead cannons skipped shrapnel over the water in myriad tiny explosions. Though she could no longer fear death she ducked, huddled by the bow of the motorboat as if her life still mattered, as if she were still a discrete entity from the monstrous submarine that shadowed them. The top of the gunwale splintered into missiles, stinging her cheekbone. When she touched a hand to her face, something in her startled that the blood slicking her palm was still red.

She crawled to her knees and peered through the shattered plexiglass. The seastead's cannons blazed pillars of flame. Edgar wove a jagged pathway through the churning water, the motorboat a fragile target but not an easy one. The *Retribution* shrilled, a scream drawn from the lungs of the dead men in its belly. Its pale appendages knifed through the water, carrying the motorboat in its wake, towards the looming city-ship.

A shell smashed into the water off the motorboat's starboard side, carrying them first impossibly high, then violently downwards, washed under by a wave of ice and salt. Blythe clung to what she could, the jagged edge of the fiberglass slicing her fingers. Seawater flooded her nose, her mouth. She couldn't tell the sky from the depths.

Her breath, when they broke through the surface, burned her throat.

From the stern, Bailey yelled, "They shot out the motor."

It was an understatement. The back end of the boat was shredded and taking on water. Between the ebb current and the violent spasms of the *Retribution*, they were still drifting roughly towards the seastead, though they'd miss colliding with it by a long shot.

And worse, there was no way back.

Edgar grabbed the emergency oar, hellbent on moving the crippled boat onward. He'd lost weight—they all had—and if the storm and the gunfire didn't blow him off the side of the boat, the force of resisting the waves would crack him in half.

There was one dingy, stashed under the deck. She breathed a silent thanks that it inflated. The little motor didn't stand much chance against the waves and the shooting, but it was better than nothing.

"Get in," she told Bailey.

"What?"

"The boat's taking on water. We have to lighten the load."

The kid was shellshocked, staring goggle-eyed at the seastead, closer than anyone from the city had ever been to it. At the restive coils of bone that fumed beneath the waves.

"Move."

Bailey splayed, a clumsy starfish, into the lifeboat. "You too," she told Edgar.

Her supervisor's eyes welled with tears.

"I'm going with the *Retribution*," Blythe said.

The sky cracked in blinding white.

"I know," Edgar said. She had to read his lips. He was quiet at the best of times, even without the storm. He had always been so soft-spoken. It was the only thing his students ever complained about in their evaluations. "But someone still needs to drive the boat." He stabbed the oar into the water for emphasis.

"Maybe I could—" Blythe said, and then stopped. As if she could come up with some clever last minute save that would let them save the day, blow up the seastead, and get away with their lives.

"Not you," Edgar said. "I'm group lead."

"The world's ended," Blythe said. "No one gives a shit that you have tenure."

"You always deserved it." Edgar's cold hand wrapped around hers. "In our next lives, maybe you'll be the one stuck doing all the paperwork."

"Please," she tried again.

"Whatever you are," Edgar said, "whatever you've become. You were always a hell of a scientist." He turned back to the bow, propelling the boat forward in torturous increments. "Let's both go do what we both need to."

Her blood was saline. Her nerves were dark, blind things flourishing in the crushing pressure of the ocean floor. Already she was its organ, its senses, already she was its expansive biome, the skein of her skin liquid and mercurial. But her body remained pitifully, stubbornly human, incapable of embracing its cruelty.

With the last of her willpower, she shoved the dinghy off the back of the boat. Bailey was a bright speck in the monstrous ocean, disappearing over the crest of a wave.

The storm was a triviality to the thing waiting in the depths, for whom storms were merely skitters of wind across its bones. Shackled to it, Blythe watched the clouds swell and burst as if from a distance. Minutes ago, it had been an obstacle, like the cold, like the cannon fire raking across the waves. How had it seemed so important?

With Edgar doomed and Bailey moving away from the blast radius,

Blythe stood, shakily, a hive of voices roaring in her ears.

It was brighter than day. Searchlights scampered and glittered over the fog, the teeth at the peak of each wave, a blinding kaleidoscope that seared her eyes. The whisper in the back of her skull urging surrender, for an escape that flickered in and out of probability.

She closed her eyes and dove off the back of the boat, seconds before Edgar's boat struck the seastead.

The *Retribution*'s arms rose up to embrace her. Shards of bone pierced her ribs, the base of her brain. Her flesh rippled, became first water, mutable and liquid, and then bulletproof.

She should have felt Edgar's death. She should have surfaced, to witness, but the thud of the impact and the explosion came too unexpectedly, the fireball a slash of yellow in the corner of her vision. She did look, then, from where she floated, suspended in ink and bone. But the storm was too thick to see, a Turner abstraction, light and fire and nothing of the crumpled prow of the ferry, nothing of her mentor and friend rendered in charcoal, melting into the motorboat's cockpit. She couldn't see if it had damaged the SVAR ship, if any of their careful planning and Edgar's sacrifice had been worth it.

It should have been the only thing in the world that mattered. But the world was now so very small.

Her consciousness darted across the *Retribution*'s shell. Its tendrils, each one a sensory organ, and then deeper, to the microbial network that spread through the oceans and tributaries, to the labyrinthian Pattern that wove the earth together. To the names humans had given to the depths—midnight, hadal, abyssal—the language of poetry they'd resorted to for the places where the terminology of science failed.

She was there, in every single drop of water, and she was here, a wreck of a body hanging above the ruined ships.

The shore was on fire. The embattled city clashed with the occupiers, as they always had, the wars of humans something distant and immaterial. On the other side of the continent, they were fighting just as fruitlessly. A fragment of her consciousness, divided amongst the creature's limbs and woven through dimensions, strained towards it.

Jonah was there. Her heart was a shell, and no longer remembered love, but the parts of her that were human, her muscle memory, her tastebuds, the tips of her fingers and her breasts and her sex, shivered in relief that he was still alive and fighting. A tiny figure at the mouth of a great demon, he fired at it, and with its death, his long-buried name withered a little further.

I'm sorry, she mouthed, but if he heard, he gave no indication.

She fell deeper, past where the twilight of the mirror world hardened first into black, and then into a bleak, eldritch light, vast carpets of pale gold ooze, the phosphorescent beacons of deep sea fish.

She had been drowning all her life. In her mother's womb, water had laid claim to her. She had heard its voice before any human tongue.

She cast out for Bailey, for Kenny, for Kitty, for everyone she'd known at the university who had resisted in ways large and small, now embroiled in a pitched battle against the SVAR. Her joined consciousness could not fathom their importance or tease out their individual souls from the masses of humanity, the guilty who had awakened it and the innocent who would suffer under its wrath. She urged its rage forward, towards the seastead.

A strange last act, to give a god a conscience.

At last, at the bottom of the well, there was Laura. No longer a metaphor or a mirage, but the real girl, standing barefoot in a bedroom larger than the closet she'd had in Blythe's apartment, frowning at the last two buttons on a starched school blouse. Teenage, and crying, and very much alive.

The *Retribution* did not deal in illusion or ambiguity. This was her daughter in the present. Such a small thing, a girl's life. One single human. Before the creature blinked one giant stone eye, she would be an old woman. Before it took a breath, she would be dust.

Her ossified heart recalled wanting. Wishing. Needing, of all things, this one thing above anything else in the world.

The wanting fell away. Her will, her choices, the carefully constructed architecture of her life and career sloughed away, into the abyss. The grief that she had carried on her back, raw and skinned and writhing and heavier than lead, shook loose from her, drowned in the monster's maw.

Her consciousness danced along a bony limb, across mountains and prairie, threaded through the earth and river. To her home, the Red River that had given her life, to her mother and her kin, and further inland, following the ley lines of the Blight to her daughter.

The *Retribution*'s many mouths had never formed human words. It took all her strength, all her intention, to shape it into sound.

Laura.

For a split second, she was as impervious to Blythe's presence as Jonah had been. Blythe could almost convince herself that the connection was a hallucination, a last flicker of her mind before it was absorbed along with all of the *Retribution*'s other victims.

And then she looked up.

Her face hadn't changed. Jonah's black eyes, welling with adolescent tears, Jonah's long, straight hair; Blythe's heart-shaped jawline.

Blythe had a moment to commit to memory the spartan details of the bedroom, the military folds of the bedsheets, the cross and the small portrait of Director Atherton over the headboard. Her creature-mind cared nothing about the implications, the Baroque machinations of human politics. That Laura was captive behind enemy lines, and by joining with the entity, Blythe forfeited the chance to burn heaven and earth to rescue her.

Laura brought her hands together, knuckles whitening. She was holding a scrap of fabric, pulling and stretching at it. Blythe watched her, still at first, then pacing, clawing at the little piece of cloth for long seconds before, at last, raising her head again.

"Mom?" she asked.

Her hands lit up.

No, the part of Blythe that was still Blythe argued, with God, with the *Retribution*, with her miracle daughter, alight with magic. But there was no argument to be had.

The vast and unknowable cosmos, the eternities beneath the sea, the molten hatred at the heart of the earth, it all narrowed down into a spark of magic held between the palms of a girl. For the first time in her forty-two years of life, she *saw*. There was no contradiction, no choice to be made. The version of herself that forsook knowledge and eternity to cross the country in search of her daughter, and the version of herself that already existed, spread across every drop of water in every universe, were simultaneous, a superimposition of a woman and a god-monster. The end of the month and the end of the world.

I'm here, she called, pointlessly, hopelessly. Her joined mind knew no distinction between her human body and her daughter's, between water and blood. *I'm here, I am*, and then, after an eternity, she both was and wasn't.

The storm met her fury. They turned on the crippled seastead, at the beating hearts and frantic minds within. Their long coils of bone unwound, crumpled cast iron and concrete, stabbing through bodies as they dragged the seastead into their mouths. Things that had been alive, separate consciousnesses, were subsumed into their biomass. They devoured histories and memories.

When the hollow wreckage of the seastead emerged again, reshaped and reconfigured, it was devoid of life and breath, and for a moment, for long eternities, they were at peace.

Epilogue

The visitors had gone, and Amelia was mopping lakes of corrosive acid froth from the floor. The glass child hadn't moved in several hours, and were it not for her certainty that Miriam was somewhere beyond the reaches of death, Amelia would have doubted that she was alive at all. She kept one eye on the child while her gloved hands moved of their own will, quick darting circles to avoid the smash of an elongated, taloned arm. There was always one spot she'd missed. The linoleum sizzled and warped where she'd left the spittle too long, a ring of black rot spreading from its perimeter. The heat leached through her industrial strength gloves.

He was late, and she busied herself with arranging the handful of intact toys, ensuring that they were within Miriam's frame of vision. There'd been more than enough time for the Director to return from whatever Train stop he used to record his address. She knew the consequences of leaving Miriam alone, and besides, Miriam was only a child. Her own son was so very far away, and even if she didn't know the difference, it wouldn't have been right to abandon her.

She wouldn't resent the girl, surrounded by her vivisected toys, her mermaid mural and the warmth of her room. Her comfort or lack thereof made no difference to Ebrahim, if he was even still alive. Her rage bubbled and whistled in her gut and she pushed it down. Angry women did not survive very long.

She could bring some of the picture books she'd bought for Ebrahim, gathering dust in a box in her shared room. How old was the child? Regardless, it must have been a long time since anyone had read to her.

Just after midnight, he arrived at last, still dressed in the suit that was, in Amelia's eyes, gratuitous for a radio address. He knelt in front of his daughter and, avoiding her mandibles, fasted a thin gold cross on a chain around her neck. Amelia would have to remove it, so she didn't choke on it or end up with it fused into her shell, but she could do that after he'd left.

"Merry Christmas, Miriam," Quinn Atherton said.

"Merry Christmas, sir," Amelia echoed.

The hatred in his eyes when he looked up at her might have slit her throat. "Shouldn't you be on your way?" he asked. "It's past curfew."

Amelia blurted a stuttering apology, pulled her hat down over her ears, and threw her coat over her nurse's scrubs. She stumbled and nearly fell in her rush to leave.

Outside, confetti flecks of white floated over the stilled city. It was too cold for a heavy snowfall, but the sidewalks and streets glittered like quartz, slick and bright. At the end of the street, out of view of the girl's window, three bodies swayed below the bridge, frost-kissed lips bulged and purple. They had been dead for days. No one thought of burying the bodies—in the cold of the superwinter, they would keep until spring.

At the intersection, a tank rolled past her, and Amelia reached for her pass card, but it kept moving. The yellow square of light at the top of the hospital watched her scurry across the road.

The wind was already picking up, and pass or not, a Cleaner wouldn't hesitate to shoot her on sight. She paused only to take in a splash of graffiti on a wall, the words, sagging at the end as if the artist had finished in a hurry. *We are winning.*

She had enough time to wonder what that was supposed to mean before, in her coat pocket, her phone began to ring.

Glossary & Translations

American Trade Zone: The economic federation composed of the American Rump State, the Free States, and the Silicon Valley Autonomous Region

American Rump State: Colloquial name for the country formerly known as the United States of America, now much reduced in size and power

"Apisis piko ni-nistohtēm nehiyawēwin": nêhiyawêwin for "I only understand a little of the Cree Language"

Blight: A magical disaster with its origin point in Ottawa, Canada, which caused worldwide devastation and millions of deaths

Broom Closet: The nickname for the office given to federal government consultants on magic, housed on Laurier Ave. in Ottawa

Cascade: A global event that caused the return of magic to the world

Cleaners: Paramilitary force employed by the Dominion

DEC: Dominion Exchange Credits, a currency used to buy luxuries such as coffee, chocolate, and medication

Demons: Colloquial name for humans or animals permanently altered by magic

The Dominion of Canada: The government of the country formerly known as Canada

Egregore: A magical being created through collective belief

Focus: Any object or process used to channel magic. You could use a wand, but you'd look like a dork.

Free States: The secessionist states of the former US, now a theocracy

Geas: A curse compelling its subject to take or avoid a particular action

Iron Alliance: A confederation of Cree, Métis, Saulteaux, and Assiniboine communities opposing the Dominion

Mackenzie-Papineaus: An Ontario-based movement opposing the Dominion

MAI: Magic Affected Individual. Technical term for a human capable of controlling magical forces. Otherwise known as a wizard.

nehiyaw: An Indigenous Nation, also known as the Cree

Night Beats: A paranormal police procedural, off the air following its eighth season and a magical apocalypse

Otipemisiwak: Another name for the Métis, translates to "those that rule themselves"

"Pēh ēkwāna kā-kicikāwit": nêhiyawêwin for "this person is a slowpoke"

PKOLS: A mountain in Victoria, known by settlers as Mount Douglas

Skwxwú7mesh-ulh Temíx̱w: An Indigenous Nation, also known as the Squamish

Somebody Else's Problem Field: You've read Douglas Adams, haven't you?

SVAR: Silicon Valley Autonomous Region, the secessionist West Coast states, now a libertarian paradise

Unencumbrances: A series of violent purges and deportations that followed the Blight

Walsingham Institute: A right-wing think tank, run by one of Alycia Curtis's shell companies

Ward: A visual spell used to conceal or protect a person or place. Can be drawn, painted, or tattooed.

Wellsprings: Concentrated areas of magic

W̱SÁNEĆ: An Indigenous Nation, also known as the Saanich

Note: I am tragically unilingual. Where possible and appropriate, I have tried to use Indigenous names for places and peoples. I owe a debt of gratitude to Romeo Côté, Julian Gunn, www.firstvoices.com, and Cree: Language of the Plains, Language Lab Workshop by Jean L. Okimāsis for the translations. Any mistakes are my own and I welcome corrections.

Acknowledgements

Well, where would I even start with the gratitude? With the original Kickstarter backers? Everyone who read, reviewed, or talked *Cascade* up to their friends? Going back further, everyone who has ever taken a stand against fascism and lit the torch for which my fumbling hands desperately grasp? I just feel like I would leave someone out.

Nevertheless, without the following people, you would not be reading this book:

Zilla Novikov, my cookbook co-author, my partner in crime, my *Night Beats* co-founder, my eternal cheerleader and enabler. If it takes a village to write a novel, she is that village's wise woman.

Julian Gunn, the anchor to my hapless climber, is a fixer of West Coast geography, a font of vulture lore, and the kind of brilliant wordsmith who challenges me to be a better writer. Much of this book was written during our Tuesday writing sessions.

Rachel Schwartz-Narbonne, corrector of science facts, warrior for climate justice, and perpetual voice of reason, is why the improbable events of this story are plausible.

Anna Otto, my oldest writing friend and collaborator, has an eye for detail, critical voice, and knowledge of the inner workings of the mind that brought these characters to life.

Dale Stromberg is the best structural editor I know and took this story from a hot mess to an actual novel.

Romeo Côté, for their cultural expertise as a Métis anarchist, incredible research skills, and top-notch sensitivity reading.

Tim Whitney: I'm sorry about the submarines. Thank you for fixing them.

Michelle Patricia Browne, for the hilarious live reaction posts as much as the brainstorming.

Marten Norr, whose phenomenal artistic talent graces the cover and map for this book.

Kit Fisher, for doing real-life chaos magick with the sigil.

Reccia Mandelcorn, whose support and encouragement have been there since the beginning. Literally.

Geoffrey Dow, my publisher, who at this point can no longer claim he didn't know what working with me would be like, and yet chose to publish me anyway.

Last but not least, to my wonderful gentleman consort, Rob Mound, who not only went over the science and economics of my brave new world with a fine toothed comb, but also kept up my morale during the writing process.

And of course thanks to the many folks with whom I brainstormed and fact-checked: Rohan O'Duill, Holly Brown, Julian Spurlock, Mary Alexandria Kelly, Emily Dawn Kelly, Raven, Nethilia, Ryszard Merey, Tucker Lieberman, Rachel Corsini, Nicole Northwood, Emma Berglund, Shirley Meier, Brook Dunn, and all my wonderful Discord friends in Night Beets, Cats and Eldritch Horrors, LGBTQI+ Critique Group, Rewilding Our Stories, and the Magpie's Flock. There are so many more people who fielded strange questions or spoke an inspirational turn of phrase or who otherwise inspired something that found its way into the book.

Finally, thanks to you, dear reader, who in an age of algorithmic cruelty and machine-driven slop, chose to read the work of a human author, in long-form, designed and illustrated by humans. You presumably read the first one and then came back for more punishment, and for that I am overjoyed.

About the Author

Photo by Alana Boltwood

Rachel A. Rosen is an activist, graphic designer, and for her sins, a high school teacher. In a previous life, she published two long running anarchist 'zines and designed the uniform for the Christie Pits Hardball League.

She is the author of Cascade, this novel's predecessor, and, with Zilla Novikov, the co-author of *The Sad Bastard Cookbook: Food You Can Make So You Don't Die*. More of her writing can be found in *Beyond Human: Tales of the New Us*, *Instant Classic (That No One Will Read)*, and *The Dance*.

Rachel co-hosts the Aurora Award-nominated *Wizards & Spaceships* podcast with David L. Clink (www.wizardsandspaceships.ca), and designs book covers in her theoretical spare time.

She lives in Tkaronto (Toronto), where she is the harried personal assistant to two cats. Her website is www.rachelrosen.ca.

Also published by the BumblePuppy Press

www.bppress.ca

Carl Dow

The Old Man's Last Sauna
Black Grass
Wildflowers: The Women Who Made McCord Chronicle
(forthcoming)
Beyond the Blood (forthcoming)

A. A. Milne

The ~~Woke~~ Inclusive Winnie-the-Pooh
The ~~Woke~~ Inclusive The House at Pooh Corner
(Both edited and with commentary by Geoffrey Dow)

Jules Paivio

Life Is Good: A Memoir (forthcoming)

Rachel A. Rosen

Cascade: The Sleep of Reason, Book I
Blight: The Sleep of Reason, Book II
So Human As I Am

Adrienne Stephenson and Marie-Andrée Auclair

Skipping Stones

PRAISE FOR

CASCADE

"Finally, something to make the hope-punks shut the fuck up.

"A near-perfect blend of implacable horror, gallows humor, and ecological apocalypse. It seems almost absurd that a novel about chaos magic and bureaucrat magicians (even if they are embedded in the sociopathic morass of Canadian politics) can somehow feel more viscerally relevant than all the earnest mainstream novels and Suzuki-Foundation bulletins you could stuff into a ballot box. Pay attention, people: all magic aside, we're far closer to this future than any of our rulers will ever admit.

"Rachel A. Rosen is some kind of twisted genius. I wish I had even half her moves." — Peter Watts, author of *Blindsight*

"Finally, an urban fantasy that kills the cop — and the rest of the government — in your head. Relentlessly radical and often hilarious, Cascade will change the way you look at magic, and the state, forever." — Nick Mamatas, author of *The Second Shooter*

"Cascade is an excellent introduction to the imaginative prose of Rachel A. Rosen. Her debut novel takes us to a futuristic North America filled with vividly realized characters surrounded by magic and the possible end of the world. One of the few novels I've read recently in a single weekend. Sharp and thought-provoking, with thrilling moments and crackling with compelling ideas, I wouldn't miss this one. I'm looking forward to her next instalment!" — Bryan Thao Worra, author of *Before We Remember We Dream*

"Rachel A. Rosen's *Cascade* is one of the best books I've read this year. She brings a unique blend of magic environmentalism, Canadian politicking, and indigenous and queer rights to the table. I never thought I would be so interested in the near-futuristic Canadian political process!" — Marsha Altman, author of *The Darcys and the Bingleys*

www.ingramcontent.com/pod-product-compliance
Lightning Source LLC
Chambersburg PA
CBHW031030030726
47497CB00004B/1084